THE
QUEEN
AND THE
SCHOLAR

Book II of The Comus Duology

Sonya Lawson

The right of Sonya Lawson to be identified as the author of this work has been asserted by him/her in accordance with the Copyright, Designs and Patents Act 1988.

No part of this publication may be reproduced, stored in a retrieval system, or transmitted in any form or by any means without the prior written permission of the publisher, nor be otherwise circulated in any form of binding or cover other than that in which it was published and without a similar condition being imposed on the subsequent purchaser.

This book is a work of fiction. Names, items, characters, places and incidents are products of the author's imagination or are used fictitiously. Any resemblance to actual events or locales or persons, living or dead, is entirely coincidental.

Cover Design, Formatting, and Editing by:
Partners in Crime Book Services

Copyright © 2022 Sonya Lawson
All rights reserved.
No part of this book may be reproduced or transmitted in any form or by
any means without written permission of the author.

Names, characters, businesses, places, events and incidents are either the products of the author's imagination or used in a fictitious
manner. Any resemblance to actual persons, living or dead, or actual events is purely coincidental.

TABLE OF CONTENTS

DEDICATION

To my family - by blood and by bond. I love you all.

And to those I miss every day who aren't here to read this. You're still rolling around in my head and my heart. Love you, too.

A NOTE TO READERS

This novel contains violence, references to and representations of PTSD and domestic violence, captivity, and descriptions of consensual sexual activity.

PART I - NIN

The Tumult of Loud Mirth

This was the place, as well as I may guess,
Whence even now the tumult of loud mirth
Was rife, and perfect in my listening ear,
Yet naught but single darkness do I find.
What might this be? A thousand fantasies
Begin to throng into my memory
Of calling shapes, and beck'ning shadows dire,
And airy tongues that syllable men's names
On sands and shores and desert wildernesses.

John Milton, *Comus*, 1634

CHAPTER 1

"Are you taking a seat, Princess Nin?" Michel asked, a hint of exasperation in his voice as he gestured in the direction where both the Mae Queen and Princess of the Green Council chairs rested, unoccupied. His cherubic face distorted for a moment, pulled down in a massive frown, although he hid his displeasure quickly. It appeared he wished to begin The Council Meeting.

Nin, however, was undecided. Picking the proper seat was a minor issue, but it was one of a vast variety of issues crowding her mind at the moment.

It was mere days after the Battle for The Palace, which was what every Fae from The Falls was calling it. Nin was still reeling from the events — her second captivity with Comus, all she learned of his treachery and plans to take over Fae, her new knowledge of the Mae Queen, Comus escaping capture when Mosi's forces retook The Palace. It was a lot to process, as the humans would say, and Nin was uncertain about much of it. However, she had done her duty. She immediately informed The Council of all she learned, including her dream vision of the Mae Queen and the implications.

Most of Fae mourned the loss of the Queen privately many years ago, but little official talk of what happened without the Mae Queen ruling occurred in her absence. Hushed whispers and vague discussions were all any in Fae entertained for the last few decades, partly out of uncertainty, partly from fear, and partly from grief. When she first disappeared, Comus filled her void quickly, taking The Palace and holding Fae in his maniacal grasp for over three decades. The Fae of The Falls searched for their Queen to no avail, and Nin's confession underscored a sad fact all would face: the Mae Queen was no more. Even if she was something, a form of energy which retained her consciousness of self and could visit Nin in dreams, she could no longer rule Fae.

This left another power vacuum; one many were eager to fill before another dark power rose to disrupt the relative peace and prosperity usually enjoyed in Fae. Or before Comus came back. He was, after all, still out there, loose in the realm. The Council, sticking with noble protocol, pushed for Nin to take her place as monarch. She became Princess of the Green long ago, which made her the rightful heir to The Fae Throne. Others, for a variety of reasons both logical and illogical, wished to take the crown, even if their discontent filtered down through mere murmurs.

Nin had always been liked by many in Fae, but every person in power had detractors. It happened that Nin's detractors had many, many reasons to rail against her. Nin did not begrudge them this, as she blamed herself for the dark days Fae endured over the past twenty years and battled her own self recriminations and doubts. However, she also felt responsible for Fae, which meant she would take the crown because her power made her the monarch, even if she doubted her ability to lead effectively based on past mistakes.

"I will not take the Queen's seat as I am not yet Queen," Nin stated flatly. The Council Chamber was returned to its past state — one of the large carved tables dominated the center of the room with the members sitting around it in high-backed seats. The Mae Queen's seat — known by this name as no one alive remembered a time before the Mae Queen's rule — was slightly bigger and higher, but not obviously overpowering. She sat for eons apart from, but mostly a part of, the proceedings of The Council. Nin could not take that seat in good conscience. At least not until her official coronation, until she became Queen. She slanted a stare at Michel and firmly said, "I shall remain standing for this business. If it does not concern me, it should not concern you."

Serge and Mo took small steps inward, crowding their sister slightly. They were likely unaware they did such a thing. It was pure protective instinct from her brothers. It both annoyed and heartened Nin. Her mother smiled at her brightly from her seat on The Council, star-strewn black eyes and hair gleaming in the flicker of light filling the chamber. As did Sten, whom she had not seen in many decades at this point. She had almost forgotten the dichotomy of this Fae — the wild and fierce nature combined with soft kindness. She smiled back, happy to see he held no ill will toward her. Andrés looked bored, as always, and Nin was struck for the first time how closely he resembled the cartoonish human depictions of devils, sharp features, slick hair, mustache and goatee, and a level of dangerous beauty some could call mesmerizing. Beside his smoldering looks sat Jane. She fanned herself as she so often did, the instrument meticulously matching her formal brocade and velvet gown and her immaculate wide-eyed face, looking nervously between Nin and a clearly offended Michel.

"Princess, I did not wish to insinuate…" Michel started to justify, but Sten cut him off with a growl that surprised most in the room. He was a famed Fae warrior, yet as a member of The Council he consistently showed patience and calm. Until this day. The massive Fae thumped his chair with his fist, his wild blond beard and mass of braids and curls shaking slightly with the force, and said, "There is no need to elaborate or continue, Michel. We are all tired and have much work to do. Nin is correct. She is free to do as she pleases. Let us move forward."

With a sigh and a roll of his eyes at the outburst of his fellow Council Member, Michel proceeded. "Very well. As you are all aware, we must crown our Princess of the Green as Queen soon. The disarray of the Mae Queen's original disappearance caused a great many problems. We must forestall similar occurrences. To wit, we plan an immediate coronation of our new Queen."

"Is a coronation absolutely necessary?" Andrés drawled, not even bothering to look up from a study of his nails.

"Of course it is," Michel huffed out.

"There is no 'of course' in this situation, Michel," Inanna added, nodding toward her daughter. "Nin's rise to Queen is unprecedented in any of our lifetimes, and we on The Council are among the oldest living Fae. We may need more time to plan and consider."

"I have already taken the initiative, as per usual," Michel said with a flourish, beckoning figures from the back of the room to step forward.

It was Gin, her cousin and one of the leading scholars in Fae, and Sabrina. Gin, in their scholar robes and ever-present wide smile and sparkling dark eyes, was not an unusual figure in this space. However, it was still jarring for Nin to see Sabrina in this environment, her tall friend filled with nervous energy even while she swept the room with a keen, blue-eyed gaze. She was Nin's bonded, her sister through love and magic if not blood, but seeing her, a human, in Fae, when no human had been safe in Fae for so long, made her nervous. It was still dangerous for her here in many ways. But Nin's friend was fierce and intelligent. With guidance and protection, Nin knew she would prosper here.

She proved this as she stepped forward. She gave a jaunty wave to Nin, Serge, and Mo. She smiled widely at The Council. Her smile melted when her eyes landed on Michel, who she apparently disliked immensely if the curl of her lip and the cut of her eye were accurate depictions of her regard. Gin, standing beside Sabrina and watching her give Michel the look humans called a "side eye," stifled a laugh, then gave a hasty bow.

A beat later, Sabrina followed suit, taking a small step back to give Gin the floor. Sabrina could lead, but she was also intelligent enough to realize when she should follow, and Gin was a person to follow when discussing Fae research and scholarship. So, she stood a little behind Gin, straight and tall, while her hands made small, barely noticeable thumps against the pale fabric of the muslin dress stretching across the swell of her midriff and hips. Nin noticed because she was concerned for her friend and attuned to her nervous energy — both because she cared deeply and remained emotionally connected to Sabrina through their magical bond. When out of the corner of her vision she caught Mo's focused attention in the same area, she smirked, thinking her eldest brother had other reasons to stare.

"Council, at the behest of Michel the Learned, I and Sabrina the Scholar spent time in The Palace Library. We found a long-forgotten reference to coronations. Sabrina then cross-referenced this with texts in my personal library and discovered a brief description of what a coronation ceremony should be in Fae."

"Should be?" Sten asked, leaning forward with interest.

"Yes. Allow Sabrina the Scholar to tell you more."

Thrust into the spotlight, Sabrina looked around momentarily in surprise, then schooled her face. Her hands, a sure sign of her nervousness at all times, danced in front of her as she looked at The Council with cool, professional eyes. "'Should' is the correct term. As Council Member Inanna asserted previously, there is no actual record of a coronation because all we have found are vague references and generic renditions of a time before the Mae Queen. No records, at least in terms of what we have had the time to explore, exist of the Mae Queen's coronation.

Hell, only a few mentions of the Queen before her popped up. We've discovered an outline of what a potential coronation should look like based on Fae traditions and court culture. That is all we have. Most likely all there is."

"Very well," Michel said with a dismissive hand toward Sabrina. He looked on her with open disdain during her report, his prejudice against humans quite clear in his reaction to Sabrina. "If that is all you are capable of."

"All anyone is capable of," Serge interjected, smoothly stepping up to stand beside Sabrina with bow, a sweep of his strong but lithe arm, and a gentle shake to ensure his black curls artfully fell back into position.

Nin might wonder at Serge jumping to defend her friend, if she had not been privy to the playful banter which marked the growing friendship between the pair, and she had not noticed the way every muscle in Mosi's body stiffened at the look of contempt Michel threw toward her. His dark skin vibrated with tension, and his eyes, so like their mother's, turned to black flames. Serge, observant as always, eyed Mo's tightly clenched fist before sliding up to stand with Sabrina.

"Please, dear Council, forgive my interruption, but I do feel I have much to add to the current conversation. As a onetime advisor to the Mae Queen, and a Fae courtier, I am well-versed in the protocols of nobility and court culture. This is a situation where we must, as the humans say, fly blind. There is no established etiquette or protocol. The closest I know of is the naming ceremony for Princes and Princesses of the Green. That, at least, has happened in the past and is well documented."

"Quite right, Sergius," Gin interjected with a nod to his cousin. "What Sabrina and I uncovered appears to mimic the naming ceremony with a few key differences."

Nin decided enough was enough at this point. She did not like seeing her friends and family questioned by the likes of Michel, who looked down on most in Fae. "What I am hearing is that there is no official record or procedure for a coronation ceremony. Is this correct?" Sabrina, Gin, and Serge all nodded. "Very well," she breathed, a hint of resignation in her voice. "My coronation must occur soon in order to protect Fae. Natural forces outside our control connect my power to the fate and safety of the realm. It is a responsibility the Mae Queen taught me when I was her pupil. One she reiterated often after I was named Princess of the Green. My earth magic ties me to the land and its people, and the monarch of Fae must have that bond for all in Fae to prosper. The realm has suffered under Comus' rule because of this. I must take the crown soon to rectify at least this one issue."

"Agreed," Michel said, looking pleased to have Nin affirm the ideas he stated earlier.

"However," she continued, cutting into any speech Michel was about to give, "the process itself is not completely irrelevant. Much of the magic in the Naming connects the Princes and Princesses of the Green to the land. A similar connection must occur during the coronation. Because of this, we will take a small amount of time. One week. In that week, Gin and Sabrina shall research more to ensure nothing is missed. I will commune with the land to strengthen my connection prior to the ceremony. Sergius will discuss protocol with his fellow courtiers. This

Council shall meet again in seven days' time to solidify coronation plans. To allow any Fae who wish to attend enough time to plan their own journeys to The Palace, we announce the coronation date today, before final plans are created."

"What of security?" her stoic brother, Mo, asked. It was his area of expertise, so it was no surprise he voiced concerns here.

"I trust you to take care of the logistics, Mosi," she replied.

"If any Fae is allowed to attend…" Mosi added, pushing back against his younger sister.

"They will feel welcome in The Palace and personally connected to their new Queen, necessary elements if they are to find comfort and security in their monarch," Nin explained with a little bite in her voice. "It must be this way, Mosi. Plan accordingly."

"May I be of assistance in this?" Sten asked Nin.

"As you wish," she answered.

"This is all well and good, but what of the rest of The Council?" Michel asked, obviously feeling slighted he was not more directly consulted in the moment.

"You will review and finalize all plans for the event." After a brief pause, Nin added, "Of course, you, Michel, will be a part of the events of the day in some way, I am sure." At this, Jane smiled and gave a quick clap, the first real addition she made to the conversation up to this point, while Michel looked on, mollified. A vote was called, all agreed on the plan Nin presented, and The Council moved on to other business.

Nin's attention floated in and out. She knew she should closely follow the decisions made by The

Council and be mindful of their current discussions in case such issues became pressing in the future. Now, however, all she could concentrate on was what would happen in a few short days. She would become Queen of Fae. And Nin worried she was ill prepared for the task looming before her.

CHAPTER 2

Nin plunged her hands into the black soil, kneading clumps loose, turning and churning to aerate the dirt. It was the cusp of spring and summer, and the Royal Gardens were a riot of color. Housed in the massive courtyard of The Palace, the gardens encompassed six square acres and were a landmark of Fae. These gardens were kept by the Queen and her Prince/Princess of the Green, the only Fae in the realm with earth magics. Over eons, earth magic Fae poured magic and sweat into this ground again and again, creating a breathtaking botanical display many traveled from across the realm to see. Some even speculated The Palace grew around this spot — the seat of Fae power first being a garden, then a Palace.

Before her captivity, Nin spent many hours here with the Mae Queen, ensuring beauty shined, helping plants along as they needed. Coaxing the earth in their own unique way. However, it had been decades since there was a gardener here. Comus locked the Royal Garden gates, refused any Fae entry into this special place. It was now Nin's job to remake and reshape the space after years of neglect. If it seemed like a daunting task, it was not. Little was required from her, the centuries of careful tending and the general Fae preference for wildness in their tended spaces meant there was no need to raise beds or weed acres of land. There was a great deal of pruning and trimming to do, but it was quick work for one as experienced as she.

She stood amongst the whispering roses, a breed of flower that emitted both a sweet smell and a soft tinkle of sound, like distant bells on the wind. These blooms enjoyed their trimming and tending, singing in their special language as she told them how, like a beautician, she would give them a new, stylish shape. She churned their soil, careful to help stimulate growth while also not disturbing the earth too close to the roots, ensuring the right mix was still there for life to grow where it would.

She was in deep concentration, listening and smelling and feeling in the one place in this Palace that still felt true to her, when Sabrina shuffled up from behind her. She knelt by Nin, silent for a time, studying what was around them as well as what Nin was doing, her head cocked as she listened to the soft music the roses made.

"Gran used to do this for her tomatoes. Said she had to get her hands in, not use some tool. Claimed it made them juicier," Sabrina recalled as she watched Nin crumble the dark, wet dirt in her hands.

"Yet another example of your grandmother's wisdom," Nin muttered, turning to smile at her friend. She looked Sabrina up and down, happy to see she was in her comfortable clothes — dirty blonde hair pulled back in a messy bun, a pair of Pumas on her feet, fresh yet worn jeans, and a tee with Shakespeare in sunglasses on the front that said "Get Lit." The number of nerdy, pun-centered tee-shirts her friend owned was astonishing, but a quirk of her wardrobe that felt true to who Sabrina was. Nin let the last of her handful of dirt fall to the ground, patting it lovingly in place, before she wiped her hands on her own faded work jeans.

Sabrina followed her movements, humor alight in her eyes. "Looks like you got visited by the clothes fairy, too," she teased, nodding toward Nin's human work ensemble.

Nin chuckled. "Not a hard feat, as we are all some form of fairy here, no?"

"True. It was a surprise, waking up to my suitcase filled with my clothes from back home."

"Who would do such a thing?" Nin said, smiling and knocking her shoulder against Sabrina's before rising. Sabrina wobbled, her balance always a little off somehow, and almost went over. Nin reached down a steady hand, offering her a lift. While Sabrina loomed at least a full head over Nin, she lacked Fae power and strength, and her clumsiness, while endearing and part of who she was, reminded Nin of her friend's fragile position here in her realm.

Sabrina wiped her hands along her thighs and faced Nin fully, "Thanks. For that and the clothes. I do love the robes and dresses here in Fae, but a girl's gotta have jeans and tees."

"You are most welcome, my friend. However, do not tell any of this, as I traveled back to the human realm with the help of Serge but without my guard. I think many, including Mo, would be quite upset over my outing.”

“First, yeah, it likely wasn’t the smartest idea, given what’s out there,” Sabrina replied, vaguely referencing Comus, “though you can hold your own. Second, I still very much appreciate it and won’t narc on you. Snitches get stitches after all. Third, are we ever going to talk about the fact that your brother has obviously spent a lot of time in the human realm? Like, loads.”

Nin laughed. “Yes. He apparently traveled often to the human realm via a thin spot for many, many years. He confessed as much to me when we went back to Wilde.”

“I knew it. His speech patterns are a little less Fae, a little more human. He also laughs at more of my jokes than other Fae. I appreciate that in a man.”

Nin looped her arm in Sabrina’s and steered them towards the garden path. They often walked and talked in the human realm. The simple action made Nin feel comforted. “Sergius is appreciated by many.”

“Yep. Can totally see that. He oozes charm all over the place. Could make a person lose their head.”

“Many people I know in Fae have spent time lost in Sergius. Likely the same is true of humans. Even the Mae Queen hinted she had, at one time, enjoyed my brother’s company in her bed.”

“Oh, the royal tea comes out!” she shouted, then started laughing at herself. “Didn’t mean that pun. You know — royal tea, royalty. Still a good one. Speaking of royalty, I guess I’ve been a little too familiar with you, right? Like, I need to address you formally. What works? Princess? To-Be Queen? Your Grace? Sorry, but I'm not all that up on these things," Sabrina rambled out in a joking manner, as was her way, but it made Nin stiffen. She did not need the reminder from her friend.

Nin stopped in front of a large magnolia tree, leaving Sabrina on the path to walk beneath pale pink blossoms beginning to peek out from their buds and leave their heady floral scent in the air. She stroked its bark, feeling the vitality there, the assurance of what it was and where it was rooted. She sometimes envied the things of the earth because of that constant assurance. They knew what and where they were always, how they fit into their own surroundings.

"Hey, lady?" Sabrina called from behind her, touching her lightly on her shoulder. "You okay? I'm sorry I said that. I was just joking around, but this shit has got to be weird for you right now, so I shouldn't joke."

"No, my friend. It is fine. I know you only tease. I am simply overwhelmed by the prospect."

"You'd have to be. Anyone would. Plus, you went through a lot in the past weeks. You also went through a lot over the past decades if I have my timeline right. You have every reason to feel overwhelmed right now."

Nin patted the tree trunk and looked back over her shoulder toward her friend. She could not face her fully. "What if I'm a horrible Queen?" she whispered.

"I think you'd be a horrible Queen if you didn't consider that question," Sabrina fired back at her. Nin nodded. Her friend drew up to her side and slung her arm over her shoulder. "I can't tell you the

future. I'm no seer. I can say you are a great friend —
kind, caring, considerate, helpful, funny, loyal,
strong, thoughtful. I'm not the only one who thinks
so, as evidenced by all the love you get from your
family. Those things will work in your favor as a
monarch, too. I'm not crazy about monarchy as a
general political system, but knowing you makes me
feel better about this monarchy."

"I feel I will never be as strong and reliable
as the Mae Queen."

"You aren't the Mae Queen. You're you. I
understand comparison is hard to let go of, but you
have to try. You'll have your own strengths and
weaknesses."

"But the people…" Nin muttered.

"Will find things to love and hate about you,
as they would with any leader. That's the way it goes
for people in power. I'm sure the same could be said
when you were a part of The Court and Council as
Princess of the Green; some liked you and some
didn't. All you can do is what you feel is right and
true. Keep that up and most will think you're good."

Nin shook her head and reached for Sabrina
as tears rimmed her eyes. She was glad to voice these
ideas to her friend, even if in a hesitant manner. It
helped ease some feelings, though doubt and guilt
still lurked and gnawed at the edges of her thoughts.
The deep hug helped her as well.

Sabrina pulled back, putting Nin at arm's
length and staring deep into her eyes. "Lady. This
will be hard. No lie. Hard in many ways you and I
can predict and in several ways we can't. Please
know you are not alone. You can always say these
things to me, talk out things with me. I'll keep it all
locked away for you. I'll be here as long as you need

me. I generally don't like to speak for people, but I'm certain Gin and Serge and Mo and your mom would all say the same, too."

Nin closed her eyes, heaved in a deep breath, and slowly let it out, allowing Sabina's words and faith to fall over her as she did. Her friend was wise and true. She trusted her. It was herself she did not trust. That would have to be put aside. The realm needed her. She grabbed her friend's arm again and gave it a squeeze before leading them out from under the magnolia. They talked of more as they walked, and each step, each beat of conversation, made Nin feel more grounded.

Nin paced The Consort Chamber, thinking about her earlier conversation with Sabrina. It was a smaller version of the Royal Chambers situated down the hall from those rooms, which was fine for Nin. She had no need for large spaces. There was also no need to return to those specific rooms, the setting for so much pain and fear in her distant and not-so-distant past.

A knock sounded on her bedchamber door, meaning the guard admitted someone. She cracked it open, peaking her eye through out of caution, to find her mother smiling brightly at her. She blew a kiss toward Nin, who smiled and returned the gesture. As Inanna did when she was a child, her mother pretended to grab the kiss and hold it to her chest, her heart.

Inanna let out a laugh, high and merry, and whispered, "Let me in, love."

Nin opened the door wide and watched her mother stroll into the room. She was grace personified for Nin, her head always high, her steps always soft but sure and steady. She never seemed to hesitate, always wore her heart in her eyes, and exuded beauty inside and out. It was a pleasure to be in her presence, and Nin missed her greatly over the past few decades.

A female gnome trailed behind her, and Nin did not notice the woman until she went to shut the door. Scurrying past with a notebook and small case, the gnome came to a halt behind Nin before giving a deep bow.

"Princess," she said in the baritone most gnomes seemed to have, "a pleasure to be of service."

Nin furrowed her brow, looking to her mother, who now lounged on her freshly made bed. "Nin, this is Vola. I met her in The Falls, and she is an absolute wonder with a needle. She also produces the most flattering creations. I took the liberty of commissioning her to design your coronation gown."

"Right," Nin replied, sitting down by her mother and scooping up her hand. It was good to touch and be close. To smell her and feel her and hear her voice. It was comfort. "A dress will be needed, and I did not consider this. Surely I would have realized eventually, but…"

"But nothing, dear. You are busy. Have much on your mind — past, present, and future concerns. I took the initiative, hoping to complete one task for you."

"Thank you." Tears climbed her throat, something that happened often in her mother's presence now. She pushed that feeling down. She needed to move forward with her mother, to be able to connect without sadness. When she managed that feat, she stopped to consider the gnome now bustling in her closet, presumably making preparations for a fitting. "Why did you not call on Lette for my gown?" Lette was Nin's dressmaker, or at least the one she favored when she was an active member of The Court and Council as Princess of the Green. Comus had forced whatever he liked on her, and no formal gowns were needed for her quiet life in the human realm, so it had been some time since she relied on Lette.

"Oh, Nin. Lette passed long ago. I thought you knew of this. I am so sorry." Her mother squeezed her hand, looking into her eyes with a mix of her spoken sorrow and the unspoken worry that tinged her gaze so often when she looked on her daughter these days.

"When?" she managed to ask around her hurt.

"I do not know the exact date, my daughter. She died…during your original captivity in The Palace. Word passed down many years before your first escape from Comus."

Nin hung her head at this. If Lette did not make it to The Falls, she was either outright killed by Comus because of her connection to Nin or rounded up in any number of raids Comus instigated during his reign of terror. Either way, she felt Lette's loss settle firmly around her shoulders.

"No," her mother stated, placing a finger beneath Nin's chin, and raising her head so they looked into each other's eyes. "No need to hang your head. It is past and was not your doing."

"You and I disagree on that," she returned.

"Listen to your mother, dear. This. Was. Not. Your Fault. Not Lette, not Comus, not your pain nor the pain of any other Fae caused by him and his devilry. All rests on his head alone."

" '*Isn't it pretty to think so,* '" Nin quoted from a novel Sabrina once lent to her. It was a snarky reply, and one that had her mother giving her sharp eyes.

"Young lady, you may be Princess of the Green. You may soon be Queen. However, you are still my daughter, and I will have none of your disrespect."

"Sorry, Mother. You do not deserve that. I am just…"

"Tired. Worried. Overwhelmed. Hurting. I see all of this, dear. Let me help. Let the rest of your family help. We will guide you true."

It was so close to what Sabrina said earlier it sparked more than a little hope. It even echoed what the Mae Queen told her in her vision. She must accept help from those who loved her, those whom she loved. On a sigh, she let her head fall toward her mother's shoulder, resting there for beats as she took in her scent and the warmth of her skin and the strength she found there.

"As always, you are right," she said, "as I am sure you are correct in your evaluation of Vola's work. Let us see what armor she has dreamed for me."

Inanna chuckled and wrapped Nin in her arms again, squeezing tightly and kissing the top of her hair. She rose and offered her hand to her daughter. "Yes. Let us see. Vola is to visit Sabrina next. She requires a proper gown for the event as well."

"I may come along for that fitting," Nin said with a smile. "Sabrina will be delighted at the experience."

"I do believe you're right. She is a delightful and frequently delighted human in general, your Sabrina. Or should I say Mosi's Sabrina?" her mother asked with a slide of her eye and a hint of a smile.

"Come now, Mother. Mosi long ago grew into a man and has had many lovers over his centuries. If you wish to know how he feels, ask him yourself. Do not try to acquire such information from me."

"I only thought Sabrina may have mentioned…"

"Sabrina has said nothing, yet even if she had, I would not share it with you," Nin interjected, a slight tease in her voice but still indicating a firm stance on the subject. She knew her mother meant well and asked out of a curiosity born from care and love. However, knowing them both well, neither Mo nor Sabrina would appreciate her nosing. In truth, she had her own ideas about the pair, but like everyone else, she would have to wait to see what came to pass. Nin was a firm believer in the idea that, no matter the love and care you held for a person, you were not entitled to the parts of themselves they were not willing to openly give to you. It was fine to ask; it was not fine to press strongly and expect answers. Hers was a belief born of time and experience, some good and some traumatic, and she would stick to it even in the face of her persistent mother.

"No fair," her mother said on a fake pout.

"Sadly, as you and life taught me, few things are fair unless you strive to make them so."

"Too true. The wisdom of our soon-to-be Queen already shines," Inanna replied with a proud smile.

Nin felt those words and that look, allowed them to wash over her, taking away a small bit of doubt. It would come back later, surely. For now, it was good to let go of bigger worries while giving time and space to a small issue, like the proper dress to wear when one is to be crowned Queen.

CHAPTER 3

Nin clasped her hands tightly in front of her abdomen, pulling her core out and up to ensure she stood straight. Her five-foot frame could not stand tall, no matter her posture, but she could maintain a regal stance. She took a deep breath, counting to ten as the air expanded her lungs. She blew out on a ten count, quietly expelling worry and focusing on what came next.

The large wooden doors to The Throne Room were shut tight before her, but she could still hear the murmur of voices from within. There was a crowd, all come to witness the coronation of a new Queen. Some came in support and hope, others to look on with condemnation and disdain. That was the way of things, she knew, but it left a nasty taste in her mouth. She did her breathing practice again and took a moment to look down at herself.

Vola was an exceptional creator, as her mother claimed. The dress she wore was a ball gown with a sweetheart neckline constructed in a gold material that flickered like candlelight as she moved. Birch branches, created with iridescent white and metallic brown thread, reached upward from the bottom hem, coiling up and around, intertwining across her petite frame. A cape reached down her shoulders, connecting at her neckline, and flowed behind her. It was a deep emerald green, a field of woven leaves that mimicked the overhang of deep, old forests. The cape rustled when she moved, creating the illusion of wind whispering through trees. It was a dress to awe and symbolize. It was renewal, new beginnings. And it was regal. It was earth magic in costume form. Good armor for this day.

She heard the creak of those large wooden doors before she saw them open, which gave her sufficient time to school her face. They spread slowly, revealing inch by inch the mass of people packed into The Throne Room. Her mother, dressed in a Persian blue gossamer gown, stood with a proud smile before her. Sergius, handsome in his navy-blue tunic with silver embellishments, gave a swift and deep bow before reaching out a smooth, strong olive hand toward her. He grinned and she gave a quick, small smile back before returning to her neutral expression, taking the hand of her brother, one that looked so like her own, one that helped mold her in many ways, and let time and memories and closeness weave its own spell of calm. Serge heaved his own sigh, one of love and remembrance, and with a rare serious quirk of the brow, he tucked Nin into the crook of his arm, patting her there, holding her there in love and protection as their mother did on her other side.

It was decided at the last Council Meeting Inanna and Sergius would accompany her to The Throne, flanking her as she walked the length of the room. It was partially for show — her family was a powerful one in Fae. It was partially for protection, as both were well-versed in physical and magical defenses. For Nin, it was mostly for comfort. Her father passed long ago, her mother and brothers her only close family. Inanna was a prominent member of The Council, had served as such for centuries at this point, so it made sense for her to participate. She was also her mother and held her arm tightly in a way that showed support and offered strength.

Mosi, as the eldest, would normally take the lead here, but he had duties to attend as the Chief General of Fae. He was more suited to security and protection. Sergius was the courtier, the one who spent his life in Court, advising the Mae Queen and navigating the etiquette and politics of this place, helping her in the years she spent here, first as a pupil, then as Princess of the Green. He was a leader in this space. It was fitting in many ways he led her to her new Throne as he would hold an official, sanctioned position beside it in short order. Only discussed in passing thus far, she and all in her family assumed he would become her Vizer soon. She would need one, a single Fae to help advise during the early days of her reign and beyond. Sergius was the obvious choice, because of his talents, his knowledge, and the mutual love felt between the two. All that was needed was a bit more time to settle, a bit more time for Fae to become accustomed to Nin as their Queen before she started putting her family in high-ranking positions they did not already hold within the realm.

Despite the strength and assurance from her family on her arms, she could not help but remember the last time she walked the length of this room in front of an audience, and that was the real reason she needed them physically by her side. She gripped the arms offered to her, digging in a shade too hard, as she thought of Comus and the horrors she witnessed only weeks before. She looked at the marble in front of the dais, seeing spilled innards and the mangled body of the Wisp male flash for a moment. Nin sought out Chief Allera earlier, asked as gently as possible for the name of the male she saw tortured and murdered as she sat chained in this room. He was Pelpa, a loyal leader in Allera's ranks, and a supporter of her and the Mae Queen. She would remember him, say his name and honor him. Now, however, she needed to refocus, reshape her thoughts for what was ahead.

Nin spied Mosi at the front, off to the right and facing the mass of people in the room. He scanned the crowd with his eyes while his body remained rigid. He wore a bronze-colored cape detailed with a filigree pattern in a thread that looked like spun rose gold. It might well be, with his metal magics. It was his only nod to the formality of the occasion. Mo was still dressed in his leathers and laced boots, his fighting gear always at the ready. He skimmed the crowd and stopped momentarily when his eyes passed over Nin. He smiled slightly, not giving too much away, but a warmth suffused his face that Nin felt all the way down to her bones. It was nice to see and feel his pride.

At the end of the runner, positioned away from the other Fae and flanked by a guard Mosi likely posted there, stood Sabrina. She was tall and beautiful, dressed in another Vola creation — a lilac satin mermaid cut gown that accentuated her ample curves, hugging her body to the knees and flaring out in a soft cascade of tiered violet tulle. She was still Sabrina, so she fidgeted nervously in her usual, unconscious manner. When she noticed Nin's eyes on her, she lit up and gave a low wave she thought would be missed by others, though such was impossible. She was in a room full of Fae, all of whom likely heard of the human bonded to their soon-to-be-Queen, her new name as Scholar, and the fact she was the soul who freed Nin from Comus' blasted chair. They were hungry for any knowledge of her, so she would never be unnoticed in Fae.

Oblivious to these facts or choosing to ignore the Fae eyes on her, Sabrina gave Nin a long look and a beaming smile. Feeling the warmth from the look and their bond, Nin turned a wide smile her way for just a moment before looking with soft eyes over to Gin, who stood beside Sabrina. They were in dress robes, a supple beige fabric that refracted light, casting a riot of colors around them whenever they moved, refracting off the smooth skin of their sharp cheekbones, skimming off the sheen of their always-mussed black hair. It was a spelled fabric reserved for Scholars and Nin always loved to see her cousin dressed this way. It was a gorgeous thing — the fabric and the magic that made it — and was Gin's standard attire for any official business or event. That brought its own brand of comfort, a small flash of beauty Nin knew and could rely on now and in the future.

The murmurs of a crowd this size dulled as Nin reached the foot of the stairs. Situated a few steps above the marble floor was Michel. He smiled with pride of place. Nin disliked he was there at this time, but it could not be helped. He was the head of The Council, and as such, it was agreed he was the only one with authority to complete the crowning ceremony as they had devised it. His position of prominence in these events stroked an already hefty ego but was unavoidable. Pushing her slight annoyance aside, she patted her mother's hand lightly and Inanna could not hold back the happy tears she shed. Serge turned and bowed over her hand, giving her a secret grin and a swift kiss to her knuckles before softly whispering, "Off you go, Little One." His voice had a small hitch, and his eyes had a shine that mirrored their mother's. Nin looked away before she herself got emotional. She had to remain composed, regal and aloof. That was the way of Queens.

She moved, back stiff and head high, toward Michel, who held The Crown of Fae in his hands. It was simple in design, golden stems and flowers woven in a thick circle with a large triangular emerald bracketed front and center. The Mae Queen had not worn it day-to-day, only putting it on for official events. Most often it was locked away in the vaults of The Palace with all the other Royal jewels and gifts. Nin would wear it today, then stow it away for weeks, pulling it out at the next major Court event such as the summer solstice, as the Mae Queen did before her. Still, it was a thing of beauty and awe and history that made her nervous.

She stopped in front of Michel and knelt on a velvet cushion placed there for her. It was the last time she would be required to kneel in front of any person and the idea struck her full force in the moment. Michel cleared his throat, signaling to all he was about to begin the ceremony they cobbled together from old hypotheticals and past Namings.

"I, Michel the Learned, head of The Council of Fae, stand before you to name Nin, Princess of the Green, as Queen of Fae. Princess Nin, you are tasked with ruling all of Fae, ensuring the comfort and protection of all people within this realm. Your earth magics call you to this task, as the Great Mother intended. Like the First Queen, you must connect people and place, Fae and earth, to create stability and prosperity for all. Do you so swear to protect and secure, with magics and might?"

"I so swear," she answered loudly, surprising herself with the strong, firm tone she projected.

"Do you so swear to guide true, with wisdom and care?"

"I so swear."

"Do you so swear to uphold Fae law, with fairness and justice?"

"I so swear."

"Do you so swear to unite our realm, all Fae in all lands?"

"I so swear."

Michel nodded gravely and set The Crown of Fae on Nin's head. It was weighty, much heavier than she thought it would be, but that could be in her imagination. Regardless, it fit snug, coming to rest at the top curve of her forehead. She did not know what it looked like to others. She was not sure if she wanted to know what it looked like on her. It was now there regardless, in fact and theory, for as long as she lived.

Michel's voice thundered as he finished the prescribed ritual. Speaking Faeish, joining words, he produced a small bag from his formal Scholar robes, upturning it over Nin's extended hand. Black earth from her gardens, the Royal Gardens, fell as Michel boomed and Nin made her own personal vows to her people, her land, herself. "Rise, Queen Nin, and greet your people for the first time as their rightful ruler." She rose gracefully, and Michel bent before her. She slowly turned, and like a wave, all Fae present went down to the floor. Many she knew and some she had never seen before. All now rested on their knees with heads bowed in her direction. It was uncomfortable, seeing a large group instantly kneel before her en masse. She was now Queen of Fae, however, and would become accustomed to this. Or so she hoped.

CHAPTER 4

"I still believe this was not the best plan," Mo grumbled under his breath to Nin. The top half of his face was obscured by his mask, a gleaming piece of hammered silver that left enough room for his dark eyes to stare around the room. It matched his silver coat and pantaloons, and white shirt with silver embroidery. Mosi rarely wore courtly clothes, but all were required to do so when there was a ball. And the masquerade ball celebrating Queen Nin's coronation was in full swing. Much to Nin's brother's dismay.

"Mosi," Nin sighed, "I am tired and ready for this long day to end. However, we do what we must. You know this. I would appreciate less grumbling from you."

He looked on his younger sister with concern. "I apologize. This is not your doing. I was beside you at Council meetings as this was planned. You and I both questioned the choice."

"Oh, pish posh," someone said with a tinkle of a giggle. Nin looked up from her whispers with her brother to see Jane of the Dale sliding up beside the siblings. "Always so serious, Mosi. It is good for you to get out of your leathers and be merry on occasion."

"I would much rather be in my gear, protecting my Queen within a crowd that was not masked and costumed. This is a security nightmare," he bit back.

"Nonsense. All is well. See?" Jane said, stretching her arm wide toward the crowd milling and laughing in The Throne Room. "Appeasing courtiers is a crucial part of a successful monarchy, and it has been too long since a proper ball."

Nin nodded because Jane was correct. It was important to keep courtiers happy or her rule would be tiresome at best, dangerous at worst. Courtiers were moneyed Noble Fae, those with land and means and political power over certain parts of the realm. Occasionally a Fae may become a courtier through merit, rising in the ranks because of courage or service or intelligence. Most, however, were rulers of their own small sections of Fae, even if many had hidden for decades under Comus. It was both smart and kind to allow this celebration — a moment of reverie working to bring everyone together, acknowledge their position in Fae, and hopefully endear them to their new Queen.

"It did not need to be a costume ball," Mo groused under his breath, stubborn until the end. He was stung by the fact others were given control of security for the evening's festivities. It was also agreed Nin's family needed to be part of the celebration. Seen and heard and interacting within the crowd in a show of support. A captain in his guard was tasked with security, which was a hard thing for one such as Mosi, who was a protective and proactive Fae accustomed to being in charge in all things. Nin saw that more than anything it made her brother anxious, and she sympathized with the feeling. She herself was often anxious these days, though she tried her best not to let such feelings have a voice or show on her face.

She reached for his arm, patting it gently. He looked down at this motion and then into her eyes. "All is well, brother. Do your best to relax."

"I do not relax well," he admitted.

A burst of laughter came from the crowd then as Sergius stopped beside Jane, who fanned herself at his approach. "That's an understatement. However, even you must learn to celebrate today," he teased. Serge wore his coronation outfit, adding a mask made from deep navy feathers to the top half of his face. In fact, Nin's family were all still dressed in their coronation outfits, with the exception of Mo. Another decision made for appearances and unity over opulence and excess.

"Oh, you," Jane tittered, swatting Serge's arm with her ever-present fan as he smirked down at her.

Mo stared hard at his brother but said no more. The comment hit its mark, the type of brilliant and tactical courtier response Serge was so adept at giving. It teased on the surface, but also reminded his brother of the importance of appearances and perceptions on this night. Nin was awed by her brothers in different ways, as each possessed their own particular skills. Serge's words, even when not infused with his magics, were often both useful and artful.

"We are all in celebration this evening, for the future of Fae," Nin added gracefully.

"Yes. Quite," Mo harrumphed. "For the bright future of Fae, helmed by my lovely sister, the Queen."

Jane, distracted by someone in the crowd, waved her fan behind her and dipped into a low curtsy before Nin. "Your Grace, Queen Nin, let me say that I am delighted to follow you. We on The Council know you will have a glorious reign. You are a true blessing to Fae."

"Dear Jane, please rise, and know that I thank you and The Council for all you have done to protect Fae since the loss of the Mae Queen. You are the blessing."

Jane blushed prettily, and Nin thought of all the Mae Queen said about this woman and the depths she often hid behind her practiced behavior. Years ago, the Mae Queen spoke of her affinity for alchemical magics, her shrewd social and political insights, her ability to be what was needed and endear herself in the moment. It was good for Nin to remember the observations her Queen once made, to not underestimate those around her.

Jane pulled her out of her observations with an effortless reply. "I am unworthy of such praise from my Queen, but I ever strive to serve as needed," she stated. "I will leave you to your revelry." With another, briefer dip, Jane melted into the crowd outside the cleared circle of protection around Nin.

Soon, Sabrina and Gin strolled up, arm-and-arm, to take Jane's place next to the three siblings. "This is awesome," Sabrina breathed. "So cool. I thought I knew what a Fae ball would be like, but this is beyond my imagination."

Nin looked around the room, trying to see it from Sabrina's perspective. She had been raised in The Fae Court, had attended countless balls as the Queen's student then as Princess of the Green. She was used to this. Taking a moment to assess what was actually there and not dismiss it as usual made her feel her own sense of awe and wonder. The Throne Room was transformed. The burgundy runner was gone and the actual Throne and dais were hidden behind a dark green velvet curtain. A sheet of twinkling lights in a variety of soft hues, created through the magic of Court decorators, hung on the high ceiling, leaving a pleasing glow around the space. The rough-hewn stone walls and smooth marble floors sparkled, as if strewn with glitter that did not shake loose or fade. Large vine and flower installations hung around the room in complicated spherical patterns. Rounded, solid silver tables, piled high with fresh fruits and nuts and cheeses, dotted the room. Oblong gold tables lined the walls at intervals, spots where drinks flowed readily in crystal goblets that reflected their own shimmer. A trio of Fae musicians wove their own magic, filling the dance space with music that did not overwhelm conversation in any other part of the space. The Fae courtiers themselves shone brightly, with fabric and jewels and metal and their own magical embellishments. It would be beautiful and exciting for a human. For Fae who had never attended a Court Ball even. Nin was happy for such a reminder.

She smiled at her friend. "Glad you approve, dear friend. Vola outdid herself with your dress. You dazzle this evening."

"This old thing," Sabrina said with a laugh, skimming her hands over the tight-fitting purple fabric, a small blush on her cheeks. Nin knew her friend sometimes had reservations about her looks where she and others saw a pleasing feminine softness to her rounded body, the curves that held not just to her hips and breasts, so she was happy to sense her friend was pleased not with the gown, but with herself in the gown. "It's beautiful. Stunning, really. So are these." She touched the mask across her eyes, a clump of tightly woven living ivy dotted with bright African violets and amethysts accentuating the hazy blue of her eyes, then gestured to the matching belt hung from her hips. "Thanks."

Nin nodded and looked at her eldest brother when she noticed him move slightly. He did not fidget. It was not in his nature. Every move Mo made was calculated and controlled. Yet, for a blink of a second, he seemed to bend toward Sabrina, like a fish on a line, unable to stop. He righted himself quickly enough, and Sabrina seemed wholly unaware. Nin caught Serge's eye, wanting to see if he also noticed. He smiled broadly and wiggled his eyebrows. Nin could not help her burst of laughter.

Mo cut eyes to his siblings but then bowed slightly toward Sabrina. "You are lovely this evening. As always," he said with an actual smile. For Mo, such open and honest admiration was as much of a declaration as any flowery words. Sabrina blushed and fidgeted, as was her way, but she looked Mo up and down with a hunger Nin had never seen her friend express. All of this made her heart warm at the idea of two people she loved finding something to desire and cherish in one another.

"Well, apparently I don't get any compliments from my family this evening," Serge fake grumbled.

"You and I both, cousin," Gin added with a grin.

"All of you are lovely and gorgeous and talented and you know it," Sabrina said, waving her hand around. "Don't act like you don't."

More teasing and chatter commenced, and Nin was happy for this brief respite with these people. Others would eventually interrupt, coming to pay respects or curry favor or learn what they could to use it against her later. That was the way of Fae courtiers — at least enough of them to be an expected occurrence at formal events. Nin held the teasing and talk close to her chest, wrapping herself in the warmth it expressed, adding it to the armor she needed to finish this first ball with her head held high. It was reprieve and reassurance and Queen Nin savored it.

However, when Gin and Sabrina were in the middle of exchanging amusing anecdotes about teaching, a commotion sounded across the vast room. The group stopped talking and searched for the source. They found it several yards away, just in time to see a figure in a black robe and full skull mask shove Inanna to the hard marble floor. Mosi tensed for half a beat before bursting into action. In a blink he was across the room, throwing the robed figure against a table as he wrapped his hand around their throat.

Nin and the others were about to rush over themselves, when two blurs slammed into Gin and Serge. She whipped her head back and forth, seeing Fae dressed similarly to the one who attacked her mother now straddling her stunned brother and cousin. Sabrina grabbed her hand quickly, standing tall next to her friend with concern in her eyes.

A fourth robed figure stopped directly in front of Nin. They hissed, "For our Prince Comus, our true ruler," and threw themselves at Nin. They pulled a large iron dagger from their robes and hissed at the contact with the weapon, their only outward reaction for the way the metal bit into their own skin, eyes and mind trained only on their target. Nin was momentarily stunned by the series of events, all obviously orchestrated to allow for this attack. She pulled herself up, prepared to deflect and redirect the blow as Mosi taught her so many years ago. Those who planned this attempt on her life must have forgotten she was a fighter and skilled with a weapon. There was a reason she and her magic had been restrained in Comus' Court. She would remind them of this tonight.

Before she could do so, she was shoved to the side at the last possible second. Nin watched with horror as she listed toward the ground and the robed and masked assassin tackled Sabrina, as her friend had quickly thrown herself in harm's way. A fragile human determined through love and loyalty to protect a Fae. She had once again saved her, even if she did not need saving in the moment, sacrificed her own body to help her.

"No!" Nin screamed, scrambling over to where the Fae and Sabrina lay tangled on the floor. Before she was within touching distance, the smell of blood slapped her across the face. Other screams and yells, the tackling of bodies to marble, and the rush of people from the room, filled the air, but Nin's only concern in that moment was Sabrina. She wrenched the robed figure off her friend, prepared to subdue them, but found the source of the blood smell. The iron knife was embedded in their chest to the hilt.

Tangled around it was ivy that connected back to Sabrina's mask and belt. Her friend blinked rapidly, shocked by what happened. Possibly even stunned by a heavy fall to the hard floor. Otherwise surprisingly whole and unharmed.

"What?" Sabrina asked, shaking her head and looking up. "Nin? What was that?" she asked with a stunned tone to her voice. Nin was unsure what part of the string of events Sabrina questioned as so much happened in a quick succession. Regardless, she had no real breath to answer. Relief tried to chase off the fear and pain in her chest to no avail, and emotions sealed her throat. All she could do was pull Sabrina into a fierce hug.

Mosi was soon by her side, looking over Sabrina with a hard glint in his eye. Something close to a growl sounded in his chest as he pushed out words. "Sabrina. Are you well?"

Serge and Gin joined them as Nin and Mosi helped Sabrina stand. The ivy snapped away, breaking the tie between Sabrina and the assassin. "Physically, yes. I think. Though my head hurts a bit. Marble flooring is hard."

Nin moved to check her head but Mo beat her to it, gently turning Sabrina around to examine the back of her head. "Borjigin," he barked harshly. "It has not been long since her last head injury. Please. Check her."

Gin investigated, saying, "There is no blood, but there will likely be bruising. Possibly swelling. She will need a poultice and some tea for the headache, but I do not believe she is in any danger." Gin patted Sabrina and eased her into their arms so she rested there while still standing. "I do, however, need to get her to her room to ensure this."

Nin and Mo both heaved a sigh of relief. "Yes, do that," Nin said absentmindedly, her thoughts turned to the curling ivy around the hilt of that blade now that she was certain her friend was fine.

"Quick thinking, Little One," Serge said, following the direction of her gaze.

In answer to his look, and the likely assumptions of her family around her, Nin whispered, "I did not do this," in a voice so soft, only their tight group could hear her response.

"What did you say?" Serge questioned, though he obviously heard her. He looked both confused and alarmed.

"Explain," Mosi ordered. In his anger and alarm, he apparently forgot she was not to be ordered to do anything any longer. She was Queen. The shock of events caused such formalities to fall away.

After taking a moment to ask her guard to push back, widen the clearing around them so no one was close enough to possibly pick up her hushed words, she elaborated. "I did not do this. I was prepared to physically attack when Sabrina pushed me aside. I did not call on any magics." She looked to her brothers and cousin, confused and unsure of what happened.

"I...I felt..." Sabrina stammered, fidgeting and biting her lip. "I mean, I don't know for sure, but I think I may have done it."

"Impossible," Serge said, shaking his head.

"Nothing is truly impossible," Gin added, "and our Sabrina has proven that herself, time and again, while in Fae."

"How can this be?" Mo asked.

"I do not know. Yet answers must wait. Sabrina needs rest and you have other concerns to attend." Gin cut eyes to the now struggling robed figures pinned in place by multiple guards.

Nin felt herself harden and started giving orders in a loud tone for all to hear. "There is much to do. Guard, take the prisoners to the Hold. A contingent must stay here, ensuring all in attendance are safe and accounted for after these events. Many ran, so search The Palace grounds. Contact any from the guest list who cannot be located in The Palace so we can ascertain when and how they left this night. Question every being in attendance. Gin, please check on my mother, then take both she and Sabrina to Sabrina's chambers. Tend her head and discuss what she felt during the attack. Mosi and Sergius, I need you with me."

All bowed and went about their business, fulfilling the Queen's demands.

CHAPTER 5

The Hold was a moldy, damp place, as one would expect. The difference in many representations of dungeons, however, was the greenery. Small, circular windows with jagged iron spikes inhibited escape to some extent. The briars, on the other hand, held all at bay. Thick and lush, with vibrant green leaves, they curled up every wall. They were rooted below the stone floor, the structure itself built around the plants. Their branches were thick as Nin's forearms in some spots, from eons of growth and care. The thorns, ranging from finger width and length to tiny pinpricks, were all razor sharp and deadly. These plants had a purpose — to snare and entrap. They were raised to it and performed their job well without much encouragement, though all living things flourished when helped along.

Queen Nin felt a prick of sadness as the sibling trio strolled down the leafy hall. She should have visited the briars earlier. Checked they were well after long decades under Comus' dubious care. Comus did enjoy his confinement and torture activities, so it came as no real surprise the briars appeared well tended. She did stop in her progress for a moment, reaching out to stroke a particularly wicked thorn on the wall, offer feelings of remorse, and give assurances of her future care. The briars trembled in acknowledgment, creating a wave of rustling leaves that traveled in front of the trio, leading them down the arched hallway.

Sergius and Mosi were a half-step behind their sister. Enough space to show respect and adhere to etiquette, but close enough to whisper amongst themselves. Nin could not see their faces, but both clipped out comments and replies. That was normal for Mo, even if his voice was a shade harder, had more edge and heat than usual. Serge's normal lilt, light and airy, was now gilded, as hot and unyielding as molten gold. Nin knew if she looked back, she would see the turmoil and fire reflected in his golden-brown eyes.

"It must be someone from The Falls," Serge bit out.

"We are uncertain a traitor exists," Nin replied, hedging because she needed to consider all scenarios.

"Sergius is correct. A traitor within The Falls, someone in leadership, is the only possible explanation. How else did Comus know of our plans to contact you in the human realm? How else could he have followed us to you without our knowledge? Anyone of consequence in The Falls attended the ball," Mo reasoned with clipped, hushed tones.

"Not everyone was privy to the security measures in place. That would require more access, implying the culprit was not only in leadership, but directly privy to discussions within The Council," Nin countered.

"Yes," Serge hissed. "The only people who knew enough about our mission to find you and the particulars of the ball this evening were on The Fae Council. Or, at the very least, connected to a Council Member in such an intimate way as to gain the knowledge without reservation or suspicion."

"If that is the case, we can trust no one," Mo said solemnly.

"Then we trust no one," Nin stated firmly, stiffening her spine, her suspicions confirmed by her brothers. "Mother is exempt, of course. As are Gin and Sabrina, as well as the two of you. That is our circle, the only people we can be free with until we find the one working with Comus. We must find them swiftly."

"Agreed," Mo and Serge said simultaneously.

Nin stopped several feet from a cracked door. The sounds of hands hitting flesh echoed down the hall. Mo stepped up beside his sister and looked down at her. "Are you certain?" he asked.

"I am no Queen if I cannot," she said. He nodded at her and gave a quick squeeze to her hand, sweeping in front to secure the room. Nin, then Serge, followed quickly.

The Fae tied to a chair with blistering steel chains was bloodied from the guard. Mo had approved this, of course, but it still sat heavy with Nin. She did not let it show, sliding into her haughtiest expression, allowing only disdain and anger to seep into her features. She stood regal and looked down on the Fae for long, silent beats.

"What is your name?" she asked. A stare was the only reply she received.

"Your Queen asked you a question," Mo ground out, shoving the Fae in the ribs with the blunt end of his spear, which he had popped into his tight grip upon entering the cell.

"I see no Queen, only a Princess to be reprimanded," the Fae spat, blood and saliva dripping from his mouth.

"Very well," Nin sighed. She had no time for these games. If semantics were so important to this Fae, she had other means at her disposal to get more words from them. "Sergius," she said, tilting her head to her brother, "I would like answers."

"My Pleasure, Queen Nin," he said coldly, a slice of malice in his voice. He crouched down, catching the Fae's quickly swelling eyes. His voice bounded and echoed around the room, the compulsion so clear it nearly snagged everyone else in its snare. It did not do so because Serge was an expert at his brand of magics, his intention focused and clear. The Fae in the chair was his only real target, and if the others in the room felt something, it was because he poured so much magic into his honeyed voice that the residual slivers were slightly hypnotic. "What. Is. Your. Name?" he asked with slow clarity.

The man in front of them struggled, attempting to keep his mouth firmly closed, but Serge's magic was too strong for this Fae to effectively combat. "Hillet of the Wood," he finally admitted.

"What. Was. Your. Purpose?"

The Fae did not try to resist this time. He let his words fly. "To assassinate the Queen in order to ensure Prince Comus took his rightful place on The Throne of Fae."

"How. Did. You. Enter. The. Ball?"

"I was given access by a Fae guest, the same Fae who planned the attack. We four soldiers were allowed into The Palace after the coronation, waited in a room far from the crowd until the ball was well underway. With our masks, no one knew who we were or questioned us. We walked right into The Throne Room without pause or resistance and remained aloof until the agreed-upon signal. Then, we struck."

"Who. Commanded. You?"

This question caused more struggle. The Fae did not want to reveal the culprit. Or maybe he could not, urged to silence by other magical means now warring with Serge's compulsion spell. He twisted in his seat and screwed his mouth shut, sweat forming from the effort he expended to remain silent.

Serge tried again, adding more force to his words. "WHO. COMMANDED. YOU?"

The man panted and squirmed, thrashing his head. Then, he fell still with his head hung low. Nin held her breath, expecting an answer. The Fae looked up at her and she saw hatred in his eyes and a triumphant smirk on his lips. The smirk turned into a wide smile with gritted teeth, and Nin watched as blood started leaking through, dripping over his lips and down his chin. He opened his mouth, a torrent of red expelled from a rattling cough, and croaked out, "Long may he reign," before the light left his eyes and his head hung lifeless.

Mo shot up, cursing loudly. He turned on the guards. "Did you see him ingest anything?" When they shook their heads, he howled, "Go check the other captives." However, the faint commotion they heard from adjoining rooms already told the story. When the guards returned, the trio was not surprised that all were now dead.

Serge was studying the Fae closely, opening one of his dead eyes wide. "I am no expert. Gin must take a look at these bodies for us to be sure, but I say it was poison. He was lucky or we had bad timing. Either way, my compulsion failed in the end." He sighed before standing up from his crouch. "At least we know it was about Comus and not some other, newer threat. We also now know for sure there is a traitor in our midst."

"Not reassuring," Mo gritted out, anger radiating off him. He turned to the guard, "Gather all the captives and lay them in one room. Borjigin the Scholar will investigate. You are to guard these bodies until they tell you it is fine to dispose of them."

"Dispose of them?" Nin asked, head cocked. "They were traitors and criminals, assassins and liars. Yet we are not. They will be given a burial in the earth, in honor of the Great Mother, as all Fae are accorded."

"Yes, your Grace." Mo said with a small bow. "Do as I say and your Queen commands," he added for the guards. "Queen Nin. Shall we?"

She nodded curtly, allowing Mosi to check the hallway and lead her out of the room. Serge needed no urging and followed behind.

When the siblings reached a bend in the hall, well away from the guards now standing over dead bodies, they stopped to regroup. "Now?" Serge asked, looking between his brother and sister. Mo, for once, looked to Nin instead of taking the lead.

"We say the captives died before we could interrogate them about the attempt on our Queen and quietly investigate on our own," Nin said firmly. Turning to Mosi, she asked, "Do you trust the guards who witnessed what occurred tonight?"

Mosi thought for a moment, "I would say yes, but we must be vigilant. I will keep them sequestered and occupied so they do not have the opportunity to speak of these events."

Nin nodded in agreement. "Good. I would like you to also handpick a new guard to increase security. For me, Mother, Serge, Gin, and Sabrina at least. It should be quiet, and not obvious, but effective."

"As you wish," he said, but his eyes shone with pride and Nin knew he approved of her decision. It should not have mattered overly much, other concerns pressed in on her, her family, her realm. Still, the look warmed and heartened her.

"Serge," she said, turning to her other brother, "you must be my eyes and ears in The Court. I will discuss these events with Mother as she will be our inside contact within The Council, the only one we can fully trust. Stealth is required, but we must work to uncover the one who executed this plot. None of us are safe from attack until this is done."

Serge tilted his head in agreement, but then frowned and looked between Nin and Mo. "This is all well and good, but we have yet to discuss one issue that may be of great importance in what lies ahead." Nin furrowed her brow, as did Mo, and Serge sighed. "Sabrina? The magic she claims to have? That's a very big unknown in all of this, and if we are all in danger, it could hinder or help us."

Nin crumbled. She watched worry etch into Mosi's face. He clearly cared for her friend, as did she. Sadly, there were no ready answers at the moment. "I told you true earlier. I did not use magic during the attack. I do not know how Sabrina did this. If it is even possible for a human without magic to somehow develop it. Magic was cast earlier, and it was earth magics at that. It smelled slightly different, tasted a little different on the air. It was either Sabrina or an unknown earth magic practitioner. Neither seem likely, but those are the only logical options."

"Gin is with her now. They witnessed these events just as we did. They are surely discussing it with Sabrina. Their knowledge also better positions them to determine what happened and how it happened," Mo added.

Serge quickly replied, "Yes. All true. We must consider all possibilities and long-term implications. If there is another Fae with earth magics, they should be found and brought into the fold. They have a rightful place in The Court as a Prince or Princess. If it was Sabrina...I do not know."

"Both of you are correct. We need to think through the implications, but we cannot fully do that until we understand what happened. Gin is our best source of information on that front. Let us leave the Hold, find our family, reveal what we know, and dig deeper into this magic question. Only then can we make more solid plans," Nin declared. Her brothers nodded and all three broke their huddle and assumed their positions — Mo leading for defense, Nin protected in the middle, Serge vigilant from the rear. The group turned and marched on, toward their

family, toward the certainty of more questions while
harboring the hope of more answers.

CHAPTER 6

Nin sat beside Sabrina on the bed. Her friend looked nervous and unsure, the tell-tale fidgeting manifesting as her hands rubbed together, fluttered over her lap, smoothed down the perfectly made bed, doing anything to remain in motion. She changed, replacing her gown with pajamas. Gin also changed, switching from their dress robes to their everyday robes. Inanna had only just left to change herself, yet the conversation they needed to have could not wait, and her mother agreed to let her children fill her in on the particulars after their discussion.

Gin hovered near Sabrina on the bed, taking care of her while she, Serge, and Mo had been busy in the Hold. Nin was anxious to see her friend, to possibly discover a few answers, but when she stopped to consider it, she felt like the events of the evening — what occurred in The Throne Room and with the captive — clung to her now heavy gown in a way that made her skin feel itchy and tight.

Serge, of course, showed no sign of discomfort from his perch on a high-back chair placed in the far corner of the room. He was all seriousness, no smirk in sight, poised and nonplussed as always. Mo stood at attention in front of the closed door, a stony sentry. He rarely looked fully at ease, but now his body was taut. His eyes sparked and a muscle in his jaw flickered as he silently ground his teeth. Her brother was very upset and had every reason to be. She also suspected the view of a distressed Sabrina set him more on edge.

"Come, Sabrina. There is no need to fear," Nin called to her friend. "You may say anything in this room with us."

Gin gave an encouraging nod and smile, as they likely assured her of this earlier. Sabrina deflated, her body folding slightly in on itself, as she expelled a quick puff of air. "I know," she said, staring intently down at her blanket and not at any individual in the room. "I know. I just…it's weird. And I didn't tell anyone about the weirdness earlier, so I feel bad about it. I didn't even know what was going on. Still don't. Not for sure. Though, talking through things with Gin, we might have some ideas. At least a theory or two."

"Sabrina, do not fret so," Serge called from his perch, and Nin felt the tendrils of his magic there, a little burst of calm to wash over their friend and help her along with her confession. The spell was no compulsion, yet it was not, strictly speaking, the most honorable thing. Manipulating emotions is tricky business, especially when humans without magical defenses were involved. Nin, however, did not press the matter.

"I can feel what you're doing," Sabrina snapped, finally bringing her eyes up to the room to give Serge a hard stare.

"No harm meant, Sabrina," Serge replied, hands up in mock surrender. He held a question in his eyes, likely the same question Nin had. How had Sabrina recognized his magic so quickly? Yes, if attuned to the magical abilities of a particular Fae, a human could eventually figure out when magic was being used on them, particularly with word magics. Even without knowledge or connection, word magics had a weight and tug humans could sense after a minute or two if the spell was not masked in some way. Sabrina was a quick study and would learn to feel it when Serge used such on her. Still, it should have taken her more time to discern and was an additional curiosity.

"Yes. Yes. Yes. Okay. So, let's just get this out there. I think, and Gin seems to agree after our little chat, that some of Nin's magic leaked into me during that whole iron-chair-slash-rescue incident."

Nin stared at her friend in confusion. It could not be. Magic was not transferable.

"How is this possible?" Mo asked.

"The chair, as Nin told us from Comus' own ramblings, was designed to leech her magic and transfer it to him. It is not completely outside the realm of possibility to suppose it could have worked with Sabrina," Gin said as they looked down on their friend with curiosity.

"Comus already holds magic, so, logically, his body could take in additional magic. Sabrina did not have magic. We would have felt it long ago if that were the case. How can a non-magical human suddenly hold magic if they never did so before?" Serge questioned, processing the information aloud for himself.

"Does magic even require such?" Nin countered. "We do not know, because we only know those born with magics or those born without. We cannot say how magic would or would not be able to operate in or through a person with no natural abilities."

"That is not strictly true, my Queen," Gin answered. "There is one famous tale of transfer of magic to the non-magical."

All in the room wondered to themselves, until Mo barked out a laugh, apparently picking up on Gin's allusion more quickly than the others. "You are in jest, Gin. Are you suggesting the New Eve Tale applies to this event?"

Nin blinked rapidly, implications skittering around her head. The New Eve Tale was the founding story of Fae, the creation myth. It involved the birth of a single Fae, a woman with earth magics, from the union of earth, the Great Mother, and sky. Knowing she would be lonely, the Great Mother molded more Fae from various elements in the realm, taking small gifts from the first Fae woman and passing them to the newly created Fae, thus sharing her magics with those who had none, those who then founded the rest of Fae and passed these gifts down the generations. Some believed it was truth, some believed it only an allegory. Regardless, it was a tale all Fae knew from infancy.

"Impossible," Serge whispered, moving forward in his chair.

Nin caught herself quickly, shook off her shock, and turned to Sabrina and Gin. "Let us set aside the New Eve Tale for now. I would like to hear more about how you two are certain this transfer occurred."

"Well…" Sabrina hesitated. "That's what makes me feel a bit bad. Because I knew something weird was going on and I didn't say anything."

"Because you were unsure and afraid," Gin encouraged. "There is no harm in this form of protection. Now we in this room are here to help. It is best they know the details."

With a nod, Sabrina visibly steeled herself and began her story. "Do y'all remember when I freed Nin from the chair? She shot up like a rocket and I was blown back? I told everyone I was fine, and I was. Except I was a little tingly. I don't really know how to explain it. It was like static electricity sparked under my skin instead of on top of it. And there was this hum, similar to if I listened to music a little too loudly for too long. It was more pronounced right after, when everything was hectic and we were all trying to get our shit together after the battle and whatnot. Slowly, both faded to the background. I barely noticed it unless I was close to the chair, which is why I would only help study the thing when Gin directly asked me to do so. My body felt tight and hot and weird when I was around it too long."

She paused for a moment then continued after a quick glance at Nin and Mo, "Sometimes, when I felt strongly, like certain emotions or physical sensations came up, the spark and hum would flair. Other than that, it stayed in the background."

"What did you feel this evening?" Nin asked, taking her friend's hand and giving a reassuring squeeze.

"Everything was a blur, what with your super speeds. Though, oddly, that too looked different than it had before. Like I could see it better? Anyway, by the time I knew what was happening, it was already going down, so I just reacted. I pushed you aside, the Fae hit me. Right before, that spark was super-hot under my skin, and the hum was really loud, and my body felt heavier, like I was weighted to the ground. I expected pain from the knife, but that never came. I did feel — no, I mean, I knew, somehow, when I was under that man, that I did something to him to protect Nin and myself. It was a bone-deep certainty, though I didn't know what it was until I saw the vines from my belt connected to the dagger in his chest."

The room was silent for long beats after Sabrina's confession. Nin never considered this possibility, but all Sabrina said made sense within the context of recent events. It also connected to how Nin felt her own magic working at times. She looked at her friend and gave a small, reassuring smile, though she did not feel much reassurance herself. This was wholly new territory, and there was little to help them predict what the results of suddenly acquiring earth magics could mean for Sabrina now or in the future.

"Well, that's that," Serge said, slapping his knees as he pulled himself out of his chair. "Looks like our Sabrina got herself some magic."

"Yippee," Sabrina replied flatly.

Serge chuckled and moved closer, chucking Sabrina on the chin like he often did to Nin when she was child. "No need for sarcasm. Will it be hard?

Yes. Do we know what to expect? No. Are you
totally safe right now? No, none of us are."

"Your words are unhelpful," Mo ground out,
not liking the direction of Serge's thoughts.

"Am I wrong?" he asked their brother, who
still stood stiff at the door. Mo gave a curt shake and
Serge continued. "Even so, we will handle this. Just
as we will handle the traitor."

Gin gave a gasp. "It is certain, then? There
is a traitor?"

"Likely one of The Council or a Fae closely
connected to a Council Member," Mo said with heat.

Gin blinked rapidly, both his dark brows and
bowed mouth turned down at his frown. "Then it
really is us, together, against whatever is out there
waiting."

"Yep," Serge grinned. "It'll be questionable.
Likely dangerous. It might be good fun, too. I like a
little mystery and intrigue in my life. With a spy and
Sabrina's newfound powers, we appear to have
plenty of both."

"You should not be so flippant about this
business," Mo ground out.

"Better to be dire and sour, like you?" Serge
countered.

"Let it be," Nin sighed, not in the mood for
the verbal sparring of her brothers. Much had
happened in the last hours. In the last weeks. They all
needed a rest but were unlikely to get it. Sitting here,
now, her focus was on Sabrina.

"Sabrina, my sister, do you still feel and
hear these things?" she asked.

Sabrina cocked her head and squinted her
eyes in concentration. "Yes," she answered. "Sparks
and hums are still chugging away in the background."

"Then you must begin learning how our magic works and how it can be channeled. Lucky for you, we have the best teacher present," she commanded, nodding toward Gin.

"It would be an honor to teach our Sabrina," they said with a bow. "I am certain she will be a diligent student. However, I would suggest I not teach her alone." They turned toward Nin and added, "If your magics transferred to her, it would be best for you to participate in the lessons as well."

"Fair enough," Nin said, then rose from the bed. "It is decided."

"Who decided?" Mo started to argue, then stopped, cutting eyes at Nin. "I do not mean offense, sister. I feel in this room you are Nin, not Queen."

"I am always Queen," Nin said, pulling herself as tall as her five-foot frame would allow. "But you are correct, Mo. In this room, or more aptly, with this group of people, I do not wish to be blindly followed. What say you all, then, to my proposal?"

Gin and Serge nodded basic agreement. Sabrina looked sad and hesitant but said, "Sure. Why not? I mean, if I have this inside me now, I'd much rather have a handle on it so it can be useful, or at the very least, not harmful."

Mo stepped closer to the bed, reaching out with a hand but pulling back before he touched Sabrina, "Are you certain? You wish to train rather than study?"

"Oh, no. There is no 'rather than.' I'll be doing lots of research about this. I'm a Scholar after all. I'm sure Gin will do the same. For now, with what we know, lessons seem the most logical step forward." She beamed up at Mosi then, her nervousness shed for a moment, and said, "Thanks for checking in on what I might prefer, though. Much appreciated." Mo was frozen by her broad, true smile. Dazed even. It made Nin happy to see it, even with all that hung over their group. Sabrina's smile and Mo's dazed look held promise and hope. They would surely need both in abundance in the days ahead.

"That is settled, then," Nin called, gathering her skirts as she stood to leave. "Let us leave Sabrina to sleep. For myself, I will be glad to be rid of this gown and tucked in my own bed." She gave everyone in the room tight hugs before pulling on her more regal demeanor as Mo preceded her out the door to escort her to the Consort Chambers.

CHAPTER 7

Nin ordered her guard to stand outside the Practice Chamber doors. There were minor protestations from her head guard, but they did not push back when she calmly stated her orders a second time. She was their Queen, and if she had reason for secrecy in a secured room within The Palace, they could not step in her path. Nin knew no one needed to be in the room where they would teach Sabrina about her newly acquired magics. Sabrina's abilities were a secret her inner circle would keep close for as long as possible. Her magics would surface one day regardless. Magics were not meant to be kept hidden. Nin, above most others in Fae, knew the consequences of suppressing magics. The goal for these lessons was not to keep Sabrina's magic a secret indefinitely, but rather to help her friend develop these new magics before she was forced to show or use her power in some instance. Preparation was key.

Today was for Sabrina and her introduction to magic. The Practice Chamber, with its cavernous interior for large demonstrations and small, darkened alcoves for more private work, was the perfect place for this. It is where the Mae Queen trained her in earth magics. Nin remembered those lessons fondly, with a tinge of grief, as her steps echoed across the large, empty space, heading toward the third alcove on the far wall — the only spot where small flickers of candlelight were visible.

The plan was for Gin to enter first, long before the others, to determine the best space for their purpose on a given training day. Sabrina followed after, and Nin would come in last, minimizing the amount of people who knew all three gathered in the room as best they could. No one knew of Sabrina's powers, so more teachers could not be brought in for instruction. Gin was enough, however, and Nin was the only Fae who could help her with any earth magic questions. The three other secret-bearers were not in attendance in deference to Sabrina's nerves. She was anxious, and the fewer people present, the less anxious she would be. She was also less nervous with Nin and Gin in general. She may have known Nin longer, but Sabrina bonded with Gin in a number of important ways while in Fae. Nin felt their connection was solid. She was happy for her friend and her cousin in this. Both were exceptional, kind individuals who deserved excellent friends in their lives.

Pushing through the small magical haze obscuring a clear view of the interior space, Nin stepped fully into the alcove to find Gin and Sabrina chatting on a bench. These spaces shaded most actions in their interior, allowing small amounts of light to be visible so as to mark when they were in use. Because of this, the blaze of candles in the room momentarily dazed Nin when she stepped over the threshold. The rough-hewn walls and stone floor gave the room a cave-like feel, as if they had secreted away to a small, unknown spot deep within a mountain. That illusion was broken by the large table and bench along one wall, the blackboard with chalk and cloth that ran the length of the far wall, and the massive chandelier that cast a bright glow around the entire space. If it was a cave, it was a cave obviously designed for learning.

"My Queen," Gin said with a small bow.

"Sup?" Sabrina added with a cheeky, lop-sided grin.

"No need for formalities when it is only us, Gin. Surely you know this?"

"Of course, Nin. Whatever you need," they replied, staring into her eyes with a hint of sympathy and too much knowing. Gin was astute and kind, a combination that endeared them to many but also brought with it an ability to see beyond an action or desire into the reasoning behind it. In this instance, Gin showed all they knew about Nin's wish to cling to some form of normalcy with a strong but thoughtful look. They gave it to her without judgment or reservation, yet it was still a hard thing to realize when another recognizes the vulnerabilities often hidden behind words and deeds.

She gave a slight nod. "Thank you, dear cousin."

Gin waved off the thanks and turned to Sabrina, "Now we are all in attendance, are you ready to begin?"

"I guess so," Sabrina said, starting to twist her hands in her tell-tale sign of nerves. "Before we start, do you have a syllabus or an outline or something? I'd like to know what I'm getting into here."

"No," Gin answered. "We do not have a solid outline for the instruction of magic. Each individual is different, so teaching the basics of magic is always dependent on the student. I can present you a broad overview of our first few lessons if you'd like?" Sabrina urged Gin on and they continued, "Our beginning concerns magical basics, including simple universal spells and magical theory. This first lesson will focus on calling forth your magic and intention. Next, we will explore affinity, what types of magic the power inside you is drawn toward. Only then will we practice release and casting, which is how you can effectively use your magic."

"So, three basic lessons?" Sabrina asked. "That doesn't seem like much."

"Three lessons are not the norm," Nin asserted, moving to stand in line with Gin in front of Sabrina, "but these are extenuating circumstances."

"Quite true," Gin assented. "You are a quick study, as we already know. We are also unsure of the depth and breadth of your magic or whether it will last or dissipate. Because of these factors, our lessons are slightly amended from what a Fae child would go through when first studying their magics with an instructor."

"Do not think of this all as lesser than," Nin quickly added. "You are an exceptional case. You are also an adult whom we know we can push forward quicker. These lessons will be lengthier and more difficult than the basic lessons offered to Fae children.”

“Ok. Gotcha. I’m not starting like a kid, even if I’m new to magic like a kid. Thanks for placating my ego. And we begin with the three basic foundations and go from there, depending on what happens during these lessons.”

“Exactly. See, already such a good pupil.” Gin smiled.

“I was always a good student, Gin. Wouldn’t be a Scholar if I wasn’t,” Sabrina said in mock affront.

“Yes. Yes. So very smart and good, my Sabrina,” Nin teased. “Let us begin.”

“Right. I’m sure our Nin has much to do, so we should get started,” Gin said as they moved over to the chalkboard. “First we must discuss the basics of magical theory, the way we think of magic.” They paused for a moment and regrouped. “It may be better to say the way we, as Fae, think with magic, as it is slightly different from the way humans contend with thinking and their own consciousness.”

Sabrina looked puzzled but remained silent as Gin continued, “Magic is a connected energy that flows through the Fae. You described it as a hum and spark. That is how many describe it. The physical sensation of magic at work in the body.” Gin paused here, looking intently at Sabrina to emphasize their next point. “Physical sensation is not the only internal issue we must consider. To be truly adept at magic, one must understand how it functions in the mind. How it may affect the way you, as a human, have been conditioned to think.”

“Magic isn’t just a feeling, but also a way of thinking,” Sabrina said with a hint of hesitation.

When Gin nodded, she continued, firm in voice but unsure in idea. "Okay. Right. The thing is, how do I know how my thinking is different? Or how do I make my thinking different? How will that make me different?" The last question was softer, more hesitant, piercing into the heart of Nin as she heard the worry there.

Gin leaned in and held Sabrina's hand. "It must be hard to think one must change a part of themselves that they hold so dear. Let me assure you, Sabrina, you will not be someone else. You will remain our lovely and intelligent friend."

Nin gave an enthusiastic but silent affirmation and Gin pulled back, continuing their lecture. "One big difference between Fae and humans, or with humans who hold no magic, is that they often divide their mind unnecessarily. They assume focus implies singularity, but the mind thrives on connectivity and joint processes. The mind, Fae or human, functions in this way. Humans have become adept at ignoring the connected, simultaneous action of the mind. To perform magic well, you must first practice focusing on multiple things at once."

"It is like multitasking within your mind," Nin said, hoping a more relatable analogy would help Sabrina grasp the concept more quickly.

"That doesn't seem too bad," Sabrina replied with a shrug. "Thinking on multiple things at once may be a little hectic at first, but feasible. Are there ways to practice without using magic?"

"Yes," Gin grinned, pulling a book from an inner fold of their robe. "This is the best way, although the exercises are meant for small children. It is a good place for you to start, and I suspect you will breeze through the process quickly."

Sabrina took a moment to flip through the book, a slight frown on her face until she looked back at the inside cover. "This was yours, lady," she said with a laugh, holding the book up to Nin, who smiled in acknowledgement and memory.

"I learned a great deal from the book, but more from my first official Fae teacher," she quipped, gesturing toward Gin with a gentle smile.

"I'm sure," Sabrina said, shutting the book gently. "Uh, I just want to say thanks, before we go deeper into all of this. To you both. For taking the time to help me get through this."

"No problem," Nin called, parroting one of Sabrina's favorite sayings with a grin.

"It is truly my pleasure," Gin said on a small bow. They were not one to linger when teaching, therefore Gin quickly moved on, knowing Sabrina had at least a theoretical understanding of what they discussed when referencing magic as a thought process. "Now, let us consider the physicality of magic, as magic works in and flows through the mind, but also manifests in the body as well as outside it. It is important to remember magic flows both inside and outside of us, and in Fae, everything has a touch of magic." Gin began to draw a figure on the board, a person with squiggly two-way arrows inside their bodies that then also radiated outward. "Our studies of magic have yet to determine the origin, whether the Fae realm or Fae people is the ultimate source of magic here. Either way, we as magical creatures are dependent on the land of Fae in some ways. Our magic effects that outside of us, space and people, and Fae is a place where such magic is sustained and supported. It is cyclical. Our minds think through and with magic, our bodies contain magic and put it out into the realm, and the realm itself seeps magic back into us."

"That's why Fae lose power the longer they stay in the human realm? Why humans start to get ill if they stay in Fae without being bonded to a Fae?" Sabrina asked, staring intently at Gin's diagram.

"Yes. Or so we believe. There is no definitive proof of this, but it is a foundational theory for Fae scholars — the land of Fae helps create and sustain magic so that Fae can harness and use it."

"This is also why earth magic is so powerful, so revered? It directly connects to all of the literal earth, which sustains all of Fae, and it is not subject to the same diminishing of power in the human realm?"

"Quick study," Nin beamed.

"I'm more than a pretty face, lady," Sabrina replied with a laugh.

"Yes. Nicely done, Sabrina. You are exactly right. Earth magics are generally more powerful, last longer, and connect to all facets of the earth. Nin can use a variety of different magics at full strength. For example, we all know Mosi has metal magics. That is connected to the earth, of course, as the earth is the source of metal. The same with water magics and stone magics and other things. Even word magics spring from the earth in theory, as they connect to Fae people, who are also a product of the earth. However, any one person with any one of these magics has an affinity to that single form of magic. They can do basic spells in other forms, some more than others, but they cannot do all. Nin, or anyone with earth magics, can do all this and also directly commune with the earth, hence her connection with plants. As we have witnessed ourselves, she can even sustain for years while outside Fae. Our creation tales highlight earth magics, which is one reason our rulers have all had earth magic affinity. However, on a more practical level, they are more rare and far more powerful than other Fae. There are also theories that earth magic monarchs allow the literal earth of Fae to thrive. We saw a downturn in certain natural areas when Comus ruled the castle, so that theory may well be proven fact soon enough.”

"Because of Nin, I likely have earth magics?” Sabrina added.

"That is my assumption, yes,” Gin said. “It makes logical sense that an earth affinity would come with her magic seeping into you from that chair. After all, it was the endgame of Comus, to acquire earth magics to make his takeover of Fae complete. We also have proof. You literally used earth magics at the ball.”

"Okay. So. The basic idea is that magic connects to multiplicity of thought. As a form of energy, it flows in and through and outside of a person. The ultimate goal, then, must be to develop a way to control thought and physical manifestation to your advantage.”

Nin jumped in here, “Yes, which is what these lessons are about. As children we are taught thinking mechanisms and flow first because to not control your magic can be dangerous.” She swallowed hard, hating to bring up these memories, but she must for the sake of her friend’s understanding, so Sabrina could realize the serious repercussions that could arise from uncontrolled magics. “I know this from experience. When I first

escaped captivity, my magic was deadly and out of
control. A similar thing happened before Comus
locked me in the chair and when you freed me from
up, though to a lesser degree." She looked seriously
at Sabrina, adding, "This is why lessons are crucial,
even if we do not know the limits of your magic as of
now. Uncontrolled, unwieldy magic is a danger to
you and those around you."

Sabrina looked nervous, but replied,
"Understood," with gravity. She took this seriously,
as Nin knew she would.

"Now, we have some basic theory. Please,
ask any questions you have along the way, but let us
jump right into practice," Gin encouraged, as they
moved away from the chalkboard to stand directly in
front of Sabrina. "The first thing you need to do is
connect with that energy inside. This part is similar to
human forms of meditation. Do you meditate?"

"Not regularly or anything, but sure. I've
done it."

"Good. Now, close your eyes, try to clear
your mind first, then focus on your body. Narrow
down on what you physically feel and sense inside
yourself." Gin waited a few minutes, as Sabrina took
measured breaths in and out, ensuring she was
comfortable with these sensations before softly
asking, "Do you feel it?"

"Yes," Sabrina whispered. She cleared her
throat, adding a bit louder, "I can feel and hear it like
before."

"Very good," Gin encouraged. "Next, bring
in conscious thought. Allow your mind to think on
the sensations you feel with physical senses. Connect
them with conscious, active thought of what they are.
Attempt to pick up on that distinction as it is

important. There is a difference between the physical sensation as thought and your active consideration of what the physical sensation means or how it functions in relation to any other number of reactions, sensations, or ideas." Gin paused as Sabrina frowned with her eyes closed before they offered more information and instruction, a brief moment for her to collect what had already been given and prepare for what would come.

Gin's voice became calmer, subtler, guiding her like a guru in the human realm. "What I ask of you is difficult and complex work. Mental visualization may help. Imagine a bridge in your mind. On one side is what your body feels and knows. On the other is your mind, how it both processes and deals with those feelings. Have the two meet in the middle, walk the bridge. Make it a specific and conscious action, this joining. Take all the time necessary. Give me a signal when you can both think and feel the sensations in a way that is connected and simultaneous to you."

Several minutes passed with Sabrina in full internal concentration before she gave a small, silent signal for Gin to proceed. "Now, I want you to open your eyes and rise. Which is your dominant hand?" When Sabrina held up her right, Gin continued, "Okay. Take your right hand and hold it at a comfortable height in front of you, palm up."

Nin leaned forward, slightly mesmerized by the process, remembering fondly how Gin led her down this same path so long ago. It made her own magic practically purr inside her.

"Good, good. The next step is difficult, so do not become discouraged. You must endeavor to join the mental and physical work of magic. Keep the multiple thoughts and sensations at the forefront of your mind, continue to allow your thinking to be simultaneously active and internal. With that focus and ability, direct your magic, as much as you can, to the tip of your middle finger on your right hand. With will and clear intention, use your mind to direct the physical manifestation of energy you feel all over your body to that one spot and that one spot only. To do this properly, you must think through the process, feel the sensation, and will the sensation to gather in one place."

Sabrina stood, silently concentrating on her upturned hand for twenty minutes, willing her mind and body to function in an entirely new way. Her eyes strained and a muscle ticked in her clenched jaw, but she finally spoke up. "I feel it. I feel it all pent up there," she said with a bit of awe.

"Okay. Now, repeat this word while maintaining that concentration: ISPISSP." Once Sabrina had the pronunciation down, struggling to keep her mind in two places at once, Gin continued. "You're doing so great, Sabrina. Now, that word, in Fae, means spark. It is a very basic spell that, in theory, should create a spark of magic." Rubbing their hands together and stepping away from Sabrina, Gin gave the final instructions. "All you have to do now is maintain concentration on your finger, say the word with clear intention to create a spark firmly set in your mind, and you'll produce it. It may take a number of tries, but keep attempting the spell, again and again, until it happens."

Nin watched, nearly holding her breath, as Sabrina started. She said the word at least twenty times, stopping to refocus and regroup every so often. Finally, after long minutes, Sabrina's words and intentions melded, and a white spark, clear as lightning across a cloudy sky, leapt up from her fingertip and danced there for a moment before dissipating.

"Ohmygod," Sabrina said in a rush. "Do you see that shit?" she asked Nin, looking both amazed and pleased with herself. "I did magic. Like, really and truly made something happen with magic."

"That you did, my friend," Nin said, reaching over to hug Sabrina. She hugged back, bouncing on her feet slightly with excitement.

"Very good, Sabrina. Very good. Now, again."

"Again?" Sabrina asked, pulling from Nin.

Nin chuckled and moved to sit at the bench. "Oh, this will take a while yet, Sabrina. Gin, while an excellent teacher, is a taskmaster at heart."

"It is only because practice is important," Gin called back to her before turning to face Sabrina again. "Yes, Sabrina. Again. And again. And again. Until the spark appears on the first try several times in a row."

"Makes sense, I guess," Sabrina grumbled.

Nin sat back and watched. There was little for her to do in the moment to help Gin or Sabrina, but she wanted to remain with her friend through this in solidarity. Watching Gin teach brought back bittersweet memories of her own time as a pupil, a small smile and soft stab of grief at what she was, who she was, before everything changed for her and all of Fae.

CHAPTER 8

Nin felt drained as she lay awake in her bed, though she did little during the first late-night magic lesson. Sabrina was not a bad student — far from it in fact. She was enthusiastic and attentive. Gin knew what they were doing, and Nin tried to follow their lead, adding what they knew when and where the information was needed. For this first lesson, at least, that meant Nin spent a great deal of time on the sideline, watching Sabrina and Gin work, and adding information and encouragement wherever she could. She was there for support for now as more specific lessons in earth magic would have to come later, and she was so proud of her friend's progress. Even with all the love and encouragement and pride present, the first lesson left her with complex emotions she needed to sort through on her own.

First and foremost, the need for such lessons made her feel guilty and helpless. She blamed herself for the state of Sabrina in general. She was the sole reason she was here. Her friend had traveled across realms to help her, and for her troubles she was imbibed with magic that could do any number of things to her physical, mental, or emotional well-being and she was forced to play the student, working to control a gift that was thrust upon her without her consent. Just like the binding. Just like so much with Sabrina now. It was enough to make Nin weep for them both, for what she and Sabrina had and would endure, and for the guilt she felt over it all. Sabrina, her family, all of Fae — it all not only rested on her shoulders but was a direct result of how she failed at so many important things in her life. She was barely over one hundred and felt like a child bumbling through life. The only difference being what she did echoed out because of who she was, giving her actions grave consequences for everyone in her realm.

The Mae Queen had thousands of years to adjust, and logically Nin knew she may well have felt these same feelings as Nin, especially when her reign began. Yet, Nin could not imagine her in this position. She was so poised, so decisive, so regal in all ways. Even as a mentor, she taught with grace and strength, showing care while guiding Nin in the intricacies of their shared magics. Nin feared she might not be able to help Fae or Sabrina. Not properly. Though she had little choice either way. Events trickled down and gathered to form pressing needs, and although Nin was hesitant and self-conscious and unsure of how well she would do, she always did what needed to be done in the moment, as long as she recognized what that was. The problem was, she knew she could be swayed, knew from experience with Comus before his change, her ideas of what were necessary could shift based on the manipulation of others. It made her not trust herself, and she was more than aware the same distrust trickled down from her to The Court and the people, making all of Fae feel a little less safe and a little more wary of her as Queen.

She burrowed into the cloud of her mattress, flinging her forearm across her eyes. Even in the dark of her room, she needed something, an extra layer between her and the world, to help her mind disassociate enough to get much-needed rest. Tomorrow would bring more worries, more ways she must confront and attempt to correct her past failures. It was exhausting to constantly be reminded of all the mistakes made, of all the ways she did not live up to what the Mae Queen was for her people. Yet, she would try, day in and day out, to help her people, her family, and her friend through this maze. Hopefully, together, they would get clear and find peace.

The next day, after a fretful night in bed, Nin sat, anxious, on The Throne. Of course, no one looking at her would know this. It was an official Court Audience Day, the first of her reign. The first following the assassination attempt. She sat, still and poised, her back straight, hands resting on her lap, ankles crossed beneath the gold sheath dress she wore. Like the Mae Queen before her, she did not don The Crown of Fae, deciding to wear The Court

Singlet instead — a simple gold chain with scattered emeralds draped across her forehead. She did not fidget or slump or express her stress in a physical way. She looked cool and calm, the monarch Fae needed in trying times. Inside, however, her heart raced, and her mind flipped from one awful scenario to another.

She heard a petal-soft whisper at her side. "Calm," Serge said, not looking down or over to her as he stood at attention to her right. As a life-long courtier, it made sense to have him with her here as her adviser. He would become her Vizer soon, after what felt like an appropriate period of time to ward off overt rumblings of nepotism from the courtiers. He waited patiently, serving her well all the while, which served as both familial comfort and political boon for her. He was a shrewd political mind, and he was also her brother, the one who played games with her late into the night when she was a child and helped her get into good forms of trouble in later years. They shared blood and time and love so it was more than savvy having him near — it was a slice of safety and comfort she could cling to, if only even in her mind. She nodded an acknowledgment to his words but did not look over to him. Instead, she raised her hand to the young page at the foot of the stairs. It was the sign for official requests to begin.

In Fae, Court Audience Days were a time to bring issues before the Queen in a public space. It was also when the Queen announced public policy changes or recognized the failings or triumphs of others in a public forum. Nin had been in attendance for many, stood by the side of the Mae Queen as she gave advice, made declarations, called for punishments and praise, as was her place when she was Princess of the Green. From such experience, she knew that, depending on the day and the attendees, Audience Days could be easy and joyful or hard and nightmarish.

Nin had little control over who came before her. She would sit in attendance for one hour and had requested a ten-minute space at the end for business she wished to conduct. Otherwise, the business brought forward was scheduled by The Fae Council, usually through Michel. However, with current events in mind, Inanna petitioned, and won a Council vote, to be The Court Audience facilitator for the first six months of Nin's rule. She trusted her mother, who looked on with a gentle smile from the bottom of the staircase in order to announce each Fae before they made their business known to The Court. Yet, the room was filled with courtiers and various important political and social figures in Fae, all craning to get a glimpse of their new Queen's methods and actions, and it made Nin feel like a child right before Affinity Day — all anticipation with the addition of forced expectations hoisted on them.

Her mother held true and eased her into the situation. The first few speakers were from prominent Fae families wishing to express their support of and gratitude for Nin. It was odd to hear such effusive praise. Something she must get used to as a monarch. She thanked all with kind words and tried to move them along as quickly as possible. It was politically important to acknowledge their power and position, to give them recognition and time. She remembered these figures, of course, but she could, at most, call them political or social acquaintances.

The final Fae in this group, however, turned a number of heads. It was Bastien of the Shores, a

powerful courtier who served centuries even though
he was known to dislike the Mae Queen. He sneered
at Nin enough in her role as Princess of the Green
that she, and most others who cared to remember,
doubted he would like her more after the events of
the past few decades. He often caused uproars
amongst the courtiers, creating minor political
upheavals the Mae Queen was forced to squash or
ignore, depending on the circumstances. He gave a
wide smile that did not reach the hard stone of his
sharp gray eyes and hesitated a beat before offering a
sweeping bow toward Nin.

"Princess Nin," he stopped as he pulled up,
pretending to be abashed by his mistake. "Oh, do
forgive me, You Grace. Queen Nin. It is only that I
remember you as Princess for so long it is automatic
for me to address you with your former title."

Nin tilted her chin down as a slight
acknowledgment but kept her eyes hard as she spoke.
"Sir Bastien. A pleasure to see you in The Palace
again."

"Thank you, Your Grace. It is lovely to see
so many back in their places again. It has been too
long. Far too long, by many accounts."

It was a quick barb that slammed into Nin's
chest where her guilt was entrenched. She blanked
for a moment, unable to respond, and a true grin
began to spread on Bastien's wide face, his amber-
colored eyebrows quirked at a smug angle. His look
said he knew his mark hit true and he would use it to
his advantage. She did not miss these political games,
but luckily, her brother was there and more than a
match for Bastien.

"Too true, Sir Bastien. While our Queen
gathered knowledge and strength, was in need of aid

and comfort, there were many who hid, not daring to fight against the one who overturned this Court. I can understand the impulse to cowardice myself, but those who did not confront the tyrant in his time have much to answer for in Queen Nin's Court. We who bled to return Fae to its true monarch, Queen Nin included, will remember who served her in her most trying days and who did nothing." Serge practically purred this, his voice not dripping with magic but colored with disdain.

Bastien pulled upright. "Yes. Indeed. I had my family and my people to protect, but we supported in the ways we could."

"As I am aware," Nin said, gaining her bearings and jumping into the conversation. "I thank you for showing your support, then and now."

"I, Bastien of the Shores, and all who follow me, support the true and right efforts of the Queen," he crooned.

"As you should. As I expect all faithful courtiers will, Sir Bastien," she added, pulling her haughtiest look to stare down at the man who wished to rile her on this first Audience Day, even after others tried to kill her. There was more than one way to weaken or manipulate a monarch, and Bastien's presence was an important reminder of this fact. She had shown no weakness in battle or with the assassins. She could show no weakness in this arena either. With a wave of her hand, she let him know he was dismissed, which was a move he did not care for and was something she should not have done, but it made her feel good to make him seem small in the moment. Not the best reaction, she was aware, but it was done.

Next came a parade of business matters.
Many Fae lost land, titles, and income under Comus.
Disputes over who had what, who could do what,
where new and old ventures stood, would take much
time and finesse. She listened to a number of these,
making quick decisions where so could and asking
for more formal information and a delay in rulings
when issues were particularly complex. In the end,
she made a quick declaration. There was too much to
handle at this time and she saw no way around it.

"Inanna of the Night Sky," she called to her
mother formally, after speaking with the last
scheduled Fae, a woman who needed information
about trade routes in order to keep her homespun
cloth business from toppling. It was odd to address
her mother so, but it was what was done in Court. At
least she thought it was. Who actually knew? The
Mae Queen had no blood family, and no one could
remember a time when she did, so protocols were
tricky. Best to stick with formalities at the beginning
at least. It was always easier to become less formal
over time than it was to try to establish formality
after the fact.

"Yes, Your Grace," her mother said,
standing and offering a small curtsy to her daughter.

"There is too much to be done, for me and
The Fae Council. From this day forward, until I deem
it unnecessary, we shall hold two Court Audience
Days and two Council Meetings per week. One of
each will be reserved exclusively for the concerns of
economics, infrastructure, and support programs for
all Fae in our realm. Additional issues in this vein, as
well as any political or specific Court concerns, will
share the additional day."

"As you wish, Your Grace," she said. Satisfaction shined clearly in her eyes, and Nin had to look away, the light of it hitting her heart so hard it threatened to crack her regal demeanor, showing the sad, slightly lost daughter hiding underneath the trappings of a new ruler.

"Queen Nin," Serge called, bringing her attention to him for the first time since the Bastien episode. "There is one more piece of business you wished to discuss," he urged. It was an issue she reviewed with him earlier. He fully supported the effort, but like her, knew it would not go over well with a certain segment of the courtiers. If Sergius objected, it would not matter to Nin. She would not be swayed from her purpose or her sense of justice.

"As you say. Please, Chieftain Allera, step forward."

The Wisp, called to this meeting but completely unaware why, started then zipped quickly to hover in place at the foot of the dais. "Queen Nin. It is an honor to be in your presence. The Wisps and all Lesser Fae wish to express their full allegiance to you."

Nin gave a warm and sincere smile to Allera. "Yes, Chief, and I am happy for such support. The Wisps, all Lesser Fae in fact, have done much for this monarchy. For all of Fae throughout history. In light of this, and your particular efforts in the fight against Comus, I have decided to extend The Fae Council. If you will accept my offer, I wish to offer you a seat. You have shown great courage and wisdom in leadership, which I hope will extend to all of Fae."

A loud murmur erupted. No Lesser Fae ever sat on The Fae Council. It had always been Noble

Fae only. But it was the Queen's prerogative to appoint members if there was a vacancy. As she was no longer Princess of the Green, there technically was a vacancy. This was usually never filled unless a new Prince or Princess was discovered, but she would worry about that if such a Fae was born. For now, it was only right to have at least some Lesser Fae representation on Council. She hoped more would come in the future, with Council support.

"Oh, my Queen, you honor me and mine. You honor all Lesser Fae with your consideration," Allera called, her voice tight.

"It is you who honor us. You who have always worked to make Fae what it is. You have shaped Fae and deserve fair representation in the workings of your realm. As Queen, I will ensure that happens more in the future."

"As you wish, Your Grace. In all things," Allera said on a deep bow.

"Lovely," Nin ended, pointing to her mother. "Please see Inanna of the Night Sky. She will help give you all the particulars regarding Council meetings."

More muttering, some louder than others, came. Nin ignored the scattered voices. Any Fae who could not see this was the right course of action would learn to see it as true. She was nervous and unsure of her position, but her position allowed her to do good, and while she sat on The Throne, she would do all the good possible for all in her realm.

Nin gave a stiff nod to the page and began to rise. The herald ran out to announce her departure. Serge met her on a step, took her arm, and escorted her down the stairs and along the long, carpeted walk from dais to door. When they were down the hallway, away from the courtiers and politicians and anyone else who would sneer, he stopped her.

"That was fun, Little One," he said with a sly grin. "We're about to shake things up, and I can't wait." He gave her a quick squeeze of the arm then continued walking down the hall without her, leaving Nin to smile to herself.

It was a new day, for her and all of Fae. A time ripe for correcting the mistakes of the past. She may be shaken on the inside, unsteady in ways, but if her mother and Serge were happy with today's events, she could not have done badly.

CHAPTER 9

The next morning, Nin woke to a banging on her chamber door that was loud and hard enough to cause a tremor in her bed. She was startled to sitting, at least until she heard the distinct grumble of Mo's deep timber. She huffed out an annoyed breath when it was immediately followed by the singsong call of Serge. "Time to wake, Your Grace."

She threw the door open to find her guard gone, likely scuttled off by Mosi and Sergius before their antics began. "I am Queen, you know, and should be allowed a morning of rest." She opened the door wider and stepped aside in silent invitation to allow her brothers to breeze into the room. Mo turned toward her after she closed them in, dark face and eyes lit with a broad smile she had not seen in so long, it almost made her gasp from the impact and memory. This is the older brother of her youth, the one strong and tall and protective but also patient and occasionally playful. Sergius leaned against the bed frame, his ever-present grin on his face, a spark of joy and mischief in the golden-bronzed mix of his eyes.

"What is all this then?" she asked with a flip of her wrist, happy to see her brothers in a way she had not in so long, but also tired and weary from all she endured in the past few weeks.

"It is time for an outing, Little One," Serge said, pulling an apple from inside his gray tunic and tossing it to her. "Eat breakfast, then we go."

"Do you really think it wise?" she asked, turning more to Mo, the more sensible brother, as she took a bite of the apple Serge offered.

"Do you mean any less wise than you and Serge sneaking off to the human realm alone at night?" Mo asked, the black slash of his brow raised in question.

Nin turned eyes to Serge who threw his hands up. "Do not pout at me, Nin. I didn't say anything."

"I am Chief General, commander of the guard. No one need tell me what transpires in and around The Palace. I knew when you began your little adventure what you were doing," Mo explained, arms crossed. "I had contingencies in place, so you were never far from aid if needed. Why not allow you to get yourself and Sabrina supplies?"

"Why not get something to make Sabrina happy, you mean?" Serge needled, but he only received a sharp stare from Mosi in turn.

"I am not surprised, brother. You are good at your job. To be quite honest, I was more surprised Serge and I got away with it. Though, it appears to not actually be the case." Taking another quick bite of the apple, allowing the snap of her teeth through the fruit to linger for a moment while she chewed, she added, "Where are we traveling and for what purpose?"

"The purpose is fun, Little One," Serge answered, pulling up from his lean to throw a long, muscled arm across his sister and give Nin a side hug. "Brother and I were talking and realized we, as in our little sibling trio, had done nothing together in quite some time."

"We will rectify the oversight this morning," Mo added on a low rumble.

"What of my schedule?" Nin asked. "It is important this early in my reign to appear consistent and diligent."

"True," Serge said, "but it is also important, as an individual, to take some time to yourself. Maybe even reconnect with your brothers." Turing serious in an instant, Serge leaned down to pinch her cheek with a soft, sweet grasp and whispered, "We missed our Little One all these decades."

Nin ducked her head, hiding her face so the tears at the corners of her eyes would not fall. She took deep breaths to keep herself in check before looking back up to see bright emotion on Serge and Mo's faces as well.

"I should take a brief break with my family," she said, clearing her throat to get the words out.

"No need to worry about the schedule, my Queen. I took care of your appointments, finessed as only I can, and you are free until luncheon," Serge assured, moving away from her, bending his back up and out, shaking his shining black curls hair into then out of his face quickly. "The only real question is: what are we to do with the few hours we have?"

"Something away from The Palace," Nin interjected, wanting to take the opportunity to escape, even if only for a short time.

"What about The Golden Bow?" Serge suggested.

"We are not going to a tavern," Mo said firmly.

"I second. Too many people," Nin muttered. She wanted time away from The Palace and her place as Queen. She could not do that with people around, fawning over her.

"What of the Meadowlands?" she added, thinking a nice hike through the fields would be good for them all.

"No. Too dull," Serge vetoed.

"We could go to Mother's compound. It is safe and secluded there," Mo suggested.

"Again — too dull," Serge said on a huff.

"Will Mother join us? If not, going home feels wrong in many ways," Nin said while Mo nodded in agreement.

"Got it" Serge said, perking up. "We go to the shore."

Nin and Mo both smiled wide at the mention of the shore. Nin went to her closet to change while Serge and Mo took up space in her rooms, like it was their own, as her brothers so often did.

The shore Serge spoke of was the white sand beaches of the Knaff Sea in the southeastern part of the realm. The sea stretched wide and covered a great deal of space in Fae, creating leagues of shoreline north and south. Nin, Serge, and Mo's family specifically owned a small, secluded beach hut nestled in a rocky bay that was not often visited by other Fae. It was where they went throughout Nin's life to relax together as a family, to play and lounge and take time away from the hectic nature of their lives. As she became more engrossed in events at The Palace as Princess of the Green, Nin spent less and less time here. Then, of course, her captivity with Comus and decade hiding in the human realm put more time between her and this place of peace. Now, standing on a small dune away from the one-room hut, feeling the breeze lift her thick, dark hair and smelling the brine of the air, Nin felt bittersweet. Happy to be back here, in this moment, with Mo and Serge. Also sad to have missed so much time with her family. She felt an arm reach around her and recognized the smell of Mo's magic as it lingered from their transport spells. Relaxing her stance, she let out a small yet happy hum and leaned her head against her eldest brother's shoulder.

"It changed little," Mo said, taking in his own deep breath of salty sea winds.

The sound of waves soothed as they crashed, and Nin closed her eyes to listen while leaning into her brother. "It is true. We changed much, but this place did not."

"Not every change is bad," Mo said, giving her a squeeze.

"No. Not all bad. Still…" Nin let the sentence die, unwilling to name all the bad of the past decades in this place, a haven of good memories for her and her family.

"Do you remember learning to swim in these waves?" Mo asked, the smile on his face present in the tone of his voice.

Nin laughed. "I remember floundering around for a good many hours with you trying to guide me."

"In the end, you did what was required and, eventually, you excelled," Mo recounted. After a brief pause, he offered, "In the end you always do." He planted a soft kiss on the top of her head before making his voice louder to say, "You at least learned much quicker than your brother."

"Hey," Serge added, traipsing up the dune with a large bag slung over his shoulder, "I learned to swim just fine."

"And you helped me when it was my turn. Never letting your Little One far from your sight."

"You were tricksy. Full of surprises for us. I always had to keep an eye on you," Serge answered with a chuckle.

"Too true," Mo quipped with a grin and Nin pulled away to push him teasingly.

"I was perfection. The best child," Nin said.

"The most spoiled," Mo said.

"The most stubborn," Serge added.

Nin folded her arms and said, "Your Queen…"

"Ah, but you are not Queen here, in this space, with us. You are Little One. You are Nin. And you are about to be beaten soundly in a round of sand javelin," Serge said, lightly tapping the bag he dropped to the ground with his foot.

"Do you remember the rules?" Mo asked Nin as he knelt to pull the equipment from its case.

"Of course. The rules of sand javelin are not complicated. Whoever throws their javelin farthest is the winner."

"Also, no magic," Serge added, "Meaning, no getting the sand to do your bidding, Nin, or controlling the metal of the javelin, Mo."

"You only say that because you remain jealous your word magics do nothing to help give you an advantage in this game," Mosi teased.

"You say that only because you know I can easily win if you do not use your metal magics," Serge scoffed.

"Enough, brothers," Nin said with a pretend sigh. "We all know I shall handily beat you both."

"Unlikely," Mo stated with a firm, disbelieving tone.

Serge laughed and started sliding bronze poles into one another, creating a clanging noise followed by loud clicks when worn grooves met in their proper place.

"Best out of three?" Nin suggested as she finished assembly. All agreed and she moved to test the heft of her javelin, twirling it in her hands for a few rotations before whipping the four-foot-long pole around quickly to stick the pointed end in the ground and run her fingers along the smooth surface glinting with a brownish glow in the sunshine.

"Do watch where you swing your instrument," Serge said with a bit of attitude.

"Afraid I will mar that oh-so-pretty face?" Nin said while fluttering her eyelashes at him in an exaggerated manner.

Mo barked out a laugh at her tease and Serge elbowed Nin in her ribs, hard enough to make her stumble but not hard enough to knock her to the ground. She acted annoyed but smiled, happy to have this playful mood rise up between them still despite the years and events and madness of late. Her brothers were serious, or mostly serious in the case of Sergius, when it came to duty and responsibility, yet even her more stoic and rigid eldest brother had often teased and tormented and joked with his siblings. It was good to witness it, to feel the love in such actions once again.

Mo, squaring his shoulders as if preparing for a demanding battle, stood tall and declared, "I will begin." Before either Serge or Nin could complain of the order, Mo pulled back with his powerful frame and let the javelin fly, a sailing bronze streak across a bright blue sky. It landed far down the beach, a shiny point swaying gently in the distant horizon.

"Looks like age before beauty," Serge said, deadpan.

"Which makes you next, brother," Nin replied.

"Very well. Watch and learn something, Little One." Serge made a show of stretching for a moment before letting his own javelin fly. It landed exceedingly close to Mosi's, making a winner between the two unclear from their current distance.

"Now you," Mo encouraged.

Nin looked out, squinting eyes in the sunlight, spotting her targets to beat. She reared back, putting her muscles into her throw, and let the javelin fly when her arm reached the pinnacle of her arched swing over her head.

"Impressive," Serge said, a note of contemplation and honesty in his voice. "Both of you. Truly. Yet, I believe I am the winner."

"You cannot possibly evaluate accurately from this vantage," Mo said.

"We shall see," Serge countered, zipping off at full speed to the area where the javelins landed.

Mo followed behind just as quickly, and Nin could hear their loving banter drift along the wind as she made a more leisurely pace toward the two. She was in no rush. She had a small amount of time to enjoy being Nin, Little One, in this place, before heading back to The Palace and the title of Queen. She let the sound of waves and laughter, the feel of mist and wind wash over her as she smiled at her family who took the opportunity to give her this time. Who loved her for who she was, not the duty she bore. Who were here with her on a beach, playing and laughing, in an effort to both forget and remember.

CHAPTER 10

"Again," Gin said, their firm tone the same as the last twenty times they said it. Again, Sabrina pulled the spark, the light dancing across her fingers.

"Are you going to do this over and over today?" Sabrina asked, obviously ready, in her mind at least, to move forward. "I thought the idea was to give me the basics quickly?"

Nin chuckled softly to herself before Gin cut a look her way, causing her to fall silent like a chastised pupil in a classroom.

"Yes. You are correct," Gin replied. "I must, however, ensure you have enough practice to move forward. Fae children practice their sparks for many lessons before moving to affinity."

"Fae children are also children, and do not have lessons for hours on end," Nin added in support of her friend. She rose from her bench seat and moved to give Gin a hug across their shoulders. "You are an excellent instructor, cousin. You helped so many, including me. You are helping Sabrina now. However, we are in need of stability and assurance in all areas, as you know." Nin gave Gin a sideways glance, hoping she did not need to say more. What they did in this alcove was enough of a secret without giving voice to the current physical and political dangers lurking. "I am mere days into my reign and already in dire need of assistance from those I trust."

Gin accepted this reminder gracefully, as was their way. "Of course, Nin. You and Sabrina are both correct. We need to move forward as quickly as possible. As it is more than clear Sabrina mastered intention and calling forward magics, we must determine affinity."

Nin tingled at that. If their earlier assumptions were true and the incident with the vines were indications, Sabrina would have earth magics. That was both exhilarating and worrisome. Nin would be overjoyed to have another with earth magic powers, especially someone she loved and who would support her reign. However, that would place a great deal of responsibility and attention on her human friend once her magics were more widely known. Would she be the next Princess of the Green? Could a human ever be accepted as Princess of the Green? If the Fae realized her magics could be acquired through force in some manner, would more danger come her way? There were many questions and no method to quickly ascertain answers. Their small band was doing the best they could, but eventually, more study and practice and finesse would be required. Ascertaining Sabrina's affinity was a small answer in the swirl of questions marring these early days of Nin's reign, but one required for them to properly move forward with lessons and research.

Gin's lecture broke into her thoughts and the Queen refocused on her cousin as he offered explanations to ease her friend's mind. "We have discussed affinity, or, at least as much as we know about affinity. All Fae manifest a strong connection to a certain type of magic. Every Fae can do simple, universal spells, such as the spark spell we have practiced. More complex magics require a magical energy attuned to specific elements or inclinations. We have covered many of these — our family has a fairly eclectic mix of magics — but something may jump forward we have not discussed. If that is the case, we will talk about strategy then."

"Strategy?" Sabrina questioned.

"You will need an affinity-attuned mentor at a certain point," Gin said. "I can teach you basics, can help with some other areas as well, but cannot take you far in, say, fire magics. If that is your affinity, Inanna would be your mentor. However, if you have an affinity related to kinetics, physical movement with and through magic, there is no one in our small group with that affinity. We would need to determine an appropriate mentor based on a variety of complex factors."

Sabrina nodded and began to fidget, the worry bleeding out into the movement of her hands and the shifting of her feet.

"Sabrina," she called to her friend and waited for her full attention. "This is usually a special ceremony early on in a Fae's education. It is a time to celebrate, not to fret. We learn your magics, and in many ways, your magical affinity marks specific aspects of your soul, who you are inside. And you are lovely, friend, so whatever comes will be right and true to you.”

“Nicely put, Nin,” Gin added, a smile on their face. “I do wish we could have the official ceremony, but as this is a secret for now, we will do it with us three.”

“That’s enough for me,” Sabrina said, reaching out to take Gin and Nin’s hands. “Thank you both for the help. And the words. And the friendship. And just generally being so awesome.”

“No prob,” Nin said flippantly, imitating Sabrina’s tone and stance as well as her well-used phrasing.

Sabrina barked out a laugh, gave a final squeeze to her hand, and pulled back. “Your Grace,” she said with a mock bow. The banter washed over Nin, making her feel seen and known, making the weight of her responsibilities a fraction lighter in the presence of these people she cared for and who cared for her.

“Okay. Gotcha. We have to see what I can do and, whatever happens, we’ll deal. Easy. So, how do we do this?”

“It is fairly simple in execution,” Gin said. “You have even seen it in action before. It is what I showed you at Nin’s human home when we were proving our magics.”

“The little ball of yellow light?”

“Yes. My light is yellow, because of my affinity toward general magical theory. Nin’s is green because of her earth magics. Mo’s is silver, Serge’s is red, Inanna’s is orange. The color is a physical manifestation of your magics.”

Gin moved to stand beside Sabrina, holding their right hand out. “Watch,” they said, as they repeated the phrase *ISPISSP CAKAL* and their yellow light formed a glowing ball in their palm.

"You didn't say anything last time," Sabrina observed, staring at the ball of light in their hand.

"No. I have no need to voice the command now. Pure intention is enough for many basic spells. However, you need practice and experience, so you must say the words aloud."

"Right. I just say the phrase?"

"No. You need to concentrate your magic in the palm of your hand, visualize a ball of light there, and say the words with intention," Gin said. "It may take a few tries, as with the spark, but it will come."

Sabrina nodded as Gin made her repeat ISPISSP CAKAL back again and again to ensure she had the pronunciation and intention right. Finally, they stepped aside and gave Sabrina space to try the spell.

Sabrina's eyes focused, causing lines to form and bunch across her forehead. Nin waited, breath shallow with anticipation, as her friend tried the spell a few times. There were sparks here and there, but on the seventh attempt a small bright ball, the size of a tulip bulb, formed in her hand. Sabrina stared in excitement at what she produced. Nin stared in awe for another reason entirely. The ball of light was a kaleidoscope, shifting from red to green like the holiday lights she saw every November and December in Wilde. Gin gasped as well, caught by surprise.

Sabrina grinned up at them. "So, this is it. I'm like Nin and Serge? That's what this means?"

Gin's mouth was slightly agape, and their eyes moved rapidly, taking in every detail of that small orb of light. "It appears so," they whispered.

Sabrina looked to Nin with her eyebrows raised in question. Nin stepped toward her friend, moving her face eye-level with Sabrina's palm and the magic that rested there. "It is extraordinary," Nin said, her tone sounding both intrigued and apprehensive.

"Okay. Okay. Is this reaction because y'all are happy for me or is something else happening here? Because I feel like something else is happening here," Sabrina muttered. As the worry crept into her voice, the ball of light flickered and quickly dissipated. Sabrina cursed then rubbed her hand along her pants leg, as if wiping away the feel of the light.

Gin looked serious and thoughtful, more so than usual, when they said, "To be honest, in all my long years of instruction, I have never seen anything such as this."

"What do you mean?" Sabrina demanded, now becoming more agitated.

"Sabrina, calm. Please," Nin called as she reached out to hug her. "All is well. We will come to understand this, too, as we will come to understand the rest."

"Will you please just tell me what's going on?" she said, panic now in her eyes.

"Fae do not have mixed magics," Gin began. "Each shows only one solid affinity. That is it. No dual affinity. You, however, appear to have a mixture of word and earth magics." Tilting their head to the side in thought, Gin added, "Although, if we stop to consider, it does make sense from a certain logical perspective."

"How so?" Nin asked, still holding her friend loosely. She could feel Sabrina's worry like a physical vibration and wanted to maintain contact to help soothe her.

"She was a human without magic. We assume she acquired the magic she now has through the chair, which would logically mean she acquired earth magics, hence the green. However, we also know from eons of study, magic connects to the soul or energy of a person, who and what they are as an individual. Our Sabrina, as a human, already displayed a very clear affinity for words. Hence, spellcraft and word magic."

"Nature and nurture," Sabrina said.

When Nin and Gin both looked confused, she said, "It's a standard human debate. Are we who we are because we are born that way and it is our nature, or are we who we are because we are shaped into that by outside forces, through nurturing in one form or another? My magic is a blend of both. I am naturally good with words, it seems, but earlier events, with Nin and the chair, made me into something else as well."

"This is fascinating," Gin whispered, awe and interest clear in the tilt of their head and the intent focus of their stare. It was a look Nin had seen her scholar cousin give many times, but not one she appreciated at this juncture.

"Yes. Well, I'm sure it is, Gin, but we are not to study this in any official capacity as Scholar," Nin said, pulling herself up in a stiff posture, away from Sabrina, and adding a hint of command to her voice. "Sabrina will be no experiment."

"Of course not," Gin said in affront. "How could you think I would ever…"

Sabrina gave her a reassuring squeeze on the arm as she stepped up to Gin. "You had a certain scholar-hunger look on your face, friend. I totally understand that and don't take offense. Nin was being protective, that's all. We're all good here." Turning back to Nin, she added, "I'm no guinea pig, but research into this should happen. If it's something neither of you have seen, we need to determine what it may mean. Like with me having magic in general. Seems all of it is a brave new world for everyone, Fae and human."

"Right," Gin said. "We will research this together as we will research the overall transfer of magic."

"We can also rejoice that no outsiders are needed," Nin added. "I am already enmeshed in your training, as we previously thought you would have earth magics. You and I will begin to work with your earth magic affinity. Soon, we will ask Serge to help with specific spellcraft and word magic instruction."

"Sounds like a plan," Sabrina said.

"With no time to waste, we begin," Gin stated, ever ready to move a lesson along.

Sabrina groaned. She was visibly tired and likely wished to rest, to have the time and space to consider, feel, and plan accordingly. Nin wished she could. She wished they all could. Yet she feared they had no time for such. With more mysteries and unknowns compounding each day, the fate of the people she loved, and all of Fae, may well depend on them moving forward at a rapid pace.

CHAPTER 11

Nin sat in the Queen's Council seat. Even if it felt so long ago given the avalanche of recent events, her coronation was days before, and this was the first time she sat at The Council Meeting as Queen. It felt less odd than sitting atop The Throne, as she herself sat on Council for years as Princess of the Green. She knew these Fae and their quirks well, had dealt with them on the Mae Queen's behalf many times before. Her position was changed, yes, but the flavor of this meeting was familiar enough to give her better bearings. It helped that her mother was seated close to her. Her family was also in attendance. Mo would be required for military and security reports. Serge was present as her adviser, her unspoken but soon-to-be Vizer. Gin and Sabrina sat quietly in the back of the room. They had no official business to force their attendance, nevertheless they waved happily at her from their bench along the wall, expressing moral support in presence and smiles. All worked to calm her, prepare her for her first Council meeting as Queen Nin.

Her relative ease of feeling regarding The Fae Council aside, she knew this specific meeting may well be tense. The reason for such tension sat in a new chair, smaller yet sturdy and carved as all the others, suspended at eye-level a few seats down on her right. Chieftain Allera was poised and firm. As always, ready for a battle of wills or weapons. Which was good, because the fight began as soon as Michel formally called the meeting to order.

"As Head of The Fae Council I must assert what transpired on Court Audience Day was most unusual. Unilateral decisions affecting this Council are most often presented for discussion, if not a full vote, prior to proclamation." Michel cut a quick look toward Nin filled with anger and resentment. "There was no vote. There was no debate. I see this turn of events as a blatant disregard for the place of The Fae Council."

"Michel," Sten sighed, apparently already exasperated by The Council Head, "you are dramatizing the situation. It is well within the purview of Queen Nin to name a new member to The Fae Council, as her seat is vacant. Traditionally, yes, that seat remained dormant in the event of a Prince or Princess of the Green…"

"Yes. Yes. Precisely my point, Sten. What will happen now if a Fae with earth magics is discovered?" Michel questioned.

"We will consider the options and make changes accordingly," her mother calmly replied. "It is rare that a Prince or Princess of the Green comes along at all, much less within a century or two of the last to hold the title. Beyond that, when this occurs, the discovery of powers is known for years before the Prince or Princess is even named formally and placed on The Council, if they come of age to join our ranks at all. We shall have ample time for lengthy debates and votes."

"Time in the future does not negate the disrespect this body was served in the present," Michel barked.

"You feel hurt because you were not consulted? Is that why you want to start with a tiresome debate over the issue?" Andrés said, more than a hint of reproach in his voice.

"The Fae Council has been in exile for years. We are a beacon for the Fae. As such, we must maintain our power and position within their eyes. The Queen's blatant disregard for our place in Fae society, and the new addition now seated at this venerated table, mar that in the eyes of many."

And there it was. Michel's real reason for anger. His prejudices were showing once again. Nin's eyes narrowed, and she was about to respond when Jane jumped into the debate.

"That was unforgivably rude, Michel. You do not say such things aloud," she asserted with a flutter of her fan.

"Yes, Michel. So rude to voice such opinions," Inanna bit out, eyes narrowed at Jane who blushed and ducked her head more securely behind her fan.

"Michel, your displeasure, and the true reasons behind them, are noted," Sten stated.

Visibly shaken at being called to task for his prejudiced attitudes, Michel seemed to make the decision to backtrack somewhat when he began, "I was not implying…"

"No. You were. As was clearly noted by all in this room," Sten boomed. "You have yet to give an actual response to the assertion Queen Nin was well within her rights to choose a new Council Member."

"Tradition mandates…" Michel shouted, using volume in an attempt to stop his argument from losing ground in the discussion.

"Tradition stands only as long as it is not changed," her mother snapped back.

"What, then, is our place? Our role? If not to uphold the traditions, beliefs, and values of Fae?" Michel countered.

Nin could hold her tongue no longer. "Your role as The Council is to ensure fairness and justice," she ground out through gritted teeth. "For all of Fae." Dissonant murmurs followed, but so did a smattering of supportive voices. The first meant more trouble for her in the near future, but the latter bolstered her spirits.

Michel could not counter that directly, so he decided on a different tactic. "I propose we consider a new vote, then. A change to the tradition, if you will. This change would call for Council approval on all future mandates from Queen Nin."

There was an audible gasp from several in the room.

"You step dangerously close to treason," Allera said, entering the conversation only on Queen Nin's behalf.

"We are discussing the flaunting of tradition, are we not? Why not consider this? The Fae Council should hold more power. We have held Fae together after all. We did not consort with the enemy or hide in the human realm," Michel said with a sneer.

The sentence caused Nin's stomach to churn instantaneously. Her breath left her as if she were punched in the chest. It was the voicing of every doubt she had, everything she believed others thought of her, in front of a roomful of magically and politically powerful Fae. The room itself became pure commotion. There were yells and cries from all sides. She heard Sabrina's voice clear above the din, saw her friend's face twisted in anger as Gin physically restrained her.

She felt her brothers then. They had moved from their seats in the audience to flank her chair, and the hard looks on their faces showed what they thought of Michel's words. Her mother had tears in her eyes, but they were not sad tears. No. Anyone who knew Inanna of the Night Sky knew if she shed tears from glowing eyes, they were tears of anger, and her wrath was imminent.

Nin also felt the atmosphere of the room like another physical entity. The energy was not against her. There were voices supporting Michel as words lobbed back and forth, but the majority backed their Queen. Nin suddenly knew this in her bones. It might not even be about her as a person, and she was okay with the idea. She was Queen Nin now. It would take more than this to rally mass support against her. As Michel asserted, tradition was important, ingrained even, and in Fae, tradition mandated the people rely on and follow the woman Fae with earth magics, no matter who that individual was. Her position and her magic created a bond of faith, one she would trust and, hopefully, strengthen through her actions.

She turned to Michel. "I second," she said with a loud but calm voice, causing a shocked hush to fall across the room. "Call your vote," she said.

Michel looked on her with a hint of panic in his wide eyes, and she realized the entire event was a calculated maneuver to shore up position and power in a time of political transition. It was simply bluster and bluff. He knew he was no match for her earth magics in the eyes of the people, much less the particular Fae who sat on this Council. He likely thought to get his way by manipulating an unsure and hesitant new Queen. He never imagined anyone, much less that Queen herself, would second his proposal. A day ago, she may not have done so, but every day as Queen bolstered her assurance in her magic and her place and the good she could do while on The Throne. Today was not the day to test this, and she was not the one to test at that moment.

"More discussion…" Michel hedged.

"No. You proposed the vote," Inanna seethed, though, from her words, she felt her own assurance about the outcome of the vote falling in her daughter's favor. "It has been seconded, as required. It is now your lot to call it."

Michel nodded, nervously looking around the room. He underestimated and overstepped. He was used to power and position, was used to the Mae Queen's absence and the authority it gave him, even in hiding. He was also used to Princess Nin, not Queen Nin. To his honor, he completed his mission with a strong voice despite the sweat dotting his forehead. "All in favor of requiring Council approval for any policy mandate given by Queen Nin, say 'aye'," he called. Deathly silence followed.

"All those opposed, say 'nay,'" he continued, and everyone else on the Council voiced their dissent.

"The 'nays' have it," he affirmed, sinking slightly in his chair.

"I propose a vote," Inanna said. "I call for the immediate removal of Michel the Learned from The Fae Council. He has shown a blatant disregard and prejudice against not only the Queen, but many members of our Fae community."

"A Scholar must always sit on the Council..." Michel began.

"Another shall take your place," Andrés said, uncharacteristically stoic and focused on business. "I second the proposal."

"A vote. All in favor, say 'aye,'" Inanna called. One by one, each member called aye. Even Jane, though she looked practically sick about the confrontation and set sad eyes on Michel as it occurred.

Mosi, not wasting a moment, moved to Michel's chair. "I will escort you from the chamber," he stated, with no trace of mercy or kindness in his voice or face.

"The Scholars Guild will have much to say on this matter, I assure you," Michel fumed, embarrassment and the loss of power making him lash out at the end. "Mark my words. This tyranny will not stand."

Queen Nin laughed. "You wish to hold your fellow Fae down in the name of tradition and claim tyranny when it suits you? You are dismissed. I have one final mandate for you, Michel the Learned. As of this moment, you are barred from The Palace unless given written consent by your Queen. If you ignore this decree, you will find yourself swiftly removed to the Hold."

"See!" he shrieked, now being led away by Mo, how held him in a punishing grip. "See how she silences those who voice disagreement? It is oppression. Tyranny. She is no better than Comus, I say."

In a flash, Gin was in front of Michel, and their slap echoed across the room. "How dare you say such things to defend your own prejudice and perceived power? It goes against all the Scholars Guild holds dear. Rest assured, Michel, I will be relaying all to the guild, and you will likely find yourself disbarred from our ranks as well. Our mandate is to learn, and to grow and help Fae through learning. Today, you have shown no growth or learning, only a lust for power causing you to twist words and law to achieve your own ends."

Gin's proclamation deflated the Fae, and Michel went limp. Mo practically dragged him from the room while Gin found their seat again. Nin hid her smile when she saw Sabrina give Gin a high five. It would definitely be a moment to laugh over and savor later. Now, much more business needed to be done.

Chieftain Allera called out, clear and true, a surprising voice after such commotion, "I propose a vote. Let us call Andrés of the Mountains forward as interim Head of Council until such time as a Scholar is presented and accepted by The Council."

Nin blinked rapidly in disbelief at the turn of events. Dre would be close to the bottom of her list for Council Head, but only because of his blasé attitude. He was a strong, solid Fae whose thoughtful nature was often obscured by his demeanor, so it was

not an absolutely ridiculous choice. The Fae on The
Council all voted aye in favor, save Andrés himself.
Jane giggling flirtatiously all the while.

He acquiesced to the vote, adding, "This is
ridiculous, and will likely end in disaster, but I will
do as you bid." Moving to The Council Head chair,
he slipped off the mask of indifference and became
more serious. Maybe it was not such an odd choice
after all.

The remainder of the meeting was calm after
the opening events. The Council voted on when their
second weekly meeting, as mandated by her during
her first Court Audience Day, would occur. They
discussed upcoming events and old business, heard
some issues brought forth as new business, and
adjourned after an hour without another outburst. If
someone observed all but the first ten minutes of the
meeting, they may have called it boring, but the
beginning was enough to drain the room. Nin was
relieved when it came to a close.

Her mother hurried over and gave her a
swift but fierce hug. "Love you, My Queen," she
said, loud and clear and full of residual anger on her
behalf.

"I know, Mother. You have my love as well.
All will calm soon, I assure you."

Inanna nodded and wandered off to talk with
Nin's brothers, who now stood with Gin and Sabrina
at the back of the room. They likely were voicing
their own resentments and thoughts about the
meeting. She would hear it all later. For now, she
turned to be escorted from the room, but was drawn
up short by Allera, who hovered directly behind her.

"My Queen," she said on a bow. "You honor me, and all like me. Your protection will long be remembered."

"I thank you. I do it because it is what should be done. What should have occurred long ago," she answered honestly.

"This is why it shall be remembered," Allera countered.

Considering the Wisp closely, Queen Nin leaned in for a more private word. "Chieftain Allera. I appreciate your support. I also wonder, however, why you chose to nominate Dre for Council Head. It is clear my mother would not be a wise choice. I believe you would also be seen as a favorite. Sten would be my next choice. Why was he not yours?"

Allera studied Nin's face for a moment then broke out in a grin. "It is hard for me to believe you do not notice it, Your Grace, but you do have much on your mind at present. As for why I did not pick Sten, it is clear in the way he looks at you."

When she turned slowly to where Sten was in the room, he beamed back at her, open and kind. It was just friendship with her mother and herself, correct? She thought that was all it was, but the implication from Allera was clear in her voice. She found something more there when she observed Sten. Queen Nin turned away from his smile quickly and gave her head a gentle shake.

"You truly never noticed, Your Grace. It is in both his eyes and his words, when either are on you," Chief Allera said, hovering close to Nin's ear to keep their conversation more private. "If you do not mind me saying, Queen Nin, Sten would not be a misplaced choice for Consort. This, as you know, would take him off The Council."

Consort was an official designation in Fae.
Marriage was a custom in Fae, although it was not as
tightly enforced or overtly expected as it was in much
of the human realm. The Mae Queen, however, had
never married. Had only named various Fae Consort
over the years. With the title came political power
and position, namely within The Court, as Fae
courtiers knew getting a Consort on their side in
issues could be beneficial because of their tight
connection with the Queen. Even those Fae who left
the title of Consort behind, willingly or no, were in
better political and financial positions after. It was a
spot coveted by many in earlier times, partially
because of power and partially because of the overall
beauty and allure of the Mae Queen herself.

Be that as it may, the idea of naming a
Consort never crossed Nin's mind, even if she was
currently residing in the Consort Chambers. She was
too nervous about her new position, too new overall,
facing too many issues and too many questions, to
give space to any relationship at present. More than
that, she was not emotionally or mentally ready for a
sexual or romantic relationship, had no idea when she
might be prepared for one, and did not require this
type of relationship in her life at present. Sten's
seeming attachment was good to note for a variety of
reasons, but it did not signify.

"I thank you for your information and your
honesty, Chieftain," Nin said with a slight nod. "Such
things are not for me. Not now."

Allera looked deep into Nin's eyes, a
disconcerting feeling when the Wisp's full warrior's
body was hovering at eye-level. "Understood, Your
Grace," Allera said with a whisper. With another
bow, she flew away, leaving Nin to mull over the

surprising conversation in her mind as she exited the room.

She shook off the implications and the memories they started to dredge up in her mind as she was escorted back to her chambers. There was too much to consider, too much to accomplish in a short amount of time. The courtier entertainments planned for later in the afternoon required her focus and attention. Queen Nin, only days under the crown, knew to brace. The Council Meeting would not be her only trial this day.

CHAPTER 12

Sadly, Nin was unable to abstain herself from Court entertainments planned for that afternoon. Serge urged her on, claiming it was her first full week as Queen and she did not want to appear either unable and weak or callous and flippant. Neither were good traits in a monarch, at least the type of monarch Nin wished to be, so she grumbled about rest and demands and hard days to her jovial yet pushy brother while still arriving promptly at the festivities.

One thing she learned early in her tenure as a student in The Palace was the Queen had little time alone. What one might consider official Court business — Audience Days, meetings, balls, holiday celebrations, and so forth — took up a small amount of the week. However, the Queen could not simply go off and do what she wished any other time. No. She had to be seen. She was required to interact in ways less formal but no less vital to her position and power. Hence, Court entertainments.

It was a tradition in The Fae Court for a chosen courtier to schedule a particular afternoon entertainment for the rest of The Court. It usually involved some type of performance-based art, a small food and tea banquet, and much mingling and discussion before and after. The discussion period, ostensibly reserved for small talk or evaluation of the performance, was the politically important section of the event. It is where deals were made, allegiances forged and broken, ideas were tested. In short, it was informal but crucial political work.

Queen Nin still felt slightly unsure in herself as Queen even if she was not unsure in her powers and the place of reverence they held for her people after the events earlier in the day. Luckily, however, she was surrounded by a small but fierce group of people who showed nothing but complete and total belief in her ability to lead. Specifically on this afternoon, in The Throne Room, Serge and Sabrina were by her side.

Serge was present because it was a Court event. He was her main Court adviser and always would be. She leaned on her brother's past knowledge and current understanding to navigate the treacherous waters that churned in The Fae Court at times. Sabrina was present because Nin wished it so. She liked having her friend nearby. It gave her a sense of solace and peace. Also, Sabrina had a wicked tongue, was not afraid to use it in defense of her friend, and the Fae courtiers often overlooked or underestimated her because she was a human. They did so to their detriment, but, honestly, to Nin's amusement. While Nin needed to be serious and cautious, a laugh every now and again was a good thing for anyone, even a Queen.

"Ohmigod, I thought faculty meetings were the worst," Sabrina hissed to Nin after a certain courtier finally left off their pretentious diatribe and walked away from the trio. "But this? Serge, I salute you. To do this for centuries would drive me to drink."

"I have many ways to alleviate the stress, Sabrina. Drinking is just one of them," he cooed, his tell-tale smirk firmly in place.

Nin and Sabrina both laughed but cut themselves short when Sir Bastien appeared before them. Nin turned a sharp gaze on the Fae, Serge kept his smirk in place, though it looked a little more predatory in that moment. Sabrina pulled herself into a defiant posture, hip jutted and arms crossed over her chest in clear contempt of the Fae in front of her.

Sir Bastien kept a condescending smile on his face through the gauntlet and bowed briefly to Nin. "My Queen. I was given the honor of scheduling your first entertainment during this week of celebration. I do hope you enjoy what is to come."

"I'm sure it will be informative," Serge coolly replied.

"Yep," Sabrina added, popping the word through her lips as she stared in open hostility at the Fae before her. Sir Bastien ignored her completely, not even acknowledging her presence with a disdainful slant of his gray eyes. Nin realized he had done so when he walked up, looking only at her and Serge before he bowed.

She ignored all else and latched on to this particular insult. "Sir Bastien, have you met Sabrina the Scholar? She is mine, and as such holds a prominent place in The Palace. However, that is not her only claim to position here. She did much to free Fae from the grip of Comus. She risked her life to come to our realm, bringing knowledge and power based in Fae prophecy she found in the human realm. Using both to directly help free me in my hour of need. Not all Fae can claim as much direct involvement with the liberation of our realm."

Sabrina blushed prettily, because she was not one for effusive praise, and Nin offered her a passing smile before narrowing her look back at the Fae before her. Her gaze was solid on Bastien, forcing him to acknowledge her words, and by extension, this woman who had done so much for so many in the realm.

"Yes. I was informed of such," Bastien said stiffly. He then proceeded to turn briefly toward Sabrina and offer the smallest nod of his head. "A pleasure, I'm certain, Sabrina the Scholar."

Serge was calm as ever, but Nin heard the edge of anger in his voice when he replied, "Sir Bastien, this woman saved the life of my Queen. Your Queen. She deserves more recognition than what you muster."

"No worries, Serge," Sabrina said with a flip of her hand. "Don't really feel like chatting with this one anyway." There was a sneer in her voice and on her face, before she completely turned from Sir Bastien. In the BBC costume dramas they watched together in the human realm, it would be called the cut direct. It was not an insult within The Fae Court normally. For a human to turn away from a Fae courtier, however, was more than a little dismissive. For a man like Sir Bastien, it clearly riled.

He gave a quick dip, face red and eyes hard. "My Queen," he bit out, waiting for her to dismiss him formally. She hesitated a moment. It was petty, but she felt the need to be petty. After long seconds, she audibly sniffed and waved her hand, signaling he could leave as he wished.

The trio watched him stomp away to his cohort, who huddled and whispered at the other end of The Throne Room.

"Jackass," Sabrina hissed.

Serge chuckled, as did Nin, but she also hesitated a moment and added, "That was likely not very smart of us."

"True," Serge replied. "Sir Bastien is powerful in The Fae Court and maintained that power throughout exile, which shows a great deal of cunning and savvy on his part. He is not a man to be trifled with without cause. Yet, he gave us clear cause by being a total jackass."

"He won't see it that way. Men like him never do," Sabrina wisely added.

"It has passed. Soon enough the problem of Sir Bastien will need to be more fully addressed. Now is not the time. Although, I would be delighted to see you give him the cut direct again, friend."

"I never thought I would have a chance to do that in real life," Sabrina laughed. "So much of my lit knowledge is coming in handy here. First Milton, now Burney and Austen and all those Regency romances I read for fun. It makes my nerdy heart flutter."

"As long as George R.R. Martin is not the model for the Court," Nin deadpanned.

Sabrina let out a guffaw. "Damn. Let's hope not. You better find some wood to knock on or something."

"Who is this Martin?" Serge asked, intrigued.

"Oh, boy. Let me tell you a little story about *A Song of Ice and Fire,*" Sabrina began, huddling into Serge as if ready to whisper state secrets. Her hands gesticulated, her voice rose and fell. Her joy and Serge's obvious enjoyment of Sabrina's retelling of a bloody human fantasy made Nin's heart happy. It was good to be lost in this moment with two individuals she loved fiercely, even as she knew it was fleeting.

Nin sat in an elevated seat at the back of the room, Serge and Sabrina placed slightly lower to her left and right. All eyes were turned toward the stage, a removable contraption with large green and gold curtains placed against the long wall of The Throne Room for these entertainments. Queen Nin was informed a number of poets would recite their works, something she looked forward to, especially with Sabrina in attendance. She wanted her friend to experience Fae poetry. However, the sounds of shuffling, arranging, and tuning were clearly coming through the curtains. It did not sound like a poetry reading.

Sir Bastien strolled onto the stage, sure strides planting him firmly front and center. He cleared his throat, a useless sound made to gain attention, and waited with pursed lips for the murmurs of the crowd to die down. When he believed he had the attention of all the courtiers, he began his introductions.

"Welcome, Fae Court, to our first festive entertainment since our return from exile. It also marks the first entertainment in honor of our newly crowned monarch, Queen Nin." A swell of quick applause followed, and Sir Bastien smiled widely for a moment before gesturing for quiet once again. "It is truly an honor to have you as our Queen, Your Grace. Your ... particular ... talents and concerns have already begun to bring new spirit to our Court." His tone sounded less complementary and more accusatory than the words implied, and Nin bristled. Bastien's smile turned oily and dark, and he offered a deep bow that felt almost mocking. "In light of current events, and your obvious preferences, I took the liberty of changing our scheduled performance. There will be no poetry reading this afternoon. Instead, we have a gnome symphony." With a laugh, he exited the stage, practically throwing a mocking "Enjoy" as he swaggered off.

Sabrina looked up at Nin in confusion. As a human new to Fae, she had no knowledge of these events or how they normally went. She did pick up on the thinly veiled disdain Sir Bastien always seemed to throw at Nin. Anyone could see it. Serge seethed beside her because of that disrespect.

Nin, however, steeled herself for what may come. Not the music, but the Fae reaction to it. Very rarely did a Court entertainment feature Lesser Fae. On the rare occasion it did, the focus was comedic and often based in ridicule. No Lesser Fae musicians ever played in The Throne Room, at least to Nin's knowledge, and she knew there were many courtiers who would see this as another way in which the new Queen drastically changed tradition.

The one problem for Bastien was Nin did in fact wish to drastically change traditions. She would not do so swiftly, but it would happen. The inclusion of Chieftain Allera was deserved. Allera fought bravely for years against Comus, as did all Wisps. She earned her seat at the table. It was also important to a long-term plan for more equity in Fae, more inclusion of Lesser Fae in the political structure overall. Nin would make that happen, though incrementally at first, as she and Serge predicted a great deal of pushback from the powerful. While Nin would fight on her own for what she deemed just, the brother at her side did not allow her to do so. The siblings agreed on the need and plotted in quiet moments alone. Sergius was a great support and filled to the brim with ideas to include more in the traditional Court structure. His happiness in helping implement such changes was matched only by his disdain for those Fae who would stand in their way. Her brother, a well-seasoned courtier of centuries, simply knew when, where, and how to let his disdain fly.

Sir Bastien already proved a target for Serge's wicked tongue and hard glare, and his switch in entertainment showed their mutual dislike of the Fae was well founded. He planned the afternoon as a mockery, a secondary thing to be called upon when pointing out the disaster that was Queen Nin's rule, something to use to leverage more power for himself and less influence for Nin. She was Queen, true, but the courtiers could make her rule ineffective in a number of annoying ways. They could also rebel. It happened a number of times over the centuries with the Mae Queen. It was not impossible for disgruntled Fae courtiers to raise arms against their Queen, especially if they thought they could wrest control of Fae from her.

Comus showed her weakness in the eyes of many, and Bastien was quickly working to exploit a certain view of the Queen. Whether he believed her truly incapable or was power hungry himself remained to be seen. Whatever the impulse, he was starting her reign with a bold disregard she needed to confront in a decisive manner. Serge warned her of this. She now knew they needed to formulate a plan quickly to stop this small mutiny before it turned into outright revolt.

As all this raced through Nin's mind, she remained outwardly poised and attentive. The curtain opened and showed a small band of gnome musicians, a dozen in total, seated at various instruments. Gnome music was not unknown to Noble Fae. Many enjoyed it. It was considered less refined and more rustic, like the difference between baroque and bluegrass in the human realm. To many Fae, especially those from older and more entrenched political families, the idea of listening to such music was viewed as beneath them, and Nin heard rumblings and affronted gasps even before the first note struck.

Still, when the music started, Nin lost herself in it for a time. The twang of strings, the lilt of winds, and the pounding of drums carried her away, and she smiled with true fondness on the band playing before her. Sabrina, alert after Bastien's introduction, visibly eased, and started swaying softly in her seat. Nin did not notice she did the same until she caught Sabrina's beat, then her eye, and both friends smiled widely at each other, enjoying the ebb and flow of the beautiful sound.

This lasted ten minutes, the happiness and joy. Then, the murmurs became louder. From Sir Bastien's section of seats, the area where he and his cronies sat, vocal jeering began. They laughed loudly, made disparaging remarks to and about the musicians. Others joined in the jokes, though they were fewer than Nin expected. Still, it was a rowdy contingent. Bastien himself did not participate. He simply smiled indulgently at those who did, encouraging his cohort without words, and occasionally cast a sly smile toward the trio, hunting for Nin's reaction to their antics.

Nin simmered, Serge seethed by her side, and Sabrina became more vocal in her grumbles about rude behavior. Nin leaned down to quiet her friend, knowing to remain stoic presented a stronger outward appearance, when she noticed a flash of movement from a laughing Fae in Bastien's crowd. She registered the small red ball sailing across the room but could do nothing to stop its trajectory. It hit a musician on stage, exploding in a cloud of red dust, causing the music to screech to a halt.

The Fae who lobbed the powdered ball laughed hysterically and others joined him. The shock on the face of the gnome, the laughter, the splash of red. In this room. In The Throne Room. It made Nin tremble. Sweat dampened her forehead. Phantom screams of pain, of memory, echoed in her head. Other, bloodier, reds dotted her vision. She faintly heard Sabrina and Serge calling her, but she was lost to horrors in her past. They could not bring her back.

She involuntarily flashed her eyes toward The Throne, a part of her expecting to see Comus there, smug and proud and secure in his position. It was empty. It was her Throne. Hers to care for and maintain. Just as the gnome in front of her was hers to help. Her mind cleared of memories, but a haze of anger descended, a blazing metal ball heavy in her chest. She rose, straight but jerking, and flashed rage-filled eyes at the still laughing Fae standing by a seated Bastien. Sabrina and Serge continued to call to her. She heard them, sensed the flavor of their pleas change to include a rush of panic and a tinge of fear, but she had no time to consider them at that moment. Other Fae close to her also saw her, must have witnessed her face morph into a cold block of intention and anger, because a few visibly cowered back when she caught their eyes.

There was a reason marble was used extensively in The Throne Room. It seemed these Fae had forgotten, but Nin was determined to remind them. Marble, a stone of the earth, could be called just as soil and plant. She felt the surge of cold rock as her power extended out toward the malicious Fae and heard the crack of bone before the scream. Then more screams, as Fae around him pushed back, falling over chairs and themselves to get away. In the hole left by the scattering courtiers, the Fae who had thrown the ball now crouched down, screaming. Stone encircled his legs to mid-thigh, a small mound of heavy marble crushing in on meat and bone.

The Throne Room was draped in a thick, shocked silence as Nin stormed down toward the now whimpering man.

"You think to mistreat Fae in my Court?" she hissed at him. "You think to harm and laugh as I sit idly by and do nothing?"

He trembled in pain and fear, eyes downcast, and shook his head in denial. She saw red, still only saw red, the powder now and the blood then, and could not control the shake of her anger, the scream she let rip through the air. A scream of frustration and deep-seeded pain planted long ago and allowed to grow over decades that made the room physically crackle and shake with her loosened power.

"Little One," Serge said softly, soothingly close to her ear. "Do not do this." She felt the tendrils of his calming magic in the last words, though they had no effect. She was too powerful, too far gone to be swayed by his spell. It was the nickname, the love she heard there, that made her stop. She pulled up, still angry, but she looked at the terror on the face of the Fae in front of her and felt her stomach churn with regret.

She called back the stone, freeing the Fae's body. She could not bring herself to look at the blood. Walking away, she motioned for others to help the man. As they carried him from the room, she stopped to slice her eyes at Bastien, who no longer looked smug. Panic was etched across his face. "Sir Bastien," she called, her voice as hard as the marble she commanded, "I tire of this entertainment. In future, remember to keep such afternoons calm and civil."

He bowed deeply, no mockery present in his gesture, and exited at a quick pace.

"Leave me," she muttered, and the people in the room, all except her guard, Serge, and Sabrina, scattered. Some smiled sadly in understanding at her as they left, others looked askance. Some showed fear. The gnomes gave deep, meaningful bows in thanks. She was oblivious to all of it. She held herself up by sheer will until the room was cleared, then she crumbled to the floor, tears falling freely on the marble.

Nin jerked when she felt arms around her, but the warmth and smell of Sabrina came through, and she let her friend pull her into a comforting embrace. "Shit, lady. It's okay. It's okay. You're okay," she whispered in her ear as she rocked her gently. Serge embraced both women in his long arms, creating a huddle of three close bodies, giving his sister comfort and warmth.

When her tears slowed to a trickle, she looked into Sabrina's eyes. "I am sorry," she said flatly. She apologized for much then. For what she had done, what she did not do, what she brought Sabrina and Serge and the rest of her family into simply by being who she was.

"Shush. None of that, lady," Sabrina responded in a soft but clear voice. "No need to apologize to me. And that Fae asshole needed a lesson, in my opinion, so I don't think you should apologize to him either. But I'm not an expert on courtiers."

Sabrina looked to Serge, who moved to help Nin stand. "Queens do not often need to apologize to anyone for any action, Little One. Besides, any person with a shred of intelligence understood what happened there. You may be Queen, but that doesn't mean you don't have bad memories."

Nin nodded. "I should control them better," she admitted.

"Maybe." Serge shrugged. "It is too fresh to expect you to do now. Plus, you gave everyone a wonderful demonstration of why they shouldn't mess with you. That's a good thing for a new monarch," he joked.

Nin looked up at her brother, love clearly in his eyes, and asked, "How bad is this for us?"

"It wasn't great," he honestly admitted. "It was also not terrible. Those who disprove will grumble. I imagine, with a few stories of Comus' Court planted here and there, not much else of consequence will come from it. It will, however, give Sir Bastien and his ilk reason to hesitate when attempting such spiteful actions in the future."

Nin heaved a sigh and rubbed her now swollen eyes, becoming more and more tired by the moment. "I need rest," she said.

"Sure you do. Ripping up floors in righteous indignation will do that to a person," Sabrina quipped, trying to make light of the situation. She smiled at her friend, even if the smile did not reach all the way into her blue eyes. Nin saw worry crowded there instead.

"What do I do?" Nin asked. "This cannot happen again." Nin faced her memories in a number of ways while hiding in the human realm — meditation, mindfulness, yoga, and so on. Those practices were never fully enough in the relative safety of her hiding spot in Wilde. Being here, in The Palace, made it worse, and she needed to find another way to bear the weight of painful memories.

"Do you have Fae therapists?" Sabrina asked. Nin and Serge shook their heads. "Well, I'm no therapist, but I'm an ear. Give me some of those memories, lady. Let me help carry the load."

Nin shrugged slightly but agreed in her heart, knowing it was the one thing she had not tried in the human realm and was the one thing she needed most. She must voice the horror to expel it from her system. Lucky for her, she was a monarch with friends and family. Regardless, she could not talk now, so she could not give voice to the gratitude swelling inside her. Instead, she leaned on her friend and her brother as she headed to her rooms to rest. It would not easily come, but the oblivion of sleep was required, if only for a brief period. The day had been too trying, and sadly, more like it would come soon enough.

CHAPTER 13

Her dreams were filled with red. The pain of that afternoon bled into the red of Wisp wings severed, of lashes given, of cuts and stabs and beatings she saw countless times in The Throne Room when Comus held her captive. The events of the day opened the floodgates of memory in some way, and her night was filled with all those things in her past she wished most to forget, causing her to have a fitful, restless sleep.

Her final dream was arguably the worst. It started with her in chains, shackled again to The Throne with Comus in its seat. His smile held the sweetness from her youth, the one that so often caught her breath when she thought they were in love. It grew more and more malicious, distorting his face into a caricature of menace she could not pull her focus from until he whispered, "Look."

When she slowly turned her head, there were scattered teacups littering the stairs to the dais with blood spilling from each, soaking the steps in a crimson wash that trickled down to the stone floor and spread, slowly but surely, outward. It was then she noticed the hooded figures, struggling bound and kneeling on the marble, forced to face the throne by a line of shadowy, cloaked wraiths at their backs. One by one their hoods were ripped off. Mosi. Serge. Gin. Sabrina. All captured in a straight line. All struggled. All silently screamed and twisted their faces in agony.

Nin scrambled up and away, rushing down the stairs to save those she loved, when she slipped on blood, tumbling down until she was yanked up hard, her chain tightening around her neck as it dragged her backward. Toward him. She pulled away when she felt him at her back, his body heat, even in dream, a sear across her flesh.

"Do not shy from me, my Love," he cooed in her ear. "I am here, as always, watching. Waiting." He leaned over her, placing a firm kiss on her cheek. A scream ripped from one of her family below, but she could not tell who voiced it. She let out her own wail of rage and hurt in response. One that echoed in reality and startled her awake.

Nin stared wide-eyed for a moment, breathing in pants, taking more than a few beats to realize she was safe in her chamber, curled on her side in her own bed, facing her bathroom. When she registered those surroundings, she relaxed her muscles, tight and trembling. She loosened her hands from their grip on the blanket, which she could tell was damp from the same sweat that stuck bits of hair to her face. Flopping over on her back, she brought her hands up and rubbed them down her face, taking a moment to breathe deep and steady, to listen to the quiet around her, before she began to brush her dark locks away from her face. To clear her mind of the rage and hurt and fear still crowded there from her dreams, Nin stared at the blank ceiling for long moments, not moving, just being present in the meditative ways she learned in the human realm. She was no stranger to nightmares and the methods she used to best rid herself of their residue, although the last was particularly bad and felt all too real.

When she pulled her arms down to lay them flat with upturned palms for one particular breathing exercise, she felt a crinkle. Something stiff and crisp brushed her fingertips. She reached out as she sat up, bringing the foreign object to rest in her lap. It was a dried red rose with a small slip of paper tied tightly to the stem. She froze, her mind revolting at what was in front of her. No one gave her flowers, as some Fae and humans did in celebration or courtship, as it was abhorrent to her. She was earth magics, connected to the land, and purposefully cut flowers, especially cut and dried flowers, were not a thing she appreciated. Comus knew this and, while she was captive in his Court, used the knowledge to his advantage. It was a show, a play on caring that was in actuality a harsh slap in the face.

Once she was again able to move, was unstuck from her shock at the discovery of this in her bed, her trembling hands undid the tie and flipped over what she knew would be a note. She saw what she suspected she would see. It was Comus' formal script flourishing and exaggerated even in the two-word message: *"Soon, Love."* Reading it, Nin let out a long, loud scream, equal parts rage and fear.

The scene in Nin's chamber was different from the last time Mosi stood in the same spot early in the morning. Nin paced, fear, anger, and worry propelling her feet to do something, a burst of activity that was uncharacteristic but understandable given the flood of events over the past twenty-four hours. Mo glowered, his jaw flexed, and he ground his teeth audibly as he seethed.

"How?" he managed to bite out.

"I do not know. What of the guards?"

"All accounted for, all trusted and appointed by me from my unit in The Falls."

Her back ramrod straight, she eased herself down into a chair beside her closet doors, willing herself to stop and focus, to think through this.

"I do not remember hearing the door and opening or closing it without sound is no easy feat." They both looked to the doors, intricately carved large oak curves that took effort to heave open, even for most Fae.

"Are we certain..." Mo started to ask but stopped himself short.

"It is fine to ask, brother. We should explore all options. Yes. I am absolutely certain this is from Comus, that somehow Comus or one sent directly by him left this for me. He is the only one who would give me a dried rose, and I know the shape and curve of his hand well." Mo nodded and she continued, "While I would like to say I was certain it was not on or in my bed when I fell asleep, of that I cannot fully attest. Yesterday was trying in many ways, and I was depleted when I entered this room. I very well could have missed seeing it."

"Guards are only present outside your chambers when you are in your chambers," he muttered, thinking. "As it stands, we are certain only that this is from Comus. We are uncertain when it was left or who may have left it." Mo sucked in a deep breath and continued, "You need a guard stationed inside your room."

"Absolutely not," Nin breathed out, another type of fear gripping her throat.

"Nin, I know you may think…"

"No, Mosi. Listen to me. I will order you as Queen if I must, but please, listen to me as your sister. As one you trust. I cannot have that. I cannot have someone in my room, watching me as I sleep. It is too much like my past."

Mo blinked for a moment, taking in her words, then sagged a bit. He moved to her, bending to be face-to-face and lay his hand on her knee in a comforting gesture. "I now see and understand, Little One. But what of me? Or Serge? Or Gin? Or Mother? Another Fae we trust. You trust."

She shook her head, sadness in her voice. "I fear it would not matter. It would chafe regardless. I am sorry."

"No need for apologies, Nin. None of this is caused by you. We only need to adapt and prepare."

Standing up, he offered her his strong hand to hold, and she took it, using his gentle pull to right herself quickly. "Surely Gin knows of stronger wards we could place on this chamber?" she said, thinking aloud. "It is the Consort Rooms. There are some protections, but it is not as heavily warded as the Royal Chambers."

"What of moving there?"

"Also impossible," Nin answered, suppressing a shudder.

"Very well. The guard will search the room for any additional clues or tokens left behind." Mo then cocked his head. "Telling Borjigin is the proper move, but it will mean also telling the others, especially if Gin requires help with research or placement of wards."

"I know. They will not take this well," Nin grumbled.

"Only because they worry."

"I have given them more than enough worry to last a Fae lifetime," Nin stated, her flat tone hiding the guilt and frustration she attempted to bury in the growing pit of her stomach.

Mo was there, in her face, quick and quiet as the warrior he was, his dark eyes flashes of lightning in a night sky. "No, Nin. Again, the blame is not yours. It is not your doing, nor your burden to bear alone. We are here to help because we care for you." He reached forward, giving her a swift but fierce hug, breathing her in for a moment before whispering in her ear. "We have you, Little One, and we shall never let you go again."

Tears pricked her eyes as she nodded into his shoulder, unable to voice her assent because of the cry that held fast in her throat. Finally pulling away, she said, "We must take measures for the others, as well. They will be unhappy about the events because of what they mean in terms of Comus and I, but I worry for them as well. If Comus can reach me, he can easily reach any of them. Even you.

And Sabrina is especially vulnerable. As a human, she may well be a target of his particular brand of loathing."

Mo stiffened at the idea of her friend in danger and ground his teeth. "He will not touch her," he gritted out.

"Agreed. Yet we must prepare for the worst while we hope for the best. I've been mulling over this for some time, and have yet to discuss it with Sabrina, but I think it best for her to begin combat training."

Mo quirked an eyebrow at this, thinking for a moment before blurting, "I will train her."

"Of course you will, brother. You trained me and Sergius and many a soldier and guard. You are the best choice." With a small smile she added, "For a variety of reasons.

"However," Nin added, "let me broach the subject with her. At a lesson."

"Very well," Mo said, moving closer to the door. "Should I call the others for a debriefing?"

"Yes. I only ask you to wait one moment. Let me change and we will go find the others. Meet in another room. I need to be away from here for a time."

Mo gave her a sad smile of understanding and took up position between her and the door, acting as personal guard and protective brother. "I shall be here."

"Yes, you will," she answered with certainty, turning to go about her business so they could do something, anything, that might let her feel in control once again.

CHAPTER 14

"Are you sure you're up for this?" Sabrina asked, her voice soft and hesitant.

"Yes, Sabrina. I am fine. We must continue our lessons," Nin answered firmly. It was only hours after they had met to discuss the intrusion of Comus into The Palace, into her very room, but the Queen rested and felt ready to do something, anything, beyond obsessively replaying all the events of the previous day in her mind. Helping Sabrina offered her the best necessary distraction, a task to take her mind off the lingering memories and doubts that crowded her head while also giving her the opportunity to actively engage with one of the few people in the realm who calmed her merely by being present.

"Okay. If you're sure…" Sabrina said, doubt lingering. Yet, she showed trust in her friends' words by preparing. "Let's do this," she replied, a determined smile on her face.

They were in the same alcove, secreted away for another magic lesson. Gin was absent. Off to the Scholar's Guild to deal with Michel, the appointment of a new Council Member, and discuss more powerful wards with a few trusted people in his ranks. Nin was left to teach alone for the first time. It was an odd position for her, something she never endeavored, but Sabrina was an excellent pupil and the lessons were vital. Queen Nin knew everyone needed preparation if Fae like Bastien, and whoever the traitor was, and Comus himself, kept up their machinations. Mosi and Sergius were each covertly working in their own areas of expertise. Mosi received regular updates from guards, especially those in close proximity to all Council Members. Serge schmoozed and chatted and flirted, all with an edge toward more information and finding both possible allies and enemies in The Fae Court.

No one outside the circle knew of Sabrina's powers, hopefully, which gave her friend an edge. That edge was maintained only if she honed her magics and could use them when the time was right. It was protection for Sabrina, a vulnerable human in their world, but also protection for everyone else in their group. Who knew when or where the next attack would occur, how it would go, and who would be the target? Nin felt drained, physically and emotionally, but bolstered by the prospect of helping her friend in a tangible way.

"Yes, let us begin," Nin said. "Gin gave you homework, correct?"

Sabrina's smile screwed up brighter. "Yep. Gave me all the homework. And, the good student I am, I did it. No problem."

"Nicely done. What was the homework again?" Nin asked, wanting Sabrina to explain in her own words, a strategy the Mae Queen often used on her and she found exceedingly helpful.

Sabrina chuckled, a teacher herself so fully aware of the trick Nin employed in their lesson. "Gin asked me to memorize two simple spells. One involving my ball of light. One involving the morning glory." Sabrina patted a potted, sapphire toned ipomoea on the table next to her.

"Yes. Good. Now a demonstration, if you please. Show me the affinity orb first."

Sabrina visibly centered herself as her breathing turned rhythmic and her eyes narrowed on the empty spot on her upturned palm. She whispered the light spell and it came immediately, the reddish green orb sparking with life. Nin was happy, but not surprised, at the level of control Sabrina already commanded over her newly acquired magics. As her friend asserted previously, though in jest, she was an excellent student. At this rate, Sabrina would master the basics in short order and need to turn to a more specialized education.

"Excellent, Sabrina. You did that so quickly. Very impressive. Now, continue."

Sabrina, maintaining focus, said, "KALLI," the word ringing clear and true in the alcove. She lowered her hand, eyes to the light, and the ball stayed, hovering at chest height.

"Good. Good. Now, with your intention, move it," Nin instructed.

"What? Like, how, exactly do you mean?" Sabrina questioned, never taking her eyes from the glowing swirl of red and green in front of her.

"Oh, yes. Intention. As we said before, it is the foundation of all controlled magic. You have established a connection with word and thought, now push that thought. Think about what you wish the orb to do. See it clearly in your mind. Focus on this intentional outcome and make the light move to another part of the room."

"Okay. Yeah. Sure. Got it." Sabrina gritted in obvious concentration, her brow furrowed as she stared at the light.

Nin did not need to wait long. After a few beats, the light rose in the air, hovering at eye level before inching its way up toward the ceiling. After a minute, the light shimmered high above their heads, skimming the rock above them.

"Very good. Very good, indeed, friend. Try it quickly now. Instead of incrementally, focus your intention on a specific spot somewhere in the room and call the light to that spot in your mind."

Sabrina concentrated in silence, the ball hovered near the ceiling, and in a blink, it zipped down and across the room to land directly in front of the chalkboard. Sabrina laughed while still maintaining concentration because the ball did not quiver once. "I got this," she whispered to herself.

"Yes. You surely do," Nin affirmed, proud of and happy for her friend. "Now, blink it out."

Sabrina looked away from the ball, blinked her own eyes, and the light shuttered then disappeared. Nin clapped softly, smiling at her. "So very good, lovely. Now, for the more difficult spell. Gin asked you to do the BEEGOR spell, correct?"

Sabrina nodded and Nin carried on. "It is a more advanced spell, one connected directly to earth magics. Not every Fae can command flowers. How did it work for you?"

Sabrina chewed her lip, fidgeted a bit, and shook her head, "It didn't. Not really. I could do it a little, but not much."

"That is perfectly fine, Sabrina. You are doing so well but remember this is all new to you and there will be places you may stumble. It is understandable. Even expected. I would actually be slightly frightened if you automatically did everything perfectly on your first try."

Sabrina slumped a bit, hunching her shoulders forward and hanging her head. She looked up at Nin and confessed, "It's hard. I haven't dealt with hard learning in a long while. Words, books, study like that comes easy, almost naturally, for me. This magic stuff is more difficult to grasp."

"No, the earth magics are more difficult to grasp. I suspect, if Serge were to come help you, the word magics you have would come more easily, feel more effortless. This is my fault, friend, not yours."

"Let's not talk about fault or blame again. Magic is amazing. I feel it running through me, energizing my body. My mind is more nimble, quicker than before, and not to brag or anything, but I was pretty damn quick already. It's awesome. Like, in the true sense of the word — full of awe. That comes from you and I'm happy to have it. End of discussion."

Nin still held on to guilt she could not easily shake off, but she moved along so they could continue their lesson.

"What I intended to express was the idea that magic, overall, is new and will take time, but you are grasping the basics at a rapid pace. The earth magics, however, are likely disconnected from your internal affinities because they are a direct infusion of my magics. The word magics may come quicker, even the more difficult spells. However, earth magic is more powerful, a better defense in many ways, so we must work together to develop these skills as well."

"Makes sense," Sabrina said, tilting her head in thought. "Okay. So, tell me, what do you feel when you use your earth magics? I think knowing more directly what you experience might help me emulate a bit better."

"It is hard for me to pinpoint now, as my magics are second nature at this point. I feel a similar static and hum, as you described. That is the general feel of magics for all, I believe. I do also feel a heat in my torso, and a heaviness at my feet. It is something I discussed with the Mae Queen when she was my mentor. She felt the same sensations, although she claimed to also feel the heat throughout her limbs. She believed the heat was the gathering of power, the heaviness a link that connects us to earth, be it soil or stone or wood beneath our feet."

"Maybe I should search for and try to pull on those feelings when I do the spell?" she offered.

"You are such a good teacher, you practically teach yourself," Nin said, agreeing with Sabrina's tactic.

Sabrina shook her head, likely to clear her thoughts, and closed her eyes. She opened them quickly as she whispered, "BEEGOR." Nothing happened. Sabrina repeated the process, again and again, asserting the spell more forcefully as she went until she yelled it, causing the words to echo in the alcove. With that yell, however, Sabrina's eyes widened and a grin spread across her face as Nin noticed the petals of the flower begin to open from their nighttime position. The ipomoea bloomed, proud and full, as a squeal of delight slipped from Sabrina. Nin clapped, both impressed with her friend and happy at Sabrina's obvious joy in completing the task.

Sabrina whirled to face her. "I'd made it shudder some before, but never that. Not until you helped. Thanks, lady."

"It is my purpose as your teacher in these lessons, Sabrina. No thanks are required."

"Gratitude is always good, Nin," she said, moving up to give Nin a quick hug. "And, that time, I felt it. What you talked about. It was faint, but heat and weight were there in the background too."

"I am happy to hear it."

"Yep. Now, I need to practice calling on that feeling."

"As it is not your true affinity, I do believe it will remain more difficult for you. It will take diligence and practice."

"Pfft," Sabrina scoffed. "I'll practice until I'm exhausted and I'll get it down." She considered Nin for a moment and added, "You know, it really is different."

"What is different?"

"The feeling of earth magic. The thing that makes you, you. It feels different to me. The other, basic magic stuff feels like breathing techniques in a way. It's mostly natural but I need to think about it to give it purpose or rhythm. The earth magic is harder, less natural to me, but oddly feels like it wants to be connected outward and not just inward. Like it flows through and out rather than being all internal. It's definitely a stronger power, but it feels wilder to me, less controllable."

"It could be your affinity issues," Nin guessed.

"No, I think it's more, but I can't know for sure until I start trying our word magics. I think the feeling is connected to what makes earth magic so special. What makes you so special, Nin. It's powerful, a restrained wildness. It's also both internal and external, a power meant to serve the individual and the community and the environment."

Nin blinked away tears at what her friend said. "Thank you, Sabrina. For everything. I am glad to hear you believe I am all those things. I am also glad I have you to talk to about earth magics. It is lonely, being the only one."

Sabrina grabbed Nin's hand and squeezed. "Anytime. You know that, you beautiful land mermaid."

Nin laughed at the Leslie Knope line, happy to have her friend there but also happy. Sabrina gave her a way out of a heavy conversation she did not wish to have at the moment. "Should we mark this on our calendars, an anniversary of the day you learned how to feel earth magics?"

"Yep. I'll even buy you a waffle maker," Sabrina quipped, and both friends laughed together, easing the stress from the lesson, the previous day, the chaos both felt in the past few weeks by leaning on to each other, feeling the laughter lift a small amount of weight. There was still a great deal on their shoulders, on their minds, but Nin thought about how good it felt to joke with her friend once again. How relieved she was they could still easily slip into that when with each other.

"I do miss television," Nin finally said. "Especially those sitcoms."

"Your Queenliness," Sabrina joked, shoving Nin's shoulder, "Command someone to get a TV, Blu-ray player, and some seasons of shows for you. Easy peasy."

"I do not know if they will work here. Surely the iron would make it difficult."

"There's very little iron in those things, if any. It's all plastic, baby. At least I think so. Who knows?"

"Then perhaps I shall. My second royal decree will be a demand to acquire humorous shows for me and my friend,"

"Seems legit," Sabrina laughed.

"Quite," Nin said, rising. "First, hopefully, comes a truly restful night's sleep. I am exhausted."

"I imagine so." Sabrina stood and wiped her hands on her pants as if she completed some hard and dirty manual task. "Our work here is done. For now. You have any homework for me?"

"Only practice. Gin has a basic earth magics primer, old and exceedingly rare. It helped me greatly before I began lessons with the Mae Queen. They said they would retrieve it on their trip to the guild. When they return, they will give you more instructions regarding that text. Take the ipomoea. You must practice speaking with the flower now, not forcing your spell through. That will also help you hone this form of magic. For this, call on those powers, those feelings we discussed, bring them up, and say 'ROBBGRA.' Focus on the plant. Try to sense its connection to the world around it, the earth and air. You may not be able to open a link, which is perfectly fine. Practice nonetheless and we will review and try together in the next lesson."

Sabrina agreed, and they gave each other a warm, tight hug before Nin departed. The guards were outside and still unsure of who Nin met in this nightly rendezvous. Best to keep it that way as long as possible. Nin thought it was good to have these moments alone with her friend, where she could laugh freely, talk openly, and not be Queen Nin for brief periods.

CHAPTER 15

A hazy early dawn light filtered into her bedchamber as a sound, much like a clearing of a throat, startled Nin awake. Her heart hammered in her chest, and she searched the dim light for an intruder with a maiming spell poised on the tip of her tongue. Nin did not let it fly as she found the Mae Queen sitting straight and proud, ankles crossed, staring around the bedroom with a sly smile. "I do remember this place fondly," she said with a sigh.

"My Queen," Nin stated, sitting up straight in bed and bowing as much as she could from her position.

"Oh, none of that, child. You are Queen now."

"Then that makes you?"

"Something else," she said. The Mae Queen was well versed in the political art of non-replies.

Nin sniffed, tired and annoyed. "It would be helpful, Your Grace, to know more about your condition."

The Mae Queen laughed, "Surely it would. As you wish, Queen. However, I can only give you what I know, which is surprisingly little. I myself was visited on occasion, in the early years of my reign, by my predecessor. She did not rule as long as I, and that was eons ago, but she was a formidable force nonetheless. My mentor. I vaguely remember it was…disconcerting to say the least. I do understand your frustration."

Nin pushed herself from the bed during this speech, rounding the side to come sit on the floor in front of the Mae Queen with legs crossed, ready to listen.

"Oh, my," she gasped, looking down at Nin, "you are so different, yet I still see that little girl I first met on a New Eve Telling, then the teenager who sat in front of me to learn more of our earth magics." The Mae Queen stared for a moment, lost in those memories, until she pulled herself up and shook her head. "Forgive me, child, my reminisces. Memories, thoughts, feelings, they are what ground me when I am aware."

Nin simply cocked her head, allowing the Mae Queen to continue at her own pace. "Where was I? Oh, yes. My predecessor, Queen Ra, visited me as well, for a time. She came with warnings and visions and smatterings of advice. I saw her five times total. My early years as Queen were rather bloody and treacherous. Queen Ra told me she was the manifestation of her magics, filtered back into the earth, lingering in an in-between space until fully absorbed. I suppose I am the same. It feels that way. I

come when you are in need, connect only with you
and the cycles of the earth when I realize it. One day
I will stop realizing. When that day will be, why and
how it will come, I do not know. All I can say is your
fear and hesitation call to me. I am still here, in your
dream space at least, to answer your call."

"Our earth magics connect us," Nin stated
plainly.

"Yes. They connect us, while living, to the
earth. When our lives are over, our bodies no more,
our magic does not immediately dissipate. It lingers,
clinging to others with similar power. It may even
feed on the shared power, allowing our consciousness
to stay on longer than it should."

"I am glad for it," Nin whispered, pulling
her knees up to hug against her chest.

"As am I," the Mae Queen answered.

"Yet..." Nin said, "no one knows where or
when or how you died? Why is that? Is it like that for
all earth magic wielders? Will I mysteriously vanish
as well?"

"Oh, no, Queen Nin. Queen Ra died in front
of many soldiers, bloody on a battlefield. The
treachery of another took my life, but that is a story I
cannot tell."

"Why?"

"I do not rightly know. I am unable to
discuss certain subjects outright, issues or concerns
or people who directly relate to your present
predicaments."

"Then your death has to do with all this?"
Nin asked, vaguely waving a hand around.

"Yes. It is a mystery now, but more will be
revealed. Only I cannot do so."

Nodding and not wanting to waste the Mae Queen's visit with questions leading to nowhere and nothing, Nin decided to press on more concrete concerns. "Very well. Why did you come now?"

"Your pain over the last few days called to me," the Mae Queen answered softly.

"Yes. I had a long, trying time of late."

"Understandable. It will also not be your last trying time. There will be many during your reign."

"If my reign lasts," Nin grumbled.

"Ah, and that, as they say, is the rub," the Mae Queen answered. "The true purpose. The Fae Court and Council have always been precarious places. You know this, child. You were practically raised in them. Such machinations should offer no surprise. As for Comus, you must expect him to rear his head until he is no more."

"The events were not a surprise from a coldly logical perspective. That does not make them feel any less overwhelming."

"You have suffered dearly, Queen Nin. It has changed the way you think and act. Some in Fae need to realize this and learn to tread more lightly. They will. Yet, there are larger issues you ignore in your pain and uncertainty."

"Such as?" Nin asked.

"Such as the traitor in your garden. You decisively took The Fae Council in hand. Well done, that. Now, The Fae Court will also be more hesitant, although your tactics were less methodical there. However, you need to focus much more on Fae as a realm, and the traitor, the one who allows Comus and his followers constant entry into your world."

"I am focused on the traitor. I have an inner circle I trust and we are…"

"Doing too little to track the Fae responsible," the Mae Queen finished. Nin could not exactly counter her point. They had done little thus far.

The Mae Queen continued, "Use your inner circle — all intelligent, skilled, and powerful beings. Once again, you need their help."

Nin agreed, so said nothing in reply. The traitor needed to be found to keep all safe in Fae and ensure her reign. She was still unsure of one point. "What did you mean by focusing on the Fae realm?" she asked.

"You have not tended the garden," Mae Queen answered.

Nin froze in shock at her own disregard. She had forgotten. It was ridiculous of her, but she forgot the central purpose of the Royal Gardens in her coronation week. They connected the Queen with Fae, quite literally. The Queen poured her magic into the plants nurtured, the soil turned, the water poured. It went directly back into the earth, creating the link between the land and the Queen. The benefits of this, fertile ground, hearty plants, the cycle of earth and life and vitality overall, were reinforced in that exchange. It was why having a Queen with earth magics was so important. It was what kept Fae working properly.

The Mae Queen read the horror of her mistake on her face and reached for Nin. "Child, it is fine. There are many years left before true damage would be done. I myself had to be reminded of this. Like I said, my beginnings as Queen were also rather busy." Coming off her seat and kneeling down by Nin, she said, "All I do is remind. Push you to make the connection. Strengthening it will help Fae. It will also help you feel surer and more grounded. What strengthens Fae strengthens you, and vice versa."

"I must do the work," Nin said, pulling her head up to stare at the opposite wall, in the general direction of the Royal Gardens.

"Tend your garden. In all ways literal and figurative. There are things that need help along, encouragement and reinforcement, if you will. Pruning and culling is also required."

"Yes. I understand," Nin answered, pulling back to the Mae Queen.

"I know you do, child," she said to Nin, bringing her hand up to stroke Nin's cheek. "You only needed a hint to remember. Nothing more or less than I did when in your position."

"But we are not the same," Nin said, again feeling a swell of negative comparison.

"We are not. Never were, and never shall be," the Mae Queen answered firmly. "I was what Fae needed in my time. You are what Fae needs at this time. When that will change, only the magic knows. For now, know you are right because the very magic of the earth wills it so. Trust in this, child."

As before, the Mae Queen cocked her head as if hearing a call only she could recognize. "I must go. Again, I do not know when I will return to you or if I will return at all. If this is goodbye, so be it. Go with my faith and love, child."

Nin closed her eyes, felt the briefest brush of phantom lips on her forehead, then opened her eyes to an empty space where the Mae Queen once stood. She curled herself on the hard floor, not crying overmuch on this occasion, although a few tears were shed. She willed herself up — to bed, to sleep, to the

prospect of awakening to bright sunlight and a day of
work in her gardens.

CHAPTER 16

"Don't you think he's taken enough of a beating?" Sabrina huffed, her breath coming in soft pants from the strain of using her newly acquired magics.

"That is a scarecrow," Nin stated in a cool, matter-of-fact manner. "He has neither physical nor emotional needs."

"It's a joke, lady, though I've taken quite a beating and could use a break," Sabrina grumbled back while undoing the messy ponytail at the base of her skull. She ran her hands through the dirty blond strands, shaking it out before pulling back into a more secure bun. She placed her hands on her full hips and gave a disgruntled look to her friend.

Nin was undeterred. Gin was again absent, so Nin tried to be as steadfast in her instruction as her cousin was in theirs. "Again," she said, crossing her arms at her chest and cocking her hip out in an imitation of her friend's human attitude, ready to take whatever guff Sabrina wanted to send her way.

Sabrina took a moment to stare, eying Nin from head to foot, seeing not courtly attire but something far more similar to what Nin wore in the human world, though her Fae garb often featured far more leather: tight but rugged leather work pants, a thick linen undershirt skimming closely to her torso, and a flowing woolen overshirt, opened and with the long, loose sleeves rolled up to her elbows. Nin missed her comfortable work boots at times, and she may well use them when in her garden on occasion, but her sleek leather knee boots still served her well when she was not forced to wear dresses and gowns. Sabrina took it all in, smirked, and bowed deep, adding a flourishing sweep of her arms, "Why, yes, Your Grace. Whatever you wish, Your Grace." From anyone else, Nin might bristle at the mockery. Coming from Sabrina, she knew it was all in jest, so she smiled back.

"Always the jester," she laughed, moving to stand the scarecrow tall on its stand for the dozenth time that evening. "Again," Queen Nin repeated.

Sabrina wasted no time now, instead concentrating hard on the straw man in front of her. She focused, said, "KALLI," and in no time the fake Fae was hurtling from its place on the post, across the expanse of the alcove. At the end, a nest of vines rested, coaxed there at the beginning of the lesson by Nin. Before the scarecrow landed, Sabrina shouted, "BEEGOR," and the vines surged up, catching the figure right before it hit the stone floor, encircling it tightly and pulling it back toward the mass of now writhing vines waiting to add their own fresh, green tangles to the snare.

Sabrina spun around to Nin, sweat on her brow. "This magic business is rougher than I imagined, but I'm getting it. It's hard to think, talk out loud, talk internally to the plant, and focus on overall intention even as that intention changes. It's a lot."

"Yes," Nin agreed, but pulled up to grab Sabrina's shoulder. "Yet, you complete the tasks, every time, with minimal effort."

"I wouldn't call this minimal effort," Sabrina replied as she wiped gently at the small sheen of sweat gathered at her brow.

"Sabrina, it takes months for Fae children to reach this level, to intentionally perform basic and affinity specific spells at the same time. It is a wonder you do such after only several days of practice." Nin was truly in awe of her friend: her ability to study and learn, her quick and nimble mind, her adaptability to all the changes in life. She felt far less sure of herself than Sabrina seemed to feel, and Fae was her home, the monarchy a duty she had prepared for since she was a young girl. She realized, on some level, she was somewhat jealous of her. She was also wracked with guilt over being the reason her friend must rise to this occasion even while happy her friend was here, by her side, as she floundered. It was a complex set of emotions for her and something she struggled with daily.

"We've been at this for an hour now. Surely we can call it a night?" Sabrina asked, moving to sit at a bench before Nin even gave her leave to break.

"I suppose you have done well enough for tonight's lesson," Nin answered. She sat down softly by her friend, leaning her shoulder into Sabrina. "Before we part, there are things to discuss."

"What?" Sabrina asked, pausing to take a large gulp of the water skin she brought along to practice.

"You completed your first defensive spells — one basic and one affinity specific. However, earth magic is not your most natural affinity. It is time we discuss bringing Serge into your lessons, adding word magics to your practice."

"Sure," Sabrina said with a shrug, seemingly unconcerned.

"I do not wish to bring another person into your lessons unless you are comfortable, Sabrina," Nin insisted, being explicitly clear with her friend. She wanted her to know discussion was possible.

"I know you'd never make me do something I wasn't comfortable with," Sabrina said, affection for Nin warm in her voice. "I was super nervous and anxious at first. I'm better now. More solid in what's in here," she said, tapping her head with her middle finger. "Besides, I know Serge. He might flirt and joke, but he can be serious when it calls for it. He's a good brother to you. He might even be a good teacher. Who knows?"

More hesitantly, Nin asked, "What of Mosi possibly instructing you on defense?"

"Is that necessary?" Sabrina asked in return, looking down to play with her fingers, a sure sign of the effect the question had on her nervous ticks.

"He is far better at such things than Gin or I, at least in terms of basic and universal defensive tactics coupled with affinity spells. It is part of being a military leader."

"Makes sense," Sabrina answered after a beat, although this was said more softly, with less assurance on her part.

"I do not pry," Nin said, "but know, if there is something involving Mo you wished to discuss with me, it would stay between us. He is my brother, yes. However, you are also mine, in a different way. I would keep your counsel."

Sabrina looked at Nin for a beat and gave a wry smile. "There's nothing to discuss, and because of what you just said, nothing to ever really discuss about me and Mo."

"I feel that may change as I see what grows between you flourish continually," Nin said, raising a hand to pause her friend when she moved to object. "No need for more negative assertions. I believe you believe what you say. Know only that if more comes, I am here to talk. I support you both in whatever you choose."

Sabrina visibly swallowed, head down, eyes cast to the grooves in the stone floor. "It's not that I don't want…"

Nin touched her friend lightly on the shoulder. "I need no justifications or explanations. I see and I say. Maybe that is not my place. I wished to let you know it would warm my heart to see you both happy, and I would be a safe place for you to discuss whatever you may feel. That is all."

"Am I the same?" Sabrina whispered, slowly turning her head to look straight at Nin.

"Whatever do you mean?"

"Am I a safe place for you? A person you can safely talk to about whatever is on your mind?" Before Nin could respond, Sabrina pressed forward as she pulled up head up and cocked it toward Nin, "Because, I've given you time and space to talk, and like you I don't want to push or pry, but it seems to me that out of all the creatures in Fae, you may be the one most in need of a helpful ear."

Nin stilled, silently staring at her friend. What Sabrina said was true, of course. Nin had much on her mind. "It is hard for me to share," she finally admitted.

"Understandable. When you're groomed to be a monarch, I'm sure keeping secrets and looking after yourself is part of the standard curriculum," Sabrina replied, leaning back so she struck a more comfortable pose, her shoulders and head resting against the curved stone wall.

They sat in silence for a few beats, Sabrina relaxed and Nin rigid at her side, until Nin finally said, "I saw the Mae Queen again."

Sabrina cracked open an eye to look at her friend. "And what'd she say this time?"

"I need to tend my garden."

"More than your literal garden in The Palace, I assume," Sabrina surmised.

"Yes, although that is an important part of Fae Queen magic, and a duty I have been lax about in my reign."

Sabrina huffed a small laugh, and Nin looked at her with brows furrowed.

"You mean your super long reign that's lasted about a week," Sabrina sarcastically said. Before Nin could reply, she went on, "You need to cut yourself some slack, lady. You may be Queen of Fae, but you can't possibly be every single thing to every single person in Fae. That's not sustainable."

Nin agreed, but it still nagged at her. "The Mae Queen…" she began, but Sabrina bolted upright and stopped her short.

"First, the Mae Queen is not here. You are. Second, the Mae Queen was her, you are you, so inherently you must be two completely different and separate people who will do different things. It's perfectly logical and expected. Third, and honey, I say this with kindness and an eye toward your feelings, but the Mae Queen wasn't likely as great and all-powerful as you think she was. You think that because she was your Queen and you loved her, as your Queen and mentor and a person with a huge influence on your life. She surely had her faults, which you justified or forgave. Give yourself the same grace, Your Grace."

Nin sat in silence, digesting Sabrina's acute observations, before echoing her friend in her own softly whispered, "Makes sense." She shook her head and looked at Sabrina, hearing the plea for answers in her own voice when she said "I feel so untried, so unsteady. Like I should not be Queen even if my powers are central to the monarchy." She paused for a moment, cleared her throat, and was tentative when she began her next confession,
"Sometimes…sometimes I think about my powers as good and true but me, Nin the individual, as the thing that is wrong and does not fit The Throne."

"That's impostor syndrome talking," Sabrina stated. "It's standard for academics in the human realm. A lot of people in different professions, actually. You somehow get it in your mind that you fooled everyone, you're this impostor that shouldn't have your position or skill or whatever, and at any moment you'll be exposed as the fraud you surely are."

Nin nodded, thinking Sabrina saw so sharply right into the heart of her.

Sabrina sighed, "Sadly lady, it happens to the best of us. I've felt it often. Even here and now."

"But you're handling all this so well," Nin asserted, waving her hand around aimlessly, trying to indicate every single thing about Fae and their current situation in one ineffective gesture.

"You feel me, right, at least bits of my emotions, through the bond we have? Because I get flashes from you sometimes too. But beyond that, you know me, in a deep place, like I know you. You can tell what I feel when I fidget and crack jokes. That's a sure sign of my nerves. And, lady, we all have them. I've dealt with them all my life. When I started getting in front of classrooms full of judgy late teens in college as a TA, I developed a way to push through. May not be the healthiest way to go about it, but I discovered you have to fake it 'til you make it."

"Meaning?" Nin said, leaning close, thinking her friend had some answer to her constant self-doubt.

"You pretend long enough that you're where you're supposed to be and are good at what you do, it eventually becomes true in your mind. Well, maybe not permanently true. You still have doubts. But the act of pretending can start to feel awfully real after some time. Helps even more when it's already real and true outside your head. Occasionally, we need to tell our mind things over and over again to make ourselves believe in the good in us." She stopped there, considering, before pressing on with her thoughts. "Listening to other people tell you you're the shit and exactly where and who you should be really does help, too. Here, in this alcove, I feel strong and right because you and Gin give me that, show me through your words and actions you believe I'm doing well. Words, others and our own, seep down deep. Maybe you need to pretend a bit, but also listen to us when we say you got this, you're doing well, and you're a good Queen."

"No one's said that yet. Not explicitly," Nin replied, moving to wipe the tears she felt clinging to the corners of her eyes.

"What?"

"I am a good Queen."

"That's on me then," Sabrina said, quickly grabbing her friend in a fierce hug, "because you are. Really and truly. Barely a week and you brought Michel the idiot down, established some civil rights for the Lesser Fae, and survived an assassination attempt. You even put a beating on that one Fae who was mean to those gnomes."

Nin scoffed at this. "That incident did not show good queenship."

"I think it did. He was an ass and you schooled him, like a good Queen should," Sabrina sniffed in response. "Besides, the laundry list I gave all happened in a few days, lady. It amazes me you still stand, much less show intelligence and kindness and forethought. You're awe-inspiring, truly. And a very, very good Queen."

"I did not realize I needed to hear such words spoken," Nin admitted.

"We all need encouragement sometimes, whether you're a fancy Fae Queen or a lowly, simple human."

"You, friend, are no simple human. You are fierce, strong, loyal, intelligent, articulate, and exactly who and what I need by my side."

"I'll always be there, you know? By your side. You get ride or die from me, Nin."

Nin felt better, somehow lighter, and knew she would turn to Sabrina again after this. She needed to remind herself to do so more often. Needed to remember she had good, strong, true people who loved and believed in her. That in and of itself said a great deal about who she was as a Fae and a Queen. Rising, she grabbed Sabrina's hand and turned the conversation to more joyful matters as she slowly led them out of the alcove and across the practice space. They walked, arm and arm, as they often had back in the human realm, and it felt comforting to do it in Fae again. It was a way to connect back to who she was through the bond she had with her friend.

It occurred to her she may have missed this in the Mae Queen's "tend your garden" analogy. She needed to see to the Royal Gardens. More concern and care regarding the hidden traitor must be taken. She also must tend her own garden, weed out the bad and focus on the good, the things like connection and love that would not only sustain her, but allow her to thrive.

CHAPTER 17

Gin threw Nin a quick smile before they began. "Hello, esteemed Council. First, I must humbly apologize for my behavior during the last Fae Council Meeting I attended."

"It was nothing," Dre drolled with a wave of his hand.

"I feel it was something, Council Head, so do accept my apology. However, I will not linger on such, as there is much to report. I returned minutes ago from my meeting with the Scholars Guild. During this meeting with Scholar leadership, not only was Michel stripped of his rank and title, he was expelled outright from the guild. He is no longer a member."

"As is just," Sten grumbled from his position at the table. Chieftain Allera gave a cry in agreement and Nin saw her mother nod, although the tight look on her face at the mention of Michel did not fade. Nin knew Inanna held a grudge for those she loved.

"Although provided by the guild, Michel was allowed to keep his home in the area of The Falls. He was heavily fined for his actions, but left with enough to live a simple, contemplative life." Pursing their lips in thought, Gin added, "I honestly do not feel Michel will be a bother after this episode. He took his banishment from The Council and the Scholars Guild with a heavy heart but did not express resentment toward others. He seemed resigned and remorseful, or at the very least resigned and appropriately deflated. The Scholars Guild leaves any further punishment up to Queen Nin and the whole of The Fae Council. They will not intervene on his behalf if you feel further measures are warranted."

Eyes turned to Nin to gauge her reaction. She had no love for Michel, never had. In fact, she disliked the man for numerous decades. Despite her dislike, she knew even in the moment it occurred Michel's outburst was more about ego and power than true rebellion. "I have no wish to impart further punishments on the Fae," she said with a detached air.

"If Queen Nin is satisfied with this outcome, I believe the rest of The Council will follow suit. Would anyone like to make a case for additional punishments and sanctions on Michel?" After a few beats of silence passed, Andrés replied, "Very well. I call for a vote on the matter of Michel's punishments."

"Second," Jane jumped in, looking eager. Whether she was eager to please Dre or get the business of Michel behind The Council, Nin could not determine from her expression alone.

Andrés nodded and called the vote. "All in favor of leaving Michel's punishments as they stand, say 'aye.'" Ayes sounded all around, although it made Nin stifle a smile when she heard the disgruntled way her mother voiced her assent.

"Very well. It is over and done. Let us move on. Borjigin, I do believe there is more business to discuss from the Scholar's Guild?" Dre prompted.

"Oh, yes. I am also to introduce the guild's presumptive replacement for Michel." Gin turned behind them and motioned toward a Fae who looked an awful lot like old human renditions of Father Christmas. His robes were a deep burgundy, and as he walked, Nin caught glimpses of a dark, lush fur lining. A hood draped down his back, replacing the usual cowl around the neck of a Scholar, which worked to accentuate his slight hunch. The Fae himself was wrinkled yet rounded, with flowing white hair and beard and rosy cheeks. He stooped, his back bent, but still tall enough his eyes scanned the room easily. They took in the scene before with a contemplative gleam.

"Allow me to present Pytor the Lettered. I am sure he is familiar to a number of The Council, as he had been leader of the Scholar Scribes for many centuries. However, I am happy to formally present his credentials if any should require," Gin announced.

"Nonsense," Jane quipped. "Who does not know of Pytor the Lettered? He is a well-respected member of the guild who has done much to preserve the history and tradition of the Fae." A true note of respect sounded in her voice, which surprised Nin.

She did not allow this to show, and merely looked on, keeping a stoic face, not hinting at the fact she knew little of this Pytor beyond vague references over the years. He never appeared in Court, at least not in her time there as mentor then Princess. Her mother offered no objections. She smiled warmly at the Fae. That was enough for Nin to proceed and keep her questions for private conversations with Gin and Inanna at a later time.

"Yes. Yes. Well said," Dre called out, a little touch of his past flippant affect bleeding through. "Pytor the Lettered, would you like to introduce yourself? Add anything of your credentials or concerns before this Council."

"No, Andrés of the Mountains," he said, his voice a husky rasp. "I have no comments prior to deliberations."

Andrés moved forward quickly, calling and casting the vote to make Pytor an official member of The Council, with Nin casting her vote in favor as well. Afterward, The Council Head looked extraordinarily pleased with himself, a bit of the old mischievous gleam leaking back into his dark eyes. He turned to Pytor and said, "Now that is completed, you are officially a member of The Fae Council. You may come to have your seat, to begin service to the realm immediately. You may also take your rightful place as Head of The Fae Council."

At that, murmurs raised, as did eyebrows. "Andrés," Inanna said, "this cannot be. It is not the way."

"And why not? My tenure as Head was presented as a temporary measure. The Head Council Member has always been the residing representative from the Scholars Guild. That is how a humbug like Michel got the position in the first place. Pytor is now that representative, therefore he should be Head."

"If I may?" Pytor asked Inanna. When she nodded, he turned to Dre, "I believe you know the mandate, Andrés, but perhaps a reminder is required. A probationary period is set for all new Council Members. As such, I cannot be named Head until after the rise and fall of three moon cycles."

"Much has occurred of late, and precedence has been overturned before," Andrés countered. Nin thought to herself he must really want out of his position to make this point so strongly. She understood, however. Leadership was not fun, and Dre liked to have fun.

"Such a change requires a vote, and I doubt it will pass," Sten added.

"We need you to remain, Dre," Jane encouraged with a beaming smile and a flurry of batting lashes.

"Very well," he barked. "However, we will return to this after three moons, and you will be taking over my temporary duties."

Pytor nodded and shuffled around the table, heaving himself up to rest with a soft groan on his open Council seat.

"As Council is now fully sat, I have business to address," Jane said with a serious tone. "Summer solstice will be upon us soon, and we must plan the festivities."

Nin stifled a groan at this. Parties were not important now. However, the discussion allowed her to observe those seated at her leisure, as she felt no need to interject on such a topic. Her mother was no traitor, and Chieftain Allera was too new to be the traitor, never mind the fact both would be killed by Comus on sight rather than bargained with in any way. Pytor was also too new. This left Sten, Dre, and

Jane. She did not want to think any of these Fae were capable. She knew each all her life, from childhood at her mother's knee to her own time on The Council and beyond. She laughed and cried with each in some way, lived with them at least at the periphery of her life for so long it brought a stab of hurt to think they would betray not only her, but all of Fae. She was making no decisions on this now, especially without more information. She searched through the smattering of attendees and spotted Serge, leaned with casual ease against a wall, staring as she did. She caught his eye and widened her own, he offered a nod in return. Serge was on the hunt as well, and he was a much better political tracker than she. He would have insight for them soon enough.

Nin turned back into the actual substance of the conversation when she heard Dre huff. "Tradition. I have grown sick of the word. It is all we discuss, how we must or must not follow tradition, how we must or must not do a thing in the name of tradition."

"Andrés, it is true there is much discussion of tradition, but it is important in this time of transition to consider such matters carefully," Inanna soothed.

"Quite right, Inanna," Jane added. "Tradition for the simple sake of tradition should be questioned, of course, but in the areas where we can utilize tradition to bring stability to our realm, we should do so."

"Agreed," Allera firmly stated. "And, might I add, Lesser Fae are generally in favor of celebrations such as these as it is often a time when we are included without question or issue."

"True," Andrés said, drawing out the word. "The summer solstice festival is always merry, and we could use merriment now. To bring our realm together and give all something to look forward to in the near future. I have no problem with this in theory. I also do not want to take The Council time away from more pressing issues for this event. Jane, would you be willing to hold off on voting, make decisions on your own for a time, and bring business of the celebration before The Council when you have a solid plan in place?"

Jane nodded quickly and fanned herself, joy at being placed in charge of the event clear on her face.

"Any objections?" Andrés asked, looking around The Council table. No one spoke up, so he added, "Very well. Jane is now tasked with creating a festive and inclusive summer solstice celebration, and we will consider and vote on her plans at a later date. Now, let us move on to other matters."

Mo presented his current defense report to The Council. Sten discussed shipping and commerce concerns. Inanna revealed what she knew of food shortages and infrastructure issues from her role as Audience Day liaison. None of it was good. People were hurting, they were unhappy, and they needed aid from The Palace. The Council made plans of protection, strategized how to straighten supply issues, and mandated how aid should be distributed. It was logical and thoughtful, but also hard on Nin's heart. She was Queen, tasked with helping all of Fae, and they needed so much help. The Council did a great deal, yes, but she must do more.

When discussion turned to planting in the vast farmlands of the realm, Nin perked up as she knew this was an area where she could provide more active aid. She interrupted her mother who was reciting current needs based on requests she fielded in her role as facilitator for Court Audience Day.

"I will go," she said firmly.

"My Queen?" Inanna asked for clarity.

Sitting herself straighter, she said, "I shall tour the farmlands over the summer, ensuring all is well with what has been planted. It is a duty not often attended, but one decidedly in my powers as Queen."

"The security of such an endeavor would be a logistical nightmare," Sten objected.

"My concern is the land and the people. It is my duty as Queen to help in this way, as it has been a hard few decades for the Fae who sustain our lands through their toil in the fields. I trust those better trained with security measures to plan accordingly."

"Sten is not wrong, Your Grace. More consideration should be taken…" Dre began, but Nin raised a hand to stop him short.

"My decision was not an instance for discussion, but rather a statement of fact. I will do this, after the summer solstice celebration. If Council would like to help, or offer an envoy to aid in my cause, such matters could be discussed and planned here. I am now only telling you what will happen. What you wish to do with the information is The Council's sole concern. Leave the rest to me and my advisers."

"I think it's lovely," Jane exclaimed, "and gives me grand ideas for festival themes and directions."

"A kind and thoughtful idea and a practical help, my Queen," Chieftain Allera said, punctuating her sentiment by pounding her fist on the arm of her chair, a sign of applause and agreement amongst the Wisps.

Nin nodded, glad to have two eager supporters. Inanna voiced her own happiness at the idea, and a gruff Sten and a quiet Dre followed suit in their own way. She was correct in asserting she did not need Council approval, but support was an affirming thing to receive, nonetheless. The meeting continued for a short time after this, but Nin was elsewhere. She was in her mind, in the fields and streams and valleys of Fae, her hands in the earth, helping restore it and nourish it for her people. It was tangible and useful and connected to who she was before she became Queen, all points that eased a small amount of her unease in the monarchy. If she could find more ways to offer direct aid based on who she was as Nin, being Queen Nin may start to feel more right and true.

CHAPTER 18

"Why am I up at the butt crack of dawn again?" Sabrina groused, a slight pout on her lips as they entered the Royal Gardens.

"Another lesson. A new type of lesson connected to your earth magics."

"Hence the gardens," Sabrina said, still slightly disgruntled in tone but perking up by the second. At first, they discussed the banquet that evening, what each would wear, what Sabrina could expect from the event. Eventually, as they tread deeper into sections unfamiliar to her, Sabrina began to talk less and study her surroundings more. She was always observant in the way of most scholars, and as they ventured further, Sabrina asked Nin more and more questions about what she saw. She stopped in her tracks at one point, mesmerized by the song of the trills. It was a plant unlike any in the human realm. The vines looked similar enough to most in

the human world, populated with deep green leaves
that clung to the ground and wound up a large trellis.
The flowers resembled foxglove but were crystalline
— transparent with shimmering streaks that threw off
a rainbow of sparkle in the light shining from the
overhead glass. They also sang in the breeze. The
petals formed small hollows that acted as pipes,
whistling sweet songs when the wind blew in from
the various windows and vents around the massive
garden space.

"Doesn't that scare off pollinators?" she
asked with her head cocked, closely listening to the
gentle sound that mimicked the melody of a pan
flute.

"Oh, no. There are creatures of Fae attracted
to sound as well as smell and sight."

Sabrina gave a soft "huh" in return, reaching
up to gently stroke the shining petal closest to her and
study it more fully. After a moment she turned back
and waved her hand forward with a smile,
encouraging Nin to continue. The Queen laughed at
this. Who else but her friend, her family, would
command her in this offhand way?

They reached a secluded section of the
garden and turned off the path, pushing through a
discrete passageway within a small section of
overgrown juniper bushes. Once through the
scratchy, fragrant evergreens, they arrived at their
destination, Nin's favorite spot in the Royal Gardens.
It was a small field overflowing with a plant much
like the human realm's sorghum. The grain, instead
of featuring brown or reddish granules, were a deep
blue, the color of the night sky when the last streaks
of daylight and coral dusk exit before blackness falls.

"Oh, lady. These are lovely. Really," Sabrina called, moving further into the patch of foliage while remaining careful, sidestepping and scooting her way around so as to not disturb the individual plants. She skimmed her hands across the waist-high stalks and caught the scent, something like a mix of soil, fresh grass, and nightfall.

"Come, my Sabrina," Nin called her back. "Let us move to our purpose here." She then led her friend around the outer edge of the small field until they hit a stone bench, roughly hewn but clearly carved with purpose, next to a barren, tilled section of soil butting against one edge of the vibrant blue plants.

"The Mae Queen had this placed for me," Nin said, stroking the upper edge of the bench. "It was, and I think still is, my favorite spot in the garden. A hidden place of beauty in a very public space." Nin turned to Sabrina and continued. "I was shy, am still in many ways. Uncertain and unsure. But I am now Queen and do as I must for my people and my realm. Still. Still. It is good to have a place of quiet few have discovered."

"It's awfully pretty here. That's true," Sabrina said. "Thank you for sharing it with me."

"The Mae Queen offered it to me as a refuge of sorts. I offer it to you in return. It is now not just mine, but ours. The two in Fae with our particular affinity."

Sabrina nodded and took a few moments to look around the space. "Okay. Right. What's today's lesson? I'm ready to get my hands dirty." She clapped those hands together then rubbed them down the jeans-and-tee-shirt combo she wore to all her lessons in order to remain mobile, and maybe more importantly, comfortable.

"Today's lesson is more about focus and emergence," Nin started, pulling a small pouch from a hidden pocket in her leather pants hidden under the hem of her pale pink oversized tunic. It was standard gear for work in the gardens, more so now because of the extra pockets she recently had sown in after her time in the human realm. Pockets were quite handy after all.

"I do not think I mentioned before, but Mosi knew Serge and I escaped to the human realm," Nin offered because she suddenly thought of the information.

Sabrina let out a gasp. "Oooohhhh. I bet you got in trouble," she sing-songed.

"No. Actually, he was fine with it. Mostly because he knew about it when it occurred and made sure we were safe. The additional bonus of this information was it was quite easy to convince him to escort me back himself so I could pick up these from around the greenhouse in Wilde." Nin held the small brown sack up by her fingers, then untied the tiny leather cords holding it closed. When she finally spilled the contents onto her palm, hundreds of minuscule feathered seeds floated down. Dandelion seeds.

Sabrina stared at Nin's palm several beats, her eyes blinking quickly, before looking back up into Nin's eyes, which were also shining with emotion. "Oh," she breathed.

Nin stepped closer, clasping her free hand on Sabrina's arm and offering a squeeze. "You must know it was truly a pleasure, a gift to you and to myself, to give you the final drops of your Gran's wine mixed with my magic. You must also know that your willingness to save me, to do all in your power to help me because you care for me, is a blessing I can never truly repay."

Sabrina opened her mouth to protest the last, but Nin cut her off quickly. "No. Please, friend. Let me say what I brought you here to say." Sabrina held her tongue and Nin closed her eyes for a moment before looking out at her favorite spot in the Royal Gardens. "You may not wish to make more wine in the future, although we discussed this in the past. You may also not choose to stay long in Fae, and that is your right. Two things will be certain regardless. You and I will always be connected, by bond and magic, and love and memory. And you will always have a place by my side. Today, I teach you more magic, a spell we will use to make that promise more tangible."

With that, Nin blew gently across the dandelion seeds, sending them out with breath and intention and magic to the tilled soil beside the bench. She and Sabrina worked the spell to call forth plants, to ask for growth from seedling to flower, the same spell Nin used what felt like so long ago to create the piece of magic in the token she gave her friend. In a matter of minutes, bright spring dandelions, sunshine yellow and vibrant green, poked through in clusters in what was once bare earth.

Nin and Sabrina sat at the bench in silence, looking over their work. "You know most humans, at least most humans where I'm from, think those are weeds because they grow everywhere and spread too quickly."

Nin answered, "I hope they do. I hope they take root, spread, and thrive in this place."

"I have a feeling they will. And they'll be happy about it," Sabrina whispered, taking Nin's hand and giving it a strong squeeze.

CHAPTER 19

Sergius, his arm firmly wrapped around Nin's, stopped their stroll around The Throne Room as a fellow Fae drew near. "Incoming," he whispered in a snarky tone that made Nin suppress a laugh. Serge's face remained pleasant; a wide smile screwed on tight as the courtier bowed deep to his Queen.

"Queen Nin, I am your servant, as always," the Fae muttered, still in his bow.

It took a beat for Nin to realize he would not rise on his own, so she replied, "A pleasure to see you again, Tinnon. Please, do rise. No need for such strict formalities on a banquet day."

Tinnon, bright green eyes sparkling and a sincere smile on his lips, returned, "Yes, my Queen, although I do feel I must do my duty to establish routine."

It was no outright confession of intention, but no true courtier would give such a thing. It was all sly implication and innuendo unless directly confronted with need, sword, or magic. Nin was steadier on her feet, surer of herself in this moment, and needed no reminders of the games of The Fae Court. Tinnon, a powerful courtier and merchant, was visibly showing those gathered in this room his loyalty to his Queen. She appreciated all forms of support but offered only a slight nod and slow smile in acceptance.

"May I add," he interjected, hesitating over her hand before she extended it openly in offer. He took it in a slight grip and bowed his head over it, offering a swift and gentle kiss, before continuing, "Your Grace looks exceptionally lovely this evening. Green is your color."

"As it is for many of the earth," Serge added.

"True. True. Her beauty and her power both shine, making Fae better for it."

The continued flattery, though expected for a monarch, was too much for Nin. She swiftly changed the subject. "Tinnon. I am happy you joined us this evening. As a merchant, one who owns many ships, I assume, you may be of assistance. The Council, just yesterday, was debating a number of supply issues involving shipping. How does your business fair? Is there an issue you wish to add to future Council discussions? Ideas to alleviate such issues you could put forward?"

Tinnon lit up, as he was a Fae always happy to talk business, and described his shipping woes, and solutions, to Nin in detail. So much detail, in fact, her mind may have wandered a bit toward the end. Luckily, she did notice his inflection and homed in on his ending question. "Would The Council wish to discuss more in-depth?"

"Surely they would. Sten of the Salt Seas is currently in charge of our efforts."

Tinnon nodded. "Of course. Sten knows boats well, although he spent more time on military vessels than merchant ships." He bowed again but popped up quickly this time. "I will leave you, Queen Nin, to your brother's jovial company and seek out Sten. I am now awash in ideas and suggestions."

As Tinnon strolled away, Serge leaned in to snidely ask, "How angry will Sten be for the interruption?"

Nin grinned and waved the idea away. "Sten is all accommodation." Her smile faded as doubts crept in. "However, who knows how true the appearance is?"

Serge pulled close, whispering, "This is no place for such conversations, but I highly doubt Sten is our traitor."

"Then it is Dre or Jane?"

Serge heaved a sigh, "Neither seems likely, I know. They may be other options outside The Council to consider. Realistically, all are suspect until more proof is offered."

A pair of Fae ladies strolled close by, pausing to give deep curtsies and warm smiles to their Queen. She waved them on and straightened. "You were right before. This is not the place, nor the time. We do need to have a long conversation about this. Soon."

"In that, we are agreed," he said, his head whipping around and his eyes narrowing in an alarmingly quick manner. Nin searched out the end of his stare and landed on Sir Bastien, who barely cleared the doors before her brother, and others, pinned him with a hard gaze.

It was no surprise he was present. His childish push during the entertainment caused him to lick his wounds and not surface for a brief period, but men like Bastien did not stay hidden for long. They enjoyed their position too much. Today's banquet was a basic gathering of The Fae Court, not an official celebration. Festivities like this occurred often. The Fae liked a good party, and the courtiers were no exception. Nin may rather be in her rooms, enjoying time alone with those close to her, but she knew this part of the game as well. She needed to see and be seen, to provide fun and frivolity as she ruled, in order to counter the machinations of Fae courtiers such as Bastien.

Serge practically hissed beside her, and Nin looked up with a laugh. "Down, brother. No need for claws."

"I'd gladly claw his face, if you only asked, dear sister," he said with a smile. Nin was unsure if he smiled because of her joke or the thought of clawing Bastien.

"Not necessary at the moment," she said.

"It may well be necessary," he said. "His plans are not done."

"Certainly not. I do, however, think they may have undergone a revision recently."

"True. Still best to keep a close watch."

"Look at that slimy asshole," Nin heard Sabrina grunt from behind them. She turned slightly to smile back at her friend, who quickly took her place on Nin's other side. "The nerve and the gall of that son of a bitch," she practically spat. "He better not start anything with you or any other Fae here, whatever their position. I'll show him what Kentucky can do."

Nin laughed at Sabrina's hackles. "Love, you have yet to train enough for a duel," she teased.

"Don't need to call a duel. Just have to walk up and kick him in the balls," she muttered.

Serge let out a sharp laugh. "A straightforward and effective plan. I approve."

"Don't encourage her," Nin sighed. "She may well do it."

"No one would deserve it more," Serge quipped. He stiffened then, but in a different way, before he melted into a soft sigh. Following his look once again, she saw another courtier she had not seen in ages, Adias, had entered the room.

"Who's that?" Sabrina asked, obviously also noticing where her friends looked.

"That is a good time," Serge said, a smirk forming on his lips.

"He sure looks like it, but maybe a little more info?"

"He is a Fae courtier, of course. Adias of the Red Wood," Nin filled in for her. Deadpan, she added, "He and Serge know each other."

"Whoa," Sabrina breathed, when Adias noticed their regard and turned hard, sultry eyes on Serge. "That look makes me shiver, and it's not even directed at me."

"Adias and I have much to discuss," Serge said, turning to bow over Nin's hand.

"Yep. Whole lot of discussion is going to happen there. For sure," Sabrina added sarcastically.

"I'll still have strength for you, love," Serge teased, "if you desire."

"You know you can't handle all this," Sabrina joked, stroking her hands from shoulders to belly to hip and offering a teasing shimmy in her blue silk sheath dress. "Stop wasting my time and go get some of that man."

Serge gave a mock salute, a jaunty smile, and turned to slink across the room and greet his old lover. Nin knew he would stay long at the banquet, lingering in case he was needed at her side. He would also make far more enjoyable plans for late in the night.

"I feel like I need to fan myself. Where's one of Jane's frilly fans when a woman needs it?" Sabrina said.

"Mo can help you if you require. He is across the room there," Nin said in fake innocence, pointing out her eldest brother, who stood at attention not far from a banquet table laden with food.

"Har har," Sabrina bit out. "Oh-so clever, Your Grace."

"Why is it you only call me 'Your Grace' when you are being sarcastic?" Nin asked.

"Does it bother you?" Sabrina countered, now all seriousness.

"No. I find it amusing and fitting from you. I am simply curious."

"Well, to me, you're Nin. Took a lot to get there from Nina. But you're my friend, my person. It's hard to think of you as Queen sometimes. Plus, I figure most leaders need people to tease them every now and again."

"All valid points," Nin said, reaching down to squeeze her friend's hand. "Please continue the practice."

"Yes, my liege," Sabrina said in a deep rasp, which caused Nin to burst into laughter. A few Fae looked on, smiling. A fewer number looked over with harder eyes. No matter to Nin. Catching a moment of joy in this Throne Room was worth any number of looks.

"Speak of the devil," Sabrina said, and Nin turned her head to see Jane strolling in their direction. She waved her fan happily at the pair from a short distance and Sabrina audibly swallowed a laugh.

"My Queen, Sabrina the Scholar," Jane said, curtsying deep to the two friends. "A true pleasure to see two women enjoying each other's company."

"Facts," Sabrina said with a smile. "A pleasure for you to join in, too, Jane."

Jane blushed prettily and tittered a bit, before moving to the side Serge left. "Queen Nin, I was hoping for a brief moment to discuss summer solstice festivities."

"With that, I'm out," Sabrina said. "I will say, before leaving you two to it, I'm always in favor of a ball where I can wear an awesome gown. Maybe not a costume ball this time, though."

"Yes. Yes. Of course," Jan replied hastily, as Nin watched her friend wave to her mother. Inanna, in fiery orange, was holding court in her own way, in the opposite corner of the room.

"I'm going to see what your mom's up to," Sabrina called as she stepped away, more than happy to bypass any Council party planning business.

Jane chattered by Nin's side as she watched her friend move toward her mother, who laughed loudly at something the Fae beside her said. Seeing her mother laugh like that, the joy spread across her face, her smile wide and true, her dark eyes bright, made Nin feel her own joy. She also knew Sabrina would add to the laughter, she always did, and the idea brought its own joy as well.

Sabrina stopped for a moment, caught in a group of Fae crowded a few feet from the food on offer. Andrés lingered there as well, leaning close to say something to her friend that produced a hearty laugh and a dazzling smile. She gave some cheeky retort, if Dre's sly grin was any indication, and side-stepped The Fae Council Head, her awkward shuffle endearing in its own way. Nin spotted a rapid shadow moving out of the corner of her eye, swift and with intent, toward her friend. Before she could say anything or move to protect, the shadow became flesh and slammed hard into Sabrina's side. Cries went up, a gasp came from Jane as she clutched Nin's arm in surprise and horror, but Nin had no time for niceties. She ripped out of Jane's grasp and moved in a flash to Sabrina. She did not move to confront her attacker, sensing Andrés, Mo, and Serge already there. Sabrina was the priority. Queen Nin skidded on her knees, stopping at her friend's side seconds before Gin and her mother crowded in as well. Sadly, no other Fae moved, afraid to touch the human out of either prejudice or knowledge of her connection to Nin.

Sabrina was fully prone, staring at the vast ceiling of The Throne Room without movement. She did not even pull in breath. Small tears welled and fell, trailing from the corner of her eyes, down her temples, and into her mass of hair, now loose and disheveled from the impact. Nin's breath was caught in horror and fear, until Sabrina sucked in an audible gasp of air. Nin's heart stuttered to see it, but only for a moment, as the breath caused Sabrina to let out a pain-filled moan.

"I think…" she said, slowly licking her lips and steadying herself before continuing on, "I think something's broken."

Gin looked pale and sad, shaking their head. They did not voice concerns or denials, only pulling their hand up to look at the blood resting there. Seeing this, Nin yelped as if she felt the cut herself, even though she had no idea where it was or what it was from. She looked to see tears freely falling from her mother's face, the face laughing not long ago. A scream for their mother from Serge and a bark of orders from Dre brought her up short. She swiftly patted Sabrina's leg, leaving her to Gin and Nin's care. The Queen vaguely registered Serge screaming at Mo, Dre shouting of murder, as she heard hard flesh hitting flesh in the silence echoing in The Throne Room.

"Is she?" Nin asked, unable to even form a full question.

"She is hurt, but there is no need for third-person. She's right here," Sabrina wheezed out.

"Still, love. No movement from you," Gin chastised, finally wiping their hand on their robe before reaching for the medicinals they always carried. "I shall stop your bleeding here and now, but we must move you immediately so I can fully evaluate your condition. I need to know. Can you feel your limbs?"

Fear again stabbed into Nin. She had not considered the real damage such a collision could do to Sabrina. A Fae could take such a hit with little to no internal injuries. It may well be different for a human. She watched with rapt attention as her friend winced from effort.

"Yes," she wheezed out, a pained but heartening sound for Nin.

"Good. Good. Then ribs are likely all that are broken. Painful but straightforward healing. To be safe, I must examine you immediately."

Nin nodded, her tongue still stuck in her mouth, unable to move. She heard more cries and fighting sounds in the direction of her family and snapped out of her stupor. "Are we sure she can be moved?"

"I will stabilize her just in case, but if she has sensation, she should be fine if we are careful during her transport. A complete evaluation will reveal more."

Nodding decisively, Nin yelled for guards. A mass converged, already close, ready to do her bidding. She noticed some move from further out and she looked to her family and saw much commotion. She was needed there as well.

Not even looking at those around her, she started shouting commands. "Listen to any command Borjigin gives as if it were my own. Follow all their directions exactly. Above all, be exceedingly careful with Sabrina the Scholar. She is mine."

"I'm fine, lady," Sabrina attempted to assert, but the strain in her voice, the sweat on her brow, and the blood on Gin's robe told a different story.

"Hush. You be still and silent. Do as you are told as well, though I know it is difficult for you."

"Yes, Your Grace," she said with a wane smile, trying to joke and reassure even now.

Nin paused over her friend, willing her magic forward, thinking of protection and healing

with all her intention, hoping her magics connected
with and helped Sabrina's magics in some way in this
moment. It was not unheard of in dire circumstances
for those bonded to do this, to offer healing
intentions. The fact Sabrina carried within her some
of Nin's magic already would only help in this
process, or so she hoped.

"I will come to you as soon as I am able,
although we both know I leave you only because you
are in the best of hands," she whispered to her friend.
All Sabrina gave her in return was a nod as she
slammed her mouth shut to block the cries of pain
caused by whatever it was Gin did at her side.

"She is prepped. Now we must fly," Gin
said.

Nin waved him and a group of guards on,
calling more to surround and protect as they exited
The Throne Room. Watching this brought more to
Nin's mind. Pulling herself up, she began
commanding. "Bar the door. No Fae exits this room
but by my leave."

A captain bowed in reply, quickly turning to
a group and barking his own orders. Nin searched for
her family as she moved forward. Serge stood out in
the crowd, looking down at the floor. However,
circling courtiers blocked her way and she was not
close enough to see her mother or Mo among the
throng of onlookers. She screamed out, "Move for
your Queen," and the Fae gathered round started as if
waking from a daze. One by one, they bowed,
dipping down to the floor, as they created space for
her to move freely to the center of their attention.

She saw the tableau now. Andrés, eyes
downcast and furrowed as he stood surveying the
carnage. Serge, anger and sadness and worry fighting

across his face. The Fae attacker was nothing but a pile of bloody and broken flesh, his gasps of pain and gurgles of breath the only mark he still lived. A few feet away sat her mother, gently holding Mo and whispering in his ears to calm him. Mo, dazed, sat limp, arms at his side, bloodied up to his elbows.

Nin pulled Serge to her as she moved, creating a triad around Mo when both siblings crouched low in front of him. "Brother. Listen. Please. She is safe with Gin."

"She lives?" he croaked, a stark pain clear in his inky eyes.

"Yes, brother. Yes. I am here. See? It would not be so if she were not safe and alive."

Her mother reassured, as did Serge, and Mo took deep breaths, returning to calm. However, when he looked down at his bloodied hands, he froze. "Does her attacker live?"

"I believe so, although I don't give a shit if he does," Serge bit out.

"Yes. He will be detained," Nin assured him in a gentle voice.

"I may have cost us much," Mo whispered.

"He attacked Sabrina and deserved what he got. Beyond your ties, how you may feel, she is the bonded human of our Queen, and as such is to be protected. No Fae will question your actions, brother." Serge stated plainly, fighting the rage Nin saw barely contained his molten eyes.

"What about intelligence? Information?" Mo asked, looking up at Nin.

"He may still offer us knowledge. He may not. I also do not give a shit," she said, rising tall and proud, anger crisp and clear like ice in her veins.

"Mosi. Brother. I need you. Sabrina needs you. We must interrogate all Fae present, find what we can," Nin called to Mo, bending at her waist to clap her still-seated brother by his neck. "Can you do this? For us? For her?" she asked with a hard edge to her voice.

"Yes. For you and Sabrina," he replied, pulling himself up straight after a deep breath in and out. He was at attention again, the alert soldier on a mission. Pulling himself swiftly from the ground, he wiped as much blood as he could from his hands before turning to Nin. "I should wash…"

"No," she said, hardness in her voice. "Let the blood remind them."

Queen Nin turned to the crowd, cutting looks across the Fae she knew and those she barely met. She ached with wrath, the need to lash out and hurt someone or something because one she loved hurt. She would not. She could not if she wished to be a just Queen. She would, however, call for documented and thorough interrogations for all present. If one did not give answers she liked, time in the Hold would follow. Queen Nin was done with hesitant, defensive posture. A plan of attack was now in order.

PART II – SABRINA

Proportional Strength

In a place
Less warranted than this, or less secure,
I cannot be, that I should suffer to change it.
Eye me, blest Providence, and square my trial
To my proportional strength.

John Milton, *Comus*, 1634

CHAPTER 1

The impact was a blur. Literally. She didn't see the thing that slammed into her, but the impact felt like the weight and force of a semi. Something hit her side without warning and she felt the rip of flesh and crack of bone while her magic, new and unsure, went haywire, crackling under her skin and screaming in her brain. It was all a jumble of agony and unknowns. When she realized she was motionless on the cold marble floor, she sucked in a breath, only for pain to become all she knew for a twisted second. Her body and mind told her ribs and other things were likely broken. She also felt a heat at her side like deep cuts she suffered before, only more jagged. And she smelled pennies, the tangy iron of her human blood, but forced herself not to look to confirm or despair.

She heard murmurs around her and was able to answer Nin and Gin's questions. She even vaguely heard Mo, or so she thought. It was a rage-filled, guttural scream she somehow associated with Mo even though she never heard it before. The bulk of her mind, however, was focused on not screaming her head off, not sinking deep into the bright pain or dreamy unconsciousness that hovered on the edge of her mind. She clung to jokes and the sound of Nin's voice, adding her own when she could, until she screwed her mouth shut to lock in the howls clawing up her throat as Gin tended to the wound on her side.

Nin rose and hands gently lifted Sabrina from the ground. She knew they tried to be careful, but it was still too much. She locked her body, going rigid in an attempt to blot out the pain of movement.

"Sabrina," Gin called, their face swimming above her. "Do not fight. Rest."

"Easier said than done," she hissed.

"Love, let go. We have you. Find peace in the dark."

"Was never much of a fan," she replied.

Shaking their head, Gin focused on Sabrina and softly touched her forehead, seemingly the one place on her body where she had no pain. He did some spell, something her magic recognized but she was too weak, too lacking in intention, to counter. And then there was only blackness waiting at the edges of her brain snapped inward, taking her under.

Sabrina woke with a yelp. "Hey," she called. "That hurts."

"Of course it does, Sabrina," Gin said, popping up from her side. "I attempt to knit your bones. It is no easy task, for you or me."

Now knowing it was Gin working on her, she eased back down, laying as still as possible. She did move her eyes around the room, noticing a much larger guard presence than she ever had.

"What gives with all the guards?" she wondered aloud, though more to herself than to anyone else.

"You were attacked," Gin stated matter-of-factly.

"Duh. Know that Gin. You wouldn't be magically mending bones if I hadn't been."

"Then logically deduce the answer from your knowledge instead of asking," Gin sniped.

Sabrina blanched a bit, taken aback by the snark. It was not normal for the usually calm and patient Fae.

Gin pinched the bridge of their nose, let out a deep breath, and looked down at her. "I do apologize, Sabrina. Such outbursts are uncalled for and undignified."

"Everyone gets snippy now and again, Gin. It's fine."

"I am no natural healer, as you know," Gin continued, apparently deciding to gloss over her statement. "It makes a complex process that much harder. However, I do not feel it prudent to call on a more skilled hand at this time. Not until we know more."

"We're keeping it in the family?" Sabrina asked, though the wheeze of pain undermined the joke Gin would not likely get anyway.

"Yes. For now, at least. The others are currently in interrogations, and I must know more before proceeding. However, the longer you go without care, the more difficult it will be to provide. Hence, my completing a task I know but cannot perform easily."

"You got this," she said, going for encouragement. Best to have a confident hand mending your bones.

Gin nodded and focused on her side again. Sabrina left them to it, biting back whimpers from the scrapes of pain caused by Gin's healing and the multitude of questions racing through her mind. She was unsure, and Sabrina hated being unsure. Sadly, it was a feeling she was used to in this new place.

"So, no clue about what happened?" she finally asked after a few minutes of quiet.

Gin merely shook their head, never breaking concentration or looking up from their work at her side. Fine by Sabrina. In fact, she'd rather have a quiet but effective doctor than a chatty, ineffective one any day.

A few more minutes of silent work ensued until the door barged open. Inanna glided in the room. She always glided, at least to Sabrina's eyes, the flowing, brightly colored gowns she favored and the silken ink of her hair always somehow catching a breeze, even in rooms where there wasn't even a hint of a draft. A knack a model might call finding your own wind, though it felt unintentional and effortless from Nin's mom. Right then, however, there was a shake to her step. No wonder, given the blood splattered across her sunset orange gown.

"What in the…" Sabrina called, trying to sit up on instinct. Gin sensed her movements before they

even began and kept her pinned in place with a strong
arm. The androgynous, bookish look Gin embodied
hid the same Fae strength others so often put on
display and the unyielding arm on her torso, gentle
yet immovable in her position and health and
humanity, was an effective reminder for Sabrina.

Turning slightly away, they called with a
note of concern, "Aunt Inanna. Are you well?"

"Yes. Yes. I am fine."

"Then who isn't fine?" Sabrina countered.
"You've got an awful lot of blood on you for
everyone to be fine." She pointedly eyed Gin's arm
across her stomach, waiting for them to take it back
while showing she could be trusted to stay in place, at
least for now. Gin shook their head and eased up with
a soft smile before turning their full attention back to
her wounded side.

Inanna looked down at herself as if only
then noticing the bucket of blood splattered across
her front and heaved out a heavy sigh before
rounding the bed to look down at Sabrina. "I promise,
Sabrina. I am well. All in the family are well. I will
explain further but first I must know how you fair."

"Peachy," Sabrina said through gritted teeth.
Gin hit a particularly sensitive spot with their magics
at the wrong moment for it to be believable.

"Her wound is knitting nicely and will
quickly heal without issue," Gin called to their aunt
while still concentrating on their work. "Her bones,
however, are another story. Nearly all the ribs on her
right side are broken. Some were crushed. Her left
side fairs better. It is a minor miracle no greater
damage was done to her internal organs or spine
given the extent of her injuries. They will heal, but

healing will require much skill on my part, and rest on hers."

"Is there any way I can assist you?" Inanna asked Gin.

"Please, talk with Sabrina while I work. I need to remain focused and cannot engage in conversation. Sabrina needs distractions from the small pains she will continue to feel as I finish."

"Yep. And I have questions. Like, what exactly happened out there?" Sabrina asked.

"I know little more than you," Inanna admitted, pulling a small chair from Sabrina's vanity and sitting down by the bed. She absentmindedly waved two fingers toward the sconces on the wall, the fire within glowing brighter, lighting the room more effectively for Gin's ministrations at her side.

"Thank you, Auntie," Gin called while still focused on Sabrina.

"You are most welcome," she replied, before taking up Sabrina's hand and giving her an affectionate squeeze. "A Fae, for reasons not fully known, attacked you. It was not a courtier, but an outsider, much like the assassins who targeted Nin before."

"Not surprising," Sabrina said. "I take it they're not talking about who may have encouraged them to do this?"

"They cannot talk, at least not at the moment." When Sabrina stared at Inanna with knitted eyebrows, she elaborated a small bit. "Mosi stopped the attacker."

"I'm sure he did. That's his job. He and others stopped the earlier assassins, too."

"No, Sabrina," Inanna said, shaking her head slightly. "Mo was…very upset. He reacted strongly. The attacker is now physically unable to speak because of this."

Swallowing hard, heart thudding, Sabrina croaked, "What?"

"The Fae lives. He is not dead," Inanna rushed to assure her. "He is badly beaten but alive. For now."

Sabrina did not know what to think of this, how to process the complex set of emotions swelling inside. Part of her, an admittedly bloodthirsty part of her, was happy. At the same time, she was confused by what she thought had to be an overreaction on Mo's part. She was also thankful, and scared, and concerned for him and how he was feeling. It was a lot more than she needed. So, like all the other times complex feelings surrounding Mo cropped up, she shoved them aside, deciding to focus on other issues instead.

"Nin's good?" she asked. She knew her friend was fine when she left The Throne Room, but best to check. Things turned on a dime in this place.

"Yes. As is Serge. Mo also, after he calmed," Inanna reassured.

"Any other injuries?" Sabrina continued.

"None. You may or may not have been the sole target. Mo reached your attacker directly after he collided with you."

"What of his weapon?" Gin asked, pulling their eyes from Sabrina's side for a scant second.

"What weapon?"

"The weapon used to slice into Sabrina. She was crushed by the impact, but a dagger or a similar instrument was used to cut into her side. It barely missed her organs. Another stroke of luck," they answered, going back to healing.

Whipping her head toward the nearest guard, Inanna called, "You. Go to The Throne Room at once. Tell your captain to pass word of a weapon to Queen Nin."

The guard looked slightly nervous, but he held ground. "My apologies, my Lady, but Queen Nin ordered us to attend to Borjigin the Scholar's needs as he healed Sabrina the Scholar."

"Do as my aunt, your Queen's mother, bids. I have no need of your hands here and we are well guarded without you."

Chain of command satisfied, the guard hastily exited the room.

"So much power, Gin. You could have them do anything," Sabrina teased, attempting to ease the tension.

"I will keep this in mind," they said, a ghost of a smile on their lips. *They must be close to done if they are easing up,* Sabrina thought. It was good, too, as she was tired of being prodded with magic healing that was, admittedly, convenient but still hurt like hell. They said earlier she needed rest, and Sabrina was more than ready for it.

CHAPTER 2

Gin was adamant about the rest, so they forced Inanna and the guard from the room. However, it didn't last long — all were back and waiting when Sabrina opened her eyes from a much-needed nap. Sabrina did not know if it was a whole Fae thing or her specific Fae friend group thing, but they were silent and eerily still until she directly addressed the room at large with a husky, "Yo."

Gin checked her bandages and the knitting of her bones, which she confessed to them still stung in fits and bursts. It was not a pleasant feeling. Inanna fussed over her, fluffing her pillows, offering her water and sweets she smuggled from the kitchen. "There was much left over from the interrupted banquet," Inanna muttered.

"I bet," Sabrina laughed, taking a glossy confection from Inanna and popping it into her mouth. It tasted sweet and tangy, an unfamiliar fruitiness on her tongue.

"Oh my God, this is great. What is it?" she rushed out when she finished chewing.

"The sweet or the fruit?" Inanna asked in turn.

"Both. I need a whole lot of both. Immediately. You know, for recovery and whatnot."

Gin and Inanna both chuckled, but Gin replied, "I was about to prescribe that very treatment. How did you know?"

"Hey, now. You are throwing an awful lot of sarcasm around for someone not used to it a few weeks ago. Might want to lay off. It's a nasty human habit. Very unbecoming of a distinguished Fae such as yourself."

"But you can…" Gin began, but Sabrina cut him off.

"I'm a heathen human. I do what I want."

Inanna laughed again, putting her hand to her chest, "Now, now. You two will have me needing medicine after this. It's like watching my children bicker." She said the last as if it were a bad thing, but a fond smile danced across her lips. Sabrina was no fool. She realized Inanna was likely a firm mother when her children were young. Despite whatever toughness she had as a mother, in the present her three children all loved her with the fierceness and loyalty displayed only to those who gave it back. She may have been demanding in some respects, but she was loving and loyal, there was no doubt.

"Back to the initial question," Inanna continued, "which we lost momentarily. The fruit is called porpha. It is like a mix of the grapes and plums you have in your realm. We also have both here, but porpha are used in many desserts as they have both a tart and sweet taste. The pastry you just had is called a porphalet. Buttered crust, porpha filling, cracked sugar topping. If you truly wish for more, I will send for them."

"Oh, no. Not now, at least. You've managed to smuggle in an entire tray of things. Would be a shame not to try all those first before asking for more."

"As you wish," Inanna said, reaching up from her bedside seat to brush a lock of Sabrina's hair behind her ears. The gesture was sweet, and Sabrina knew it was likely unconscious, but it had been so long since she felt those off-handed maternal touches it left an ache in her chest.

The three talked softly and amiably, Gin making sure Sabrina stayed mostly reclined the entire time, until a commotion outside caught their attention. The hurried shuffle of heavy feet turned to silence before the door swung open and Nin rushed into the room to engulf Sabrina in a tight embrace.

"Oh, my friend. I am so glad to see you awake. How do you fare? How is your pain? I am so very sorry," Nin rushed out while holding tight to her friend.

"Lady, hey. I'm fine. I'm good. You do need to be mindful of the ribs, though," Sabrina replied, offering comfort, but letting out a squeak with her reminder as Nin hugged a little too hard a little too close to her tender areas.

Nin pulled back, situating herself inches from Sabrina face and studying her closely. "I do apologize. For your ribs and your situation. It is all my doing."

Sabrina huffed out angrily, "Not this again. We're not going down this road every single time I stub my toe in Fae. It's. Not. Your. Fault. The dude who jumped me is guilty, not you."

"I see no need to be flippant at this juncture," Nin said with some attitude.

"Well, I see no need for you to continually beat yourself up over me. I'm here. I'm good. All will be well. Stop looking for things to pile on your shoulders. You got enough there already."

Nin studied her for a moment then gave a weak smile and slow nod, a sign she took in what Sabrina said and would not keep talking about it. At least for now. Sabrina suspected it would be a long while before this was not the first conversation topic for them whenever something happened to her in Fae. Nin needed to get it through her head, and Sabrina would keep reminding her as long as she needed to do it. Nin blamed herself for a lot, Sabrina did not want to be part of the list in any way.

Nin's face was perfection, something Sabrina tried not to compare herself to too often in her own insecurity, but she could see the stress and guilt etched in the tension of her muscles and her sharp, hazel gaze. Those eyes, so like moss on an old tree, darkened with worry she wished she could ease for her. Sabrina herself worried, felt guilty over Nin's worry, or maybe even felt Nin's worry and guilt herself because of the magical bond thing. Emotions were complex enough on their own to ferret out, never mind bringing in magical bonds and connections and the multiplicity of feeling that could get all tangled up inside. Regardless, attempting to ease Nin's stress helped her because she loved her friend and she felt better when Nin felt better.

Nin was too determined to find information and answers, in any way possible, so she turned to her cousin and started playing twenty questions about Sabrina's injuries, Gin's healing, and Sabrina's recovery. This was when Sabrina felt the heat from her other side and turned her head to find Mo replaced his mother. He sat in the too-small vanity chair, rigid and tight, practically quaking in his seat. Sabrina's breath hitched at the sight, at the dark look in his eyes. He picked up her hand, turning it palm up to place a soft kiss on her wrist, sending the static and hum of Sabrina's magic into a tingling overdrive.

"My Sabrina," he whispered with a husky breath, and although she was not his, in any real way, she felt the shock of truth in the statement. "I did not protect you," he whispered, fear and pain and a little self-loathing marking the lines and curves of his tawny face.

"Not you, too," she gritted out. It was too much to take on, all the blame others piled on themselves on her behalf. Didn't they know it only caused a cycle of shame, everyone feeling guilty over something-or-another, constantly? "You're not doing this, too," she said more firmly as annoyance gave her words heat. "I get it enough from Nin. Don't need it from you. Don't you think that makes me feel guilty, all the guilt your family expresses on my behalf? Nin feels guilty because I'm here, but I feel guilty because I think of myself as a burden in Fae she shouldn't have to deal with on top of everything else. Same holds true for you, Mosi."

"Sabrina," Nin called softly, hand to her chest. "Do not say such things. You are no burden, my friend."

Cutting eyes to Nin, she said, "See? See how what I said made you feel? That's what I feel when you all go on and on about how sorry and guilty you are. We have to stop doing it. All of us. It makes everyone hurt."

Nin looked at her seriously for a moment and nodded in agreement. Sabrina could tell she took her point to heart. Mo, on the other hand, was not so inspired by her speech.

"Sabrina, I applaud your effort to ease tension and feelings in our tight circle. However, I am in charge of security in general, and your safety in particular because of who and what you are to all those in this room, all of my family. The burden does lie on me to care and protect."

Exasperated, Sabrina waved her free hand, the one Mo didn't have in a secure grip, between them and snapped, "I'm not yours to protect, and you aren't to blame for what happened tonight."

"We may debate your second point," Mo said, leaning close, "but your first is a lie, and I think you know this."

"Get a grip, Mo."

"I plan to," he said, clasping her hand even tighter while remaining gentle enough to not cause her any pain, "and I plan to keep hold." His eyes, pools of sparkling night much like his mother's, looked deep into her own and she felt heat rising. She, once again, tried to ignore it.

"Yeah. Well. Whatever," she muttered, looking around the room to avoid his gaze while trying to wrest her hand from his.

Mo smirked and threw her words back in her face, "You're not doing this." He likely meant running or hiding or denying, all things Sabrina used to keep distance from Mo these last few weeks in Fae. Apparently, he was done with those tactics. Sabrina decided to come at the issue a from a different angle.

"You can't tell me what I can or can't do," she huffed in anger, finally pulling her hand free. She crossed her arms, turning slightly away from him, but enough so that it was clear she did not want to speak with him more. She didn't even cut eyes to him when he whispered, "We shall see soon enough." Instead, she focused on the others in the room. All of them — Gin, Nin, Inanna, and the three guards — starred in open curiosity. Gin, Nin, and Inanna smiled. The guards were taken aback, likely unused to seeing anyone rebuff or question their military leader. It was enough fuel to keep the embers of Sabrina's anger steady.

"Enjoying the show, everyone?" she snapped to the room. The guards went back to stoic attention. Gin busied themselves with their medicinals. Nin and Inanna had no shame and openly grinned while looking back and forth at the two.

"As entertaining as this must be," Sabrina drawled, letting her words drip with as much sarcasm as possible, "there are more important things to discuss, like what happened tonight."

Sabrina's statement sobered everyone up quickly. Nin looked to the guards in the room and ordered, "Leave us, but remain posted outside. No one is to disturb us until I exit. The only Fae allowed to enter is Sergius the Whisperer." The guards left and Nin lost some of the rigid tilt to her posture.

"Serge is good?" Sabrina pressed.

"Yes. Yes. Perfectly fine. He is meeting with a few key Fae to test waters, see who else may or may not be trusted, but he will be along shortly."

Sabrina released breath she didn't realize she held at this announcement. The Fae she cared about were all in this room. All except Serge, whose witty banter and outrageous flirting and easy laugh wiggled their way into her heart. She needed to hear he was fine once again before anything else was discussed.

"Please," Gin said, taking a seat next to Inanna on a bench near the wall, "tell us what you know thus far." Mo and Nin supplanted them by Sabrina's sides, but they still remained close.

"Sadly, there is little to relate. The attacker is in no condition to answer questions." At this, Sabrina cut quick eyes to Mo, who looked chastised, although there was no judgment in the statement from Nin. Sabrina's anger disappeared and she reached a hand for Mo, finding his on her cover and giving him a reassuring pat, even if she could not look him in the eyes when she did it. She feared the emotion she'd find reflected there, and she'd engaged with him on that level enough for one night.

Mo took the opportunity to hold her hand once again, and she did not fight him on it. She also did not acknowledge the action, thinking ignoring it outright was her best play, at least in the moment.

Mo continued with the information. "Yes. Nothing much to report. Thanks to you, Gin, we searched for and identified a weapon used by the attacker. However, it is a basic steel dagger with a wooden handle. No clues to be found there. We interrogated all the Fae in attendance but learned little from these discussions. One Fae noticed the attacker slink into the room a few minutes before the attack. Obviously, there were less ways to hide identity this evening, so the attack needed to occur quickly. This is also the likely reason there was only one attacker. Two or more coordinating would have been easily noticed at the banquet."

"One courtier also observed the Fae staring at Sabrina when she was with me," Nin added, "and several saw the moment when he turned to attack. There were no obvious accomplices, no pressing information given, so we were forced to release the courtiers present."

"Would you like me to see to the injuries of the attacker?" Gin asked.

"No," Mo growled at the same time Nin replied, "Yes."

"Mo," Nin said calmly. "We need him to be conscious and willing to talk."

Mo didn't verbally agree, but he gave a harsh roll of his shoulders that let the room know he understood, even if he did not like the decision.

"Yes. Please. When you are able," Nin said to Gin.

"Of course." Gin added, "I will go now."

"I will accompany Borjigin," Inanna called, moving to kiss the cheeks of her children and Sabrina. "I feel you three have all handled here," she said with a smile, and both she and Gin gave a quick goodbye again as they left the room.

"How are you actually feeling, Sabrina?" Nin asked.

"I'm for sure sore. My ribs have these weird stings every now and again, which Gin says is because the bones are healing quickly. Otherwise, I'm just tired."

"You need much rest. A few days in bed will do you good," Nin replied, before cutting eyes to Mo. "However, there is one thing we must discuss before we leave you to sleep. The events of this evening make the need for your defense training with Mosi far more pressing."

"You want me to start taking lessons with Mo?"

"As soon as you are healed properly. Also, lessons with Serge should begin at the same time."

"And you?" Sabrina asked.

"I will still work with you on earth magics, but our lessons will be less scheduled, less formal. As you need defensive work, and word magic may be your true affinity, both should take precedence right now. It is the most logical step forward, the best way to prepare you in case another attack occurs."

"Sure. Okay. We already discussed it, so it's fine."

"These lessons will be slightly different," Mo said, finally adding to the conversation. "No one need know we teach you magic, that remains secret, but no Fae would question me training you on my own. What you need to learn from Serge is more stealth, more connected to others, so you will be shadowing him in The Palace instead of having traditional lessons, secreted away in an alcove."

"My schedule is what, then? Spy classes in the day and warrior classes at night?"

"Basically," Mo stated coolly.

Sabrina closed her eyes. She was tired and hurting. It was a solid plan, formulated to make her and the others safer, so she nodded in agreement, but could give no more. She was fine with most of it, really. All except the alone time with Mo. It felt dangerous in a way she was not prepared to interrogate after such a rough night.

"Good. I shall leave you, Sabrina, to rest. Rest assured I shall return in the morning to see how you progress," Mo said, leaning close to plant a soft, sweet kiss on her forehead. She shivered but kept her eyes closed, only letting out a too flippant "K," as she heard him move away.

After the door closed, Nin leaned down to run her hand over Sabrina's hair. "Oh, my dear friend. It will be fine. You will be safe. We will make sure of it." She hesitated then smirked, "Some time on your own with Mosi will also be good for the both of you. There is much there to address."

"I'm worried about staying dressed," Sabrina muttered, finally giving voice to some of the desire she felt for her friend's brother.

On a laugh, Nin added, "Again, it would be good for you both."

"Maybe. Maybe not. I'm…unsure."

Nin looked serious but unconcerned, "Sabrina. I know you well. I know my brother well. I would encourage neither if I believed it not beneficial to you both."

"I know, it's just, I feel more with Mosi. Or maybe different is a better way to phrase it? Whatever it is, it's a little much with all the other new and exciting goings on in my life. There's a lot more and different for me here overall, so do I need to even get into that? I don't know."

"True, but Mo offers a different difference. Maybe a more comforting one? You must do what makes you comfortable, but also know I think it a grand idea. Above all, I trust you will be safe with Mo, and he with you. In all ways. Being open with your feelings and concerns may be the best way forward, friend."

Sabrina chewed her lip, thinking. It wasn't an easy choice for her, to let her guard down when she rationally knew there was every reason to feel very guarded as a human in Fae. It was something she would mull over more, especially now they would be spending time alone together.

CHAPTER 3

Sabrina was sick to death of her bed when Gin finally
gave her the all clear after five days. Her ribs healed
nicely. A handy trick, that. Broken ribs normally took
weeks for a human to heal without any real help. The
stab wound, shallow and as misplaced as it was, took
two days to stitch itself together. After the initial
shock of pain and information, Gin told her it was
another piece of luck. The knife was dull, made of
steel, and the Fae who wielded it had no real skill
with the weapon. If she were Fae, allergic to iron, it
wouldn't matter. The small bits of iron infused in the
steel would have incapacitated her, maybe even
poisoned her blood. Seems her humanity wasn't all
frail and weak. She could take iron and steel on like a
champ.

    A full week after the attack, Sabrina
received a note from Mo. She was to meet him
outside her chamber one hour after dinner. Sabrina,

unthinking, traced the scrawl of Mo's handwriting across the paper. It was slanted, rushed, but precise. Much like Mo. He started with *"My Sabrina,"* something that made her heart beat a smidge harder even though her brain fought against it.

She fidgeted outside her door five minutes before she was to meet him. It was a curse and a gift, her general need to be early for everything. She twisted her hands, wiping the sweat on her jeans when she realized her palms were damp. Looking down at herself then, she considered her clothes. She didn't have leathers and kickass boots like Nin, felt she might not have the frame to pull off such a look anyway, so she wore jeans with a tight gray thermal tucked in her waistband, hiking shoes on her feet. If she asked for fighting gear, Nin would be happy to oblige. The tight leather was standard attire for most Fae she saw in informal settings, but the Fae she saw all had tight bodies unlike her own, chunkier set. It was fine, something she only gave fleeting thoughts to most days, but today for some reason the idea of what her body was compared to the Fae around her raced across her mind. She knew she could talk to Nin about it, both her fears and her need for clothes, and maybe she would. But she had other options as well.

She apparently had a mass of money stored somewhere in Fae. Sabrina didn't even know if Fae had banks like humans, but what she viewed as the unnecessary reward she received for helping her friend was sitting somewhere, collecting dust. She could use it to buy herself proper Fae clothes. She was a person who generally felt a bit awkward, back in Kentucky or here in Fae, and one sure way to make herself feel less weird in her surroundings was to take time to shop for and buy clothes that would look good on her and show a bit of her personality, too. That's why she had so many pun shirts. They looked good and fit her quirks. Standing in the hall then, remembering who she was and what made her happy in the past, she told herself she'd find some Fae store somewhere and get it all straightened out as soon as she could get away from The Palace.

On the heels of that decision, she heard the soft squeak of leather on stone and looked up to see Mosi, his long powerful legs erasing the distance between them in swift, sure strides. Sabrina had never been one to swoon over a man in uniform. Her general questioning attitude and need to know everything happening around her made her weary of authority for the sake of authority, and human men who wore uniforms usually fell into the authority category. Even here, the Fae guards, beautiful like all Fae, held little interest for her. Her prior attraction to bookish and artistic men were also usually based first in personality, a response to the mind and the spirit that became more physical over time. Even after the burst of attraction, physicality was not something she lingered on when thinking about her partners. She enjoyed their bodies, as they enjoyed hers, but her desire was a weaving of many different factors, not just lust based on looks.

She could not say the same for Mosi. Sure, she admired a great deal about him as an individual. His beauty, though, was apparent from the jump, and if she was honest with herself, it was a bit of a barrier. Something that made her nervous because it was new and butted against the insecurities she tried so hard to squash in herself. However, she felt him early, his energy or presence or whatever it was that made Mosi feel different to her than other people, whatever drew her to him like a moth to a lamp glowing in the darkness. The pull, and her attraction, grew each day as she learned more about who he was. His strength, honesty, care, fierce loyalty, sharp and strategic mind. They were all traits Sabrina found sexy as hell. Unlike previous partners, his body also called to her in an unfamiliar, nearly startling way. It was almost visceral, animalistic, and Sabrina, a person of the mind and of feelings, didn't entirely trust it.

Watching him simply walk down the hallway in a modified version of the soldier/guard uniform so many other Fae wore caused heat to pool in her stomach. His tight breeches slid under knee-high leather boots. His leather vest molded to the curves and dips of his torso, highlighting his compact but formidable muscle. The one note of flowing fabric was an orange cape dangling from the shoulder straps on his vest. Unlike other soldiers, Mo changed out the colors and patterns of these capes he wore. Must be the privilege of a Chief General of Fae. The sconce light sparkled off his dark skin, catching the deep, smooth tones and reflecting them back in flashes. Even the memory of the peek of white teeth behind full, lush lips whenever he actually grinned or smiled made her stomach whoosh like she was about to bungee jump off a bridge.

Sabrina snapped out of her contemplation of Mo when he reached her. She knew she stared and her thoughts likely telegraphed across her face when Mo gave a soft smirk. "What's up?" she said, going for nonchalance and failing as she continued to twist her hands in front of her.

Mo stared down at those hands, fluttering and active, and reached out to steady them. It made Sabrina self-conscious, so she filled the silence between them with information. "It's not a bad thing, you know. Fidgeting. It's a physical way to release stress. No harm in it."

"I did not say there was harm," Mo countered, stepping closer still.

"But you just stopped me from doing it."

Mo leaned in, pulling the hands he held up and giving them a soft kiss. Sabrina noted he sure liked to kiss her hands for some reason. "I do so because I do not like to see you nervous, especially because of my presence, and wish to help ease the feeling."

"Don't know if you can," Sabrina muttered, pulling her hands from his and looking away. "It's nice you try. It's part of me, though. The fidgets. And the rambling. All included in the Sabrina package." She ended with what she hoped was a jaunty smile.

"And what a lovely package it is," Mo said, his eyes refusing to leave her face.

"Yeah. Um, well. Shouldn't we be headed somewhere?" Sabrina asked, deflecting yet again.

Mo kept his stare for a beat then gave a curt nod. "Yes. Follow me."

Mo brought Sabrina through the maze of The Palace and outside its gates. It was the first time she'd traveled outside since her arrival through the chalk door bridging Gin's home in The Falls to The Royal Chambers in The Palace. The woods surrounding the gates were dense, crowded with a variety of trees and vines, almost like an additional natural barrier of protection. Made sense, given the fact earth magic Fae ruled this realm, under normal circumstances. It was a dense green with bursts of colors, pops of bright red flowers dotting the vines so the whole appeared slightly less formidable. The flowers offered up a sweet scent, too, the smell a happy reminder of springs spent in the woods and fields of Wilde.

Mosi called back to her a few times, ensuring she was well and followed while also giving her space and time to take in all these surroundings, her first walk in Fae in a number of weeks. She listened and looked and breathed deep, but she did not investigate too much or stray too far from Mo as the jungle incident from her intro to Fae was fresh in her mind. After a short trek through the forest without issue but with much observation, they reached a clearing. It was obviously a Fae-made clearing, as the compacted dirt was in a perfect circle, enclosed by large wooden beams. Sabrina thought it was about the size of an MMA cage, which made her snort a bit at the appropriate analogy.

"Amused?" Mo called, turning to her from the center of the ring.

"Let's get ready to rumble!" Sabrina mimicked, laughing to herself. She laughed harder when Mo looked on in confusion. "Oh, nothing. Famous human line said before people fight. A hilarious reference. Trust me."

He gave a smile and a small bow. "Undoubtedly." His teasing tone sent shivers through Sabrina. She appreciated good banter.

"Why here? Why not the practice room?" she asked, taking a moment to pull the smell of crisp forest air deep into her lungs. "It's lovely and all, but is it necessary?"

Mo slowly walked the outside of the circle, lighting small fires on what looked like massive tiki torches with a spark of his hand. "Loveliness is reason enough, at times," he answered, "but the more practical concern is your earth magics." After lighting the last torch, Mo strolled toward her while wiping his hands. "I cannot call the earth. You can. If we wish for you to do so during our practices, it is best we train in nature rather than indoors.

"The drawback," Mo added as he crouched in the dirt, "is the fact Gin revealed to me you learn best when things are written."

"Facts. And there's not a chalkboard anywhere in sight."

"No. We do have a good deal of dirt beneath our feet." With that, he tugged Sabrina down to his level and began his lesson with no preamble. He held a sturdy stick in hand and wrote "Reaction + Leverage" on the ground. "Now, our first question: What is the purpose of defense?"

"To protect," she answered, quick and sure.

"Yes. True. How do we ensure protection? What do we focus on?"

Sabrina thought silently for a moment and shook her head, preferring to hear where Mosi planned to go with his lecture.

He looked down at his writing and said, "We must decide in the moment, given our knowledge of any particular situation, what steps we take to ensure protection."

"Context is everything," Sabrina added, nearly rote. It was a phrase she repeated often to her writing students.

"Yes. Very true. Understanding the moment is important in defense and tells us whether we must react or bring leverage to bear," Mo replied, underlining the words in the dirt as he talked to add emphasis.

"Okay. Sure. I'm with you. But what do you mean with those words?"

He straightened, pulling Sabrina up with him once again. "Reaction is based on immediate and swift evaluation of surrounding elements. The attack when it occurs, unknown and when one is unprepared. Leverage is planning and research, strategic defense, an attack based in forethought of your opponent and the thorough knowledge of any particulars within the current situation. Reaction and leverage. Your two defensive options, in a broad sense."

"What do we focus on first?"

"Reaction. It requires the most practice. You already have what is needed for effective leverage, a thoughtful and agile mind keen to know and learn, do research and strategize. Reaction is immediate and necessary in dire situations, so we must work on honing your reactions first."

"Sounds like a plan," Sabrina chirped, bouncing on the balls of her feet to help relieve her nervous energy.

Mo nodded and pulled a copper suit of armor into the ring with a flick of his hand. She hadn't even noticed it crumpled on the ground and now it stood, tall and rigid, held up entirely by his metal magics. "Nin informed me of your current progress, so it should be no difficulty to repel the armor and snare it in tree branches outside the ring."

Sabrina breathed deep and focused, pulling the hum and static of her magic forward, isolating the heat she felt from the earth magics in her, reaching out with the intention to connect with a tree outside their circle and kindly ask it to help while focusing on her overall intention. She managed to hold it all in her mind, even feel out the tree and nudge of permission it granted her, then flung the spell from her lips, giving her mind direction with words and hands. The hum increased but ebbed and flowed as if performing a backdrop for action. The static feeling rippled, and she felt heat loose on her tongue and in her fingers, shooting out along with her intentions. The metal rose easily, sailing through the air, until it caught in the extended branches of a large maple. The tree cocooned the suit high above ground, suspending it mid fall.

"Impressive," Mo said, considering the armor with his head cocked to the side. He turned a smile her way, "I must add, not surprising. Your mind is a wonder I've seen work in many amazing ways."

Sabrina blushed but silently congratulated herself at the praise, more than a little happy Mo noticed her progress. "I've got this one down. A few others, too."

"I'm sure," Mo called, stepping away and behind Sabrina, "but under what conditions?" Before Sabrina could respond, the metal arm of the armor shot from the tangle of branches. It catapulted toward Sabrina, who stood motionless, like a deer confronted with car headlights along the dark country roads of Wilde. She had enough time to release a gasp when the phantom hand wrapped around her throat. It wasn't painful or tight. Surprising in a way that made her heart race and her magic flare without focus, but not actually harmful.

Mo circled around from behind, hands clasped behind his back, to look at Sabrina. "What of your magics?"

"The flying metal caught me a little off guard," she gritted out.

"It did," Mo called, a twist of two fingers calling the metal hand to his own. He looked down, his eyes darker than black ice on a wintry road and just as cold. "As did the knife used by your attacker, but that instrument caused true damage." He gripped the metal so hard Sabrina heard it pop and creak, watched it wrench and crumble like fragile glass in his hand, littering the ground with shards. They both stared at the remains until Mo whispered, "This is why we must train." Care and concern and determination swirled in the pool of his dark eyes when he said, "Again."

"You get that line from Gin and Nin?" she scoffed, attempting to defuse with sarcasm, a go-to method for her.

He looked on unphased and the only warning she received was a faint rustle of leaves before a metal foot flew at her face. It stopped centimeters from her nose, hovering as she stared it down. Mo wrenched it away, throwing it back into the tangle of branches. "Again," he said with command.

Sabrina spent the next half hour with metal flying at her face. Occasionally, Mo allowed it to actually touch her, but never in a way that was painful. He used it as a reminder of what could be. When she was finally able to quickly cast her spell after Mo said "Again," he switched it up, stopping his verbal commands and letting the metal pieces fly at random intervals without warning. After she began anticipating the sound of metal coming at her from a specific direction, he switched that as well, littering pieces around the ring and flinging them at her from random directions.

Another grueling hour went by, stress and adrenaline and a need to perform well pushing Sabrina along. She knew she was safe, would come to no harm with Mo. That didn't matter as much as her need to do well, which stemmed partly because of her natural drive to excel in any lesson, and partly from a desire to impress her current instructor. Eventually, sweat dripping down her brow and eyes shifting constantly, she was able to consistently perform the spell work, repelling whatever metal sailed her way and snaring it in Maple branches.

"Enough," Mo clipped out, and Sabrina snapped to, as if coming out of a daze. He forced a water skin into her hand and grunted, "Drink," as he led her to sit on one of the large wooden beams. He sat beside her after gently guiding her down and said, "You did very well today."

"Took me long enough," she groused in between large gulps of water.

"No. Your reflexes reacted quickly, as they did the night you protected Nin from assassins. It is, again, expected from one like you."

Sabrina couldn't stop herself from blurting "Like me?"

Mo leaned in close, gently sniffing the air between them before grumbling out, "A human miracle."

Sabrina was dazzled by the words, Mo's closeness, the smell of him, which was always an alluring combination of leather and metal and a tangy scent she could only identify as purely masculine and

all Mo. She already knew his particular combination
of smells, would recognize them anywhere. She
leaned forward as well, staring at his full lush lips,
licking her own.

A sound, part grunt and part groan, passed
over those lips, and Mo leaned forward the fraction it
took to have their foreheads rest against one another.
"I like the promise in that look, my Sabrina, but I fear
you are too tired."

Mo's words were a dash of cool water on
her overheated nerves. She pulled back abruptly,
internally lecturing herself for the lapse. "Yep. Right,
right. Too drained and not thinking."

Mo grinned, grabbing her head to hold her
gaze. "You and I both know what will come. You
may fight, and I will resist as long as you do, but it is
inevitable."

"Nothing is inevitable," Sabrina whispered,
still resisting, just as Mo pointed out.

"Oh, no? What of your human play, your
reason for entering Fae, the text you used to save our
Nin?"

"Prophecy is different," she asserted, though
there was no real conviction in her answer.

"Perhaps. Perhaps not. I am no scholar like
you, but I know this: your body sings to mine."

With that devastating line, Mo placed the
sweetest of kisses on her forehead before rising.
Offering a hand down to her, he silently beckoned
her to follow. Back to The Palace, but also, in other
ways. Sabrina hesitated a moment then took his hand.
He was right. This felt inevitable, even if she
continued to hesitate.

CHAPTER 4

It was two days after her first training session with Mosi and she was fidgeting in a different room, nervous about a different sort of lesson. Serge's chambers were smaller than Nin's, but still spacious — a decent receiving room leading into, what Sabrina guessed, was a similar bedroom, bathroom, closet set-up. Her rooms lacked the formal seating area, but she had the rest. Serge obviously needed more space, as a courtier and Court adviser.

There was a sturdy wooden table, polished to such a high gloss shine Sabrina saw her reflection clearly on the surface. It was round and made from a deep brown wood shot through with traces of gold, a perfect match for Serge's eyes. Six matching, delicate chairs surrounded the piece. It was a dining and meeting table, one Serge surely used often. Today, it was the sight of her first lesson.

"Come to my rooms for luncheon," Serge's note read in a loopy, flourishing script. "And be sure to wear something fetching."

Sabrina fretted, once again, over clothing because of the summons. She ordered some of her own clothes, including a fetching pair of fighting leathers molded to her own body type, from a designer Nin invited to The Palace for her use, but they had not come in yet. Would not be in for some time. In the end, she called for Inanna, who graciously offered her services, waltzing into Sabrina's room with a smoky blue, empire waist dress she found somewhere in The Palace.

It looked like something straight out of a *Pride and Prejudice* adaptation except the square neckline was a tad scandalous. The cap sleeves clung to a centimeter of fabric that skimmed her armpit and sides, cut dangerously low given the full swell of her breasts. A genius in fabric made the dress a sort of all-in-one design, meaning she needed no tight and restricting undergarments to hoist and plump. Those babies were firmly in place, yet also practically out in the open. Sabrina was busty, had been since puberty hit hard in middle school and her baby fat turned into soft, chubby curves in all parts of her body. She had no general aversion to showing off now and again. The uncertainty of what she would be doing her lesson today, however, made the dress feel more uncomfortable than it might on a different occasion. Sabrina quizzed Inanna, but she knew no specifics, only Serge planned a luncheon with a few courtiers and Fae leaders. She assured her she looked lovely, hinted at how Sabrina might want to wander in search of Mosi while strolling The Palace in her dress, and pecked her cheek before taking off.

Now Sabrina sat, breasts heaving like she was in some bodice-ripper, fidgeting while Serge stood by, looking her over.

"I'm happy you took my note to heart, love," Serge purred her way.

"Oh, stop it. I don't need your ridiculous flirting. Your mom picked out the dress, so go talk to her about it," Sabrina groused.

Serge put up his hands in mock surrender and chuckled, "Whatever you say. Just know Mo will not be in attendance this afternoon."

Sabrina hit him with a withering glare, and he laughed outright. "Okay, okay. Enough teasing. We have serious business to attend." He moved to the seat next to her and scooted it close. "Have you used word magic before, beyond calling on spells?" he asked.

"No."

He casually flipped his hand like it didn't matter anyway and began his lecture. "We'll dispense with general magic discussion. I hear you excel in that arena already. Let's talk specifics. Word magic has many shades and nuances and falls within two broad categories: spoken or written. Spoken, which is where my true affinity lies, is about language heard and uttered, and how that can cause desired actions or effects. Written is about the visual representation of language and the power behind making a thing spoken into a symbol."

"Like semiotics?" she asked, becoming more interested.

"I have no idea what that is," Serge said with a smile.

She waved it off, deciding it best to move on and thin over on her own, later, "Oh, nothing. A human English nerd thing. I'll explain later. Please, go on for now."

"Now that I have your permission," he said with a grin, "I will. An affinity for the written would correspond with who you are as a Scholar, a reader and writer, in the human and Fae realms."

"How will I know for sure? Simple trial and error?"

"You feel heat when you use earth magics, right?" Sabrina nodded an affirmation and Serge continued, "Well, there is a different, particular physical sensation most feel when pulling on word magics. It is described as either the feeling of a whisper or rustle. A burst of breath or pages turning running across their skin."

"Ah. So, not only is affinity different in results and connection, but each affinity also comes with a different feeling?"

"Right on the nose. Now to check. Call up your magics and try to push the feeling you get from earth magics aside. Concentrate on the words of a spell you know. Focus on saying it and seeing it in your mind. Tell me what you feel."

Sabrina followed instructions, calling up the *ISPISSP* spell in her mind as it was the one she used the most. She stomped down on the heat of the earth and focused on the Fae word itself. She repeated it in her mind, visualized it, a flash of Times New Roman on a blinking computer screen she imagined in her brain. After a breath she felt it, the soft caress across the downy hair of her arms. It was the turn of a page in a heavy book, exactly as Serge said. She popped her eyes open and whispered. "It was there. On my arms. I felt it clear as day."

"As I suspected you would." Serge smiled down, obvious joy for her discovery in his face. "You are, my dear, a true bearer of word magics. More specifically, one drawn and connected to the written word."

Sabrina smiled to herself until a thought popped into her head and she asked, "Does this mean you can't teach me?" She was suddenly nervous because of the slight differences in their magics. Maybe she needed a teacher with written word magic, and who would that even be?

"No. At least for right now. I can give you basics that relate to all word magics. It's also in our favor that a lot about learning writing magics is solitary, mostly time spent memorizing symbols from books and practicing their execution. Both things I think you have done pretty well already." At that, Serge softly whispered a Fae word and a book rose from a side table and sailed across the space to land in front of him. He smiled and said, "One benefit of word magic is you can use it for a wide variety of things. Nin needs earth to move objects. Mo needs metal. I only need my tongue." With a wide grin, he ran his pink tongue across his full lips and gave her a wink.

Sabrina laughed, shoving his shoulder playfully in response. "That's just creepy," she said.

"You wound me, dear Sabrina. Your constant rebuffing will give me an inferiority complex. I'm sure of it."

"Yeah, right. You have enough Fae fawning all over you. You don't need me."

"I suppose," he said with a mock sigh and a sly smile. He reached up to open the large leather book in front of them, flipping pages slowly as he explained. "This, my dear, is a book of runes and glyphs. Each entry gives you a symbol you can trace on paper or in the air. Added with intention and a nonverbal spell, it can allow your magic to push through the writing."

"Will I not have to say spells anymore?"

"Not these at least. Others, yes, for now. Eventually, like all Fae, you'll be able to perform simple spells without speaking, unless the casting requires it for power or purpose." Serge stopped for a moment, looking around the room before muttering, "Before everyone arrives, let us give you a small test."

He flipped quickly to a page with a large whooshing symbol on it. To Sabrina it looked like an equal sign, except each line had a gradual upward tilt and ended with a sharp, straight downward stroke. "This," Serge said, pointing to the symbol, "is the rune used to push something away from you." He pointed next to a familiar Faeish word beside the symbol on the page. "Nin and Mo say you already know the spell and use it well. Let's see if you can write it effectively."

He instructed Sabrina to trace the symbol several times in the page without thinking of intention or the Fae command KALLI. She practiced, and when she told him she had the form and shape down, he instructed her to push the unlit candelabra at the center of the table over.

Serge offered a bit of instruction, but not much. "Basic mechanics are the same as what you've previously practiced. You think about what you want, form your intention. You also call your magic forward. Look for the sensation you felt earlier and focus on it. The change is you do not speak the word aloud. Simply think it as you write the symbol in the air with your finger."

Sabrina concentrated, simultaneously performing the list of instructions he gave. It took a few tries, and a few fails, before it happened, although it did come quicker than the other spells she attempted so far and somehow felt more natural. In only five minutes she was able to fling the candelabra over without speaking the repelling spell aloud. It seemed Nin was right; her word affinity would come swiftly and feel more connected to her somehow.

"Fabulous," Serge said, clapping her on the back in a brotherly move. "That took no time at all. However, I must warn you this takes a great deal of practice. Other spells will not come as easily. This was simpler because you were already familiar with it. Others will take more time and focus."

Serge hesitated a moment, lost in thought, a playful look on his face. "I want you to use something else during lunch with some Fae. I always say it's often better to learn by doing."

Sabrina reeled back in surprise. "Won't they know I'm doing magic."

"Not if you're doing it right," he challenged, and flipped through the book briefly until he found the right spell for her to attempt over lunch.

Nin sat at the head of the table and Sabrina was happy with this turn of events. She hadn't expected her friend to be here for her lesson and felt bolstered by her presence. She was less formal, but still regal, sitting straight and proud, and Sabrina felt supported even without her words. The hug she received when Nin strolled in with her guards, the rushed encouragement before others arrived, was enough. No more was needed in the moment as Sabrina sat at her friend's left.

Serge sat at Nin's right, alternating glances between Sabrina and the man to her left, Adias, who seemed to be a quiet but lovely table companion so far. Sten sat beside Serge, talking animatedly with his hands as a large salad was served to each guest. Sabrina took a bite of hers, savoring the crisp feel and taste, the burst of sweetness from berries and the crunch of seeds adding nicely to the dish. She swallowed quickly, though, when she heard Serge clear throat and looked up to him running a finger along the edge of his chilled wine glass.

This was the signal, one they established after Sabrina practiced her rune and spell combo. The plan was to engage in conversation with Adias, who was apparently not as magically gifted as the other Fae in the room, and use her new knowledge to get him to voice a feeling or idea he had that he would not normally say out loud.

It was a form of compulsion, something she felt a little icky about using. Nin, also, did not approve, saying it was too close to the darker sides of word magic. Serge assured both the plan was fine, Adias was a loyal and neutral choice, and there would be no adverse consequences. Sabrina mumbled, Nin worried, but both agreed to the plan.

Now, Sabrina engaged Adias in actual conversation, in particular asking him about the outfit he wore to the banquet, the place where she first saw him. He was kind enough to elaborate when she explained she wished to expand her current wardrobe. He talked about the Fae who made his formal attire and Sabrina plastered a pleasant smile on her face as she worked a spell in her mind. She focused, cast intention, pulled the gentle wind of her word magic forward, and visualized the word *TUTNG* as she traced a mark on the tablecloth without looking down at it, hoping it looked like her usual human fidgeting to Sten and Adias, if either Fae noticed her movement at all. It was more complex, a series of lines and swirls written in a specific order. After several failed attempts, she felt the magic expel from her, like she did with earth magics she used, and she abruptly asked Adias a question, cutting him off in mid-sentence: "And how did you feel after the banquet?"

Adias stared at her, head tilted, eyes wide, as words spilled from his mouth. "I was glad all were well, but honestly, very put out Serge was unavailable later in the evening because of you." He brought a hand to his lips and blinked hard. His voice reverberated, snagging the attention of all in the room, and everyone seated around the table stared at the Fae for a moment. Sten looked angry, as did Nin. Serge was momentarily shocked, stunned by the words and the results of his lesson.

"Oh, my. Sabrina the Scholar, do forgive me for such an outburst. I did not mean…"

Sabrina fidgeted for real, nervous and unsure of what to say to the Fae she forced to speak and who remained visibly mortified by what he revealed. Serge interjected after a few silent seconds, saying, "Your words caused no offense, dear Adias. I assure you. Sabrina and I do not mind. Neither does our lovely Queen. Right, my Queen?"

Nin pulled in a long breath, staring at Adias then cutting harsh eyes toward Serge, before giving a curt nod. "As you say, brother."

"Now see, here," Sten began, looking from Nin to Sabrina and obviously feeling a need to defend.

"Sten, please, it is of no consequence. Truly. As your Queen says," Serge stated calmly, though there was a hiss of warning in the last sentence, a bit of a reminder to Sten. Nin acquiesced, and as Queen, he should not overstep her claim on the matter.

Sten bit his lip, puffed his chest for a moment, but deflated, looking down at his plate with a small pout.

Sabrina looked on at the horrified Adias, who practically trembled. She felt bad. She did this, causing his pain and worry. "Please, Adias, I take no offense, as Serge said. Queen Nin takes no offense either. We're all good," she ended, with a pat on his hand, now balled into a fist on the table.

Serge frowned, looking on at Adias distress. "Friend," he called, staring straight at Adias until he snagged his gaze. "All is well," he said, but he did more than say. Sabrina could feel the breathy whisper of his magic, quickly seeing he used his words to calm the Fae next to her.

Adias trembled for a moment, but a shake of his head preceded a slow smile, and he turned back to Sabrina. "Thank you for your reassurance. I really did not mean to imply it was your fault. The attack was horrific, and I am truly happy you are well."

Sabrina recognized sincerity in his words, knew he spoke the truth, whether that was because of magic or her own intuition, and again felt a pang of guilt. That was the thing with words. They could so easily be twisted, misinterpreted, lost or change meaning on a whim. It made her hesitant about her own powers, fearful of them in a way.

The lunch continued amiably after the incident, and the two Fae unaware of her magics did not act as if they caught on to her during their lunch. Sten shook off his snit, Nin eased a bit, and they were all laughing at one of Serge's stories by the time the final plates were cleared.

"It has been a lovely luncheon, brother. Truly. I appreciate the time spent with all of you," Nin said magnanimously. "However," she added, "there are a number of things I wish to discuss with Serge and Sabrina, so if Sten and Adias could please excuse us?"

Sten quickly rose, shook hands with Serge, bowed to Sabrina, and bowed deep, for a touch too long, over Nin's offered hand before leaving. Adias bowed and waved as well, leaving with a soft smile on his handsome face.

Once the door firmly closed behind them, Nin reeled on her brother. "I told you," she hissed. "What you played out today was unkind at best."

"Agreed," Sabrina called quickly, folding her arms across her bulging chest and landing a hard stare at Sergius. "Not cool."

Serge, for his part, looked contrite and remorseful. "You're both right. I am sorry. In my own way, I will make it up to Adias. It was wrong of me to set him up in that manner. It was equally wrong for me to ask Sabrina to do it, without her really knowing what it meant. It is no justification, but I did not think on what Sabrina would be able to coax from him, only that she should try to do it to help hone her powers." He looked sadly over to her and asked, "Forgive me?"

"I forgive you, Serge," she loudly exhaled. "That doesn't get you off the hook, though."

"True," Nin added, a hint of bite in her voice. "You must be more mindful in future. You are sometimes sloppy with your magics, unconcerned with consequences. Ends do not always justify means, brother."

"I have done much to help you and others," Serge added, becoming defensive.

"You have also done harm. Like today." Nin focused sad eyes intently on him. "Sergius, I saw what you did during the fight in The Royal Chambers." There was a pause, where something stark and raw flashed across Serge's face, a regret Sabrina wanted to soothe even if she was unsure of the cause. Nin must have felt the same, as she reached to gently squeeze her brother's bicep before she continued, "I know the immense power you have. It is a testament to your character that you do not wield it more often; do not fall into that trap, turn into someone far more sinister. Trust me, I have seen the sinister turn of word magics firsthand. For long years in this very Palace. I ask you now not to test the bounds of that power for everyday matters, but only when absolutely necessary."

Serge swallowed hard, looked at his sister, and raised a hand to her cheek. "I often forget the core of Comus' power, Little One. It must be hard for you to see these magics at work."

Sabrina didn't know this before, and her breath caught in her throat. She realized it must be another reason she studied with Serge rather than

Nin, even if her friend didn't fully admit that to herself. It made Sabrina's heart hurt. She leaned over, slinging an arm around Nin, who sagged into the half-embrace. "Oh, lady. I'm sorry. You shouldn't be here for this. It's likely too much, too soon."

"I wished to be here for you," she whispered, "but you may be correct."

"Okay. That's decided. It's just me and Serge here for the word magic practice in the future," she stated firmly while squeezing her friend close.

Serge agreed, but Nin mumbled, "You cannot order me around. I am Queen."

"In a very strict sense, but you know it is best, so you should agree also," Serge said firmly.

"As you wish," she said, pulling herself from Sabrina's hold after patting her friend's arm lightly. A light gleamed in her eye before she added, "Although, seeing Sabrina in such finery is a reason to return."

Serge barked out a surprised laugh and Sabrina acted offended. "I'll tell you what I told your brother earlier — your mother picked it out. Talk to her if you have comments about it."

"I'm thinking you need more like these," Serge said, standing to come to Sabrina's side and offer a hand. When she took it, he twirled her. "Don't you agree, my Queen?"

"Quite," she answered, smile firmly back in place.

Sabrina pretended to be offended but took the continued teasing well. She learned a great deal that day, about many different things, and it was nice to end those lessons with laughter.

CHAPTER 5

She felt him before she saw or heard him, a warmth at her back as she paced beside the outer gate of The Palace. It was time for another defense lesson with Mosi. She received another note, but this time she wrote back, adding extra flourish to her words as she asked to meet at the gate rather than her bedroom. Seemed like a waste of time when they both knew where they were going now. She would have suggested meeting in the woods, but she knew Mo wouldn't like the idea. He'd bristle at the thought of her outside the gates without him, even if for a few minutes' walk.

He was all slow, sincere smiles and hard, heated stares as he strolled her way from across the courtyard. Her breath hitched, like usual, and she let herself imagine, for a moment, what it would be like to see him stroll toward her, with that smile and those eyes, from across her bedroom. Heat sparked under her skin at the idea and she knew she blushed.

Mo could apparently guess why she blushed so brightly at the sight of him, as his smile became more knowing. He dipped in a low bow, taking her hand as he raised up and giving her a kiss on her wrist. It was usual now, something he did whenever he saw her, but that did not make it any less potent. She didn't want to give thought to the surrounding aura of his scent and how it cocooned her whenever he stepped close like that. He didn't speak, so she chose to follow suit in an effort to hold all her lustful thoughts at bay, turning without a word toward the gate.

They silently followed the same path to the training ring in the forest. All was as they left it days before. When Mo reached the center of the ring, he turned with arms crossed and finally spoke.

"Lesson two: physical reactions and defense," he boomed.

"Sparring?" Sabrina asked, head cocked in interest now.

"In a way, yes, but only in terms of physical defenses." He moved closer to her, so close she felt the strong heat of his body. "You are human, Sabrina. In many ways, more fragile than any Fae you encounter. Physical attacks will not serve you well. Fae are stronger, faster, more agile than any human, and any good Fae fighter will attempt to use this to their advantage when confronted with a human target. Just as your Fae attacker did at the banquet. There was a reason he simply slammed into you — it was an effective strategy given his speed and your particular human vulnerabilities."

"No picking fights in Fae bars, got it," she joked, before turning serious. "Mo, I know Fae are a lot stronger and faster than I am. I'm well aware of my limitations here, believe me. All this leads us to…" She left the sentence hanging, waiting for Mo to explain his overall lesson plan.

"Reactive defense maneuvers are part physical and part magical."

"Self-defense with a bit of spell work thrown in," Sabrina said, turning the idea of it over in her mind.

"Have you completed any self-defense training in the human world?" Mo asked, still too close to Sabrina.

"Yep. Took a few women's self-defense classes when I was an undergrad. My university wasn't in the safest of neighborhoods."

Mo smirked and replied, "Show me."

Sabrina shrugged, but she cackled to herself internally. She was happy to show what she could do, especially if Mo was going to stand there and take it. As he already said, Fae were stronger. He'd be fine. She lifted her left hand for a hammer strike, bringing it up and down toward the side of Mo's head. It wasn't quick enough for a Fae, and Mo easily dodged it. What he wasn't expecting was her bringing her right hand into play just in time. She swiped her hand out for a palm strike. At the last second, Mo saw the move coming and course-corrected, but not enough to completely miss the blow. It grazed up and across his left temple with a satisfying slapping sound.

Mo laughed and looked up in wonder at Sabrina. "I expect much from you, my Sabrina, yet you still manage to surprise me at every encounter. It is truly a joy to be so often surprised by another."

She blushed again but shrugged it off, taking a step back and flippantly replying, "You told me to attack you."

"Indeed, I did, and you did well, showing me your natural reaction time is strong. Very good. It is enough to throw off many Fae who would underestimate you. It would, however, not fell a Fae." Contemplating her for a moment, he asked, "Were you trained to remove yourself from a hold?"

Sabrina nodded, but her head barely moved before Moe spun around her in a blur. He pulled her back hard against his front, but not hard enough to hurt. His arms circled her waist, and he held firm. He whispered, his lips barely connecting with her ear, "How do you get away, my Sabrina?"

Her heart hammered in her chest, fear and lust racing through her system. She was not truly afraid of Mo because she trusted him. Still, the speed and ease of his movements reminded her of their differences, of the vulnerability she had in Fae in general. The lust, well, it was almost always present around Mo, it simply came to the forefront with the intimate way his lips touched her ear and his arms hugged her plump torso a fraction of an inch below her heavy breasts. She breathed deep, fought those feelings to establish calm, and lifted her foot to stomp down hard on top of Mo's. He side-stepped, easily moving out of her way.

She reared her head forward and back, going for a headbutt, but he also moved his head back quickly. She bent forward again, making Mo believe she would try a second headbutt. Instead, she crouched down slightly, firmly planting her feet and curving her back while leaning forward as fast as she could. This brought Mo off his feet, dangling over the curve of her back for a moment. She took advantage of his disorientation, grabbing his index and middle fingers on one hand and bending them back hard. He jerked his hand away before she damaged his fingers. The force caused Sabrina to wobble, and they both tumbled to the ground.

Mo's speed saved her any bruises. He flipped her over, landing on his back and cushioning her fall. He chuckled and said, "Not the most graceful of examples."

Sabrina scrambled off of him, hoping she didn't hurt him in the fall while also trying not to imagine what it would be like to flip herself, take his mouth to hers, wrap her legs around that hard waist. "Never claimed to be graceful," she said, rising to her knees, then her feet.

Mo dusted himself off and said, "You continue to surprise, but that was not successful. Now, we must practice basic defensive moves. You have a foundation of sorts, one that is solid yet requires more time and energy to perfect. We want muscle memory."

Grumbling, Sabrina asked, "More homework?"

"You must practice these moves, the motions themselves, every day. Even if you do not have someone to help you practice." Giving her a heated look up and down, he added, "Although, I am more than happy to provide you with a body."

"That sounded a little too much like Serge," Sabrina laughed.

"I can flirt as well as my brother," Mo replied. "I gave him instructions on occasion."

"Mo the player," she quipped.

"Player of what?" he asked, confused.

Sabrina laughed. "Never mind. A silly human joke. Let's move on. I think we still have to mix magic into all of this?"

Mo nodded and pulled closer to start training her. It would be a long lesson.

Mo stared, unwavering, unmoving, patiently waiting. She gritted her teeth and planted her feet as he taught her, bracing for what came next. Once she'd gotten some basic physical moves down, they added a bit of word magic, with Mo instructing her to use the KALLI rune. Because of this, the armor came back into play. The metal man attacked and Sabrina defended with moves and magic. It followed the same ritual, first with Mo's verbal warning, then with no warning.

Sabrina dripped sweat, exhausted from physical and magical exertion, but fully alert to her surroundings. It was a part of her magic, she knew, as she never felt this way before. Her brain worked harder and faster in general, but the earth magics leached from Nin gave her a primal connection to everything around her out in this forest. It fed her energy, even when she wasn't using earth magic, and her magic, in turn, fed her body with its static and hum and gentle breaths of air over skin. She was bone tired, more than ready to call it a night, but also mentally steady and strong, willing to take it as long as Mo dished it out.

She heard the rattle of metal a second before the empty but sturdy armor gripped her from behind. She leaned forward, as she had with Mo earlier, lifting metal feet from the ground. At the same time, she pulled her magic forward, focused her intention, called the spell in her mind and traced the sigil quickly with her finger in open air. The metal frame quivered and jumped, popping up into the air as if pulled by an invisible string, landing in a heap a few feet behind her.

Sabrina paused, catching her breath as she leaned over with her hands on her knees. Mo walked up to her slowly and placed a hand at the small of her back, tracing a small circle there. It sent shivers up her spine, forcing her to shoot up straight and step smoothly out of his touch.

He appeared unbothered by her seeking distance, only offering a small smile her way in response. "You've done well, my Sabrina. I believe we are finished for the evening."

Sabrina sagged a bit in relief, ready to get back to The Palace, her room, and her large, steaming bathtub. Lost in that thought, a ghost of a smile on her lips, she didn't fight Mo as he reached for her hand, holding it while leading her away from the practice ring. They walked hand-in-hand, in comfortable silence. Sabrina focused on the odd tired but invigorated feeling she had after two hours of training. When they stepped through the gate, Mo kept walking her, directing them both toward her room. He spoke only when they reached her door.

"This is where I shall leave you for the evening, my Sabrina," he said, but he didn't release her hand or move to leave.

Sabrina shifted on the balls of her feet, unable to fidget in other ways because Mo gripped one hand. "Um, Mo? I want to say thanks. You've put a lot of time and effort into this, all to help protect me. I suspect it would be easier for you to wash your hands of it, or say you'll protect me yourself or set more guards on me or something. But this…this lets me have a hand in it. Gives me more control. That's, well, I really appreciate it, is all I want to say."

Mo whipped his free hand up, pressing on the back of Sabrina's neck and pulling her forward. Her head tilted up as he tilted down, and she thought he was going in for a kiss, something that made her tense and tingle all at once. Instead, he gently rested his forehead against hers as he had done before in the forest and breathed deep, closing his eyes.

"It is hard for me, in many ways," he finally admitted after a few beats. "I wish you to not only be safe, but to have peace. Our current course of action is the best way to achieve that, even if I would fight the entire realm to protect you myself."

Sabrina swallowed hard, tears springing to her eyes. This thing between them, the visceral feelings of lust and heat, also held tenderness, and Sabrina melted a bit when he voiced them.

"Mo," she whispered, not knowing what else to say, how else to express the tug-of-war her heart and mind and body played whenever she thought of him.

The torchlight in the hallway gleamed off his dark skin, something she noticed before, but it became a soft glow that warmed her in a way when they stood this close. He pulled back, heat in his eyes, and said, "I will leave you, because you are tired and need more time. However, the time will come for us, my Sabrina."

She didn't argue or ignore or bluster. It was apparent there was something between the two. No one minded if they explored it, especially not Nin. It was getting harder and harder to deny, so she didn't say it aloud, but she nodded slightly, a small surrender in her own internal fight.

Mo beamed back at her and pulled her into him for a gentle kiss on her forehead, holding her close for long beats. "I will seek you tomorrow. Not for practice," he clarified, though he didn't elaborate on why or what they would do. He licked his lips, and Sabrina inadvertently leaned forward, drawn into the sight of his pink tongue sweeping over his full, oh-so-enticing mouth.

Mo chuckled and turned away and Sabrina watched him walk swiftly and surely down the corridor until he rounded a corner and moved out of sight. She sagged against her door, fanned herself like she was Blanche Devereaux, then pushed her way into her room. Before she closed her door, she wondered if she needed that hot bath after all, or if a cold shower was more in order.

CHAPTER 6

The days rolled on for Sabrina, and it felt like a win when she realized it had been a full two weeks since her attack, or any attack for that matter. Sure, in that time she'd healed, had a few rounds with Mo, and learned more about her word affinity with Serge, but there was no bloodshed. Seemed easy in comparison.

A secondary effect of not being in immediate danger was she started spending more time with Mosi outside of the practice ring. After the second round of training, as he promised, Mo began showing up at her door to take her to lunch and, sometimes, afternoon tea. They weren't going out. She didn't even know if Fae had brunch spots or diners or restaurants. Lunch and afternoon tea out, for them, was visiting various spots in and around The Palace, which was a small maze of a village in its own right. They had picnics in the gardens and meals in out-of-the-way sitting rooms with gorgeous stained glass. They met with a few other Fae, in and outside of their core group, on occasion, but they spent most of those hours alone.

In that time, Sabrina learned more about Mo's smile and laugh, the feel of his calm and strong hand on her own, the warmth of his eyes when focused on her. They chatted about their families, a bit of their pasts, and generally explored who each was. Lust remained, full force, but more was growing in a way that warmed Sabrina's belly differently. A very welcome feeling for her, the more afternoons they spent by each other's side.

It was a happy string of hours spent with Mosi, but the rest of the time she was in student mode. When she wasn't being quizzed by Serge or worn out, physically and emotionally, during defense practice with Mo, she was studying quietly with Gin or catching up with Nin in small pockets of time found within the Queen's overwhelming docket of duties. Today she was supposed to meet with Serge in his rooms earlier, but he changed their plans at the last minute. She was now set to meet him in The Throne Room to attend Nin's Audience Day activities. What that had to do with the written spell work she practiced, she had no clue, but she showed up a few minutes before the official party started.

She bristled a bit walking through those huge doors. It looked nothing like it did the night of the banquet, yet Sabrina was still on edge. She hadn't stepped foot in this room since the attack. Mo hammering vigilance and reaction during training made her acutely aware of the Fae who mingled and mumbled all around, and she kept a close watch out for Serge as well as any sudden or unexpected move her way.

After a moment she spotted her friend-
turned-mentor straddling one of the long backless
benches close to the front of the room, flirting with a
Fae woman Sabrina didn't know. Gin was by his
side, calmly sitting with a soft smile on their face.
Sabrina moved toward the duo. When Serge beamed
up at her and shouted, "Sabrina, love. Finally, you
arrive," she did not imagine the glare cast her way
from the Fae woman lingering at his side. It made
Sabrina smile, because if this Fae woman was jealous
of her, she'd have a hard time of it with the flirtatious
and seemingly non-monogamous object of her
affections. Serge was Serge, lovely and flirty and
sexual but seemingly committed only to his family.
She'd known him for a short time and knew this.
What the Fae woman thought she could tame, or had
the right to try to tame or change, was well beyond
her. Serge took the cold stare in as well and with a
frown muttered apologies to the woman, shooed her
away. Being Serge, he still made plans for later,
given the whispers between them and the hungry
look in the woman's eyes.

Sabrina gave a finger wave at the Fae's final
scowl her way and turned to her mentors. "Really,
Serge?" she asked, not needing to elaborate.

"What can I say, I'm insatiable." He
chuckled.

"Incorrigible is more like it," she quipped,
plopping down by Gin, who laughed with her. "That
doesn't seem like a good idea, though."

"I am well aware of her thoughts and have
been open. If she does not listen to what I tell her in
honesty…" Serge shrugged, putting it back on the
Fae woman. It wasn't Sabrina's business, and she did
think Serge would be honest and open, so she let it

go, choosing to bump shoulders with Gin and give them a smile as a hello.

"How are you, friend?" they called, reaching over to pat Sabrina's hand.

Turning serious, Serge also asked, "Are you fine?"

"I'm all good," she called, confused by the very sudden turn toward concern for her. "Why?"

"Sergius told me he observed you avoiding crowds of Fae. And The Throne Room," Gin said softly.

"This is like some aversion therapy session?" she asked, looking over to Serge.

"I do not know that particular method, but if it means throwing you in the deep with the sharks once again, then sure. That's what this is," he said coolly, not even a hint of shame.

"You didn't think to, say, discuss the issue with me first, rather than simply telling me to come here?"

"Best to get it over and done with," he said. "Besides, I know you can take care of yourself. Mo's told me about your training."

"This group is worse than *Gossip Girl*, always up in everyone's business," she groused, folding her arms across her chest in a pseudo-snit.

"We wish you well," Gin assured her, "and trust you heal in all ways. We only want to ensure you are receiving all the support you require."

"I just like the gossip," Serge countered.

"Stop it," Gin said, reaching behind Sabrina's back to slap their cousin's shoulder.

"Oh, all right. I'll be serious for now," he replied, turning to fully face Sabrina. "Love, you have healed physically. You do well in defense training, which Mo tells me about because it is clearly connected to what you are learning, or still need to learn, in our affinity lessons. However, you need to push yourself more in another area. You are, whether you wish to admit this or not, a major figure within The Fae Court. You are Sabrina the Scholar, a human magically bound to Nin, who is Queen. You are also a human who sacrificed much for the benefit of Fae. All this gives you both supporters and enemies. You cannot properly defend yourself without knowing more about this side of our realm."

"Hence a lesson in politics, not magic," she replied.

"Precisely, my star pupil," Serge said, slinging his arm across her shoulders and pulling her in close. He leaned over to whisper in her ear. "There are enemies who will not offer physical attacks, but who can hurt us and those we love nonetheless."

Sabrina nodded and he pulled away. "Lesson here today: watch and learn. I must be away, to stand with Queen Nin as counsel. You and Gin are to sit and observe what passes. We will discuss afterward." He pulled himself up, grabbed Sabrina's eye and held it, making sure she watched him in all liquid grace as he rose and fit an aloof smirk on his face. He said nothing, gave her no hints at purpose, but Sabrina was a quick study and good with implied meaning. It was a mask Serge allowed Sabrina to clearly see slip into place, and that in and of itself was a lesson she needed to remember. Something she recently spoke about with Nin, before the attack. Sometimes you had to act the part no matter what was going on behind your eyes. If she knew this, others did as well, and some would mask feelings or intentions that could hurt those she cared for, especially Nin. Politics was a game. She'd always known this, on a theoretical level, but she had never been in politics. Now she was knee deep in it, and, as Serge said, she needed to learn to swim more securely with the sharks that populated this ocean.

Serge climbed the steps, taking position slightly behind and next to The Throne. Moments later, fanfare marked the entrance of Queen Nin, dressed in a fine golden gown, escorted through the room by her mother. Inanna stopped at the foot of the stairs, taking her place behind a small podium to direct the events of the day. Nin climbed steadily up, turning to smile at the Fae in attendance, an extra nod slyly thrown in when her eyes skimmed over Gin and Sabrina seated so close to the dais.

To be honest, it was all a bit boring for Sabrina. Gin whispered explanations of Fae relationships and customs to her as the first few people trickled down the aisle to address their Queen about some matter or another. It was the dull business of government, and even though Sabrina knew this was important to the healthy function of a community, it didn't make it any more enjoyable to watch.

All the while, she took in Gin's instruction while scanning the room, studying the Fae she could see without craning her neck in an obvious way. She gained little information. She did note who spoke with who, remembered faces she had seen before, and started making connections, ones that would help her learn more in the future.

Eventually, some action occurred at the dais. Two Fae were presented to Nin. One was a small farmer, a man in the process of plowing and sowing his plot of land. The other was a large landowner, who came before his Queen claiming a track of the plowed land was actually his, intended as a pasture for one of his many, many flocks. The farmer brought forward deeds and titles — paper evidence of his claim. The landowner, with his wealth, asserted he had been gifted the land long ago by a Fae courtier, who backed up the claim as a witness.

Nin looked over the materials, heard the arguments, and rendered her verdict in favor of the farmer.

"You would side with one such as him over your own courtier?" the landowner scoffed.

"I would side with evidence," Nin asserted.

"She sides against us at every turn, even hurts us for amusement," the courtier grumbled.

Sabrina knew he referenced the fiasco at the entertainment. It still hung in the air, and likely would for a while, a sticking point courtiers upset with their Queen could call on as proof of a trend in mishandling situations. It was enough to make Sabrina's blood boil, and if Gin had not reached for her hand, squeezed it gently as a reminder, she might have jumped up and started cussing. She didn't like seeing her friend abused and maligned in this way.

Nin, however, had it under control. She coolly looked down at the courtier for long beats, enough that the Fae became visibly uncomfortable with the scrutiny. "Please, do tell me what amusement I am to receive from two prominent Fae attempting to wrest the livelihood from a small farmer? All when our realm is in the midst of food shortages and supply issues? We must be helping, not hindering, the Fae who grow our food."

"My flocks require more," the landowner whined, before Nin cut them off with a simple raised hand.

"They have ample room to roam freely on your lands. My decision is final."

Sabrina heard murmurs. Some seemed in support. Some protested. It was the way, she supposed, no matter the leader. It may have been a cliche that "you can't please everybody," but cliche status did not make something less true. Nin would continue to fight and scrape, in small and large ways, her entire reign. She felt a pang for her friend, realizing the struggle her entire life as Queen would hold.

Sabrina sat, watching Nin and Serge, learning bits and pieces of history from Gin, until Audience Day formally ended with a call of trumpets and the pointed opening of the large wooden doors. The bulk of the Fae filed out, although some lingered to speak softly in tight clusters. A tension she didn't realize she held eased from her shoulders as the crowd thinned. Serge and Gin were right, she'd been avoiding Fae in large groups for the past two weeks. It was good of them to force her in a controlled manner, get her to recognize the behavior so she could manage it. She smiled, thinking Serge was a sounder judge of people and a more caring friend than some might think because of his general demeanor. She saw the heart of him though, in his care for Nin and the rest of his family, in his joking but patient way with her as her teacher.

Gin's tap on her leg brought her out of her thoughts as her gaze followed their gesture toward dais. She looked up to see Nin disappear behind the curtain and Serge beckoning them forward with the crook of a finger. She and Gin climbed the steps. Pausing to look back out over The Throne Room at the top, she noted the height and distance, feeling a bit sad and cold up there.

Serge came behind her, leaning down to her ear. The soft smell of mint, the lingering hints of Serge's magic, hit her then and made her oddly happy. Recognizing his scent was familiar meant she had a clear connection, in time and place, to this person she truly enjoyed. It was nice. Her initial connection with Nin was broadening her circle, giving her more friends, more family, and it warmed her heart to have so much here in this strange new world.

"Nin wants to speak with you. There's a room through the back curtain." Serge cocked his head in the direction where a sliver of dark space peeked out from the folds of fabric.

When she slipped through the crack, she found a short hallway leading to a tiny room. Inside was a small settee and side table. A rocking chair sat in one corner. And that was it. No other furniture or decor or object cluttered the room. It felt like an in-between space to her, a landing pad to move in and out of but not to linger in, what she imagined a small green room in the back of a theater might look like. Nin was perched on the edge of the settee, visibly tight and showing strain.

"Sup?" Sabrina called, hoping to bring some levity to her tired-looking friend.

"Sabrina. Friend. Please, come sit with me."

Sabrina moved close and sat beside the Queen, who remained rigid and at attention to begin with. She visibly relaxed as slow and silent minutes passed. It wasn't awkward. Sabrina didn't think she needed to fill the void with needless talk, or to act or be a certain way, even though a Queen sat next to her. In this space, with just the two of them, it was Sabrina and Nin. Sabrina lounged comfortably herself, quickly moving from an up-right position to a slumped rest against the wall behind her.

After a few minutes, Nin let out a soft hum and turned her head to her friend. "Sorry I am not more pleasant company. Thank you for sitting with me."

"No problem, lady. Any time. You know that. That's why you called me back here," Sabrina answered with a cheeky grin.

Nin chuckled, relaxing more into her seat. "These days are very…tiring."

"I bet," she replied, adding, "though, you did well out there. All stately and fair and whatnot. You also look gorg in that gold."

Nin shook her head, worrying her lip briefly. "Not all feel as you."

"They won't. Ever." Sabrina stared at her friend, telling her the truth, but adding more. "I do and will. Same with Serge. Gin. Your mom. Mo. Lots of Fae I heard out there. You're a good ruler."

"Thank you," Nin said in answer. "I am attempting to follow your advice. Put on a solid face, tell myself repeatedly I am where and as I should be, and listen to those I trust."

"It seems to be working fine and dandy," she said. "No one out there would guess you were slumped in here next to a human, muttering about shit."

Nin laughed then, full out. "I suppose not. It is their loss, however, as it is good counsel indeed."

She closed her eyes briefly then changed the subject. "What of you? How go your lessons?"

"They're fine. Serge and Mo are both a pain in the ass, in different ways."

"I hear you excel, as always. You impress my brothers. They may well have been taken with you early on, but they are demanding instructors with high expectations, so such praise is hard to come by from those two."

"Oh, whatever. I do okay, I guess. Still need a lot of practice."

Nin cut eyes to Sabrina then, looking her friend up and down. "If I do not get to doubt, you do not get to downplay. It is the same. You must listen to those you trust when they say you do well."

Sabrina puffed air through her lips, but she couldn't argue the point. "As always, it's easier to dish out advice than take it."

"Agreed," Nin nodded, "but let us try. Together." Taking her friend's hand and giving a tight squeeze, she said, "We always seem better together."

"That's truth," Sabrina affirmed.

The two friends talked for longer, about this and that. Sabrina told her of her new clothes and her books and her study. Nin talked of her changes to the Royal Garden and plans for more entertainments that may actually be enjoyable. When Serge called to them, reminding Nin of another appointment, she mumbled but readied herself to leave.

"Oh, I almost forgot," she called right before exiting. "Mother informed me she is holding a family dinner tomorrow night. You are invited of course." Sabrina's heart swelled at the forgone inclusion.

"However," Nin hedged, turning back, "I wished to make a request, if you would oblige?"

"Whatever you need," Sabrina said without hesitation.

"Would you make macaroni and cheese?"

Sabrina laughed, a deep and familiar tug in her gut. Her macaroni and cheese was well known, and it was the one thing she cooked that Nin loved above everything else. "Do y'all even have macaroni noodles here?" Sabrina had seen and eaten very good Fae cheese, so that was a certainty.

"Something similar, though I will have someone acquire the usual ingredients from the human realm. I want the rest of my family to experience it."

Sabrina's heart swelled more, again so easily included in this big, funny, and lovely Fae clan. "You got it. Where will I cook it?"

"I will ensure they open space for you in The Palace Kitchens," she said, excitement sparking her voice and eyes.

Sabrina moved up to hug Nin before she left, happy for the time they had, glad of her friend and her new family. The Fae realm was a whole lot of new, and it definitely wasn't all bad.

CHAPTER 7

The trip to Inanna's home didn't involve a magic cable car, like her trip to The Falls. She also didn't walk there or use the magic chalk Gin reserved for special occasions. Gin spelled her there. It was the first time since coming to Fae she was spelled between locations, and it felt less harsh than the spell work that allowed her to travel from the human to Fae realm. Also, unlike that trip, she could sense and taste the magic, smell the hint of Gin, an odor their magic always seemed to have. Nin said it was myrrh, but because Sabrina only knew of it from Nativity stories and never actually smelled it in the human realm, she couldn't confirm. However, like Nin and Mo and Serge, Gin's feel and smell was familiar and comforting even if she couldn't accurately identify what it was.

This doesn't mean it was a pleasant trip for Sabrina, even if it was slightly less dramatic for her.

She still stagger-stepped on landing, and felt a whoosh low in her tummy that, although momentary, made her think she might puke.

Gin patted her shoulder and chirped, "A quick and painless travel."

Sabrina muttered "Sure. Easy peasy," but bit off the remainder of her sarcastic retort when she spied Inanna's home. Or, more aptly, her compound. It was more than a home. The big house looked like an old manor — two massive stories with an impressive stairway leading to beautifully carved heavy metal doors etched with flames. The structure was wide enough Sabrina couldn't see the sides from her position a football field away from the impressive front entrance. She could see hedges and gravel rows winding in front of and around the house in the distance, and at her back she found an imposing metal and wood gate connected to a large stone wall, stretching tall and wide until it disappeared in a tangle of thick, dense briar bushes that somehow managed to appear clean and tidy rather than unruly. Sabrina figured it was Nin's doing and smiled at the thought of her friend growing something as protection for her mother.

She heard Gin shuffling toward the door and pulled her eyes away from her surroundings to follow on their heels. When they climbed the wide steps, the doors flung open, with Inanna waiting to engulf both Gin and Sabrina in tight, warm hugs.

"Welcome," she said, her excitement bubbling.

"Aunt Inanna, thank you for having me in your home."

"My pleasure, Borjigin. You are always welcome," she said, patting their arm and waving them inside. "Sabrina, welcome for the first time. I am overjoyed to have you here, a new member to the family." She grabbed Sabrina's hand to stop her as Gin disappeared deeper into the house and looked into her eyes. Inanna paused for a moment, tears coming up quickly, "It has been far too long since all of my children have been under my roof again, and I have you, new daughter, to thank for their safe return."

"Oh, Inanna. We've done this. I don't deserve all the credit, but I'll admit I'm beyond happy to see your family here and whole, and to be considered a part of it."

Inanna pulled herself up on a deep inward breath and turned on her brilliant smile to match the happiness present in her starry eyes, quickly wiping away the few tears she shed in the moment. "Yes. You are correct. It is a night of joy, not past sorrow. Come in, come in. The rest of the family is already present." She looped her arm through Sabrina's, a cozy way to connect and walk with another she obviously passed down to her daughter, and pulled the new addition to her family inside.

Sabrina gawked at the artwork and tapestries in the grand foyer. She imagined, from the outside and entrance, they'd be eating in a fancy formal dining room. However, Inanna wound them through rooms until they reached a small, cozy chamber, big enough to hold a large hearth and a solid oak table with seating for eight. There were, however, only six in attendance.

Nin sat to the right of the head, waving happily at Sabrina as she entered. Serge smirked and raised his wine glass. Mo, who sat to the left of the head of the table, gave her a long, deep look she reciprocated. Gin, over beside a small bar, poured a glass of wine and called to Sabrina, "Would you like one as well?"

She nodded to them as Inanna led her to the seat beside Nin. She said, "We like to keep family dinners more informal," apparently feeling the need to explain why they weren't in some other room in the massive home.

"I think it's perfect," Sabrina said, plopping herself down in the sturdy oak chair topped with a fluffy orange velvet cushion. "Fits right in with my contribution," she added, as she set the burlap sack on the table.

Nin clapped her hands in excitement. "Oh, Sabrina. Thank you so much. All of you are in for a special surprise. Our Sabrina makes the best macaroni and cheese." The rest of the Fae nodded politely, but none were as excited as Nin. "It will not disappoint," she promised the table, but turned to Sabrina and added, "I hope it was not serious trouble making it in Fae."

"Nope," Sabrina answered. "The Palace chef gave me plenty of space and you got me the ingredients from my realm. All good." She pulled the large wooden bowl from the sack, tugged off the fitted stone lid with a bit of effort, and presented it to her friend. "See? Just like usual."

"Lovely, Sabrina," Inanna said, taking her seat at the head of the table. "We thank you for it," she added, cutting a look to the other Fae in the room who followed their mother's / aunt's polite lead and thanked Sabrina accordingly.

The sound of heavy footsteps had Sabrina whipping around to the entrance, but the door did not open. "Do not worry," Serge called. "Only Little One's guard taking their positions."

Sabrina understood this. Nin needed guards even in her mother's home. It was logical and also a touch sad for her friend, who ignored the comment completely.

Inanna, a more than gracious host, began to serve dinner family-style. Although she likely had servants in this massive house, Sabrina saw none, and the small room felt like it could be dining rooms in any number of homes she knew in the human realm rather than in a fancy mansion in Fae. Most of that had to do with the company. They all laughed together easily, eating and telling jokes as the night went on, the drinks flowed, and the food disappeared — including Sabrina's mac and cheese, which everyone loved.

However, as time passed, Serge's brotherly teasing of Mo became a smidge more antagonistic. What started as friendly banter turned into snide remarks. It was a side of Serge she had never seen, and one she did not like. Inanna attempted to shut it down, as did Nin and Gin, but he kept it up.

At one point, when discussing some old game he was better at than his brother, Serge flippantly threw a hand in Sabrina's direction, saying, "It is no surprise brother dear can't win this prize either."

Mo seethed at Serge's side, snapping, "Sabrina is no prize to be won."

Serge snorted. "You wouldn't know that regardless, would you?"

Inanna, Nin, and Gin were speechless, staring aghast at Serge. Sabrina's cheeks flamed and she felt both embarrassed and awkward. Mo stared at her a beat and pushed from his chair, towering over his lounging brother. "Stop such nonsense immediately. Apologize to Sabrina."

"Oh, lovely Sabrina," he crooned, reaching over the table to trace a finger along her hand before she pulled it out of his reach. "I mean no disrespect. In fact, I can show you how sorry I am if you follow me to my rooms."

Gasps sounded all around, and Mo smacked the wine goblet from his brother's other hand. It flew across the room, hitting the wall with a hard thud, splashing drops of red across the golden wallpaper. He breathed rapid and hard, like a dragon about to unleash flames. Serge looked on calmly, no apparent worry on his face or in his frame. Mo, with fists clenched, turned toward Inanna and said, "Please excuse me, Mother," before storming from the room.

Sabrina was stunned by the outburst from Serge. Where did this come from? He flirted, true, but always in an offhand way. Even that mostly stopped when they all started her lessons. After they had grown closer with one another. After it was more than clear Mosi had an interest in Sabrina, pursuing her openly.

"That's some bullshit," she whispered, staring at the door. She whipped her head around, staring daggers at Serge. "I cannot believe you just did that. Are you insane? Mosi could rip you apart."

"He could try," Serge said on a shrug.

"Oh, no. He would. Easily. Beyond that, he's your brother. Why treat him like that? I've heard you say some shameless things, seen you do a few, but this was beyond. I don't even want to look at you right now. You're acting like a complete and utter ass, and you need to apologize to Mo right now."

"You don't require an apology?" he asked.

"No. I don't give a shit. But Mo does. He loves you, everyone here. All he wants in life is to protect you all, to keep you safe and happy. He deserves so much better from you."

"It's not all he wants," Serge repeated, staring at her.

"Is that what this is about?" Sabrina yelled, rising from her chair and planting her hands firmly on the tabletop. "Getting your stoic and honorable brother to admit he wants to get in my pants?"

"No," Serge said, meeting her gaze openly and honestly, "this was about getting a reaction out of you."

Sabrina pulled back. "What?"

"Sergius," Nin hissed, standing to back up her friend.

"It was time for a push, Little One. Stay calm." He sighed and rose himself, coming around the table. "I mean no disrespect, and I apologize for my words. They were for a purpose. Mosi is cautious and respectful, but open about his desire for you. You, however? With you, I wanted to see how you felt, how you would react in his defense. He beat a Fae near to death for you. I want that same loyalty returned to my brother."

"Sergius, that is a dirty trick, and I am appalled you would question Sabrina's motives or loyalty in such a manner," Inanna chided.

"I do it for Mosi, Mother. However, I will concede I may have gone too far, and for that I apologize."

He turned to fully face Sabrina, a surprising amount of earnestness in his face. "Dear friend, know I trust in you much. You have proven yourself over and over again. But we cannot pretend there is no difference between platonic and romantic attachment. I fear for my brother's heart. That is all."

"Sabrina owes you no explanations or proof. Both she and Mosi are grown and capable of their own decisions in this arena. Sabrina, a human, has done more for this realm, this family, than many others alive today. I will not have you treat her with such callous disregard, even if it is an unintended consequence of your misplaced protection." Nin gritted out.

"Little One…" he said, reaching for her.

"No," she said, sidestepping him, "you play games with people and do not consider what it can do to their hearts or minds."

Serge hung his head and sighed. "Yes. I will do better," he said, "but we cannot forget these games are useful in our life."

"In politics, perhaps. However, it is a quick slide into dark waters, brother. I only ask you to take more heed and not subject those you care about to your machinations. For now, leave it for Court business."

He nodded slowly and apologized again before leaving the room. Nin also apologized, but it was not her fault, so Sabrina stopped her short. She was about to take her seat again, when Inanna called to her, "Sabrina, Mosi likes to sit in the courtyard, by the fountain, when he is troubled."

Sabrina took the hint and took her leave, after getting clear directions from Nin followed by some more concrete help in the form of a chatty and accommodating guard who appeared a little concerned for his general. He walked her to the closest exit and pointed out the fountains in the distance. She stepped out into the night to see how Mo was after all the drama. Serge's question of her and her intentions took root too, so she walked slowly, contemplating the decision she had already been very close to making.

CHAPTER 8

Sabrina found Mo seated on a metal bench, facing a bronze fountain featuring a phoenix rising from dying flames. The bird was aged, the patina green in most spots, with deep brown patches peeking through here and there. More brilliant flashes of bronze showed, splashing against the trickle of water that spread out and down the outstretched wings of the bird. It was beautiful and intricate, unlike most centuries-old bronze pieces Sabrina had seen in pictures in the human realm, but similar enough for her to appreciate the change in style and subject matter.

She walked up to the bench and sat silently, watching Mo stare at the soft trickle of water in the brief flashes of firelight thrown from lanterns dotting the gravel pathway around the fountain. He said nothing, simply studying the fountain intently, until Sabrina whispered, "It's a beautiful statue."

He turned, eyeing Sabrina and giving a soft smile. He leaned back on the bench and grabbed Sabrina's hand in his so she was pulled back slightly with him, relaxing into the metal somehow. "It was a present to my mother, from Fannon, long ago," he finally said.

"Fannon?" she asked.

With a sad smile, he turned to explain. "Nin's father. They were together, Mother and Fannon, for a few centuries before Nin was born. Sadly, he died in a forge accident a decade later."

"Oh," Sabrina puffed out, remembering hazily some mention of Fannon now, or at least Nin's father, wondering why she never bothered to ask about him before. "He had metal magics like you?"

"Yes. He forged fabulous weapons, but as you can see, he was an artist at heart. He called Mother his phoenix as an endearment, a reference to her own fire magics and the life she led before."

Sabrina nodded, not wanting to pry, but Mosi continued, "Mother has lived long, even by Fae standards, and not all those years were happy. While she cared for my father and Sergius' father, her care was based more in friendship, respect, and a mutual desire for children. She loved Fannon, and I never saw her happiness shine quite as bright with any other Fae. It has dimmed considerably since he passed."

Sabrina was saddened for Inanna, who was lovely, kind, and fierce. The phoenix seemed fitting for her. "She did have love, though. There's something to be said for that."

"Yes, there is," Mo replied, looking hard and deep into her eyes. She was transfixed, under a spell that didn't actually involve any Fae magics. Eventually, she blurted, "Serge apologized."

Mo's eyes turned a little mean and his face became a neutral mask. "I will have my own words with Sergius."

Sabrina spoke up, placing her free hand on Mo's knee, turning her body more toward him as she did. "He was an ass, don't get me wrong, and he deserves a smack upside the head. But he explained some things after you left. He did it out of loyalty to you. He wasn't actually pushing you. He was pushing me to react for you." She turned her head away then, unable to face him as she went on. "He said he had to be sure of me, not you. Like, sure I cared for you. Would come to your defense."

"Did you?" he whispered, suddenly close and hot at her side.

Chuckling, she answered, "Yeah. So did Nin. Don't think he was ready for that heat."

"Mother will rail at him as well, though I am unsure why she did not immediately move to stop his antics earlier."

Sabrina shrugged, looking up at his face now so close to hers. "Maybe she needed answers, too. She's your mother, after all. This family is pretty protective all around."

"True," he said, reaching up to run a hand across her cheek. "Do you think she was happy with the turn of events?"

"I think she was pissed at Serge, but happy to see me so riled up on your behalf. As was Nin, though she already knew how I felt. How else do you think I found you out here?"

"That is no matter. I am only happy you did. That you sit with me here and now."

She arched closer, softly echoing back Serge's question from earlier, "That's all you want? Me to sit here beside you?" She pushed into his hold in a way he could not mistake.

"No, it is not all I want. However, I do not wish to confuse you or press my suit when you are not ready or willing," he admitted.

Sabrina turned her lips toward his hand, kissing the inside of his wrist slightly, as he had done to her so many times. His breath hitched audibly, and his hand spasmed in a delightful way.

"Sabrina," he moaned, bringing his other hand to her face and pulling them together, a hairspace between their lips at this point. "I need the words."

"I want you, Mo," she admitted, fully and completely, for the first time out loud. "I want every part of you. Right now."

Mo's lips crashed down on hers, a dark wave stealing her breath, drowning her in deep desire. She tasted wine and spice and the now so familiar scent of Mo. Her heart beat a frantic rhythm in her chest as she felt his arms melt around her, one sliding down around her lower back, one going up to fist her hair. She groaned down his throat when he pulled tighter and his tongue caressed her own. Heat bloomed in her core, starting low and spreading out to tingle across her body. Her magic hummed and throbbed, pulsing to a new beat she couldn't quite place until Mosi's chest pressed so tightly against her own, she recognized the thrum and pulse of his heartbeat somehow. It matched her magic, surely matched his own.

In a flash, Mo's head reared up, flashing dark eyes and furrowed brows across the dark expanse beyond the small fountain area. "Someone comes," he said, his voice ragged in a way that left Sabrina satisfied with herself. "Do you wish…" he began, but Sabrina cut him off.

She jumped up, enthusiastic and impatiently, pulling him with her. "Hell yeah, I wish. Where to, Mosi?"

"Are you certain?" he asked again, pulling her in a loose hold along her hips, pressing his forehead down on hers in a heavy sigh she knew was an attempt to calm his desires if she wanted to stop now.

"More than certain," she said.

He gave a curt nod then and pulled her into his arms. "Just as last time, it may be best you close your eyes." As soon as she did, she felt the rush of speed, but even Fae speed seemed too slow for the beat and pulse of need that ripped through her body.

Mo set her down gently on her feet, though she wobbled from both the speed of her physical transition from one place to another and the lust that pounded in her veins. He kissed her forehead and said, "You may open your eyes now."

He swiftly stepped aside to give her space, another nonverbal question of consent on his part she very much appreciated. Her eyes blinked and adjusted, taking in the bedroom around her. It was sparse, consisting of little more than a bed, a dresser, and a rigid chair next to a darkened window. From where she stood facing the bed, two doors were visible, slightly ajar and to her left. The little she could see indicated they were a closet and bathroom situation. It was efficient, like Mo, but also refined like him as well. The walls were a soft gray wallpaper with some sort of fine texture beckoning her to walk up and stroke it. His bedding was silver, metallic thread lacing through the fabrics that could very well be metals given Mo's affinity. The frame, dresser, and chair were utilitarian but sturdy and finely made. If she'd been asked to describe a place where Mosi would sleep, her guess would have been similar to what she saw, which made her a bit giddy in her knowledge of this man.

After giving her a few beats to take in her surroundings, to re-orient herself after his swift exit from the fountain, Mo reached out and gently rested his hand on the small of her back. "Sabrina?" he whispered, and when she looked at him for more, his eyes showed a mass of lust and uncertainty. All she wanted was to wash both away.

She turned toward him, lacing her hands behind his neck to gently tug his head down to hers, to encourage him to meet her waiting lips. He did, a dark roiling cloud about to burst into a torrent of rain. Mo moved his lips over hers in a rush, hungry for her in a way Sabrina appreciated and mirrored. She wanted him just as much and it was heady to realize they had the same need, same level of desire.

He pulled away, his eyes dark pools searing into her when she managed to languidly open her own after that stellar kiss. He cocked his head in question as his hands began to roam, first to skim down her sides and back up her back. His eyes

279

followed his hands, and as they went down to her hips, he licked his lips as if he couldn't help himself.

She took the time then to do her own exploring, with eyes and hands, feeling every inch of his upper body she could touch, rushing over him as if she had only minutes to memorize every dip and curve and line. When his hands thumped at the clasp at the back of her dress, the point that kept everything waist-high up on her garment, she shuttered, but was momentarily frozen with doubt. She tried, constantly, to keep the little nagging bits about her body at bay, especially in situations like this. But it was Mo, and she wanted him so badly, and he was so good and felt so right, and what if she wasn't what he expected.

He sensed her hesitancy or saw the uncertainty in her eyes and pulled her in his arms to whisper in her ear. "Sabrina, if you are unsure, unready, we do not need to do this now."

"No. No. I want to. I want you. I just. Well. I'm human, you know. Not Fae. And I don't look like all the Fae I've seen around."

Mo pulled back, a wrinkle of question marring his smooth forehead. "Do you think I do not see you? Know you?" He paused then, swallowing hard before softly saying, "Think of where my hands have touched and wished to see and know more?"

"No, but still. You know? Imagination versus reality and all that."

"Sabrina," he called, cradling her face in the palm of his hands and pulling her gaze up to meet his own. "If you wish to stop, we stop. There is no question in this. If, however, for some reason you feel you are not what I want, what I've dreamed of every night since I first laid eyes on you in the human realm, then you are mistaken, and I would ask you to give me the opportunity to dissuade you of incorrect notion you seem to harbor."

She pulled in a breath, closed her eyes, and nodded, more to herself than to Mo. She was in her own head about this. Everything Mo said, everything he did, showed care and concern and respect, but also lust and heat and desire. He wanted her, and she was not about to let her hang-ups and internal comparisons get in the way of that. Steeling herself, finding her own heat and pulse and tapping into it to let it guide her true, she opened her eyes and said, "Dissuade away," with the best sexy smirk she had in her.

Mo skimmed her shoulders with a reverent caress, leaning down to kiss the fabric where his fingers skimmed. Each kiss was a punctuation of need, a mark of want. He circled her again, going for her zipper, tugging it down slowly as his tongue began to lick and suck on the swoop where her neck met shoulder. A shudder racked Sabrina and her desire ramped up, as did her wish to see and feel more of Mosi. She reached for the laces on his breastplate as her zipper hit the end of its path.

They were a frantic mass of untying and unbuttoning and hurried contortions to free themselves. Soon, Sabrina was naked save a small slip and her underwear. Mo looked like a God molded in bronze and poured into leather short pants. Both took a moment to stop and appreciate. Sabrina panted, quite literally, and the momentum of her chest snagged Mo's eyes, his gaze caught there in open admiration. She laughed softly to herself but stepped forward and blocked his view for a moment. She reached down, finger tracing the loosening tops of his pants, and looked at him from a breath away.

"Mosi, are you certain? You've asked me enough, and all I can think about is how much I want you. You, though. Are you sure?"

He closed his eyes briefly, a small smile on his lips, before pulling Sabrina's lower body flush with his so she felt the shocking outline of his arousal in his pants. "I am more than certain, my Sabrina, but I do appreciate your willingness to ask." He dipped down then and took her mouth, ending the conversation there. They broke apart only to finish undressing, to stare at each other's naked bodies for the first time for a few slow beats.

A deep grumble ripped from Mosi's chest before he grabbed her hand, hurrying her onto his bed. He crawled over her naked body, staring her down from feet to head as he moved slowly up, placing haphazard, scorching kisses across her prickling skin. He licked at her dimpled hips and nuzzled her soft, rounded belly. Her nipples ached to be touched, and his mouth did not disappoint her there before moving forward after long minutes. When he stared down at her from arm's length, his face hovering over her own, his look softened. There was something like wonder there. Keeping himself balanced on one hand he took the other and traced the lines of her face, moving from forehead to eyes to cheeks to mouth to chin and down her neck. "I've thought of this often," he confessed, "the way you would look in my bed. My imagination does not compare to reality."

Sabrina blushed, turning away for a second, unused to the honesty and stark care she saw in his eyes. This wasn't her first time in a man's bed. Far from it. It was, however, different. The feelings and connections were more visceral somehow and it made her feel slightly vulnerable. Sex was sex, yet this was something else. She knew it before they even began. The pulse of her blood and her magic told her as much and she needed a moment to process. Mo gave her that, bending down to his elbows and nestling his face in her messy hair to break eye contact for a few seconds.

A few seconds was all she needed though, as desire spurred her on past her nerves about what was between them, her body almost of its own accord arching up off the bed to meet his, rubbing across him in a way that brought a hiss from his mouth. He pulled back up, connected once again eye-to-eye, and Sabrina found comfort in the nightfall of his gaze.

"Are you ready, my love?" Mo said, and it brought a hitch to Sabrina. Others used "love" with her as a term of endearment, but Mo meant it in a specific way she could no longer deny.

"Yes, Mosi," she called, bringing her arms up to his shoulders, trailing them down his strong arms, gripping him there because in this position she could not hold his hand. He nodded, leaned down to kiss her lips briefly, before pushing back up to watch her face as he nudged her legs open. She moved then, fishing down with her own hand to help guide him inside of her. She let out a small gasp from the newness of him, the stretch she felt, but their frantic kisses had left her more than ready, easy to slide into even if it was a tad snug.

Mo puffed out a breath, resting his forehead gently on Sabrina's as she softly panted and squirmed, willing him to move. "There is so much more I wish to do to you, to make you feel. This is the first time such things will not happen, and for that

I am sorry. Yet, we have time. Other nights and days."

Sabrina, filled with need and the spark and hum of magic under her skin that someone matched the pulse and heat she felt from all of Mo, inside and out, rolled her hips and spoke in a broken rasp she barely recognized. "Soon. Yes. We have a future," she admitted, "but for now, more. Please, Mosi. More."

He did not make her wait. He pulled back with his hips and thrust forward, creating a pace that built and built until he moved his hand down between the two of them while staring at Sabrina, touching her in just the right spot with the right amount of pressure to make her scream over the edge. An edge he quickly followed her over.

CHAPTER 9

The following evening, the soft knock at her bedroom made Sabrina's gut do a pleasant flip. She smiled broadly as she flung open the door to see Mo standing there, straight and stoic with his hands clasped in front of him. His heavy, neutral look, the one Sabrina thought of as cold or hard when she first met him weeks ago, melted slightly, giving way to a sly smile that spread up from his mouth and hit his dark, molten eyes. He tilted his head slightly, an acknowledgment and question rolled into one simple gesture, and Sabrina grabbed him, dragging him forward to plant a kiss on his lips.

He pulled away, too quickly in her opinion, his hands framing her face as he stared down at her. "Good evening, my Sabrina."

"Hey," she said, her voice sounding husky to her own ears.

Mo flashed his eyes at her unmade bed and gave a sigh of frustration. "There is work for us this evening."

She nodded, seeing the promise in his eyes, knowing that after work, more would come, and it filled her with a pleasant buzz. "Then let's get to it," she said, pulling from him to walk into the hallway. He followed her without hesitation or the need to retake the lead. She knew where she headed and he trusted her to get them there.

The day itself had been strange for Sabrina. She woke in Mosi's bed, curled against his warm brown body, her magic a purr in her chest, matching the cadence in Mo's. He was already awake and moved to brush hair from her eyes when he noticed her stirring. A quick kiss, a few whispers, happy hearts and minds all around, and Mo helped her return to The Palace. Their hands lingered, grasping until space forced them apart, as both went their separate ways. It wasn't harsh, but necessary as both had packed schedules for the day.

Sabrina met with Gin to study, pouring over rune books and word magic primers until lunch. Her eyes felt dry, a clear sign of how tired she was, both from studying long hours and the blissful lack of sleep from the night before. Gin, for their part, smiled openly and asked how she was, but did not pry. It wasn't their way. They did make a soft comment about how it was odd to smell Mo's magic in a study room where he was not in attendance, a sly joke made with a grin and the lift of an eyebrow, a subtle acknowledgment they knew the outlines of her evening and approved.

The two scholars ate a quick lunch then went to Sabrina's first Scholars Guild meeting; an informal event held in The Palace between the large quarterly gatherings of scholars from across Fae. Pytor and Gin were leaders, so they sat toward the head of a massive black table. Sabrina, still unsure of her place in Fae, much less this specific guild, sat toward the back to better observe and take in the events. She soon found she didn't need to worry. While the topics were slightly different, and involved the discussion of magic and magical research, it was still familiar to her. In fact, take these Fae and plop them down in a faculty meeting at a college or university, and they'd fit right in. Sabrina chuckled to herself as they poured over the meaning of a single phrase in a decree they wished to draft for fifteen minutes straight because she had been here before and now had far fewer reservations. Seems scholars in both realms had particular characteristics, and though Sabrina was annoyed more often than not by this in the human realm, she found comfort in the familiarity of it in Fae.

After she spent more time studying in one of the smaller Palace libraries, she wondered for a moment if she could pop in and hang out in Gin's much more awesome home library in The Falls through the chalk door she figured was still up in The Royal Chambers, but it was a fleeting wish. She didn't want to go in that room where the iron chair probably still sat. Plus, she couldn't go traipsing around Fae by herself and she knew it, so Palace libraries it was. She had a quick private chat with Nin over a later-than-usual afternoon tea where her friend appeared distracted. It was fun, as always, even if both made a point to specifically not discuss something the other either did not know (on the part of Sabrina) or silently agreed to just let rest for now (on the part of Nin). She managed a quick solo dinner before preparing for her defense training, anticipation a live wire up and down her spine.

Reviewing her day, she suddenly realized she had no idea what Mo did on a daily basis. What the contours of his day entailed when he wasn't training her or taking her on lunch and tea dates or attending some meeting where she watched his cool competence at work. She stopped, feeling a flash of shame for never asking. He looked down at her, a silent question in his eyes, and she shook off the worst feelings. "What'd you do today?" she asked, slowing her pace so they meandered rather than reaching the training ring too quickly.

"I met with my seconds. Discussed strategic plans with a few high-ranking Fae officials. Toured Palace fortifications for inspection."

"That a normal day for you?"

He smiled down at her and took her hand. "You wish to know more of my days?"

"Well, yeah. You know an awful lot about mine. Seems you and everyone else are always exchanging info about what and how I'm doing. I realized I don't know much about what your days are like. Sorry about that."

Mo stopped her, his brow furrowed. "Do not apologize, Sabrina. I believe all of us forget you are new to Fae, new to us, because you feel so vital here. Much takes up space in your mind, as it should. You are still finding your place."

"Sure, but—"

"Sabrina, it is fine. I take no offense. I am happy you ask now, but it is of no consequence. What we do with our days together is far more interesting."

Sabrina reached up and gave Mo a quick kiss in response. She was happy with him, thankful he understood it was no slight to him personally that she was focused on other issues. There was a lot going on in her mind, all the time, in Fae. It took getting used to, for sure. She did, however, make a mental note to be more proactive with Mosi, and she knew she would. She would listen to his stories and share his frustrations. She did actually care, and she wanted to learn all she could about him even before this moment. Her learning was simply inhibited by the business of surviving day-to-day in a new, dangerous magical realm and her previous hesitancy to connect with Mo on a more romantic level.

They reached the ring and Mo took on his stern trainer look, focusing on the task at hand. "This evening, we grapple."

"Grapple. You mean like wrestling?"

He confirmed but went about clearing a wide area of leaves and debris. Sabrina shrugged and waited, arms crossed, to see what came next. Once he was satisfied with the clearing he created, he unhooked his belt, vest, and cape, leaving only a thin undershirt and his leather pants and boots in place. It made Sabrina's hands twitch to stroke the expanse of chest and smattering of curly dark hair she saw from the opening at the top of his shirt, but she restrained herself and focused on his words.

"To this point, we practiced defenses against advancing advisories. However, you may be forced into close combat, unable to use the same physical or magic techniques. As before, we shall start with the physical portion, then practice bringing your magic forward in this scenario."

He crooked his finger and she strolled toward him, stopping when he put his palm out about a foot away from his body, placing his hands on her shoulders. She wore an old sweatshirt, as she still hadn't received her Fae wardrobe, but she felt the heat of those hands, and her magic lingered in the place he held her, making her skin crackle from the inside out.

"Have you wrestled before?" he asked.

"Not really." Sabrina shrugged it off. "I'm familiar with the overall concept, though."

"We will spend more time on basics then. We may even wait for our next lesson to bring magic forward. Grappling can be exhausting work and, as always, we want to practice enough for you to develop automatic reactions."

She nodded and Mo dove into explanations, showing her, step-by-step, a set of moves and counter moves while emphasizing the random nature of such attacks. It made sense to Sabrina. It was the difference between Greco-Roman wrestling in the Olympics and a bar fight. You might know how to put someone in a hold or get out of a hold, but when there were no official rules, it would all become far more frantic and wilder.

After an hour of moving through slow scenarios with her as both defender and attacker, Mo asked, "Are you prepared to grapple in a more serious way?"

"Yes," she breathed, already slightly winded by their long work and the constant tingle of Mo's hands on her body. She was also a little annoyed. He seemed far less affected by her than she was by him.

Mo wasted no time and dove for her torso. She managed to push him up, and they grappled in a

crouch for a long minute before Mo swiped a foot out
from under her, bringing her to her butt. She
scrambled, but he was a flash, pinning her down with
his hands at her wrists and knees on her thighs,
pulling her arms firmly above her head. She bucked,
kicked her feet as best she could, tried to wriggle
away, but nothing worked. He was an immovable
stone above her, his stoic face set in place.

"Now that was embarrassingly quick," she
huffed out.

"Not so. You simply need more practice,"
Mo countered, but he didn't let her go.

She waited. One beat, then two, expecting
him to call out, "Again." Only, he didn't. His face
was neutral but he held her tight, staring down at her.
It made her feel flushed with nerves and desire.

"Mosi?" she called, wiggling slightly in his
grip.

He let out a puff of air that sounded an awful
lot like "damn" and bent forward, bringing his body
down on hers and searing her mouth with a hard, long
kiss. His heat and smell enveloped her, and she
ground against him, letting out a whoosh of breath
when she felt the hardness in his leathers press
against the juncture of her thighs. Apparently, he was
not nearly as unaffected as she thought.

He whispered, "I need you," against her
mouth, taking a moment to breathe deep. He kept her
hands pinned in one of his own, but moved the other
down her body, hovering over her breasts when she
hitched a harsh breath in. However, he had a clear
goal. He cupped her over the crotch of her jeans, and
she let a deep moan slide down his throat. Ripping
the zipper down, he dove into her panties, and

Sabrina could do nothing but pant and writhe. She wanted to do nothing else.

He pulled away from her lips and looked at her with those vibrant onyx eyes. "I wish to watch you." Staring down at her as his hand made her climb higher and higher, he watched her face closely until her orgasm hit like a lightning bolt, jolting her body and her magic, wrenching a soft scream from her throat. He bent down then, planting kisses on her face as she caught her breath.

He rested his head against her neck and said, "I am sorry."

She laughed. "Sorry for giving me an orgasm. Don't ever apologize for that."

"No. This is defense practice. It is crucial. I should not do such things here and now. I must control myself in the future. You felt..."

"Like electricity dancing across my skin whenever you touch me," she interjected. "I was already goo. I'm not complaining, although I get your point. We need to have a clear separation between work time and play time."

Mo rolled off her and she missed his weight and heft until he slid close to her side and threw a heavy arm across her stomach. "You describe the feeling well, my Sabrina. Such a way with words you have." A dark thought flashed across his face and his grin fell as he confessed, "I would be devastated if you were unprepared for another attack. We do not know when Comus will strike again."

"What?" she asked as Mo stiffened by her side. That got her attention even more. "What about Comus?" she demanded, bending her body up on her elbows and staring in confusion at Mosi.

He closed his eyes, a sure sign of resignation, and explained. "Early this afternoon, your attacker woke long enough to swear allegiance to Comus, deride the attack on Nin but disparage you, and then inflict a mortal wound on themself."

"You didn't think this was important information I should know immediately?" she seethed, reaching down to zip and button her jeans before scrambling up awkwardly to her feet.

Mo bounded up to meet her far more gracefully, and calmly replied, "I did not."

"Are you shitting me?" she said, shaking at the audacity of this man.

"I do not understand what that means," he said with his head cocked, "but if you want to ensure I speak true, I do. I did not think it was important information for you to know at this time. Neither did Nin."

That last part was a blow to the stomach. Mo, sure. She could see it, him thinking he knew best. She'd seen him do it with his sister when she first set eyes on him in Nin's nursery. He was unyielding in his loyalty but also, sometimes, in his protection. Not exactly a red flag, although it was something that would require a lot of discussion and boundary setting in the near future. Still, it was not a surprise. Nin's reaction did surprise her.

"Nin approved this crap?"

"Yes. She and I are the only ones who know."

"Was she planning on telling me?"

"I cannot speak for my Queen."

"Were you?" She asked in a strained voice because his reaction, though somewhat understandable, cut.

He paused for a moment and simply replied, "No."

"Oh, but lost in a haze of horniness you let it all slip out? Lovely. Just fabulous." She started to pace, gearing up to let her emotions fly. "That's some bullshit, and you know it. You talk, every damn time we're out here, about preparation and practice. About knowing how to react appropriately. You think I can do that without all the information? How am I supposed to defend myself if I don't know anything important about the threats I may be facing?"

Mosi stood at attention, taking all her words in, and replied, "You are correct."

Sabrina did a double take at this. It was a quick turnaround. "You agree with me all of a sudden? Just like that?"

"I cannot say I would make a different decision if I went into the past, but your assessment is correct. I did not provide you with information you might possibly need to defend yourself in the future. For that I apologize."

"Why, though?" she huffed out, losing steam at his admission of guilt and his logical assessment of the situation.

"I wish only to protect you," he whispered, "even if I know you must learn to protect yourself."

It was exactly what she said about him to Serge last night. It was who he was, a part of him she knew and accepted. That did not mean they shouldn't address it. She closed in on him, putting a hand to his chest as he breathed deep and closed his eyes. "Mosi, that is who you are, and it is something I find lovely, your fierce drive to protect the people you care about. You have to be logical about it, even when it's hard to do. You and I both know leaving me blind to threats is not protective, it's possessive. There's a difference."

Mo nodded, reaching for her hand at his chest and covering it. "I worry so much, about…"

"Everyone. Yes. I know. Your family knows. It makes you a great general. An awesome brother. Probably a lovely partner. But, like Serge and his mouth, this instinct can go too far. You need to be aware of that, work on pulling back at a certain point."

"It is difficult for me."

"I understand. That doesn't mean you don't have to try."

He opened his eyes and shined their bright night sky down on her, a complexity of emotion playing there. "You are correct, and I am truly sorry. I will try in the future. This I swear." He lifted her hand up and kissed her wrist. "You make me better," he breathed out, and those words cozied right up alongside Sabrina's soul.

"I hope we'll make each other better," she admitted.

Mo hugged her to him, a fierce squeeze lasting long minutes, and though she was still annoyed, and still had many questions, her body and her anger eased. The argument was necessary, but ultimately good. When he released her, she felt like they were stepping off onto even more solid ground, together.

CHAPTER 10

When Mo opened the door to Sabrina's room the next morning, he let out a soft grunt in greeting. Sabrina peeked out from behind his frame to find Serge leaning against the opposite wall, finishing off an apple. She narrowed her eyes at him, but he smiled broadly in a kind and sincere way. No trace of their argument clouded his face.

"Brother," he said, nodding to Mo. Mo replied with a quick hug and pat on the back, apparently the universal dude greeting in both realms. He turned and pushed Sabrina a little further back into the room, leaving space between them and Serge so he could whisper to her. "Sergius made amends with me yesterday. He is my brother, and I am happy to forgive him, as I realize it came from a place of protection — something we both know I also must work on. It would be hypocritical of me not to forgive." He searched Sabrina's hard face and sighed,

"I know you may not be ready, and I will not ask you to forgive him on my behalf. I ask only that you listen to his apology and judge as you see fit. He is your mentor as well, and you must continue your lessons regardless. He is also genuinely contrite."

She sniffed and turned her nose up, not ready to fully give up her snit at his behavior, even if she agreed to let him have his say. Outside of her relationship with Nin or Mo, Serge was her mentor and her friend, and she would give him another chance. She would be a tad pissy about it at first, as was her right as a person who held a grudge over the treatment of someone she cared for deeply.

Mo let out a relieved breath and with a small smile, dipped down to touch her lips, and asked, "I shall see you this evening?"

Her heart, attune to his touch, thumped in overtime and her magic sang along her skin. She gave a firm, "You betcha," and a saucy wink before turning Mo around and following him out of her bedroom.

She closed the door then leaned against it with crossed arms as Mo patted Serge on the shoulder and walked down the hall. She said nothing, choosing icy silence as her greeting to mark her displeasure.

"You are a loyal one, tough to the end," Serge said, a hint of happiness in the words. He pulled himself straight and offered her a deep bow. "Sabrina, I have wronged you as I wronged Mosi. More so, in fact, as my push for answers implied negative character faults. Please believe I did not feel you to be disloyal or indifferent to Mo, only more apt to hide those feelings away."

"They are my feelings, Serge," she finally answered, pushing off the door and getting into his space. "It should be my choice to share or not."

He nodded, hands up in supplication. "That is true and fair. I did not give you an option. My behavior forced your response, and although I did it with Mo's best interests at heart, it was harmful to each of you. Please believe me when I say I am truly and deeply sorry."

Serge waited patiently for a reply, not pushing his suit. He also used no magics, which is something he could easily do to finesse the situation. Sabrina appreciated the restraint. "You can't do it again, whether you're trying to protect your brother or me. You can't get into our personal business. It has to be separate from what you and Mo have, or what you and I have."

"A fair demand I happily accept. I won't meddle in your affairs again."

Sabrina sighed. Part of her wanted to drag this out, teach Serge a lesson. Mo was right, though. He was her friend and mentor. He also acted genuine and remorseful.

"You and your brother are a pain sometimes, you know that? Both so protective and pushy," she groused, and Serge let a grin slip, knowing from her words she was in a forgiving mood.

"Something we both will endeavor to correct in the future, I'm sure."

She huffed at him loudly. "See that you do," she said in her haughtiest voice.

Serge moved quickly then to grab her into a hug, hard and deep; brotherly. As was the quick kiss to the top of her head. He pulled back, keeping his arms thrown across her shoulders but looking into her eyes with a serious expression Serge rarely wore. "I also want you to know, Sabrina, you are mine in a way as well. You were Nin's first, of course. You are Mo's in a very particular way I do not wish, even if I occasionally flirt and tease. But you are also mine."

Sabrina's heart squeezed at the affection and light in the words and his voice. "Back at you, bro," she said, attempting to lighten the mood slightly as the big emotions welled inside, gathering around her eyes and threatening tears.

Serge graciously gave her that play, easing into his usual sly and happy self. "Bro? I'm no bro, Rina," he said, chuckling her on the shoulder, and the nickname, so casually thrown out for the first time, so much a part of how the Fae in this realm and this family in particular addressed each other, made the waterworks break forward.

She grabbed Serge in a hug and he shushed her, taking her tears of joy in something new and lovely and pain at something lost long ago. "All is well, my dear. All is well. We have you now," he crooned to her.

It took a few moments to pull herself together, but she did, giving a final squeeze before she pushed away from Serge. "Alright. Enough of that. On to other business. What's up for today? Do we have a lesson?"

Again, he graciously allowed her to move on without note. "Not today. Tomorrow. Late morning, perhaps. I wish to discuss some research with you and Gin, and I need more time to prepare, gather my thoughts. Also, Jane has asked to join us for tea tomorrow afternoon. She wishes to rally our support for her summer solstice plans before she presents them to Nin and The Council."

Sabrina groaned a bit, "I'm not really much of a party planner."

"Be that as it may, it's a good lesson for you in Fae politics. A lot can be accomplished with private conversations over tea. We also need to gather more information from and about Jane. We have yet to find the traitor, after all."

Serge and Sabrina made quick plans to meet in his rooms the next day for research talk, then political tea. Sabrina, for her part, steeled herself again and went off to find Nin. She figured she may as well get all the rough discussions with this particularly loveable but sometimes infuriating band of Fae siblings out of the way.

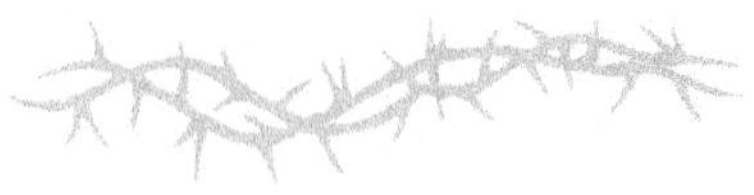

Sabrina found Nin in The Royal Gardens, which was the first place she looked, actually. She called out for her. Nin replied from a deep corner of the grounds Sabrina found through a long twisty route. When she spotted Nin, the Queen looked like a study in contradiction: pristine white and intricately embroidered day dress, thick black hair set in complicated braids in and around the gold singlet she wore most days as a sign of her royal status, and sturdy yet bulky leather work gloves smeared with mud and fertilizer. She likely looked like this because she came from or was expected at a formal meeting. It still marked a bit of who Sabrina saw her as overall, a woman ready to do whatever work necessary to set things to rights. Even if she was hurt

300

and a little angry with her friend, she could recognize and appreciate that.

"Hey," Sabrina called softly in greeting as Nin reached up to stroke a large black hanging plant that resembled gigantic upside-down tulips.

Nin turned and answered cheerily, "Hello, dear Sabrina, and good morning. How are you, my friend?"

Sabrina cut to the chase, wanting to get the conversation started before she set her hurt aside and decided to let the issue pass. Things festered between friends if not discussed, and she wanted to clear the air with Nin. "Why didn't you tell me about Comus and the attack?"

Nin froze for a second, then blinked quickly before slouching her shoulders. "Mo told you," she easily guessed, giving a final pat to the flower next to her head and moving closer to Sabrina.

"Yeah. He did. Accidently. What neither of you did was tell me on purpose. And I gotta say, it hurts. Don't you trust me with the information? Do you think I can't handle it?"

"No, no," Nin said in a rush. "Nothing like that, Sabrina. Mo was being protective, as he often is. I...well, I was feeling guilty and protective."

Sabrina threw her hands in the air in frustration. "Nin. Come on. You have to let this go. Whatever guilt you feel about me, about all this, you need to work through it. It makes you and everyone else feel bad. We talked about this the night I was attacked. I thought you understood."

"I know. However, it is difficult, particularly in regard to Comus. I feel responsible for all he did. It does not help he reached me, in actuality or by proxy, directly before he attacked you. I could have done more, been more vigilant."

"That's on him, not you," Sabrina assured. "You are not responsible for the actions of a grown ass man, especially one hundreds of years old who should have learned long ago not to be a horrible person."

"But I let him in — into the highest circles of The Palace, into my heart." Nin slumped further then, sitting down on the ground with no concern for her pristine white dress. She started crying, and it was like a dam broke. Big, wrenching sobs came. All Sabrina could do was hold her friend, whisper soothing words, and allow her the time and space to let it pass. Just as Serge did for her earlier.

When Nin quieted, long after Sabrina shooed away guards concerned by the sounds of their Queen in distress, she pulled herself up and said, "I am sorry, Sabrina. It seems my family and I do nothing but hurt you."

"Nope. Not true," she whispered back. "First of all, you're my family, and family sometimes sting. That's the way of it. They love, too, and I'm glad for that. Second, no more apologies. We seem to be going round and round in a circle with all this."

"You are correct, as always."

"You should keep that in your little head," she replied, tapping a finger at her friend's temple. "Remember: Sabrina is always correct."

Nin looked at her friend with haunted eyes, ignoring the joke, and said, "I still hear him there sometimes."

Sabrina's heart shattered in her chest at those words, at the stark pain in her friend's voice and gaze. She pulled her close, held her tight, and

with a fierce tone said, "I don't know how to stop
that. Or how to get rid of your guilt. I think they're
both tied together. I know we'll work through it,
though. Me and you."

"Me and you," Nin repeated.

"Maybe also Mo and Serge, Gin and your
mom," Sabrina added with a smile, pulling back to
look at her friend. "You are Queen, but we're here
for you. You have an entourage, lady. You've been
using it for political duty and that's great. Use us to
help ease your emotional load, too."

"I don't know how," Nin said, threading her
fingers through the grass beside them, watching as
the blades rippled in response to her touch.

"I think letting it all out is a good start."

Nin nodded and pulled in a deep breath,
releasing it at a slow, steady pace. "Again, I shall try.
Really try, this time."

"I know," Sabrina assured, "and part of
trying is talking about the attack. We know for
certain it was Comus who set a hit out on me? He
was, for whatever reason, also not too happy about
the assassination attempt?"

Nin's face hardened at that. "Yes. It makes
sense the attack on you was him and the attack on me
was a different threat. He would not wish me dead.
However, he would love to send a message to me and
The Fae Court and would think nothing of spilling
human blood to do so."

"Comus has it out for me," Sabrina stated
blandly. She felt like puking at the idea of someone
like him focusing on her in any way.

"Unlikely you, specifically. I am sorry to
say, Sabrina, but he would think of you as nothing, as
lesser than, because you are human. He knows of our

connection and disproves. It is more about me than you."

"I'm caught in the crossfire, which is why you feel guilty?" Sabrina pushed. Nin nodded in response, looking down, and Sabrina thought of a different tactic.

"Nin, you think I'm a smart, capable, intelligent woman, right?"

"Of course," she said, sounding slightly offended.

"You think I've handled myself well here?"

"You saved me, dear Sabrina. You have risen to meet every challenge and new experience faced in Fae."

"Would you say I didn't actually do all that myself, that I'm simply some pawn in this big Fae game?"

"Never," she replied immediately, the vehemence in her voice a clear indication of the honesty in her quick answer.

Sabrina stared into her friend's eyes and said, "When you think everything is on you, that it is all your fault, you take away any agency I have in this. You make it about you, which some of it is. But you disregard me. I made the choice to come here on my own. Without you anywhere around. That was my action. It's also something I would do over and over again, despite the hard hits we've taken."

Nin wiped tears from her eyes, leaving a small trace of dirt on her cheek from her dirty work gloves. "I understand your point, Sabrina. I see the logic there. However, logic does not always rule."

"Sure, but we can use it to help bolster our feelings. Like a mantra of sorts."

"Anytime I feel guilt, I remind myself of this?"

"Yep. Like, anytime you feel guilty about something to do with me, you just say to yourself, *'Sabrina is a bad bitch and deserves credit in her own life.'*"

Nin let out a harsh laugh. "Should I write this down?"

"I'll send you a note," Sabrina retorted, pulling herself up off the ground and offering Nin a hand up.

Returning to more serious matters, Nin asked, "Do you forgive me?"

"I'd forgive you a whole lot, lady. This? No problem."

Nin wove her arm in Sabrina's and pulled herself straight and tall, or as tall as her five-foot frame allowed, taking on a stiffer posture. "I will endeavor to make such forgiveness unnecessary in the future."

"That's why you got it now," Sabrina whispered, squeezing Nin's arm, letting her friend lead her through the lush gardens. "I've had hard chats with all of Inanna's children in the span of about twelve hours. Love the lot of you, but I'm ready to drop all this heaviness."

"Whatever you wish, friend," Nin answered.

"What I wish for is a good book in a long bath, immediately followed by a nap. Sadly, there's stuff to get done. Seriously, I thought I was busy teaching all those comp classes? Pfft. Nothing compared to magical Fae family shenanigans."

"Would a much calmer family dinner suffice?" Nin asked as they strolled. "Mother says she feels bad over what transpired at her table. The more likely reason, however, is she wishes to be nosy and see you and Mosi together in the same space with her own eyes. We can accomplish both with a small dinner in my chambers. If you are amenable?”

"Why not?" Sabrina shrugged. "Couldn't be any worse. Though, I have to say, even if I hate to admit it, Serge's machinations worked wonders."

Sabrina wiggled her eyebrows at Nin as her friend laughed and said, "No details. Please." They moved forward, laughing and chatting, as they so often did in the past. As they would do in the future.

CHAPTER II

Sabrina received a note from Mo shortly after returning from The Royal Gardens. All this paper passing was reminding her of pre-cellphone middle school days, which made her chuckle and wonder if she should play a quick round of MASH. She had more tangible pleasures to enjoy, however. Mo's note claimed he switched around his schedule for the day after learning she had no afternoon lessons with Serge. Yet another example of how quickly gossip passed between those two brothers. He wrote he wanted to take her out that afternoon on one of their picnics, a date of sorts after their official start as something.

The 'something' they were was still new, though, and slightly nebulous. Hard to define. A problem for another day. All she focused on was what to wear. Mo told her to wear comfortable clothes for a day of "activity," whatever that meant.

The best she could do here, with her still limited wardrobe, was jeans, hiking shoes, her trusty flannel, and a white tee-shirt with a font pun on the front: "Live Life in BOLD."

When it was almost time to meet up with Mosi, a gentle knock sounded at the door. A small sound that had butterflies dancing in her belly. She opened it with a smile to meet Mo, only to stop in surprise at what she saw in front of her.

Mo was dressed very much like her. That's to say, he looked like a human except for the slightly pointed tips of his ears his close-cropped hair always put on display. Everything else screamed 'human dude.' Squeaky clean sneakers on his feet, straight legged but roomy dark wash jeans, a tight red U of L tee-shirt plastered to his muscular chest, and a soft black jacket. Sabrina took a moment to drink him in, as she did most days in his Fae attire, too, but made a point of exaggerating the act. The clothes, especially the college shirt, was a gesture on his part, and she wanted him to easily see she understood it as such.

"My, my, my," she drawled, exaggerating her Kentucky twang a bit. "You look mighty fine there, Mosi."

He grinned back at her and pulled his jacket out by the zipper in a hesitant way, obviously new to the feel and look of the clothes he wore. "Truly? I asked Nin for suggestions. She gave me strict instructions."

"She did well," Sabrina said, pulling him close and giving a soft peck to his lips, "but all this is unnecessary, Mosi. You don't need to change your clothes for me. One, I want you to be who you are. Two, you're Fae warrior look is pretty damn hot."

Mo's eyes heated and skittered for a minute past her, into her room. He came back to her quickly, gathered himself, and replied, "You adapted to my realm in many ways, my love. I wish to show you I can as well."

The simple statement brought a surprising pinprick of tears to Sabrina's eyes, which made her a bit annoyed. She'd cried an awful lot already in the day and didn't need to shed more tears. Sucking it up, pushing the tears back, she focused on the idea. She changed, sure, and she did it happily. Not just for Mo, but for Nin and the other Fae she loved and trusted in this new realm. It was new, and a lot of change at once. To know someone other than Nin took the time to recognize, acknowledge, and act on that was touching. It burrowed under the skin, melting into her in a way that made Mo stick a little faster to her heart and mind.

"Okay then," she whispered and gave him a heated kiss in return, savoring his taste and smell as he took over the action and deepened it, extended it, leaving them both breathless when they finally broke apart.

"Any more of that and the date is canceled," Sabrina said.

"Yes. Let us leave, then, as I do wish to take you out today."

"By out, you mean out-out? Like outside-The-Palace out?" she asked with a note of excitement.

"Yes." Grabbing her hand, he led her down the hallway, out the gate, and once she was held tight in his arms and her eyes were squeezed shut, off to some unknown area of Fae.

They transported using Mo's magics and she was a little shaky upon landing but seemed to be better at the form of travel with every turn.

"Maybe I'll get totally used to this one day," she wheezed, hands on her knees and body bent slightly because the nausea still hit hard, even if it didn't last long.

"You do exceedingly well, Sabrina," Mo encouraged while rubbing slow, soft circles on her lower back to comfort her.

She raised slowly and saw the crossroads from her first step into Fae. The four forests were the same, each unique. The unusual ombre grass swayed in the soft breeze, jungle loomed, the alpine spring meadow scuttled with life, the wintry wood looked far too chilly, and the leaves fell from the autumnal scene. It was as she remembered, but the impact was no less mesmerizing.

"I never asked what this place was," she observed, spinning slowly to take it all in again.

"It is a convergence point for the mystic woods. It's a specific region of Fae where these four forests display the same seasonal weather despite the time of year. The rest of Fae has seasons which wax and wane, but the woods and meadows here are stuck in one time."

"Why? Or, how?"

Mo shrugged. "Gin could give you more specifics. Nin as well, as it is earth magics at work. I do not know the details. I know only it is a type of persistent natural magic. I do know it helps shield the detection of other forms of magic when one performs spell work here."

Sabrina nodded at this, extending the logic quickly in her mind. "Which is why The Falls was created in the jungle space over there."

Mo swooped in, pulling her into his arms and offering her a full smirk. "Exactly, my smart one. Exactly."

After a tight hug and a slow kiss, he took her hand and they headed off in the direction of the spring meadow. Sabrina was more than glad they didn't venture into the jungle again and was happy to see another part of Fae so different from what she previously explored. Here the evergreens towered tall, like redwoods but bushier, fuller, gigantic pines jutting into the crystal blue sky. Clusters of vivid wildflowers swayed in the gentle breeze, cutting the scent of needles and sap that clung in the air with a hint of sweetness. She heard the rustle of life all around. Small, furred creatures scuttled close and, when they walked further in, bands of deer roamed and ate a distance.

They walked and talked for half an hour, until a small puff of smoke signaled something ahead. Cresting a hill, Sabrina saw a cottage and large barn nestled in the valley below. It was idyllic in the extreme and brought a smile to her lips. Two Fae worked outside and they waved to Mo in recognition as they descended the peak of the hill.

"Lill. Myrr. Good to see you again, old friends," Mo greeted, pulling each into a hug when they met.

"You as well, Mosi. You as well," the woman called Myrr said. She gave a sidelong glance at Sabrina and said, "This the girl?"

Sabrina bristled a bit. She didn't like being called 'girl' when she was one, and she was well into womanhood at this point, but Mo patted her arm and smiled.

"Yes, my Sabrina. Please do meet Myrr," the Fae curtsied at this, "and Lill," the other Fae offered a sweeping bow.

"A true pleasure to meet you, Sabrina the Scholar," Lill replied.

"You know about that, huh?" she muttered.

"Aye. Not every day a human bonds with the Queen, then saves her life," Myrr answered. "It's an honor to have you at our stables, Scholar."

She appreciated the gruff kindness of Myrr, the no-nonsense way she treated her, but was hung up on something. "Stables?"

"This is what I wished to show you. Myrr and Lill's stables. The finest in our land."

Sabrina's mouth formed an O of shocked happiness. "We get to hang with horses? Wait. Y'all have horses?"

Mo laughed. "Yes. To both questions. We can ride out for a time, as well. If you know how. If you do not, we can begin lessons if you wish."

"I'm from Kentucky, Mo. I've ridden a horse." He looked at her in question because he didn't get the reference and she waved it off. "The place where I'm from in the human realm? It's known for a few things. One of those things is horses."

"Then you are pleased?" he asked, the question earnest in tone.

Sabrina realized he was unsure himself, maybe unused to things like dates or surprise events for a partner or dressing in a way that would please them. It made her heart squeeze to think of him hesitant but active, doing what he could in an effort to bring her a piece of joy.

"Yes. Very pleased. So, let's go. I want to play with the horses."

Myrr remained gruff but informative as she gave them a tour, set them up with horses, prepared them for an outing, and eventually, left them to it with an admonishment to be careful with the horses and themselves. Mo and Sabrina rode out, separate on their own beautiful mounts, but in Sabrina's mind, even more connected than they were before. It was a brief, leisurely outing, with a small picnic where Sabrina shared apples with their mounts, laughing big and full of delight at the sweep of their lips across her fingers and the happiness she felt in this place and time with Mosi.

CHAPTER 12

Late the next morning, Serge ushered Sabrina into his rooms where Gin already sat at his table, casually flipping through one of the many books stacked there. In fact, the table looked more like it should belong to Gin or Sabrina, groaning under the weight of so many volumes. Not that Serge was unintelligent, he just wasn't bookish. Or so Sabrina always thought.

She waved at a smiling Gin and sat herself down, noticing the number of books on runes and sigils before her. From the looks of it, Sabrina figured she'd have a lot more studying to do in the near future, and that thought sent a fissure of excitement down her spine. She did love a good book, as well as a solid research project. Both left her with a nerdy giddiness.

"Thank you both for coming," Serge said, as he took a seat at the head of the table. "I wish to discuss a possibility. You're each uniquely positioned to get to the bottom of a magical theory I've been mulling over in the back of my mind lately."

Sabrina was surprised to be included in this. She thought it was another lesson, or a discussion of future lessons, not an all-out theoretical debate. She felt a little unprepared to be lumped in with the likes of Gin in such a situation. Both were technically Scholars, yes, but Gin had many years under their belt — an entire Fae lifetime stretching centuries in fact. Sabrina didn't put herself in the same category.

"We've pondered, for weeks at this point, how to figure out who the traitor is amongst us, yes? We know a likely location but have yet to form a way to pin down who the person is exactly, so we must remain wary of everyone while also constantly being on guard against another attack on Nin or Sabrina."

"Um, my attack wasn't instigated by the traitor. It was direct from Comus," Sabrina interjected at that point.

"What?" Gin whispered in astonishment. Serge yelled a much different human expletive.

"Yeah. Mo and Nin learned about it, like two days ago. The traitor wasn't even supposed to attack Nin, at least according to my attacker. That one apparently upset Comus."

"Why are we just now learning about this?" Serge seethed.

Sabrina put her hands up. "Don't look at me. I already had words about keeping it from me with both your siblings. Take it up with them."

"If you are a specific target for Comus," Gin said with a mournful shake of their head, "this is very disturbing news indeed."

"Yeah, I know. It's not fun times. I had the broken ribs and knife wound to prove it, so I don't need the reminder." Turning to Serge, she said, "Does this change what you were going to discuss with us?"

"No," he bit out, "just makes me angry. It means we have two worries to contend with because I thought the traitor was doing Comus' bidding. Now…" Serge trailed off for a moment, rolling the new information around in his head before snapping back to the conversation. "It doesn't matter, at least not in reference to what we'll discuss today. We still must find the traitor, the one who attempted to assassinate Nin. They're a threat whether connected to Comus or not."

Sabrina agreed, as did Gin, and Serge continued, "I've been mulling over the possibility of using Sabrina's writing magics. Is it possible to find or develop a spell Sabrina could use on an official document, one that would, by its nature, be passed around The Council?"

Gin looked thoughtful for a moment and replied, "In theory, it may well be possible. I have never heard of such a spell. There are, of course, many ways to bespell a particular object for a general purpose, such as causing a reaction in or amplifying the power of any Fae who touched or read the object. As you well know, we have our share of cursed objects and objects of power. Crafting a spell that would cause a specific reaction in only one Fae based on a hidden fact about that Fae would be far more complicated."

Sabrina interjected, "If it's that complicated, that specialized, there's no guarantee I could pull it off."

Gin gave her an encouraging grin. "You would rise to the challenge. You already perform well above expectations. I have no doubt in you, Sabrina. I have doubts about being able to develop such a spell overall."

"We could try, yes? With your knowledge of magical theory, my understanding of word magics, and Sabrina's affinity, is it a possibility?" Serge pressed.

"Anything is a possibility," Gin said, "with the proper foundations and precedence from which to work. It is a difficult puzzle to think through, one that may be unsolvable in an appropriate timeframe, but the answer to all puzzles come out eventually."

"Yeah," Serge muttered, half to himself, "the time constraints are important. We cannot take years to work through this."

"Aren't other investigations going on?" Sabrina asked.

Gin answered, "Sergius is finessing where he can in conversations, and Mosi is having guards report on all activities based in and around The Council and its members."

"Then, if you say we can try it, that there's a chance, why not take it? The other tactics won't be abandoned. This one would just be added."

"An excellent point, Rina," Serge agreed, jumping to his feet to pace in excitement. The use of her new nickname made Sabrina beam with happiness.

Gin, looking between Serge and her for a moment, added a happy grin of their own. "Rina," they called, reaching across the table to pat the hand Sabrina placed on top of a short stack of books. "It suits."

Serge paced while talking, laying out what he knew of past word magics using similar tactics. Gin added information where they could fill in blanks or more fully explain the theory behind such a spell. In the end, they clearly mapped out research responsibilities, a solid first step in Sabrina's opinion. Gin would dig deep into the archive, seeing if they could find any reference to similar spells. Serge continued his other spy-like duties while also researching in his word magics collection, which was apparently vast. Another pleasant surprise for Sabrina, as she loved to find others who collected books. Her part entailed keeping up with her training, but escalating her study and practice of writing magics, moving on to the practice of committing spells to paper and not just tracing them in the air. It would be hard work for a long shot, but it gave Sabrina a sense of being proactive. She'd been doing a lot of learning in the name of defense. She was happy to start playing offense in some way.

Jane breezed in the room with a cart from The Palace Kitchens loaded with tea and cookies and miniature sandwiches soon after Serge, Sabrina, and Gin transferred the books to another part of Serge's suite. She stopped to flirt with the guards on the door, tittering in her usual way, fanning herself while offering them sweets from her cart, before focusing on the three friends standing around the table.

"Oh, Gin. I didn't know you'd be here," she
called in surprise, "but I am, as always, delighted to
see you." She gave a quick curtsey and beamed. "As
well as Sergius and Sabrina, of course."

"Yes, lovely Jane. It is a pleasure to host
you this afternoon," Serge drawled in his usual way,
slinking forward to scoop up Jane's hand and kiss it
slowly while eyeing her. She giggled, fluttering her
other hand to her mouth to discreetly stifle those
dainty sounds. It was odd to watch, like a play where
you knew some part of it was natural to the two Fae,
but also there was power in playing up in such a way.
Flirtation was a part of who Serge was. It was also a
calculation for him. Sabrina knew little of Jane, but
guessed her behavior was similar—part affectation,
part natural inclination.

"Oh, Serge. You are too much at times," she
said, blushing prettily and playfully swatting at him
with her ever-present fan dangling from a ribbon
secured tightly to her wrist. She strolled to the table,
acknowledging Gin's quick bow, before taking
Sabrina's hand in her own. "Sabrina the Scholar, we
have had little opportunity to socialize outside more
formal Court functions and Council endeavors. I have
been truly remiss in this. You are a fierce human, and
I do hope our time together this afternoon presents
new dynamics for our relationship."

"Uh, yeah. Sure. It's always nice to have a
friend," Sabrina answered a bit awkwardly.

"So very true!" Jane exclaimed, spinning
around in her ruby brocade gown, clapping her hands
and giving a high, short squeal of joy. "It is a lovely
time to plan a celebration. Now, I took the liberty of
having tea and a few snacks made for our chat. I do

love a good tea service, and if we are to forge ahead with plans, food and drink are in order."

"It is more than okay, dear Jane. You are all kindness and care. I should be ashamed as your host, but, sadly, I rarely feel shame." Serge smirked at his guest as pushed the tea cart closer to the table. "I'll allow you to be the de facto hostess in my suite, if you please."

"Oh, you," Jane laughed, "I am more than happy to oblige." All but Jane took their seats as she passed out cups and saucers and small plates. She poured a potent tea and placed delicate cookies and tiny crustless sandwiches on each plate.

"I have not had this spiced tea blend in many years," Gin said, bending over to smell the strong brew. "It has an unforgettable odor, one that makes me think of falling leaves and chilly air."

"It is not traditional in spring or summer, I know," Jane replied. "Yet it is a favorite of mine all year. The spices ensnare my senses."

Sabrina and Serge both muttered in agreement and drank. For her part, Sabrina took only small sips. She loved coffee and tea but couldn't drink when it was too hot. Her mouth somehow never developed a resistance to the heat, so she always needed a bit of a cooling period before diving into any steamy beverage.

Jane sat at her empty place, doctored her own tea, and nibbled at a cookie. "I do so much appreciate the time you have taken to meet me today. I have such plans for our Queen, but I want to engage you first."

"Completely understandable, Councilwoman. We are happy to help in your preparations," Serge added kindly. Sabrina wasn't exactly happy. She'd never been one for planning big events. But she wasn't about to correct him. That would be plain rude.

"Summer solstice is one of my favorite holidays," Gin added, always full of kindness and encouragement when they felt it was warranted.

Jane smiled broadly and quickly began outlining a plan that involved an outdoor festival, an open banquet, and a late-night ball for courtiers and leaders. It all sounded fine to Sabrina, who politely nodded and added soft exclamations and affirming noises when she felt necessary. For the most part, though, she stayed out of it, not knowing much about the politics, culture, or the specific traditions of this holiday in Fae.

After several minutes, she was able to take larger pulls of tea, and it reminded her of pumpkin spice in the human realm, that lovely and comforting blend of cinnamon, nutmeg, ginger, clove, and allspice. Although this version was heavier in clove and ginger, which overpowered most of the other tastes and smells. She set the cup down and watched, in an odd, detached way, her own handshake slightly. It was a wobble of her fingers, like they were too weak to grip. She noticed then her other senses were off, sounds more muffled and her eyes slow to turn and take in the rest of the room. They did, however, and spied both Serge and Gin slumped slightly in their chairs. Serge appeared to be struggling, attempting to get up out of his seat but unable to do so. A loud thump brought her roaming eyes to the Fae guards at the door who were laid out in a heap on the floor.

Jane shushed Serge and held him still with a hand on his chest until his struggle ended. She turned to Sabrina, who heard the words Jane spoke as if listening from the bottom of a well. "I am lucky you drink so slowly, human, or you would have succumbed long before Sergius and Borjigin. I am favored on this day."

With that rolling in her mind, Sabrina gave a few slow blinks, attempting to correct the haze falling over her view, until everything faded to black.

CHAPTER 13

Sabrina woke to the smell of burning wood and dried flowers. Lavender and rose and something else more cloying. She opened her eyes and saw purple everywhere. Grayish purple walls bled into a deep purple carpet crowned with mauve wing-backed chairs and a large orchid-colored tufted couch. On that couch, facing away from Sabrina while staring hazily at a large, roaring fireplace, Jane sat, slowly swaying her crossed ankles. Sabrina's head whipped to the right when she heard muffled noises and saw both Serge and Gin beside her. They sat in tall wooden chairs, bound by chains and gagged with cloth. Their eyes bulged and communicated to her as best they could without words. That was when Sabrina's head cleared fully and she felt the rough scrape of rope fiber against her wrists and ankles, and the soft whisper of fabric tied tightly around her face.

Her movements caught Jane's attention. The Fae pulled up straight and clapped her hands in delight. "Oh, good. You're awake. I did not want to harm you, but you took so long to come out of your stupor, I was afraid I had given you too much potion." She faked a pout then added, "I did not factor in how it may affect a human differently."

Sabrina struggled in her bonds, and cursed Jane with her mind and her words, but little came out beyond muffled, unintelligible screams. She went on for a minute, but stopped abruptly, knowing there was little use in fighting with her strength at the moment. It would do little to help them.

"Now you have calmed a bit," Jane called as she reached across the space between them, pausing before she touched the gag at Sabrina's mouth, "I would like to have a civil discussion. I understand that is hard for you, as a human, but I would appreciate your general cooperation."

When Jane pulled the cloth down to hang around Sabrina's neck, she couldn't hold back her retort, "Better human than a traitor, you screaming bitch."

Jane pulled back, hand to her throat in mock offense. "Well, I never. There is no cause for such words, human."

Sabrina didn't respond, choosing to stare daggers at her captor with a quiet rage as she ever-so-slowly twisted her wrists in the ropes, looking for weakness. Her bounds were so tight her fingers tingled, so tight they smashed her hands together in a way that didn't leave any room for her to trace runes in the air.

"I would say you hurt my feelings with such an outburst," Jane laughed, "but, gladly, I do not care what any human thinks of me, much less a lowly bonded thing who's a lapdog to the pretender on The Fae Throne."

Sabrina barked a laugh at that. "Pretender. Oh, please. You and I both know Nin is the only one who should be there. Let me guess, you think it should be you, with your tittering and your fanning and your sickly fawning. Groveling gets you nowhere, babe. Don't you know that?"

"Groveling got me a seat on The Fae Council decades earlier than I would otherwise. It endeared me to the Mae Queen, although I believe she had her suspicions. Suspicions well founded when I slipped her a much different draught decades ago. It gave me means and opportunity to ensnare you."

"If you think you were trusted by us, you're mistaken," Sabrina spat. "You were on the list of traitors under close watch."

"Not watched closely enough to prevent your capture, to cause Sergius or Gin to question my motives in bringing refreshments for you. You must admit, it was all too easy for the flirty and groveling Jane to swoop in and do what she wished, right under the noses of all those big, powerful Fae. My affinity for alchemy is neither flashy or a show of strength, but more than enough to create and conceal effect concoctions when needed."

Sabrina couldn't respond. Jane was right, in this at least. They should have been far more wary of her. They weren't and now they paid that price.

Jane offered a saccharine grin, knowing what Sabrina's silence meant. She looked from Sabrina to Serge and Gin, making sure all eyes were fixed on her. From the corners of her own vision,

Sabrina could see the other Fae. Gin sat rigid and straight, calm even in this moment. Serge lounged, looking unconcerned as metal fastened his body to the hard chair.

However, both their eyes were straining, looked in pain, and Sabrina blurted out "Steel?" in shock.

"Why of course, silly. If one is to keep a Fae in line, one needs steel on hand. As I said before, I was not expecting Borjigin in our little meeting. I thought it was to be Sergius and yourself. You were to have the second chain. In light of events, an unnecessary precaution. Rope does fine for the likes of you."

Her heart hurt for her friends, but she focused narrowed eyes on Jane, wanting as much information as possible from her as she worked to formulate an escape plan in the back of her mind. It was feasible, if she played it right. Jane didn't know she had magic, or at least, she didn't appear to know. She was ecstatic now about the decision to keep that tidbit a secret. It seemed to have worked, a handy card up her sleeve. She figured if she could repel and stun Jane, get Gin and Serge free quickly enough, they could team up and take her out. No problem. Sabrina needed to be free, or a bit freer, in order to do all that quickly and protect herself if Jane came back at her before Gin and Serge were prepared to help.

"Does Gin mess up things for you?" Sabrina asked, trying to buy herself time, hoping Jane didn't know how cliche it was to hear a villain lay out their plans just so the hero could escape.

"Not at all. An extra boon in fact. Comus will be more than pleased," she crowed.

The name made Sabrina's blood freeze. "Comus?" she said on a hush.

"Yes. Of course. Who else would I do all this for?" she said, gesturing toward the tied trio.

"We thought the traitor wasn't working for Comus. We heard he was angry about the assassination attempt at the coronation ball," Sabrina offered, hoping for more time to wiggle her hands loose and get them out of here.

"He may have been slightly annoyed," Jane replied with a shrug, obviously downplaying the situation. "He knew my reasons, my feelings."

"Feelings?" Sabrina asked, latching on to anything to keep Jane talking. She hit on the right note because the Fae huffed and let a long tirade fly.

"Yes," she hissed, folding her arms in a childish pout. "My feelings for Comus are true and have lasted centuries, though he thought it best to keep our love a secret until our positions were more assured. Then an upstart comes along, favored by the Queen. I know why he lied to her. Why he used her to gain power. However, he never loved her, not really. He never said he would make her Consort, give her the title and power of such a position. Which is for the best, as she never truly loved him. Not like I did. Like I still do! I have sacrificed years, loving in secret, surviving on stolen moments and quick meetings in the shadows. At the first opportunity, Nin left him and Fae. She deserves neither The Crown nor Comus' affection. She's a stain on our land, a Noble Fae who loves all those beneath us — human and Lesser Fae alike. She is an abomination, unworthy of her power or position."

Sabrina couldn't help herself. Her hands were slightly loosened, and she needed more time, but any dig at Nin made her blood boil. "If anyone's being used in this situation, it's you. From what I've heard, he offered Nin even more than some low title of Consort. I heard he wished her to rule by his side. You've been deceived by a man for centuries, Jane. It'd make me sad for you and all your pathetic baggage if you weren't so damn nasty. You're not fit to walk in Nin's shadow, let alone put yourself above her light."

"Bah!" Jane said, now fuming and starting to pace the small space between her couch and the trio tied to her chairs. "You know not of what you speak. How could you? You are a human, feeding only on your base desires, not realizing the higher callings of true love and loyalty."

"I know if someone is deserving of love and loyalty, they will not misuse you or ask you to do immoral things in their name," she spat back.

"I happily do my Comus' bidding," Jane retorted, "and smile all the while. He is all that is mighty and powerful in Fae. A true leader, not afraid to put the realm on the path to recapture our greatness and glory."

Sabrina let Jane carry on like that, not interrupting all the talk. It sounded familiar to her. Humans spouted these ideas whenever they followed a leader they knew was bad for most but good for them, spinning over and over again a tale of nostalgia for a past that was happy and wholesome only if you squint hard and forgot about the blatant mistreatment and horror of the lives many lived.

She fiddled with her ropes, turning her wrists and twisting as best she could, using Jane's distraction in her diatribe to push herself harder. She'd wiggled enough that her left hand was able to slide up a fraction, giving the fingers on her right hand enough room and range of motion to do some writing.

She hid her glee, running over the spells she knew that might break her bonds completely, when Jane's head cocked as if she heard her name called from a distance. A sinister smile spread across her face and she whispered, "Comus. He comes."

"What?" Sabrina said in a panic. Comus was like the bogeyman to her, but very much real. She never met the Fae, never wanted to, only wished a bloody and painful death on him for all he did to her Nin.

"Yes, human. He comes. Just. For. You."

Gin and Serge were now wide-eyed and looking confused. Jane let out a laugh and in a flash was inches from Gin's questioning face. "I have you to thank for this, Gin. As you well know, we're in my cottage in The Falls, a place mostly empty except for the sadly mistreated Michel. You never erased your chalk door in The Palace, the one that led right to your own home, the secret location I could never give out because of your wards and traps and magical conditions. You gave me an opening, however, and I grasped it. I only had to double-back, lead Comus through the door, to get past all your precautions and protections. Comus may well thank you for your sloppiness, but I doubt he will be so magnanimous toward the likes of you." She spit the last line, her mask slipping, rage and hate radiating in the twist of her lips, the rapid pace of her breath, the squint of her eyes.

Sabrina wished for more time, running scenarios and spells through her mind at a breakneck pace as Jane pulled back from them, placing herself in a deep curtsey beside her couch. She heard the door open, felt heavy but sure footsteps, and watched as a Fae it what looked like a Greek god costume came into her line of sight. Serge and Gin seethed at her side, but she stared, open-mouthed, at this thing in front of her as he offered his hand to Jane. Jane took it, showering kisses and muttering praise as he looked down on her with a cold disregard Jane was obviously, somehow, blind to in her fervor. After a beat, he cut hard eyes Sabrina's way, and she felt fear heavy in her chest as her magic sang a warning in her head.

CHAPTER 14

Comus strolled forward, condescension dripping from his haughty face. If she could get past who he was, what he was, Sabrina might say he was handsome: all blond curls and svelte, athletic body. She couldn't, though. Hate and fear shook her core in equal measure, and she sucked in rapid breaths when he reached out to snatch her chin between his hard fingers.

"You are the human Nin bonded?" he asked, a clear incredulous note in his voice. He scraped eyes across her body, pausing at the swell and heave of her breasts as she breathed deep and hard to keep control of her emotions and her magics, pushing those down as far as she could, hoping like hell he didn't somehow feel it all over her skin. He roughly turned her face side to side, studying her contours. Bending down, he gave a quick audible sniff, and with his head so close to her own, Sabrina reared back on instinct, trying to get as much distance from him as she could. She knew he read the fear and hate on her, and the grin on his face told Sabrina he liked seeing it.

He shrugged, wiping his hand on his clothes as if her skin sullied him somehow. "I must admit, I see no reason why. You are plain, ordinary, too fleshy and round for my taste in most areas. How any Fae can stand your smell I cannot fathom. And yet," he breathed again and cut eyes back to her, "I smell so many Fae on you. Serge is here, that makes sense. As does Nin. I have known for quite some time she erroneously bonded herself to you. There's another scent now, fresh and strong. Mosi. Yes, it seems Mosi has enjoyed this human body recently. That is simply delightful! I wished you to be a lesson to Nin, but it seems you have wound your way through her entire family."

In a blink, he was there, taking up Sabrina's entire field of vision, blue eyes icy on her as he leaned deep into her. "I will lay your broken body at their feet before I kill your lover and take Princess Nin as my own yet again."

"Queen," she said, simply and truly, and Comus backhanded her so hard she toppled over, slamming onto the floor. Pulsing black spots twinkled in her sight for a moment, the stun from the blow a screech in her ears right before the pulse and throb of pain spread across the left side of her face. Her magic screamed to respond, defend, but she pushed it down again. Knowing she would not be able to contain it, she still attempted to wait, especially with Comus now present. All she had on her side at the moment were a few spells and surprise. She needed to be strategic and wait for the best moment, the one that would give the three of them a real chance to get out of this mess whole.

"Insolent and insubordinate, as most humans," Comus said, spitting on her from above. "Stay," he commanded, like she was a dog.

Turning to the commotion at her side, he looked over the struggling Gin and Serge. From her position on the floor, Sabrina saw they fought harder against their binds. Gin looked down at her with deep concern in their eyes. Serge rocked hard in his seat, straining and twisting, doing all he could in an attempt to free himself and confront Comus, who gave him a mocking wave before turning on Jane.

"Jane, what were your instructions?" he asked, his voice a cold and quiet wind.

Jane cowered, knowing full well she did not do as he asked. "I know I was only to bring Sergius and the human, my love, but Borjigin was also in attendance. There was no way to steal away with only the two."

"No way you and your feeble mind could devise," Comus bit out. "You displease me once again. First, with that ill-advised attempt on Princess Nin's life. Now, this. Are more lashes in order?"

"No, my love. Your Grace. Please. I swear there was no other way." Jane sounded truly frightened to Sabrina's ears, and she could believe it. The pain she felt as she lay on the floor told her Comus was not above doing serious damage when he wasn't happy.

Comus, ramrod straight, stared with unwavering focus at his minion, who once again dipped into a curtsey, this one so low she was practically sitting on the floor. "Oh, do get up," he said, exasperated. "You will be punished for this, but not now. Get the human off the floor. I will not touch it again. In fact, place her facing the others."

Jane, in haste, moved some of her furnishings to make room for Sabrina, jostling her into position easily once she cleared space. She stared, blinking hard, at the bound and gagged Gin and Serge, and tried to communicate with her eyes that she was fine. Theirs reflected worry and anger back but that was all she could decipher.

Comus stepped up to the small triangle of hostages, grabbing their attention but not moving to place himself between them. "It is so much better with an uninterrupted view."

Then, Sabrina felt pain. It lasted no more than ten seconds, but if she were pushed to describe it, she would say it was like being skinned alive slowly. There was a burning scrape, piercing flashes. Above all it was deep and hot and enough to make her scream and black out.

When she came to, her head hanging down, she heard the now-familiar sound of chains rattling in frustrated anger. "Now, now, you two. Do not overexert yourself for no reason. There is nothing you can do for this thing."

Sabrina raised her head, turning her eyes to Comus, and cracked a smile. The pain faded as quickly as it came and there were no lasting effects. And, it seems, her magic didn't fly out all willy-nilly. If she could get through that, she could do it. She could hide her magic even from Comus and help them get out of there if they got the chance.

"Why do you smile so, human?" Comus asked, looking at her like she was an oddity in a curiosity shop.

"Because you're nothing but a little pissant throwing a fit because someone's better than you," she said with a cracked laugh. It wasn't the best insult in the world, but it would do.

His face went hard, his wand turned on her again, and he whispered "ISSPIRN". This time, the effect crept up on her. The burn started at her toes, slowly migrating up her body, intensifying as it went along, until tears were streaming down her face openly and she cried out in pain. The scorching heat crept up to her chest and then, as suddenly as it appeared, it stopped.

"What does it feel like to burn?" Comus asked, dipping down into her face once again. "It is a tactic you humans are ever so fond of. I thought you might find some comfort in it." Turning back away from her and ignoring the rattle of chains, Comus clasped his hands behind his back and stood firm. "You now have a taste of my magics. There is much more I can show you. I assure you of this. To avoid pain, to bring yourself a quick and merciful death, I expect obedience. Acquiescence. Such civility may be far beyond your human understanding, but you have lived in Fae for a number of weeks at this point and have seen how truly righteous beings exist. I expect an attempt at emulation at the very least." With a wink, he added, "However, I did enjoy your screams. Next, I will draw blood, so behavior or error is a boon for me, regardless."

"Kiss my ass," she spat out in response.

Comus muttered something she couldn't hear and with a flick of the wand a razor-thin slice appeared across the expanse of chest exposed in her afternoon dress. It welled, dripping quickly and freely down her body. Serge and Gin released muffled screams and Sabrina hissed in her breath at the pain that didn't relent this time, but she gritted her teeth and pushed through, offering a grimace of a smile in return.

"You bare your teeth like an animal, and you will be treated as one," Comus quipped, turning to face the two Fae opposite her. "Now, Borjigin, it has been an exceedingly long time since our last meeting. Too long in fact. I was so very sad to see you chose poorly when I rose to power. An intelligent, articulate Fae such as yourself should choose the right path, follow the true leader, the one who will lead Fae into prosperity."

Gin stared motionless, no longer trying to free themselves or speak. Comus, however, yanked their gag down. When they continued to sit still and silent, Comus lashed out yet again with his wand. Sabrina couldn't tell exactly what Comus did to cause the pain, but she could see the agony written clearly in the twist of Gin's lips. When they went limp after a few moments, they looked at Comus with pure hate, a look that was odd on Gin but more than fitting for the recipient. "I do follow the rightful ruler, the true leader of Fae: Queen Nin."

"Pity you are not more pliable now, Borjigin. I would have you on my side when I take Nin again. You would be a comfort for her." Pausing to study Gin with a tilt of his head, he finally gave a slow smile and finished with "I can still keep you with her, chained and weak if needs be."

Comus dismissed Gin, turning away to focus on Serge, who bucked and twisted in his chains, glimpses of raw and damaged skin flashing as he moved. "You were always half feral, Sergius, spending far too much time with humans, but even you should know to calm yourself when it is necessary."

Serge's body stopped struggling, but the jerking rise and fall of his chest and the anger falling off of him in waves made it seem like he still moved. Comus ignored the animosity and continued to talk at him. "Now, I cannot give you the same guarantees I give Gin. You are far too tricksy, my friend. Your magic is too similar to my own, which means I know your power. I witnessed it myself in The Royal Chambers. No, too much compulsion power, indeed. That is not to say you are my match." Comus let out a hard laugh at that before continuing. "You could never best me. It is ridiculous to even think so."

"Then release him," Sabrina said on a rasp. "Unchain him and remove his gag. Duel or whatever it is y'all do with magic. Prove it."

Comus turned to her, a savage light in his eyes. "I have nothing to prove, human. He is already bested."

With that, Comus moved at top speed toward Serge, taking his head in his hands from behind. Staring right into Sabrina's eyes, he twisted, breaking Serge's neck with a sickening crack. Sabrina and Gin both screamed, their voices rising together in horror and pain. Comus smiled and shoved Serge to the ground, chair and all, so that he landed facing Sabrina, his golden-brown eyes open but vacant. Dead.

CHAPTER 15

Sabrina discovered a handy result from all the magical mental practice she performed as she stared into Serge's dead eyes. She actively thought about the situation, knew, logically, what was happening and what she needed to do to survive. She also recognized another part of her brain was in shock. It was odd, a small, coldly logical section of her butting into the silent buzz of blankness threatening to envelope and take control. She felt, she knew, she considered on a tiny level, but a part of her brain existed in a haze, snared only by the lifeless look in those lovely eyes, eyes she was so used to seeing in laughter.

She only partially registered Gin's sobs and Comus' words as he moved away from the body. "It was always the plan — to break Nin's spirit a bit more with the death of her brother. Gin's addition only means Nin has more to lose at my hands yet again. However, I do not wish to listen to more wailing. Jane, take away the body so we may properly present this present to Nin soon. Make them cease this incessant noise while you do." Comus noticed something on his toga and lifted the fabric up to his nose, reeling back at whatever he smelt. "I have human blood on me. That will not do. Jane, do as I ask. I will return once I am free of this…contamination."

Comus floated out of Jane's home, no trace of the horror he left in his wake in her face or step. Gin's cries made no more sound, but tears rolled down their face as they looked at their cousin. Sabrina shook her head, her logical self attempting to use physical movement to dissipate the shock and trauma of what she witnessed, forcing her mind to focus solely on planning and survival.

Jane stood above Serge, staring down and heaving out a sigh. "A pity, this. A beautiful Noble Fae turning against his own interests, forced to face consequences. Pitiful, but ultimately fair, as the will of Comus ever is."

She bent down to scoop up Serge and something in Sabrina snapped. It made little sense that this was what broke open the gate and not the act itself. Maybe the murder was too quick, too surprising. Whatever the reason, Jane touching Serge made Sabrina turn into a wild, feral thing. Or, more aptly, made her magic run wild, and Sabrina rode the wave of those magics like a vengeful goddess bringing damnation down on her enemies.

The only warning Jane had was the audible snap of the ropes on Sabrina's wrists, body, and ankles. She crackled with energy, the sizzle that broke her bonds, but she lunged with her body, taking an off-guard Jane hard to the floor. She reared up, relying more on her physical instincts than her magic, and started pounding into Jane's face and body with her fists. Her magic did join in, giving force and power to her blows, protecting her while searing into Jane, who feebly batted at the blows for long moments.

She did, however, get over her surprise, and bucked Sabrina off her, crawling away and jumping to her feet with Fae speed. She pounced, knocking Sabrina into the soft couch and doing little damage. She wrapped a delicate-looking hand around Sabrina's neck and squeezed, clamping like a vise on her fragile human neck. Her magic still raged, however, and muscle memory was kicking in. Sabrina knew how to fight, how to get out of a hold, and she used that knowledge to dislodge and push away Jane before shouting "KALLI," forcing the scrambling Fae back against the sickly gray-purple walls of her cottage.

Unlucky for Jane, she had a clump of blood purple tulips in a large standing pot along that wall. Sabrina's magic cried forward, pushing the leaves and stalks and stems to grow and unfurl to an abnormal degree, curling them up and around Jane as the Fae looked on in horror.

"It can't be," she whispered.

Sabrina ignored her words, letting the magic flow, conscious of her own intention, the direction of her thoughts. A better person may have pulled back then, or at least tried to pull back. Sabrina didn't, and the thick leaves engulfed Jane's face, pushed into her open and screaming mouth, and seconds later, burst from her throat, ripping her windpipe from the inside out. There were gurgles, whistles, until Jane finally slumped down, dead but floating within a riot of tulips pinned against her wall.

Sabrina stared at Jane's body, shock once again taking over, but she heard Gin calling her in the back of her mind. She watched the blood stain Jane's dress, dripping down to the floor, and she was oddly happy the gore wasn't on Serge's body, that Nin and Mo and Inanna would not see him ripped open like this at least.

"Sabrina!" Gin screamed, their voice harsh like they'd been screaming for a while. It brought her out of her stupor, and she spun away, now sick at the sight of what she and her magic had done.

She rushed to Gin's side, using a rune to slice through the steel chains binding her friend. She threw them off and Gin fell forward on their knees, tears streaming, and reached for their cousin. They wept, pulling Serge toward them, grasping at him, calling his name. It was enough to make Sabrina's heart break all over again.

She rallied after a moment, pushing her own emotions and shock and trauma aside to help Gin recover. "Gin. Gin. I'm sorry. I'm so damn sorry. But we can't stay here. We have to go. We have to go NOW."

She urged them, pulling on their robes as they cried, until her voice and arms somehow broke through. Looking up, a mask of grief and loss, Gin nodded and held onto Sabrina's hand as she pushed them both up off the floor.

"We have to go, Gin. But you're the only one who knows how we can do it. We're in The Falls, remember? How do we get out, quick? How do we get back to The Palace from here?"

Gin nodded absently and Sabrina thought for a beat she would need to repeat herself, maybe multiple times, to get through their grief and pain, but they sucked in a hard breath, and on the exhale, said, "The cable car is too far. The Meeting House won't let us in without another leader. We don't know who we can trust here or who even is left. We must go to my cottage. Even if the door is no longer there, I am most familiar with the space. I can more easily cast a transport spell there."

"Right. Okay. Solid plan. Let's do it."

Gin paused, staring down with fresh tears at Serge. "Let us take him to his family," they whispered, bending down to mutter a few words and snap the chains still tied around his body.

Sabrina was about to tell him they didn't have time, couldn't carry him themselves, when Gin easily hoisted Serge up over their shoulders. In the chaos she again forgot they had such strength.

"We gotta motor," she muttered, turning away to find the door.

Sabrina took three steps forward and felt a whoosh of air. It was Gin, flying backward, dropping Serge as they spun straight up in the air. She heard something whistle past at speed before she saw the large metal choker crash around Gin's neck and heard his gurgle of pain and surprise. She had no time to react because her body was pulled, up, up, up too. It felt like a rope was tied around her middle, pulling her this way and that, completely out of her control. Her magic screamed and heated, word and earth, but she was held fast, the invisible rope winding up and down her body until she was immobile.

Comus stepped through the door once again, his wand aloft, his eyes calculating. He ignored both

Gin and Sabrina as he took in the scene around him. Rage infused his face when he noticed Jane in death. He stormed over, inspecting her body closely, clearly unconcerned about her death. He sniffed and poked without a second glance at Jane's face. He cared nothing that she was dead. He, however, seethed out, "How is this possible?"

He whipped around, twisting the wand and causing some pain in Gin, enough to make them scream out. "How? How? You have no earth magics. The only living Fae with earth magics is Nin. She is mine. They were to be mine. The chair was…" He stopped abruptly and rushed to Sabrina, who hovered closer to the ground so he could once again tightly grip her face in his gasping hands.

He smelled her again, this time more deeply, and his blue eyes blazed when he said, "You have magics. Not only that," he breathed deep again, "you have Nin's magics. From the chair, correct? Jane mentioned her human was the one to free her through some silly potion. I never imagined it possible, magic transferred to a non-magical human. Yet here you are, reeking of your kind and Nin's powers. It's disgusting."

Gin was quietly testing the choker around his neck when Comus spun again, demanding answers. "How can this be?"

Her friend paused before coldly saying, "The chair was your invention. Your plan. How do you not know?"

Comus screamed in rage, flicking his wand so both Sabrina and Gin were thrown to the ground. "Those magics were to be mine! I was to rule, with earth and word magics, more powerful than any before me. Nin at my side."

Gin heaved out a mirthless laugh and said, "The same combination Sabrina actually has."

Comus flung her back up, slinging her around until she faced him again. "Earth. And. Word. Magics."

Sabrina thought they were both surely dead. Part of her wanted to be, if she were honest with herself. A small part, the piece of her that wished to feel no more physical or emotional pain. If she were to die, Sabrina figured she'd be herself until the end, and quoted Milton at him in response. Even though it wasn't a line from the play that kicked all of this off, *Paradise Lost* felt far more fitting in the moment. "*'Abashed the Devil stood, And felt how awful goodness is.'*"

She smiled after his answering smack and roar, feeling blood leak down from a split lip, thinking she must look like a terrible spirit here, a crazed human smiling through blood in the hands of a raging Fae. "I'd say you hit like a girl, but that's an insult to girls in both realms," she quipped even through the pain.

Another scream tore from Comus as he turned away from her in anger and frustration, muttering about research and spells and whatnot. He pulled up close again, grinning maniacally, and vowed, "I'll make you scream as I rip the magic right out of your filthy human body, shred you to pieces, and laugh all the while."

"Try it, dick," she answered, and expected another slap to come, this one hopefully bringing unconsciousness with it, but before it could, Comus disappeared from her view. Her eyes followed him down, saw him lose a grip on his wand, watched the object go flying as she herself slammed into the floor, its magical hold on her body broken so she no longer defied gravity. She caught only a glimpse of the rest, but her heart swelled to see a thick vine wrapped up Comus' leg, crawling further up his body as he was pulled out the front door.

CHAPTER 16

Sabrina scrambled to her feet despite all the aches and pains, thanks in large part to Gin's assistance. They bolted for the door, and Sabrina felt as if she could breathe again when she viewed the sight before her. There, in a small meadow in front of Jane's cottage, stood Nin, Mosi, and an entire platoon of heavily armed Palace guards.

Mo, clasping eyes on Sabrina not only standing but moving unaided toward him, visibly jolted, relief clear across his face. However, he paused to say something to a close guard, who then walked quickly past Sabrina and Gin and into Jane's cottage. He looked for Serge, and it was like a knife wound to the chest, seeing that concern and knowing what he would soon find.

To give herself a momentary reprieve from the grief rushing like a train right for her, about to smash into the people she loved, she looked toward

Nin, who was paler than normal but rigid and upright.
Regal, even, and staring with a curled lip at a vine-
wrapped Comus suspended five feet in front of her.
He looked like Sabrina felt moments before, wrapped
foot to throat in large, creeping vines, but these
twisted and tightened, constraining and crushing at
the same time. It didn't stop his anger or
condescension, however. That was still on full
display.

"Princess Nin," he hissed.

"Queen Nin," she snapped back. "You know
this, Comus. It is time to accept the new order."

"Oh, but you look like my Princess still.
Here and in sleep." He gave a mocking laugh and
said, "All the so-called scholars at your disposal, the
keen political and strategic minds of your family, and
none checked for a passage between The Royal
Chambers and The Consort Chambers? I watched
you sleep more than once, but hearing of the blood
you shed in anger, I had to reach out to my Nin, offer
a gift, let my Lady know I was still with her in fact as
well as in spirit."

Mo cursed at this tirade. Nin took it in
stride, waving away the claim. "A mystery at one
time, yet it matters not now. Does not change our
current reality. I am Queen and you are defeated,"
she said calmly, truthfully.

"I am the rightful monarch. I am the one to
lead Fae into a new age of prosperity and
righteousness," he called, sounding more and more
demented and shrill with each word, his voice
becoming almost a whine.

Mo laughed, but it was a harsh, mirthless
sound. "Comus, you are clearly defeated. You should
spend your time begging for your Queen's mercy

rather than spouting lies once again. I do not think she will grant it, but your time would be better spent trying."

Mo would say this, something logical and thoughtful. Because he wasn't Comus, wasn't a man who would use his last breath to degrade or lash out. Sabrina knew what he was and remained on edge.

Comus gave a sickening smile at those words and replied, "Even in the face of death I will speak my truth, but I do not feel I face death today. Not from my Nin."

"I am not your Nin," she called, pulling herself even straighter, suddenly looking taller than five feet. She somehow towered, looking every bit the Queen to Sabrina, and seeing her friend in her abuser's face made tears well in her eyes.

Comus smirked and cooed in a sweet tone, "Oh, but you are, my Lady. You are mine and I am yours, always. No matter what happens today, I am inside you. A part of you forever."

Nin swallowed hard but was otherwise untouched by his words. She stalked closer to the trussed-up man, a mix of rage and self-awareness in her eyes. "That may well be, but it gives you no power, no control over me. Your power ends here, you pathetic bully. My past makes me stronger, not weaker. You made me stronger, not because you stayed with me, but because I survived all you threw my way and will thrive for many centuries still, long after you die."

It was a damn beautiful thing to hear, to see, and her heart leapt for her friend having this opportunity, speaking her truth to the man who tried so damn hard to grind her into nothing. In this moment she was more than a Queen, more than a powerful Fae, she was an elemental, growing and flourishing the ashes Comus scattered in his wake. She'd flourished, and Sabrina was happy to be present to see it, now and in the future Nin clearly manifested for herself in front of her abuser.

Comus, however, sneered, and made his move. Something whipped past Sabrina's head as Gin cursed then screamed, "The wand!" A finger loosened was enough to call the magical object to him, and Comus, getting it in his grasp, shook off the vines in a flurry of ripped and sliced greenery. Nin did not back up, but stood her ground, determination clear in her face. She said her piece, now she would back those words up with actions.

Mo sprinted across the distance at Fae speed, ready to step in for his sister. Sabrina could have told him he didn't need to do so. He likely knew that, but he wouldn't be who he was if he did not at least try to protect and save.

Comus seemed to not want interruptions, either, as he created a blast zone somehow. A wave of pulsing energy radiated from where he and Nin circled each other, driving everyone back, pushing them away until all they could do was stand and stare at the fight about to happen.

Comus faced off against Nin, half-crouched and ready to attack. First, though, he would use his words again. "Now what will you do, Princess? No one to save you. No one to step in. I doubt you have what it takes to kill a man you love."

Nin, for her part, paced leisurely but guarded, and released a hollow laugh. "I loved you once, but it was not you. It was a lie of you, one projected to trap and manipulate. That is no real love." She shrugged her shoulders then looked out for a split second, right at Sabrina and Mo and Gin huddled together, watching. "I know love. Feel it in my bones. Touch it when I put my hands to soil and hug my family close. Hear it in the way the wind caresses leaves and my friend laughs with all her body. See it in the way flowers turn toward the sun and in the shine in the eyes of the people I know deep down in my soul. What you offered was lust and empty promises, I know this now. It was nothing more. I never had you, the real you, and because of that, you never actually had me."

"I warned you before, Princess. If I do not have you, you will die. You can pontificate all you wish, but it is the truth. I will kill for you, even if it means killing you." Comus lashed out with the wand then, a slice appearing on Nin's face, a small but deep cut following the beautiful curve of her cheekbone. It was a direct hit, Comus drawing first blood, but it was the only hit he would get in this battle, because as his magic sliced, Nin's magic grabbed, and a mound of hard clay earth punched out from the ground, encasing his hand up to his fingers in a viselike hold. Tighter and tighter it crushed as Comus struggled to get free, but eventually he had to drop the wand, as the crack of bones and his screams echoed in the meadow.

Nin calmly walked up to the wand and scooped it off the ground, standing so close to Comus, who sputtered and raged without her even looking at him. In a voice that carried but still remained soft, Nin wondered aloud, "So much damage from a thing that, at one time, only wished to grow and flower in the sun."

Comus, refocusing, attempted to bespell her using his word magic, flinging complex Faeish at

Nin, a spell Sabrina didn't know but could tell was
horrible and harsh by the gasp it caused in the crowd,
the rigid intake of breath she felt from Mo and Gin
both. They didn't need to worry, though. Nin had it
covered. The spell did nothing to her.

She shimmered in a soft spark of light for a
moment and there was an odd sizzle, like bug zapper
on a Kentucky summer night, and Comus sagged
while Nin remained tall and strong. Gin whispered,
"Beautiful magic," to themselves, both mesmerized
and impressed with whatever ward Nin silently threw
up with ease.

Sabrina didn't know the spell, had no idea
why it was impressive other than it was some form of
highly effective defensive magic. However, she knew
her friend, had seen her caress plants in the same way
she caressed the wand in her hand now, and she
knew. The truly impressive magic was yet to come.

Comus, trapped and beaten, with nowhere to
go and no recourse in the magical skill he valued
above everything else, turned to screams and threats
and hateful words. Nin flicked a finger, and a section
of clay bounded from the pillar trapping his hands
and smacking into his mouth, gagging him. He was
silent, voiceless, struggling and now visibly afraid
when Nin turned back, squared her shoulders, and
pulled up into what had to be called a queenly
posture.

"I, Queen Nin, declare you, Comus of the
Isle, a scourge on Fae. A true traitor of the realm. As
such, you are bound by the punishment for all
traitors: death. As Queen, I both pass judgment in this
matter and execute the sentence. We will waste no
more time on you, now or in the future." With a pull
of her hand, the clay rose again, engulfing Comus

from foot to neck, pushing and squeezing, until he gave a final scream his gag couldn't even muffle, and his head lulled to the side. Comus was dead, defeated, no more. Nin and Fae were free of him forever.

Nin stared, not in triumph, but in serious contemplation. She wasn't happy, because what true heart could be happy after doing such a thing? She did look solid and strong in the knowledge necessary — for Fae, her family, herself. The clay retracted, pulling Comus down with it, putting his body back down in the dark earth where it might do some good.

She was a Queen in the eyes of all in that moment, the woman who ruled and saved in equal measure as she stroked the wand, then held it flat out in her extended hand. It rippled and pulsed, shooting from her hand into the ground, and a sapling rose, morphing in the blink of an eye into a fully mature tree. It looked a lot like a dogwood, although the colors were off. The trunk flashed with shimmery red bark, the flowers a pale green with a similar blood-red outline along the petals. It was arresting and mesmerizing, for Sabrina and, apparently, everyone else there, who began to slowly kneel and call out, "Queen Nin."

Her friend, though, seemed broken from a spell herself, and turned to her family. She flashed to their side, squeezing Gin then Sabrina in powerful hugs. "Are you both well? Where is Sergius?"

With that, Sabrina's heart dipped. She searched for something to say, but nothing other than tears came to her. Gin looked down, silent and shaking in their grief. Nin knew then without a word being spoken, her hand flying to her mouth as she whispered, "No," and rushed into Jane's cottage.

CHAPTER 17

Mo followed Nin into the cottage and Sabrina hesitated. She didn't want to again see Serge's body on the floor, lifeless. She didn't want to hear the cries and witness the agony of people she loved. But because she loved them, because she still held on to her love for Serge, she followed them through that door.

Nin and Mo sat on the floor by their brother and wept. It was a painful picture, the three siblings, one lost, two in grief. Sabrina moved slowly toward them, cautious in her approach. She didn't want to infringe on the moment, didn't want to misstep in this, but she wanted to offer her support, her love, her own sense of grief and loss if it would help those two get through the moment.

When she stepped close enough, Nin wrapped an arm around her leg, drawing her in a little too forcefully, bringing Sabrina down to the floor.

Her Fae strength was no match for Sabrina, but she didn't care. She'd take a bruise or two from her grief-mad friend without complaint. Gin moved toward the other end, hemming in Mo, and the quartet formed a semicircle of tears around Sergius.

Eventually, after loud cries and sobs ebbed into a more manageable trickle, Nin reached down and closed Serge's eyes. She rolled him to his back, kissed his hands, and placed them on his chest in a restful pose. Mosi bent forward, kissing his brother's forehead, pausing there for several beats as he breathed in deep. Gin smoothed their hand over his messy curls and whispered, "He would want his hair in place."

Nin pulled herself back, still holding tight to Sabrina and Mo, which caused them to scoot back with her. She muttered an apology, which both waved away, but as soon as she let go of each, Mo brought his hand around his sister, taking Sabrina's in his own, and they formed a small cradle across her back. Sabrina felt his magic, his energy, whatever you wanted to call it that she connected with so strongly, pulse in weak waves. It was off somehow, but that was no wonder. Grief did hard things to the body, to a life.

Nin wiped her eyes and looked toward Gin. "He collared you?" she asked softly, and Sabrina was brought back to all that happened in such a short period of time.

Gin nodded but seemed resigned. "It is still stuck, even after his death. I thought…"

Nin pushed up and walked on her knees towards her cousin. "I've never seen it from this angle. Let me try something." She tested the choker, studied the runes on the side, and Sabrina, from across the room, noticed one she knew.

"That one, under their right ear, means 'tighten' or 'hold tightly.' It was one of the first runes I learned, to help me with my whole repel-and-hold shtick," Sabrina offered, inadvertently looking at Jane's body, still pinned to the wall, before forcing her eyes back. Mo didn't miss the look, and he finally noticed the dead Fae there. His eyes were hard, and his nostrils flared as he squeezed Sabrina's hand in a silent acknowledgment of what she was forced to do. Sliding that feeling down as best she could, she continued, "Since his affinity was word magics, he likely used a lot of it to construct that thing."

"True," Gin said quietly. "With more research, more time, we can surely remove it."

Nin cocked her head in thought, brought her hand to trace the rune Sabrina pointed out, and let a small amount of her green light spark out. It sizzled on contact, causing the rune to glow faintly before it singed beyond recognition. With the symbol removed, or at least made ineffective, the collar disconnected and fell from Gin's neck. They rubbed the space where it lay and gave Nin a squeeze in thanks.

Slowly, deliberately breathing in and out, Nin rocked back on her butt, sitting on her heels, to look around with more attention to the cottage.

"Our assumptions were correct, Mosi." Although she did not sound remotely happy with that observation. Happiness was a ways off for all of them. Noticing Jane for the first time, she rose to examine the body, a sneer of hate on her face. Sabrina knew, in her heart, it was about the woman on the wall, but a part of her wondered how it made

Nin feel about her, what she'd done, how she'd used her magic.

Mo, his eyes clearing a bit more, pulled Sabrina, then Gin from the ground, and directed them toward the leather couch. He moved to Nin, eyeing Jane's body closer, but she brushed him off, preferring to pace in front of the large hearth. Mo himself stood at attention behind the couch, again ready for battle if needed.

"I take it you figured out we were gone pretty quick?" Sabrina asked.

"Yes," Mo said, not elaborating.

Nin looked over to him and sighed, moving to what had been Gin's chair and sitting on its edge. "Mo and…" she looked back at her dead brother, coming to face the others with tightly closed eyes again after. She swallowed hard and got it out on the second try. "Mosi and Sergius had a meeting scheduled directly after tea. When Serge did not meet him, he went to his chambers and found everything laid out for tea but no one in attendance. It took little effort to connect Jane to the disappearance, as she was already on the potential list of traitors. There were few places she could take you swiftly, especially as she did not leave via a Palace Gate. A guard heard commotion in The Royal Chambers but originally thought it was a Scholar studying the chair and did not bring it to anyone's attention until asked. We discovered, remembered the doorway then. That's how we were able to come so quickly in force."

Gin shook their head, devastation and guilt stretched across their face. "This is all my fault. If I had not created the door…"

Mo interjected, "Nin would have remained stuck to the iron chair."

"Perhaps. I also did not remove that portal as I should have done. I was careless and it cost…so much."

"Gin," Nin said in a stronger voice than she had used since finding Serge. "Look at me. I know of guilt. Of remorse. As Sabrina taught me, it serves little purpose when not truly warranted. We do not blame you. Life in Fae has been chaotic and abnormal for many weeks. You did nothing intentionally malicious. You must work to forgive yourself."

"Yep," Sabrina interjected. "Mistakes happen, but Gin, all this," she assured as she circled her finger in the air, indicating the cottage and the devastation inside it, "is on Comus. He took advantage. He plotted and schemed. He used Jane, who also gets some of the blame. You, friend, can't take on their guilt."

Mo added, "Gin, we were all aware of the door. None in this room thought to secure it. You are not to blame, cousin." He clasped them firmly on the shoulder, reassuring with his touch as much as his words.

Gin gasped in and out and nodded but looked unconvinced. It was early days, the events too fresh and raw for perspective. Sabrina vowed to keep an eye on them, to help them work through this as best she could.

"How did Jane…" Nin asked aloud, but Sabrina wanted to offer the minimal amount of explanation, so she cut her off with her answer.

"She spiked the tea with some potion. We all woke up here, chained or tied, to her and Comus together. Comus…he…he killed Serge in front of us and I went a little wild. I killed Jane."

"In defense," Mo asserted with a hard edge to his voice.

Sabrina nodded and looked up when she felt Nin hover above her. "You saved and defended me before. You avenged my brother. You are all loyalty and love, Sabrina. Do not doubt this. You did what needed to be done."

She moved away from the trio and walked back toward Sergius. "Let us leave this horrid place. Enough tears have been shed here, and sadly, more will come. I must…I must take him to Mother."

She was an awful sight to behold, blood dripping down her cheek, clay splashed and matted in her dress, her eyes wide with grief and determination, as she lifted up Serge and cradled him in her arms.

"I should do this," Mo said, stepping forward.

"No, brother. It is my duty as Queen. Sergius died in my service." She moved out the door and the rest followed in her wake. They took the doorway through Gin's cottage and Inanna's screams echoing off The Palace walls was enough to break Sabrina's heart all over again. As she wailed over the body of her son, Sabrina held on to Mosi, who nearly buckled under the combined weight of his and his mother's grief. She cast sad eyes to her friend, who stood regal and rigid, tears mixing with the blood and earth on her face.

CHAPTER 18

Sabrina watched from a distance as Nin pulled the dark earth up, cracked it open to create a cave she then lined with rocks from its depths. On the outside, she urged grass to grow and coaxed daffodils into position, forming a burial mound that managed to look serious but sunny, a bit like the Fae who would be laid to rest there.

Mo built the vault doors, gold to match the flowers that would ever-bloom for Sergius.

When he finished, Sabrina stepped up with Gin and Inanna. She and Gin studied in their restless grief, picking perfection from among Serge's books. Inanna, tears sliding down her face, put her fire behind Sabrina's writing on those doors, permanently searing into it runes and symbols and words, words, words, things in life Sergius loved.

The five worked silently, coming together to make a beautiful place for their love to stay, within

the walls of Inanna's gates, so she could light her fire
there nightly, as she wished. The magic work was not
difficult, but the cause was heavy, and occasionally
they leaned on each other and breathed through the
tears until the burial mound was completed.

      The funeral itself was a blur for Sabrina. Not
unlike those in the human realm, at least as an
expression of grief. For her part, she was so focused
on the family around her and her own grief, she
wouldn't have noticed any differences unless they
whacked her right in the face. She was glad to note
Sergius was respected, even loved, by many in Fae.
The grounds of Inanna's home were near to bursting
with Noble and Lesser Fae all there to show respect
for the loss of their Queen's sibling, but also, how
they personal felt over the loss of Serge.
      There was one issue that arose early on, but
it was squashed quickly. Groups of Fae lined up in an
informal way and it clearly angered Nin when some
came directly to her to offer condolences before
speaking to her mother. Mosi and Gin were
sometimes even ignored outright in favor of toeing to
the Queen and the Queen's mother alone. After a few
particularly harsh words for an effusive and pushy
courtier, many took the hint and the other Fae
followed the wishes of their Queen, even if it meant
contradicting what they believed to be protocol.
Inanna was moved to the front of a more defined
greeting line, Mosi by her side to help hold her steady

through the pain. Gin stood studious and silent between Mo and Nin, while Sabrina brought up the rear, making her presence known for her friend but not wishing to be a part of the reception. She felt she had no right, at least until Nin looked back at her with a mix of anger and hurt, motioning her to stand close, to be a part of her and her family's process.

"All in my family will be honored this day, if it takes all the power of The Crown of Fae to make it so," Nin hissed out of the side of her mouth when she stepped up to her side.

Sabrina reached down her hand without looking and grabbed onto Nin, squeezing her tight, trying to squeeze all the love and care and concern and pride she had for her friend in that moment and in their life together.

When the funeral ended, Nin asserted some of her monarchical power for herself. She commanded she be left alone, listening to none of the arguments made by Sabrina or Mo. She simply walked off, dismissed her guard, and told none to bother her until she returned to the house. Sabrina could give her the moment of peace if she needed it, but she wouldn't go far. She walked down the gravel path a ways, stopping after a bend that hid Nin from her sight. Turning to face where her friend would appear, she stood still, not even a fidget in her hands, and set herself up to patiently wait.

Mo, who came back to find her in this position after escorting his mother to her receiving room, slid close to her side, resting his hand on the small of her back. "You shall wait?" he asked, although he likely already knew the answer.

"Yep."

"Do you wish for me to wait with you?"

Turning to him, she pulled him into a tight
hug, rubbing her face into his chest to get a hit of the
feel and smell of him, to wipe off some of her tears.
He hugged her back hard, squeezing a bit too tight for
her human frame, but she didn't mind. It was an edge
of pain she could take. Finally pulling back to look
him in the face, she asked her own question, "What
do you need?"

He hesitated, letting a huff of air out and
releasing the rigid posture he almost always held. He
deflated slightly and shut his eyes tight before
looking in the direction where Nin likely sat alone,
back toward the house, then deep into Sabrina's eyes.
He pushed his hand up to cup her cheek and give a
soft, tiny smile. "Such choices are hard for me, but I
am certain you and Little One will care for one
another well. I shall return to Mother to ensure she
has all she requires." He stepped back, pulled her
hand up, and gave a slow kiss to the inside of her
wrist. Those actions — the kiss and the trust in who
she was and what she and Nin meant to each other —
made her heart flutter.

"I will see you soon, love," he whispered.

"Of course," she answered before he turned
and strolled down the path, taking his time when he
could run, showing her he maybe needed to regroup
alone for a bit, too.

When Nin rounded the curve and saw
Sabrina several minutes later, she finally gave into a
bit of exhaustion and seated herself on a metal bench
along the path. Nin didn't look at all surprised. "I see
you still care nothing for my title or authority," she
said in mock affront, plopping down
unceremoniously on the bench where her friend sat.

"If your orders are bunk, I don't have to do jack," Sabrina sniffed, scooting closer to her and shoving her arm. "Not going to ask how you are, because we're all doing shitty right now, and it's a pointless question. I will ask if you need to talk or be silent for a bit?"

"Silent and alone?" Nin ventured.

"Nope," Sabrina said on a pop. "You're stuck with me for now. Inanna and Mo and Gin are all taking care of each other. They'll hover over you, too, when you get in, so fair warning there. Now, it's just me and you. I'll do whatever you need me to do, except leave."

"You do enough, being here."

"Like I said, I'm not following crappy orders, Your Grace," Sabrina said in a jokey, flippant tone. She'd never say anything like it, or that sounded like it, in earshot of another. She wouldn't undermine Nin in that way. Sabrina did it only when they were alone, but thought it was important. It made Nin smile and chuckle. It seemed to ease her in some way. Sabrina was no monarch, but if she were in Nin's shoes, she'd want somebody around who she could be less formal with, who she could trust to joke with her and make fun of her in a friendly way. That type of person was dependable, reliable, and honest. She wanted to be that for her friend now and in the future.

Sabrina gave Nin a weak but genuine smile at these thoughts, but it faltered and fell quickly, a mixed look for a sad occasion. Nin shoved Sabrina's shoulder back finally and eased into a more comfortable position on the bench. Sabrina took her lead, gave Nin what she needed, and sat next to her, offering quiet but strong and unwavering support on this tough day.

Ten minutes passed in silence, then Nin rose, straightened her gown, and moved gracefully to the side to let Sabrina lift herself off the bench as well. "Shall we?" she asked, offering her arm.

"Let's do this," Sabrina called, and the two walked down the path, Sabrina strong and steady, Nin regal and poised.

Deep in the night, after they passed out from exhausting grief in Mosi's room in Inanna's house, Mo screamed. Sabrina startled awake, moving toward him. He sat, head in hands, on the bed, and when her hand hit his back, he whispered, "I am sorry, my Sabrina. It is nothing. Sleep."

She wiped sleep from her eyes and pulled up behind him, wrapping him in her arms. "Not happening," she replied firmly.

He breathed deep, in and out, and her body moved with his breath. Their magic matched now, or at least that's how she thought of it, because they had the same rhythm to their hearts, the static under their skins, and the hum she heard as background noise in her head. She didn't know how or why. There was likely some answer, something others learned long ago in Fae having to do with magical theory and chemistry or some such, but for now, for once, Sabrina wasn't overly curious to find an answer. It felt right, true, and that's what she needed, so she let it be. Mo seemed to be in the same space because he also didn't question it. Then again, he'd known they'd work for a long while before she decided to explore this feeling with him, so maybe he had more time to get used to the idea.

"You want to talk about it?" she whispered, not pushing but offering him an opening if he needed it.

He shook his head, but then he started talking, as if he didn't want to but he needed to. "When bad events occur…sometimes…I just…I have moments when I remember other bad things. And I have nightmares. These, however. All I can see are my brother's empty eyes in that dreadful purple room."

"PTSD," she guessed.

"What?" he asked, pulling her arms away. She thought he was pushing her away for a moment, but he only shifted, laying back in bed and bringing her over to lay across his chest.

"I'm not a therapist or psychologist, so I can't explain it in great detail, but it's a condition we call Post Traumatic Stress Disorder, PTSD. One symptom is nightmares based in memories. It happens a lot to soldiers and survivors of abuse. Nin shows signs of it, too. Maybe you both should talk about it, think about how you can help each other." Sabrina pushed gently, but it was still a push. She wanted to help both Fae siblings in any way she could, and she also knew framing the issue like this would hit on Mosi's need to protect, ensuring he worked through issues he had in order to help Nin work through her own issues.

Mo considered this in silence, then asked, "Could we learn more?"

"Anything you need," Sabrina said.

"You have nightmares as well," he replied, reminding her of the visions she had at night, apparently so similar to his own — Serge's dead eyes, flowers bursting through Jane's throat.

She nodded, silent on his chest, and he pulled her head up to place a sweet but deep kiss on her lips. No more talk that night, the warmth and comfort of their bodies kept the nightmares at bay until morning. Before she sank down in that solace, Sabrina knew they'd talk more, feel more, and study more later.

CHAPTER 19

A week after the funeral, Sabrina was called in an oddly formal way to a meeting with Nin. When she entered the small room located down a dark hallway of The Palace, Nin sat at the head of a large, leather-inlaid table with Mosi and Gin seated to her left. The guards ushered Sabrina through the door then shut it with a firm thump behind her.

"Sabrina, please do have a seat," Nin called, offering the chair to her right.

"What even is this place?" she asked as she made her way around the table.

"It is the Advisor Chamber," Gin answered quickly, ever ready to help people learn something new, "used exclusively for important meetings between the monarch and her specific advisers."

"I'm an official advisor now?" Sabrina said with a bit of a laugh as she took her seat.

"Precisely why I called you here today, Sabrina the Scholar," Nin answered to her surprise.

"Huh?"

"As Queen, Nin is in need of official advisors. Ones whom she can trust to give her sound and honest advice," Mo started to explain. "As Chief General, I already hold such a position. Gin is to receive a promotion within the ranks of The Scholars Guild soon, which will allow them to become part of Nin's advisory team as well."

He paused for a second to suck in a harsh breath and Sabrina blinked rapidly to push back her own tears when she realized why. "As you are aware, Sergius held a special position, unofficially, for our Nin. He would have become Vizer if..." His sentence drifted off and all sat in heavy silence, navigating their own grief for several beats.

"I am in need of a Vizer," Nin asserted into the quiet of the room, "and I choose you, Sabrina."

"I'm human, though. And I don't know anything about Fae politics."

"Yes. You would be the very first human to hold an official position within the ranks of Fae monarchy," Gin added.

"Whoa, whoa, whoa. I think, maybe, we need to back up a little and talk this through," Sabrina hedged. She was unsure of herself in Fae as it was, new to the place and the people and her magic. Adding an official and serious government position to the mix might be a little much for her.

"I have thought through the details, the issues that will surely arise because of who you are, the areas where you need more training and education. Regardless, you are the one for the role. The only one I would trust in this role."

"Isn't it unnecessary? Can't you go without a Vizer?"

"The Mae Queen had no Vizer for the last several decades of her reign, it is true, but as you yourself have said on a number of occasions, I am not the Mae Queen," Nin countered.

"Now, that's not at all what I meant, and you know it. You don't need more than whatever she had. You're enough, lady," Sabrina assured without a pause.

"You believe I can rule justly and fairly. Be a good Queen. You will also tell me if I stray from those things. Such attributes are what I need."

"And you have them, regardless of any title or position."

"So why not take the title if it does not matter?"

Stymied momentarily by the Queen's logic, Sabrina looked down at her hands as they rubbed together in her nervous state.

"Sabrina?" Gin called, waiting until she looked back up at them. "We are all new at these positions. All unsure in our own ways. However, Nin asks this of us."

"I need you," Nin whispered. "I cannot do this alone, and although I am fully aware you support me in all ways, I need someone to officially stand by my side, to be my chief advisor in all things. The only person I trust in that position is you."

Sabrina breathed deep and answered, "Lots of people aren't going to like this," on a puff of an exhale.

Nin smiled, knowing Sabrina now agreed with her plan. "Let them hate."

"Haters always gonna hate," Sabrina said, biting her lip in her nervousness but still unable to not make the reference. Nin chuckled softly, Mo and Gin looked confused, and she smiled before saying, "Whelp, we probably have a lot to discuss. Let's get this started."

Sabrina stood outside the large wooden doors of The Throne Room and fidgeted, as per usual. Mo tried to soothe her with a hand to her back and a smile, but it didn't help. "You're just going to have to deal with this for a minute," she snapped at him in her nervousness.

"It is fine, Sabrina. Do as you will," he replied. He continued to smile and hold her in a way that soothed her fraying nerves. She still worried her hands, though. That wasn't changing anytime soon.

The doors opened to loud murmurs and fanfare. Brass horns sounded, and Mo gave her a steady push forward. She walked slowly along the runner, mortified with the thought she'd get tangled in her flowing peach gown, eyes trained ahead on her destinations: Nin and the dais.

Sabrina knew what was happening, why it was needed, why she was there, but it still tied her stomach in knots. She'd do an awful lot for her friends, her Fae family, and this proved it. Surely. Why else would she agree to this mess?

It took a while, but she reached the steps without incident and kneeled before Nin, who wore her Queenly regalia, Crown of Fae and all.

"All have gathered to witness this auspicious occasion. In light of the death of Sergius the Whisperer," Nin's voice hitched a fraction, but she gave herself a beat and powered through, "new official advisors must be appointed. It has been decades since The Fae Court was graced with a Vizer, one advisor to serve above all others, to officially sit at the Queen's right hand in all matters, for all days, as long as it pleases the Queen. Sabrina the Scholar, though a human and new to our realm and our ways, has proved her mettle." She tapped Sabrina lightly on the head with a scepter and boomed, "Rise as Sabrina Vizer, Second in Fae, Right Hand to Queen Nin, with all afforded powers and privileges."

There was applause and Sabrina stumbled a little as she pulled herself up, which was too embarrassing for words but very much on brand for her. Nin smiled and nodded, taking her hand in a formal way and leading her up the stairs. Next to The Throne, a little behind and to the right, was a large but simple wooden chair with a lush green velvet seat. It was The Vizer's Chair, something some Fae servant found squirreled away in many of the attics. Sabrina would sit there and be the official number two in the entire Fae realm. Weird and surreal for her to think about, but reality nonetheless

Through the extended fanfare, Nin leaned over to whisper, "Take your seat," and Sabrina filled her role as asked. The cushion was harder than it looked, and the smell of must wafted up when she sat down, but after a few minutes it molded to her, fitting

nicely along her curves as she watched her friend
rule.

There was a ball that evening. Again.
Sabrina was excited about it, though, because she had
her own dress commissioned by her designer. And
Mo would be at her side. The friends had a few
moments between the business of making Sabrina
Vizer and when Queen Nin would be whisked away
to get prepped for the events of the evening. They did
not plan it exactly, only managed to look at each
other and decide in an instant to steal away together,
creeping off to the small room behind The Throne to
be alone.
	"Are you well?" Nin asked, clearly
concerned with how Sabrina was holding up.
	"Just peachy," Sabrina said, deadpan. When
Nin frowned, she added, "No, no. Really. I'm good.
We're all good, lady."
	"I am glad of it, as I am glad to have you by
my side."
	"I mean, who else would call you out on
your crap when you get all uppity?" Sabrina joked,
but Nin turned serious.
	"You will. I know you will. You are loyal
and loving, but good and true. Everything a Vizer
should be."
	"Thanks," Sabrina whispered, the only
response she could muster at the moment.

"Plus," Nin said, pretending to be nonchalant, "this means you have more than enough reason to stay in Fae indefinitely."

"True. I would've likely stayed anyway. Not much left in Wilde for me, not like what I have here. Plus, you and Mo are good times… though in dramatically different ways."

Nin laughed, full and loud, and for Sabrina it felt like the first time she'd heard the sound in ages. It was nice to joke and tease again, to have a moment to remind them of what used to be and what would come more easily in the future as they remained beside each other regardless of what this life decided to throw their way.

WANT MORE?

Sonya Lawson is coming out with new work at a steady clip. For current info on new releases, a chance to get freebies first, and the occasional opportunity to enter special fan giveaways, you can join her newsletter here - https://bit.ly/31xZ2o7 - or via her website at sonyalawson.com. You can also follow her on any of the platforms linked below to stay up to date on her work.

TikTok –
https://www.tiktok.com/@sonyalawsonwrites
(@sonyalawsonwrites)

Instagram –
https://www.instagram.com/sonyalawsonwrites/
(@sonyalawsonwrites)

Facebook –
https://www.facebook.com/sonyalawsonwrites

Twitter – https://twitter.com/Sonyawazhere
(@Sonyawazhere)

BookBub – https://www.bookbub.com/profile/sonya-lawson

Amazon Author Page –
https://www.amazon.com/Sonya-Lawson/e/B09P2NT6M3

Goodreads -
https://www.goodreads.com/author/show/21408437.S
onya_Lawson

ACKNOWLE DGEMENTS

I'll start with friends this time. A big thank you in particular to Sarah, Guff, and Lynn for just being the best in general, forever and always, with all the support. A special thanks to all the writing friends I've made in the past year, particularly my mastermind groups and the RRA group. You've been a source of guidance and inspiration. The CBs continue to come out in full force to support, as always. And everyone else, I hope you know you have my love.

This whole duology wouldn't be what it is without my amazing beta reader, Ellie. The women at Partners in Crime did it all, from covers to edits to formatting and everything in between. They're the best and deserve the biggest thank you I can give, so these few lines don't seem like enough. Here they are anyway. Thanks.

Again, a big thanks to my husband, who lets me rant about characters and book marketing/production while always maintaining a phenomenal level of both support and patience. My family, most far from me, are exceptionally supportive as well. Love you all.

Grief is an ending note in this novel, and a hard note so many of us carry in our hearts in real life. I'm lucky. I've experienced a whole lot of love in my life.

However, with love comes loss at some point. We're human, not nearly immortal fantasy characters. At the end of this first publishing journey, I can't help but think of all those who aren't present to read these books. So many of those now lost to me would have loved them, if for no other reason than because they loved me. It makes me both sad and blessed. Miss you still and love you always.

Finally, a big thank you to John Milton across the centuries. There would be no *Comus Duology* without *Comus* and the women he created for his play. Thank you for the words and the inspiration.

AUTHOR INFO

Sonya Lawson is a recovering academic currently writing fantasy, light and dark, in a variety of subgenres. Some might say she switches it up too much, but her stories have at least one common characteristic — sassy, intelligent, articulate women trying to do the best they can in whatever world they inhabit. While she remains a rural Kentuckian at heart, she currently lives in the Pacific Northwest where she fills her days with writing, editing, reading, walking old forests, and watching sitcoms or horror films. You can find more information about current projects and upcoming releases at sonyalawson.com.

www.ingramcontent.com/pod-product-compliance
Lightning Source LLC
Chambersburg PA
CBHW070207310726
48976CB00001B/238